Praise for A

'Prepare to fall head over heels in love with this book' *HELLO!*

'Magical and beautiful' **Josie Silver**

'An insightful, nuanced look at modern relationships, I LOVED it. *A Christmas Carol* meets *Love Actually*' **Holly Bourne**

'A heart-warming and surprisingly feminist novel of "what if"' **Laura Jane Williams**

'Has all of the feels – the messy complexities of family and friends, the power of love and a sprinkling of magic. Gorgeous' **Clare Pooley**

'Sharp, funny and poignant' **Rachel Winters**

'A warm, cosy, Christmassy delight. It's SO honest, funny and sad, and most of all it is full of hope. It tugged at ALL of my heartstrings, and I loved it to bits' **Cressida McLaughlin**

'Romantic and gloriously life-affirming' **Rachel Marks**

'So captivating I couldn't put it down. A gorgeously festive story' **Emma Cooper**

'An outstanding story about regrets, self-reflection and love, littered with relatable situations and fabulous humour. I LOVED IT!' **Roxie Cooper**

'A magical, compelling and thought-provoking story, full of depth and heart' **C. J. Skuse**

'Clever, funny and romantic. I hope the Netflix adaptation comes swiftly after' **Melinda Salisbury**

'Oh my gosh, it's wonderful! I cried so much!' **Polly Crosby**

Tom Ellen is the co-author of three critically acclaimed Young Adult novels: *Lobsters* (which was shortlisted for *The Bookseller*'s inaugural YA Book Prize), *Never Evers* and *Freshers*. His debut adult novel, *All About Us*, was published in 2020, and he has since released two books in a middle grade series: *The Cartoons That Came to Life* and *The Cartoons That Saved the World*. His books have been widely translated and are published in more than 20 countries. He is a regular contributor to *Viz* magazine, and as a journalist he has written for *Cosmopolitan, Empire, Evening Standard Magazine, Glamour, NME, Time Out, Vice, The Quietus* and many more.

Also by Tom Ellen

All About Us

The Lifeline

Tom Ellen

ONE PLACE. MANY STORIES

This novel is entirely a work of fiction. The names, characters and incidents portrayed in it are the work of the author's imagination. Any resemblance to actual persons, living or dead, events or localities is entirely coincidental.

HQ
An imprint of HarperCollins*Publishers* Ltd
1 London Bridge Street
London SE1 9GF

www.harpercollins.co.uk

HarperCollins*Publishers*
Macken House, 39/40 Mayor Street Upper,
Dublin 1, D01 C9W8, Ireland

This edition 2024

24 25 26 27 28 LBC 5 4 3 2 1
First published in Great Britain by
HQ, an imprint of HarperCollins*Publishers* Ltd 2024

A catalogue record for this book is available from the British Library.

ISBN: PB: 9780008523855

This book is set in 10.7/15.5 pt. Sabon by Type-it AS, Norway

Printed and bound in the United States of America by
Lakeside Book Company

To Carolina and Maud

PROLOGUE

26th February, five years ago
Paris, France

They both know he has to go.

For the last hour, they've been avoiding the fact. Dancing around it. Not so much an elephant in the room as a herd of the things, stampeding after them through the French capital. But now there's nowhere left to hide. There's no getting past it. It's time.

'So,' he says.

'So,' she replies.

They're standing on the Pont Alexandre III – the same bridge they'd crossed together six hours previously. Amazing, she thinks, what can happen in six hours. To the west is the Eiffel Tower, to the east the Place de la Concorde, and as the sun starts to set, colouring the Seine a deep red-gold, it's like they've stepped into a postcard. For a moment, she feels almost breathless with regret that this is it.

'Well, I should probably . . .' he says.

'Yeah. Yup. Totally.' She nods. 'Can't let the fans down.'

He laughs, and she does her best to act nonchalant. Like it's no big deal. But she wishes, more than anything, that this wasn't it. That they had one more hour together.

He puffs his cheeks out, stuffs his hands in the pockets of his coat. 'Wish I could sack this gig off, to be honest.'

She nods again, wondering for about the hundredth time why he doesn't just invite her to the bloody gig. Does it have something to do with that girl from earlier, perhaps? The one with the fringe? Is she misreading this whole situation? Paranoia tugs at her and, as if reading her mind, he says,

'So, I think you got enough material out of me, then? For the article?'

For a split second it's like she's been punched in the stomach. But then she realises he's joking. Grinning that bright, dimply grin that exposes the weirdly attractive gap between his two front teeth. 'Do you always spend the whole afternoon with your interview subjects?' he asks, nudging her foot with his.

'Sorry, did you just kick me?'

'It was a tap. A playful tap.'

'If you say so.' *Nonchalant*, she thinks, *stay nonchalant.*

'So, how are you gonna describe me, then?' he asks. 'In the article?'

'I'll probably go with "annoying". "The band's annoying frontman, Will . . ."'

'Mm-hm. Yeah. Could work. Or "sexy"?' The tip of his tongue hovers under that gap in his teeth. '"The band's sexy frontman, Will . . ."'

'Split the difference?' she says. 'Annoyingly sexy?' He laughs – a wide, open laugh – and she's suddenly very glad her cheeks are already pink from the cold.

Annoyingly sexy. It's the perfect description for him, actually.

His phone rings. He pulls it out, glances at the screen. A moment passes as he stares at it, his face unreadable. He slides it back into his jeans, unanswered. 'I really should go,' he says. But he doesn't.

He scratches the stubble below his jawline, and frowns at the setting sun. *Why don't you ask me to the gig?* she thinks. *Just ask me to the gig, you annoyingly sexy twat.*

'What's funny?' he asks as she stifles a laugh at her own internal monologue.

'Nothing, sorry.' She composes herself. He's obviously not going to ask her. Better to be the one who leaves first. She'll feel less pathetic on the train home. 'So, listen – this was really fun, and—'

'I was thinking . . .' he says. 'How long are you in Paris for?'

'Erm . . .' She wrinkles her nose. Her Eurostar leaves Gare du Nord in precisely one hour and forty-eight minutes' time. 'Not sure yet.'

'OK.' He looks down at his shoes. 'Well, I don't know what you've got going on later, but I was thinking, maybe, after I'm done with this gig, we could hang out a bit more? If you wanted.'

She has to bite the inside of her cheek to stop her smile spreading. 'Yeah. Maybe. You're not going to kick me again, are you?'

He laughs, but he still can't meet her eye. 'No, I just . . . Look, I had a really nice time today. And I'd really like it to not be over. Yet. If you want . . .'

He tails off, stumbling over his words, and her heart thumps.

She pretends to make up her mind. 'Er, yeah. All right. That'd be good.'

He runs a hand through his hair, visibly relieved. 'Cool. Great. How about we meet back here at 11 p.m.?'

'Back here?'

'This exact spot. And we can carry on. It'll be like I never left.'

She laughs. 'Yeah. OK. Back here.'

'Eleven o'clock.'

Eleven? She's in bed by eleven most nights. Probably best not to admit that to the frontman of a successful indie band.

'See you back here, then,' she says.

She wonders if he'll kiss her. Please let him kiss her. Maybe she should kiss him.

'See you.'

Still grinning, he turns and leaves. She exhales slowly and tells herself not to get carried away. After all, she barely knows this boy. But then again, why not get carried away? Didn't today feel like . . . something? Like the start of something? She grips the rail of the bridge. Screw it, she thinks. I'm getting carried away.

The sun sinks into the river, and she walks back to the Left Bank, wondering how on earth she can kill the next four hours.

CHAPTER ONE

WILL

26th February, present day
Green Shoots office, Limehouse, London

The phone is ringing.

I push aside my Tupperware containing tonight's dinner – a gluey clump of leftover tuna pasta – and feel my chest tighten as I lift the receiver.

'Hello? Green Shoots Crisis Line?'

'Oh hello . . . Is that Jack?'

The tightness slackens at the sound of my 'safe name'. It's a voice I recognise. 'Hello, Eric,' I say.

'Oh, Jack. Great to hear you. I've been trying for a while now. I was worried I wouldn't get through.'

'Yes, sorry about that. We've been busy tonight.'

This is something of an understatement. I've been volunteering at Green Shoots for almost five years now, so I know that no shift is ever the same, but this evening has been properly hard going. Some nights I sit in this dingy little basement office for hours and the phone doesn't ring once. And some nights – like tonight – I barely have time to make a cup of tea between calls.

It's nice, actually. No time to think. No time to let today's date pull me under.

So far, as well as two regular callers, I've had three very heavy first-timers: a young bloke with serious money worries, a woman who suspects her husband is cheating, and a tearful father terrified that his daughter might be self-harming. As such, it's a relief to hear a familiar voice: Eric's voice. It's a relief to know this won't be a conversation that spins out of control.

I cradle the phone in the crook of my neck and start logging the call on the computer.

'How are you tonight, Eric?'

'Oh, not so bad, Jack. Can't complain. Although that's what I'm usually ringing you to do.'

He laughs. I laugh. It's our little ritual, this: the same jokey exchange that's opened every conversation we've had for the past five years. I'm not sure how long Eric has been calling this helpline, but it's definitely since before I started here. Like so many of the other regulars, Green Shoots really is a lifeline for him. His sole connection to the outside world. He'll often tell me that mine is the only voice he has heard all day.

'Have you had your tea?' I ask, and from the computer's drop-down menu, I select '60–70' for 'age', and 'regular caller' for 'call type'.

'Oh yes. Microwave biryani. Morrisons' finest.'

'Excellent.'

'Just settling down to watch *MasterChef* now.'

From the drop-down menu, I click 'reason for call' and select 'loneliness'.

'Oh yeah? New series, isn't it?'

'That's right. They look a lovely bunch, the new contestants. They're doing desserts tonight. It's making me wish I'd bought something sweet for my pudding.'

He tries a laugh, but it doesn't quite come off.

'Are you . . . all right, Eric?'

Despite the fact that I have no idea what Eric looks like or where he lives – and he doesn't even know my real name – we've spoken on the phone pretty regularly for almost half a decade. As such, I can tell by the slightest twinge in his gravelly voice when something is off with him. And tonight, something is *definitely* off with him.

Just when I was hoping this would be an easy call.

'Oh, yes, just . . . feeling maudlin, I suppose, Jack,' he says. 'Silly, really. I had a bit to drink. Just been thinking about things.'

I stare at the computer screen. The word 'loneliness' flickers back at me from the menu.

'Anything you want to talk about?'

'Well, I . . .' His voice falters, and he takes a deep breath to steady it. 'I was putting that curry in the microwave, and I caught my hand in the door, you see. And it's funny – I looked at my hand, and . . . it was an *old man's* hand. With old-man veins and old-man liver spots. I know it sounds silly. I mean, I *am* an old man. But sometimes . . . it just catches up on you. You wonder where all the years have gone. You wonder how you ended up here.' I hear him take a swig of something. 'Alone.'

'Mm-hm,' I say softly. A 'verbal nod', they called this noise in our training sessions. Designed to let the caller know you're still on the line. Still listening.

'I just never thought I'd end up like this.' His voice is so quiet I can barely hear him. I press the receiver to my ear. 'But maybe everyone feels this way from time to time. I don't know. Do you ever look back on your life and regret things, Jack?'

Every single day. Ever since . . .

My eyes find today's date in the corner of the screen, and my stomach swoops like I've missed a step. I have to swallow hard to get my breath back. 'Ah, Eric – you know I can't talk about anything personal relating to myself. This call is about you. We're just here to listen.'

He laughs sadly. 'I know. You'd think I'd remember that after all these years.' I hear him take another swig. 'Well, I'd better let you go,' he sighs. 'There are people out there who need you much more than I do.'

'Eric, you know how much I enjoy chatting to you. Brightens up my shift every time.'

'You're a good lad, Jack. You really are.'

Trust me, Eric. I'm not.

'Ah, thank you.'

'I mean it,' he says, his slurred words sounding tougher now, more serious. 'All of you on this helpline – giving up your spare time to talk to old duffers like me. And people who are going through things much worse. You should be really proud of yourselves.'

I try to speak, but my mouth is dry. Despite the awfulness of the previous calls, this one suddenly seems worse.

Since everything fell apart, on this exact day five years ago, I've felt many things. But 'proud' is definitely not one of them. My face is boiling hot and there's a tightness spreading behind my eyes. I can't hear this stuff right now. Not today of all days.

'OK, Eric. Take care, then.'

'You too, Jack. Speak to you soon. Goodbye.'

The dial tone drills into my ear, and I can breathe again. It's just me, alone in this damp, cramped office, the rain hammering hard against the window, the word 'loneliness' still winking at me from the computer screen.

Eric doesn't know why I really do this. What made me sign up. What keeps me coming back, year after year.

Sometimes I get the mad urge to tell him.

CHAPTER TWO

ANNIE

3rd March
Shoreditch, London

'NO VAGINA CAKES!'

The email is blank, apart from that subject line. It's also marked 'High Priority'.

I peer over the top of my computer screen to see its sender – my friend and colleague Lexi – staring pointedly back at me.

I hit 'reply' and type: 'What are you on about, mate?'

I hear her sigh dramatically from across the desk, and then start hammering away at her keyboard. Her reply arrives a second later:

'No cakes that look like vaginas! I don't know how I can put it more clearly? NO VAGINA CAKES!!'

Even though we sit directly opposite each other for eight hours a day, Lex and I tend to communicate mostly by email when we're at work. This is partly because we enjoy swapping obscure *Schitt's Creek* gifs – hard to do when you're speaking out loud – but mainly so we can give the appearance to our open-plan office that we are beavering away productively. When, actually, we're just, you know, swapping obscure *Schitt's Creek* gifs.

Or, in this case, discussing Lexi's baby shower.

'Are cakes that look like vaginas actually a thing?' I write, and hit 'send'.

'Big time,' she writes back. 'Google it.'

'Yep. Sure. On a work computer. Are you TRYING to get me fired?'

I hear her snort at that, and then quickly compose herself when people look round.

'Who's organising this baby shower anyway?' I write. 'Me or you?'

'You OBVS,' comes her reply. 'But I just think there should be a line in terms of what's acceptable, and a vagina cake is that line.' She adds a gif of David Rose saying, 'Very awkward and cringey.'

'I thought you wanted it to be a surprise?' I type, adding a gif of Moira Rose selecting a particularly ridiculous wig.

'I do! But a GOOD surprise. Not a horrific vagina-cake surprise. LOOK.'

Two seconds later another email drops into my inbox. I open it and flinch – half in laughter, half disgust – at the photo Lexi has attached: a three-tier cream cake decorated to resemble a disturbingly realistic crowning baby.

'Jeez, Annie, what *are* you looking at?!'

I spin around to see my boss, Matt – the editor-in-chief of Marker Media – standing over my shoulder, grimacing at the marzipan vagina taking up half my screen.

'Sorry, I . . . Sorry.' I blush, minimising the photo, as Lexi dissolves into silent hysterics across from me. 'Just doing some . . . research. For an article.'

Matt raises his eyebrows. 'Right. Well, I look forward to reading your list of The Top Ten Most Nightmare-Inducing Cakes very soon.'

He tugs at the drawstrings on his hoodie. Like most men who work in digital media, Matt still dresses like a schoolboy on non-uniform day, despite being in his late thirties. Today, he is rocking a neon-green sweatshirt and low-slung skinny jeans that reveal half a bum cheek's worth of *Rick and Morty*-branded boxer shorts. He perches said bum cheek on the edge of my desk, and lowers his voice as he leans in to speak to me. 'On that note, actually, Annie,' he adds, 'I wanted to have a quick chat with you tomorrow about something. Whenever you've got a sec?'

Out of the corner of my eye I can see Lexi's head bobbing, meerkat-like, over her monitor.

'Yes, of course,' I tell Matt. 'Sounds good.'

'Coolio.' He raps his knuckles on my desk and slouches off.

Lexi is still pulling *what-was-that-all-about* faces at me, so I send her that gif of David Rose saying, 'I'm feeling this, like, deep, aching sense of dread.'

She writes back straight away: 'Shall we get an early lunch?'

*

'So what do you think he wants to talk to you about?' Lex asks as we weave our way down Shoreditch High Street towards Pret.

'No idea,' I say. 'Probably just a brainstorm or something. He's been on at us for weeks about getting some fresh ideas on the site. Or maybe . . .' I gawp at her in mock-terror. 'You don't think he'd fire me over that vagina-cake picture, do you?'

She snorts with laughter as we turn the corner. 'Maybe he genuinely wants to discuss that Nightmare-Inducing Cakes idea. I can one hundred per cent see that on the site.'

'Me too.'

The website we work for – Marker Media – is a *BuzzFeed* knock-off, really: silly lists, funny quizzes, weird bits of news, trivia and celebrity gossip to lighten up your lunch break. In our group of seven editorial staff, I'm the Senior Writer: a title that sounds impressive but only really serves to remind me that I'm a good five years older than everyone else here, bar Lexi and Matt.

Not that I'm complaining. For the most part, I really enjoy my job. It definitely doesn't stress me out or give me horrendous insomnia and heart palpitations, like some of my friends' jobs. And yes, I have moments when I succumb to an almost paralysing internal panic, wondering if I'll still be compiling lists of the top ten *Love Island* memes when I'm 40, and remembering that I arrived in London eight years ago with dreams of becoming a *proper author.* But mostly I'm still chuffed beyond belief that I actually get to write for a living.

'I was serious about that, by the way,' Lexi says, as we swerve a couple taking selfies in front of a Banksy mural. '*Please* don't get a vagina cake for my shower.'

'Alexie,' I sigh, 'you do realise this shower is nearly a month away, right? I probably won't even start thinking about the cake until the night before.'

She stops dead in the street, her face a mask of abject horror.

'Joking! I'm joking!' I grab her arm to get her moving again. 'I know nothing stresses you out more than sloppy admin.'

She pulls a face. 'I just want it to be nice, Annie! Nice food, nice drinks, nice games; just a nice time.' She cups her bump through her jacket and smiles at me. 'You'll understand when it's your turn . . .'

My turn. I smile back at her, though, in truth, I feel a mild stab of anxiety at the phrase. I'm 31 and Dom and I have been together nearly three years now; I suppose I should be thinking about 'my turn'. But somehow, whenever I try to picture us getting married or having kids . . . I don't know. The picture never comes fully into focus.

Lexi balks as we reach Pret. 'Ugh. Packed. I thought we could beat the rush by getting here early.' She takes a deep breath and rolls up her sleeves. 'There'd better be some falafel wraps left or I'm gonna kick off.'

As it turns out, there aren't any and she does. I pay for my sandwich and drink and tell her I'll meet her outside, once she's stop haranguing the Pret staff about how they should be better prepared to cater for pregnant women with uncontrollable hummus cravings.

As I step back onto the pavement, I catch sight of a shop across the street. A bookshop. I must have walked past it a thousand times but I've never noticed it until today. It's the kind of bookshop you see less and less these days; all flaking paint, weather-beaten sign swinging creakily above the door, and a grimy glass window that reveals an absolute treasure trove of fusty, second-hand volumes within.

Exactly the kind of bookshop Dad would have loved.

My breath catches in the back of my throat. It's been more

than a year now, but it still shocks me how suddenly – how violently – this feeling can sneak up on you.

Some days, missing him is just a dull ache – a background noise. Others, it's a stranglehold. Something that grips you by the throat when you're least expecting it.

Without thinking, I cross the street and peer through the shop's open door. Even the smell of the place reminds me of him. So many of my favourite memories feature the two of us in shops just like this one, stood side by side, digging through the shelves in silence, until one of us suddenly yelped for joy when we struck literary gold.

He made me a reader, and he played a big part in making me want to be a writer, too. All my memories of writing are linked to him. Playing Consequences when I was a kid; long after my mum and sister had got bored and sloped off, Dad and I would still be there, on the living room carpet, swapping our bits of paper back and forth, laughing like idiots at the joy of surprising each other, of taking the story somewhere completely unexpected.

My stomach flexes as I remember how excited he was about me moving down to London, about me wanting to try and make a go of writing. He was so stupidly happy even when I got the job at Marker. I showed him the site, told him it wasn't 'proper' writing – more silly quizzes and lists. But he refused to listen. All he said was: 'Annie, I am so bloody proud of you.' He was always in my corner. Always, always.

'Annie!'

Lexi's voice brings me back to earth with a jolt. I turn to see her striding out of Pret, holding a falafel wrap aloft. For a moment, the sheer effort of shifting gears – of pretending I'm

OK – seems genuinely unmanageable. I just feel so . . . *tired*. But I swallow hard, digging my nails into the heels of my hands, and the memories dissolve, the stranglehold loosens.

'You coming or what?' Lexi calls.

I take a deep breath and fix my smile back on as I cross the street to meet her.

CHAPTER THREE

WILL

3rd March
Tottenham Court Road, London

As tradition dictates, I am early to work and Dev is late.

I lean heavily against the graffitied steel shutters of MicroShop and watch the commuters shuffle past in their coats and scarves, eyes glued to their phones.

When I visited central London as a kid, Tottenham Court Road was populated almost exclusively by stores like MicroShop – huge, chaotically messy electronics havens with names that always teetered on the brink of copyright infringement. Places you could buy every gadget under the sun, and where haggling was not only tolerated but actively encouraged.

Now, though, our shop is the last one standing. It looks shabby and out of place among all the newly built chain cafés and sleek homeware stores. How long before MicroShop goes the way of AppWorld, iStore, MacPalace and all the others? How long before Dev takes me aside to tell me, sorry Will, but we're going to have to let you go?

For some reason, Eric's words from two nights ago ring out in my head: 'You wonder where all the years have gone. You wonder how you ended up here – alone.'

I'm not sure who or where I thought I'd be by the time I was 32. But it wasn't here. It wasn't this.

In my twenties, I never thought that far ahead. Life was one long party. It sounds clichéd, but it's true. I existed exclusively in the present – I felt bulletproof, immortal – and on the rare occasions I considered the future, I just imagined it would be a brighter, shinier version of what I was already going through.

I never once dreamed my life would turn out to be so *small*. I was supposed to be the next Alex Turner, the next Liam Gallagher. I was supposed to be something more than . . . this.

'Oi oi!'

A hard slap on my shoulder and the tinny screech of jungle music indicates that Dev has finally showed up. I turn to look at him, his Parka hood pulled up, enormous Beats headphones over his ears and a wide grin splitting his beard in half.

'My latest mix!' He shouts so loud that a passing businessman nearly chokes on his flat white. 'Did it last night – check it out, man!'

He takes the headphones off and clamps them over my ears. Instantly, the honking Tottenham Court Road traffic is drowned out by the tooth-rattling sounds of 'DJ Devilish' – aka 35-year-old electronics store manager, Devindra Nayar. It's like being trepanned by a pneumatic drill. Dev is nodding eagerly at me, his face fishing not very subtly for compliments.

'It's very good!' I yell. 'Your best yet!' Satisfied, he takes the headphones off me, and my ears breathe a sigh of relief.

'Was up all night working on it,' Dev says, unlocking the

storefront shutters. 'You might have to hold the fort this morning while I have a little kip in the back.'

Dev is technically my boss, but his management style is so laid-back it's almost horizontal. His uncle owns MicroShop, and Dev sees his role as store manager very much as a stepping stone on the path to becoming a world-famous drum 'n' bass DJ. For him, this job is a holding pattern, a waiting room for bigger and better things. For me, it's the final stop. I've had my shot at bigger and better, and I screwed it up royally.

It's actually not so bad, as jobs go. But after things fell apart, I didn't exactly have much choice. I've got zero qualifications, since I decided to sack off uni a few months before graduation. I never thought I'd *need* a degree. Everyone told me I was stupid not to sit my finals – Mum, Dad, Joe – but I didn't listen.

My stomach twists. I can't let my mind drift in that direction. Have to keep occupied.

'Tea?' I ask, heading for the kitchen while Dev opens the till.

'Oh, yes please. Four sugars this morning, I think, William. Let's push the boat out.' He pulls out his phone and connects it to the laptop behind the counter. 'I was thinking I might stick my mix on the shop stereo. See what the punters reckon?'

'Do it,' I tell him, even though my inkling is that the punters will most likely reckon, 'Why am I being forced to listen to aggressively loud rave music when I just want to buy some SCART cables?'

Dev nods. 'All right. Unless you want to put something on? Matter of fact: I *always* choose the tunes in this place.' He jabs a finger at me. 'What do *you* want to listen to?'

I shrug. Music used to be all I lived and breathed, but after what happened . . . Well, let's just say it's taken a back seat slightly. Anyway, as far as I know, Dev has no idea I was ever in a band, and if I have it my way, he'll never find out.

'If it's my choice,' I tell him, 'then I want to hear more of your mix.'

He nods sombrely, as if he knew this would always be the outcome. 'Your taste is flawless, I'll say that for you, William.'

His latest mix explodes through the high-quality audio equipment, rattling the shop windows and sending a cloud of pigeons skyward in the street outside.

'I'll make that tea!' I yell over the din. I'm halfway out of the door, when Dev turns the music down. 'Oh, I was gonna ask, actually, Will. D'you fancy a quick drink after we shut up tonight? I'm meeting a mate at the Rose & Crown round the corner.'

I don't turn around. I just stand hovering in the doorway. Dev's been trying to get me out for an after-work drink for nearly two years now. I don't know what stops me from going. I like Dev. A lot. But life is just easier nowadays without other people in it. A drink would mean *really* getting to know each other, and I'm not sure Dev would like what he found out.

'Ah, I can't tonight, man. Sorry. Maybe next time.'

'No worries, Will,' he says. 'Next time.'

CHAPTER FOUR

ANNIE

3rd March
Ladbroke Grove, London

When I open the door of the flat, I'm immediately hit by two things: a delicious cooking smell, followed by an intense rush of affection for Dom.

Since he usually works later than I do, making dinner is almost always left to me. Tonight, though, Dom is apparently bucking that trend and, after the day I've had, I couldn't love him more for it.

It was so weird – after seeing that bookshop, Dad stayed on my mind all afternoon, stubbornly refusing to budge. I sat tapping away at a couple of articles, occasionally batting a gif back to one of Lexi's emails, but all the time it felt like a tide was rising steadily inside me. At one point, my spiteful arsehole of a brain decided to replay memories of Dad in his last few weeks – thin, ghostly pale, yet still smiling – and I had to rush to the loo because I was scared I might actually start crying in the middle of the office. And as I splashed cold water on my boiling face, all I could think was: *when does this get easier? It* must *get easier, surely?*

I read somewhere once that grief is like weather. As in: constantly changing, impossible to predict. You might be expecting clear skies but instead you get storm clouds. That seems about right. But I'm not sure how much longer I can go on, never knowing exactly when I'm going to get caught in the pouring rain.

Now, as I hang my coat up, that hollow ache in my belly is replaced by a warm, tingling glow. After such a shit day, this is *exactly* what I needed: a scrumptious home-cooked meal, gallons of wine and Dom and I curled up on the sofa, watching crap on TV. It's times like this I feel so lucky to have him.

What's he making, I wonder, as I follow the scent down the hallway: Thai green curry? Something along those coconutty lines . . .

'Something smells a-mazing . . .'

I let the sentence tail off as I step into the kitchen. Because there are no pans bubbling away on the hobs, no half-sliced onions on the chopping board, no cookbooks splayed open on the table. There's just Dom, shovelling curry directly from a plastic container into his mouth while staring at his phone.

'Waitrose,' he says without looking up. 'I got you one as well. It was two for one on ready meals. Sorry, had to be quick with dinner tonight.'

'Oh.' I pick up my cellophane-wrapped dinner with more than a slight twinge of disappointment. 'Are you off out?'

'Mm-hm. Quiz night.'

Another twinge. My perfect evening is disintegrating fast. 'But quiz night's Thursday, isn't it?'

He mops up some sauce with a slice of white bread. 'Clare found another one at a pub round the corner. We thought we'd go along to get a bit of extra practice in. You don't mind, do you?'

'No, of course not.' Dom's weekly quiz night with mates from his old job has been a tradition since before we starting going out. The five of them worked at the same PR company for years, but they're now all at different agencies so they relish their regular chance to gossip and talk shop. Once upon a time, I might have been miffed that he hadn't asked me to join them. But having tagged along to a couple of previous quiz nights, I know I'd just spend the evening listening to them bitch about people I've never met, and trying to hide my secret dislike of Shrill Posh Clare, whose shrillness and poshness seem to get more pronounced with every glass of rosé.

Dom stands up to chuck his empty container in the recycling, and clocks the look on my face. 'You don't want me to go?' he says, frowning.

'No, no, go,' I say hesitantly. I'm very conscious of not being *that* girlfriend. For as long as we've been together, Dom's always been big on how important it is we have our own friends and our own interests and don't do *everything* together. I'm pretty sure this is down to his parents, who apparently spent every waking hour in each other's pockets, before suddenly, acrimoniously, divorcing shortly before we met. 'I was just looking forward to a night in with you, that's all,' I add.

His frown deepens. 'I can stay here if you like? It's just they'll be a team member short . . .' He takes his phone out and starts typing. 'I'll tell them I can't go.'

'Dom! Stop. Of course you should go. I'm fine.'

I'm naively hoping he might insist – sweep across the kitchen to kiss me, telling me he'd much rather a night in with me anyway. But he just shrugs and says, 'If you're sure. I've left the oven on, by the way, if you want to pop your food in.'

'And they say chivalry is dead.'

He laughs, his dark hair bouncing shaggily. He's wearing a red Muji flannel shirt – his wardrobe is made up almost exclusively of Muji flannel shirts – and his stubble has grown just past the 'scratchy' stage and into 'warm and fuzzy'. I want to go over and hug him – I want to feel comforted, loved, less alone. But the idea suddenly feels clingy and pathetic.

'How was your day?' he asks, dropping his knife and fork into the sink with a clatter.

'Yeah, it was OK,' I say. 'Though, something weird happened, actually . . .'

I tail off. Because, really, what is there to say? That I saw a shop and it made me miss my dead father? Great story. I've been telling Dom I miss Dad for the past fifteen months. It doesn't make me feel any better, and I'm sure it's not particularly thrilling for him either. So why bother?

There's no need to try now anyway, though, because he's stopped listening. He's squinting at his phone, chuckling away at some text he's just received. 'Right, I'd best be off,' he says, slipping his phone into his pocket. 'Quiz starts at half seven.'

'OK. Good luck.'

He gives me a green curry-flavoured peck on the lips. 'See you later.'

I slide my ready meal into the oven and wonder which Netflix series will most effectively take my mind off Dad. As I open the fridge to get a bag of salad, I see two full bottles of chardonnay standing there.

No scrumptious home-cooked meal, no boyfriend to curl up with. Still, at least I have gallons of wine.

CHAPTER FIVE

WILL

4th March
Harrow, Middlesex

I read an article in a Sunday paper once, in which some Hollywood actor outlined their morning routine. It was predictably ridiculous: '2.30 a.m.: wake up for 9-mile run, 4.30 a.m.: kale smoothie in cryo chamber', that sort of stuff. But it still made me reflect on my own waking ritual. Which – while just as rigidly scheduled – is definitely less beneficial for my health.

After hitting snooze on my phone's alarm, I will typically scroll listlessly through *The Guardian* app for five minutes, before my woozy brain leads me back to the same place every time: my phone's contacts section.

There are 742 numbers in here, and this morning – bleary-eyed, with my face buried in the pillow – I'm browsing the L's:

Len the Legend
Levi Sony
Linden Flat Cap

Liv Fit
Liz Irish
Liz Not Irish
Lolly B
Lonnie New Number
Lorna
LOUD KATE (whose name has been entered in all caps, as if to emphasise her loudness)

The list goes on and on and on. Suffice it to say, I have absolutely no memory of any of these people. I'm guessing they're mostly record company executives, publicists, musicians, models, hangers-on, one-night stands, people who were very briefly my Best Friend In The Whole World in some nightclub at 2 a.m., until the next day when I promptly forgot all about them. In fact, of the 742 numbers in this phone, there are only two that currently show on my 'incoming calls' list: my parents' landline and my total bastard of a landlord, Gareth.

I keep swiping, watching the faceless names glide by. It seems impossible now that I was once connected – no matter how tenuously – to 742 different people. It's like wandering through a past I can't quite believe was mine. Occasionally, my finger will hover over a random name, and I'll imagine what it would be like to call them. Whether they'd have heard about what happened. Or whether they'd have forgotten me, as I have them.

I'm halfway through inventing a hypothetical conversation with LOUD KATE (mostly her shouting at me) when my alarm bleats for the fifth time, reminding me that it really is time to get up and go to work.

As I stumble from my boxy bedroom into the even boxier

kitchen-living room, I'm struck by how strange it is that such a tiny amount of floor space can still be so cluttered. My flat is in Harrow, at the arse-end of the Tube map. Twenty-five square metres of stud wall and peeling lino, whose rent I am only able to afford due to having absolutely no social life to speak of.

I make a half-hearted attempt to tidy up, before pouring myself a bowl of porridge and feeding Milligan, my very badly behaved cat. I dump half a can of Whiskas into his bowl and surround it with a moat of Dreamies. He thanks me with a few gentle, purring headbutts to my shins.

Milligan was a gift from Mum and Dad when I first moved in here. I'd been back with them for six months after everything went to shit – six months of therapists and pills and darkness – and when I finally felt strong enough to move out, they were understandably concerned about me being on my own. They'd pushed for me to find a flatmate; I was adamant I wanted to live alone. We met in the middle on Milligan. I'm glad we did, to be honest. Some days, he's the only thing that keeps me going.

My phone buzzes on the table with a new email. It's from the Green Shoots chain – another volunteer, Linda, saying she can't do her late shift this evening, and asking if anyone else might be able to step in.

I write back straight away, saying I'll do it. It'll be my third late shift in five days. I'm sure the other volunteers must think I'm a bit odd – we're only obliged to do one shift a week. And right now, the thought of schlepping across the entire breadth of London after a full day at MicroShop is giving me second thoughts about accepting so quickly. But I just know that, come 6 p.m., I'll be glad I did. I'll be glad to hear Eric's voice, and the voices of the other regulars; glad of the familiarity and the routine. Glad of having somewhere to go besides this empty flat, where yet another night alone would otherwise stretch in front of me, the silence coaxing my brain into places I know it shouldn't stray.

The truth of it is: Green Shoots isn't just Eric's lifeline, his sole connection to the outside world. It's mine, too.

CHAPTER SIX

ANNIE

4th March
Shoreditch, London

I'm halfway into my coat when Matt pokes his head out of his office and looks in my direction.

'Annie? I know it's nearly six, but have you got time for that chat I mentioned yesterday? It'll be quick, I promise.'

I shrug my jacket back off. 'Yeah, of course. Sorry – I completely forgot.'

I've been nursing a fairly severe hangover all day after polishing off nearly an entire bottle of chardonnay by myself last night. I was conked out in bed by the time Dom got back from his night out, and he was up for a run so early this morning that I didn't even see him. The dent in the mattress and a lingering aroma of IPA were the only signs he'd actually been sleeping next to me.

I've spent most of today chain-drinking coffee and bashing out a quiz that's supposed to go live on the site tomorrow lunchtime. It's called 'How Much Of A Middle-Class Cliché

Are You?' – a brainfart I'd suggested out of desperation at the last ideas meeting. Of the twenty-four questions, nine currently revolve around avocados. That's probably too many. I should try and get that down to six, at most.

I step into Matt's glass-walled office, which is decorated with ironic prints of Super Mario in an Andy Warhol pop art style. There's a foosball table by the flipchart, and even a beanbag in the corner, onto which Matt has been known to flop during a particularly lengthy meeting.

'Here, take a seat,' he says, thankfully ushering me towards a chair rather than the bag. 'So, listen, Annie. I wanted to bend your ear about something real quick. We're looking at doing more branded content for the site – advertorial stuff.'

I frown. 'Right . . .'

'I know, I know,' Matt laughs, forming a triangle with his fingers and resting his chin on the top. 'But this wouldn't be your normal advertorial bollocks – 'Ten Reasons Why Eating Rice Krispies Will Get You Laid', or whatever. It's the chance for us to do some genuinely interesting, properly journalistic stuff – and get paid a nice chunk of change for it.'

This sounds a little too good to be true, but I nod along anyway.

'Basically,' Matt says, 'the ad guys upstairs have hooked us up with this new jeans brand called Shuvvit. They're super cool, they've got tons of cash and they want to sponsor a new series for the site. Not just a quiz or a list thing – something readers can really get their teeth into. So, we put our heads together and realised the thing that gets us most clicks at Marker is nostalgia. People sit at their desks on their lunch breaks in their dead-end jobs, and they want to be reminded of when they were young, free, single and happy. Marker can do that for them.'

'Slightly depressing as our company USP, but fine.'

He chuckles at that. 'So, listen, what these Shuvvit guys have come up with is a sponsored series called "Whatever Happened To . . ." It'll be all about bands from the past decade that were massive for a bit and then disappeared. We'll give it the proper investigative, long-read treatment: track down the former members, dig into some crazy stories from their heyday, and find out where it all went wrong and what they're up to now. It's perfect for our readers.' He leans back on his chair and shoots me a wide grin. 'And my Spotify threw up something over the weekend that I thought might make a banging first instalment in the series.'

He tugs smugly at his goatee, leaving a pause like he's Gregg Wallace about to boot someone off *MasterChef*. And then he says: 'Do you remember that group, The Defectors?'

I blink. It takes a second for the name to register. As soon as it does, it's like a switch has been flipped inside me.

'They were a sort of shit Arctic Monkeys rip-off,' Matt continues. 'Big about six or seven years ago. They were right on the brink of going major league, and then they completely fell off the radar. No clue why – or what's happened to them.'

He clocks the look on my face and throws his hands up, laughing. 'All right – rumbled! You know full well why I'm talking to you for this one. You interviewed them back in the day, right? In Paris?'

I can feel the heat in my neck rising, spreading fast to my face. 'Erm . . . think so. Might have done.'

Matt's nodding like one of those Churchill dogs. 'Oh, come

on! Stop being so modest, Annie. I looked the piece up last night. For that site you worked for before you came here. It's brilliant. Savage, though. You ripped that lead singer a new arsehole!'

I force out a laugh. I haven't thought about that article in years. I still feel pretty ashamed of it, to be honest. The person the article is *about*, though – he still drifts into my head fairly regularly, whether I want him to or not.

'So, what do you think, then?' Matt asks me. 'Since you've got previous with these guys, I was thinking you'd be the perfect person to write the piece. You could have a dig around, do a few new interviews with them, and bingo – we've got the first episode in our brand-new viral hit series!'

I swallow hard. 'Look, it's really nice of you to think of me for it, Matt. But I've already got a fair bit on with my regular stuff, and I just don't know where I'd find the time, you know?'

He nods solemnly, his chin back on the finger-triangle. 'OK, I hear you. But between you and me, Annie, times are a little tough right now with ad revenues. When push comes to shove, this kind of sponsored content is probably the only way Marker is going to survive long-term.'

'Right . . .'

'I like your writing,' he says. 'I always have. I think you'd be great for this – and if this first one with The Defectors gets enough traction, you could end up writing the whole series. You'd be responsible for one of the few sections of the site that actually makes any money!' He laughs without smiling, then adds: 'We're not talking about redundancies or anything – not yet – but taking on something like this would prove how valuable you are to the editorial team. Plus, it's a chance to do some proper, longer-form writing. You're always banging on at me in our ideas meetings about that. Here's your chance.'

He's right, annoyingly; I am always banging on about that. More importantly, though, the mention of the word 'redundancies' has filled me with a sudden and intense passion for my job that I haven't felt in a very long time. The idea of being back on the scrapheap at 31, spending all day trawling *The Guardian Jobs* website . . .

Matt pulls his phone out and squints at it, a sure sign this meeting is coming to a close. 'But, look, if you don't want it, I can always give it to Zara or Nick . . .'

Reading between the lines, it seems pretty clear what my boss is saying here: take the commission, or risk being the first piece of dead wood on the pile when the ad revenues get even drier.

I can't tell him no. I'll have to take it. But I can already feel a solid knot of anxiety forming in the pit of my stomach. Because I don't want to dig up dirt on The Defectors. I don't want to know what they're doing now and where it all went wrong.

And I *definitely* don't want to speak to Will Axford.

CHAPTER SEVEN

WILL

4th March
Green Shoots office, Limehouse

There aren't many things I've got down to a fine art, but lurking is one of them.

I can lurk with the absolute best. If lurking was an Olympic sport, I'd be up on the podium, no problem.

It's four minutes to six, and I'm doing some really top-notch lurking at the edge of a grimy East London industrial estate, just a few metres from the Green Shoots office door. The rain has just graduated from light drizzle to cats-and-dogs, and obviously any normal person would use the key in their pocket and head into the warm, dry office. But going in now – four minutes early – would mean small talk. Socialising. And I'd rather be soaked through than have to endure that.

Hence the lurking.

I check my phone. Three minutes to six. I'd like to say this is a one-off. That I just don't feel up to being chatty and cheerful on this particular evening. But truthfully, this has been my routine for the past five years.

Before I started volunteering at Green Shoots, I'd assumed that your average crisis helpline would be manned by more than one person at a time. I'd seen TV adverts for The Samaritans, with rows of volunteers in headsets sat beside each other in a big open-plan office, taking calls simultaneously. But I soon learned that Green Shoots is not your average crisis helpline.

We're a tiny operation, funded by the occasional second-hand book sale, the takings from which barely cover our communal tea bags. As such, a huge open-plan office is slightly outside of the charity's budget, and we're reduced to a single, shabby room just about big enough to house a desk and a chair.

The Green Shoots day is split into two shifts – 1 p.m. to 6 p.m. and 6 p.m. to 11 p.m. I know from the group emails that go round that having a cup of tea and a chinwag at the crossover of these shifts is very much part of the appeal for the other volunteer listeners. But for me, they're basically an occupational hazard. Which is why I'm getting soaked to the bone out here.

I check my phone again. One minute past six. Right on cue, the office door opens and I affect a purposeful stride towards it, as if I've arrived bang on time, rather than been lurking pathetically outside for the past quarter of an hour.

'Hey! Will!'

I knew from the online rota that Tanvi would be on the early shift today. She gives me a cheery wave as she spots me, fiddling with the hood on her Paddington Bear-esque raincoat. She must only be a few years older than me, but from the Green Shoots email chains I know she's married and has three young kids.

She always seems friendly, cheerful and pleased to see me. But in all the years our shifts have crossed over, I don't think I've ever said more than about forty words to her.

'Hi, Tanvi. How are you?' I say, bumping the total up to forty-five.

'Kicking myself for not bringing a bloody brolly is how I am,' she chuckles, glancing up at the driving rain. 'How are you doing?'

'Yeah, I'm OK, thanks,' I say. 'But running late. So, I'd better . . .'

I nod towards the office door and Tanvi smiles brightly again. 'Of course. I'll let you go. Have a good shift, Will.'

Once inside, I lay my damp jacket on the rusty radiator, log in to the computer, and make a strong cup of tea.

Finally, sat in the rickety office chair, blowing steam off a chipped Bart Simpson mug and waiting for the phone to ring, I feel like I can breathe properly. I'm in control. I'm doing something good.

As pathetic as it sounds, this – right here – is where everything makes sense.

CHAPTER EIGHT

ANNIE

4th March
Ladbroke Grove, London

For the second evening running, I am sat on my sofa, drunk and alone. When I was a kid, dreaming about what life might be like when I was a swanky professional writer in London, this wasn't *quite* what I had in mind.

Dom is out again – after-work drinks with clients – and I'm slumped in front of an episode of *Friends* I've seen a thousand times already, making steady headway through that second bottle of chardonnay.

I'm desperate to talk to someone about this Defectors thing, but Lexi's having dinner with her in-laws tonight, and my other best mate, Maya, is out on yet another Bumble date. For a second I even consider calling Mum or my older sister, Josie, until I remember that I haven't spoken to either of them for weeks. I decide to pour another glass of wine instead. I feel restless. Agitated.

There's no way I could talk to Dom about it, obviously. I've never even told him about that day in Paris. Not that there's anything to tell, really. But Dom gets weirdly jealous about the most insignificant things. He once sulked for an entire weekend after I mentioned that Keanu Reeves had 'nice arms'.

I go and get my dinner out of the oven – mushroom risotto from two nights ago – and then flop back on the sofa to woozily scroll Instagram. Dom has already posted a photo of his night out – him and a load of people I don't know grinning tipsily around a pub garden table. I can't help feeling envious of him being so close with his colleagues. Lexi aside, I can't imagine going for a drink with *anyone* from Marker. And Lex will be buggering off on maternity leave in a month or so. Who even knows if she'll come back afterwards? The thought of eight hours a day in the office without her makes me reach straight for the bottle of wine again.

I tap out a WhatsApp to Dom, asking what time he'll be back, but decide against sending it. Instead, I start absent-mindedly scrolling down through my other chats to see if there's anyone else I want to speak to right now.

Sure enough, after a few swipes, I find someone. Someone I want to speak to more than anything, and yet someone I will never speak to again.

Dad's profile picture beams out at me from the corner of my phone screen, our last text exchange – a banal thing about train times to Sheffield – frozen underneath it. I take another large gulp of wine as I scroll upwards through the conversation chain. It goes back years and years. All the gags and quotes and questions and book and TV recommendations are here; all the emojis and stickers and Moira Rose gifs (I bought Dad a *Schitt's Creek* boxset one Christmas – he was a confirmed Rose family fanboy from then on). I feel a lump rising in my throat. It's like some kind of sick joke. How can all this still be here when he isn't?

I take another swig of chardonnay and keep scrolling, the pain of missing him like a skewer in my stomach. It must be the wine, but I find myself actually laughing out loud when I reach a series of photos he'd sent me a few months before he died. They were taken just after he'd embarked on what would prove to be the final furlong of his chemo. The doctors had told him he would definitely be losing his hair this time around, so Dad – previously of the opinion that any man who wore a hat was a 'show-off' – decided it was now high time he embraced headgear.

He went into town one day and essentially live-streamed his hat-shopping excursion to me. He asked the sales assistant to send me photos of him as he tried on everything from straw boaters to berets to baseball caps, waiting for me to give the thumbs up or thumbs down. I scroll through the photos slowly, each one funnier and more agonisingly bittersweet than the last. I try to remember what I was thinking, what I was feeling, at the moment these photos were being sent. I knew things were serious by then. I knew the treatment wasn't working. And yet I'm still playing along with the charade, passing judgement on each photo with flip remarks like, 'Dad you are NOT Hercule Poirot' and 'Google "Jamiroquai" and you will understand why I forbid you from buying that hat.' It wasn't even that I was trying to remain upbeat for his sake. I just genuinely thought it would be OK. I honestly never thought I would lose him. It seems crazy now – completely childish and naive. But I didn't think something that horrible could actually happen. Not to my dad. Not to me.

The penultimate picture of him, in a nu-metal-style beanie

cap, gets a strangled half-laugh-half-sob out of me, before I see the photo of the one he finally bought: a smart brown Fedora with a slightly Indiana Jones-y feel to it. 'That's the one, Dad,' reads my message underneath it. 'You look very dashing xxxx.' That hat was rarely off his head over those last few months. Until he was moved to the hospice, and it just sat there on his nightstand, next to his stack of books. Like he didn't need it any more. Like he'd accepted his fate.

I reach up to wipe my eyes and my fingers come back damp and sticky with blotched mascara. I pour myself another glass of wine.

I'm not sure how long I sit here, scrolling through the messages. But by the time I blink and look up, the bottle is nearly empty and the clock says half past ten. I just feel numb now: numb with missing him, numb with wanting someone to talk to. I go to the bathroom, dry my face and resolve to pull myself together. I stick on another episode of *Friends*, and without even realising I'm doing it, I start googling Will Axford.

It's been a while since I last stalked him, but nothing's changed: he still appears to be on no forms of social media whatsoever. I should probably go to bed – my head is getting woozier by the minute – but I decide to google another member of the band instead: Simon McGillan, the drummer, who I vaguely remember from Paris. He's on Instagram, but it looks like he hasn't posted in ages. One of his most recent posts – from a few years back – is just a black square with a phone number inside it. A landline.

I type it into Google, and this is what comes up:

Green Shoots Crisis Line – you do not have to cope alone.

CHAPTER NINE

WILL

4th March
Green Shoots office, Limehouse

I've just put the phone down on Sandra – one of our more draining regular callers – when it bursts straight back to life again.

I'm already out of my chair – I've been gagging for a cup of tea for the past hour – so I'm tempted to just let it ring unanswered. But something stops me. You never know who might be on the end of that line. You never know what they might be going through. I settle back down and pick up the receiver.

'Hello, Green Shoots Crisis Line?'

'Oh . . . Hi. Sorry. Hi.'

It's a woman's voice. A voice that sounds weirdly familiar. She must have called before – although she seems almost surprised that someone has answered.

'Hi,' I say. 'How are you doing tonight?'

'I'm . . . I don't really know why I'm calling, actually.'

'That's OK. Have you called the line before?'

'No, never. I just . . .' She breaks off. 'This is weird. Sorry.'

You hear this pretty often: new callers apologising for having the audacity to phone a crisis line. For having the temerity to feel desperate or lonely or sad. For having the sheer brass neck to admit that they're in pain. Always makes me wonder how many people have chosen not to reach out for exactly that reason. How many lives have been derailed or ruined or even lost because people were too . . . *British* to seek help.

'So, how are you feeling?' I ask again. The line crackles as the woman sighs into her phone.

'Erm . . . Well, not amazing, to be honest.'

In the background, I can hear what I'm fairly sure is Janice from *Friends* loudly invoking God to express her surprise at something.

'Sorry, I'll just turn this down,' the woman says, and the TV noise fades.

'I'm sorry to hear you're not feeling great,' I tell her.

'Well, thanks.' The woman gives a forced laugh. She sounds around about my age, and she's got a nice voice – husky and full of humour, the ghost of a Northern accent just audible. I still feel like I've heard her before somewhere, but I guess after five years of listening to strangers' voices they all sort of blend into one.

'Look, I should go, actually. I don't know why I'm calling you', she says. 'There must be people with real problems trying to get through and I'm . . .' She breaks off and her voice is so quiet I can barely hear it. 'I don't know what's wrong with me.'

'Just because you're not feeling brilliant it doesn't mean there's anything wrong with you,' I say. 'We all feel not-brilliant every now and then.'

‘Yeah.’ I hear her take a large gulp of something.

‘It can help to just talk about it. If you like, you can tell me a bit about whatever it is that’s getting you down?’

There’s a pause. ‘So, that’s what this is?’ she asks. ‘People call you up and you just . . . listen?’

‘That’s it. We just listen.’

She laughs – a genuine laugh this time, nothing forced about it. ‘Well, that does sound pretty good. I mean, I’ve got people I could talk to, obviously, but they’ve heard me talk about these things before, and there’s not really anything new they can tell me.’

‘Mm-hm.’ I give a verbal nod, encouraging her to keep going. Like a lot of first-time callers, I can sense this is someone that just needs to *vent*. To open a valve and let out the thoughts that have been pinballing madly around her head for God knows how long.

‘I’ve just had a bit of a weird day, and was reminded of something that happened a long time ago, and it made me think about . . . something else that happened, and it’s funny – just when I think I’m starting to get over it, it creeps back up on me again, and I realise I’m not even close. I wanted to talk to someone, but my friends are busy and my boyfriend’s gone out, and . . .’ She cuts herself off suddenly. ‘Sorry, hearing myself say this stuff out loud makes me realise how ridiculous it all is. Talk about First World problems.’

‘Not at all,’ I say. ‘Not in the slightest.’ And I mean it. After so many years doing this, I can tell when someone is genuinely suffering.

She laughs again. ‘You’re being far too nice. If you think I’m a dick for wasting your time, you can just tell me I’m a dick. I honestly won’t mind.’

I can't help laughing, too. 'I don't think I'm technically allowed to tell you you're a dick, actually. That's not really what this helpline is for.'

'Right. I guess it would go against company policy to tell callers that they're dicks.'

'It would most likely be frowned upon, yeah.'

We both laugh this time. It's weird. It feels sort of . . . comfortable. I've felt many emotions listening to callers in this room, but 'comfortable' has never been one of them.

'Maybe,' the woman says, 'there's a gap in the market for a helpline where someone just calls you a dick and tells you to get on with it. You babble on about your so-called problems, and at the end they just say: "Yeah, get your shit together and stop being a dick." I actually think that'd be quite effective.'

I should really stop laughing so much. I have no idea what this person is going through; maybe she's deflecting her pain with humour, using it as a defence mechanism to hide how much she's struggling. The problem is, she is undeniably pretty funny. I clear my throat and try to be a bit more professional.

'For what it's worth, you wouldn't believe the number of calls we get from people in a similar position to yourself, who are feeling the exact same thing.'

'Right,' she says. 'So, I'm not a dick; I'm just staggeringly unoriginal.'

'Exactly.'

More laughter – from both of us.

I hear her take another sip of her drink. 'God, this is so weird. This is the most honest conversation I've had in months, and it's with someone I can't see and whose name I don't even know. What does that say about me?'

'It says that you're feeling low and you made the right decision to reach out for help,' I tell her firmly. 'And as for names, I'm Jack.'

'OK. Hello, Jack. Should I . . . tell you my name?'

'If you want to, you can. And if you don't want to that's fine, too. Some callers use a 'safe name' rather than their real name – they make something up, or use a different name, a name that means something to them.'

'Hmm.' I hear the rustle of the phone shifting as she moves around. I suddenly wonder where she is. What she looks like. 'Maybe I'll give myself a safe name, then.'

'If you like.'

'OK . . . Well, since you're Jack, maybe I should call myself "Rose"?'

I snort at that. 'Ha. That's definitely an option. You know, I remember point-blank refusing to see that film until about ten years after it came out.'

'What?' She sounds genuinely aghast, and it nearly makes me snort again. 'Why?'

'Because it was the most successful film of all time, and I prided myself on having not seen it.'

She lets out a long, loud groan. 'Oh God. Jack. You're not a hipster, are you? Have I got through to the only crisis line in Britain staffed by hipsters?'

'I'm ashamed to say I used to be one, yes.'

What am I doing? This is not how a first-time call is supposed to go. Even with a long-time, regular caller I shouldn't be dropping bits of personal information into the conversation – no matter how trivial or meaningless they might seem. The only thing I'm supposed to be doing is listening.

It's hard, though, because a memory is unravelling in my head; one I haven't thought about in *years*. It would have been – what – last year of GCSEs? Me and Joe, drunk in his room, playing guitar, and *Titanic* came on the telly. I dived to change the channel, outlining my twattish desire to never see the most popular movie ever made. Joe reacted in exactly the same way 'Rose' has just reacted now: he chucked a cushion at my head, and branded me a 'massive try-hard poser knobhead'.

He was always good at that, Joe: keeping me grounded. Any time my head started to swell, he'd be there to gently nudge me back to earth with a perfectly timed piss-take. I play-acted like I was annoyed at it, but I enjoyed it. I needed it. I—

'Jack? Hello?'

I snap back into the room. 'Sorry, I lost you there for a second. What was that?'

'I just asked if you've got round to seeing the film now?'

'Oh yes. Yeah. A friend forced me to watch it.'

'Well, they sound like a very good friend,' she says. 'It's a stone-cold classic.'

'Yeah, annoyingly, I did quite enjoy it in the end.' She laughs. I shake the memory from my head and try to refocus. 'So, is that what we're going with, then? Should I call you Rose?'

'Hmm. No, I don't particularly fancy being painted like one of your French girls. How about you call me . . . Pia?'

'OK,' I say. 'Pia. Nice to meet you, Pia.'

'Nice to meet you too, Jack.'

The computer fades into sleep mode and in the black screen I catch my own reflection – a silly grin plastered across my face. Weird. Can't actually remember the last time I saw myself smile.

For a second, neither of us says anything. And then:

'I lost my dad,' she says. 'About a year ago.'

'OK,' I say slowly. Even after five years, I can't help fighting the urge to say 'I'm sorry' in response to a comment like this. The first thing we were taught in training was not to express any opinion or judgement whatsoever when a caller says something along these lines. It makes sense, I guess: somebody calls and tells you their dad has just died, you say, 'Aw, I'm sorry to hear that,' and then they tell you that their dad abused or neglected or abandoned them. By expressing sadness or regret, you're making the caller feel worse about the fact they may have mixed emotions about their father's passing.

Basically, we're supposed to stay neutral until we have all the information. Which, in practice, is much harder than it sounds. Still, I manage to wrestle down my natural human instinct to offer condolence and instead say: 'Can you tell me more about that?'

I hear her take a breath. 'There's nothing to tell, really. He got ill – just a bit ill at first, and then really ill. And then he died.'

'Mm-hm.'

'I just . . . I know this is supposed to be hard. But I didn't know it would be *this* hard. I just miss him so much, and—' She swallows thickly before she speaks again. I realise I'm gripping the phone cord tight. 'It just feels like it's knocked me so far off track. And now everyone and everything else is moving forwards around me and I'm just paused, frozen, watching them all go past. I just don't know when I'm going to get over this.'

'I don't know if we do ever truly get over things like that.'

'Do you not think so?' she says quietly.

This time it's me who has to swallow hard before I can talk again. 'I don't know.'

'Mm.' She's silent for a few seconds, and I use the time to push certain memories firmly out of my head and try to get a hold on myself. Then she says: 'I was thinking the other day that grief is like weather. You can't really predict when it's going to hit, and how bad it's going to be.'

'Grief is like weather – that is good. Is that from a poem or something?'

'Not sure. I think I saw it on a tote bag, actually.'

I laugh at that, and she mock-scolds me. 'Oi! All the best life advice comes from tote bags. That's a well-known fact.'

'No, you're right,' I say. 'I do always try to keep calm and carry on, and I do like big books and I cannot lie.'

She dissolves into laughter again. It's a weirdly nice feeling, making her laugh.

When she's stopped, she lets out a gasp that lands halfway between anger and relief. 'God, it feels so good to actually talk about this.'

'That's what we're here for,' I say.

She coughs and then I can hear the smile back in her voice. 'So, you're not going to give me any advice, then, Jack? You're not going to tell me, "It gets easier"?'

I play along, but I'm smiling too. 'Definitely not, Pia. I'm just a volunteer, and I've known you for all of about eight minutes, so I can't give you any advice and I certainly can't make any sweeping judgements about your life. The whole point of this line is to listen without judgement.'

'Oh, OK. I get it . . . So, you're like a kind of phone Beefeater?'

An extremely inelegant snuffle-laugh splutters out of me. 'A what?'

'Beefeaters aren't supposed to react, are they, no matter

what you do in front of them? I remember my dad taking us to see them when we were kids, and me and my sister would jump about, sticking our tongues out at them, and they had to stay totally composed and professional. So – that's you. You're a phone Beefeater. No matter what I say, you can't react.'

My grin stretches even wider. 'Couldn't have put it better myself.'

'OK.' There's another oddly comfortable pause. Then she says: 'Well, I'd better go – there must be other people trying to get through to you.'

'How are you feeling now?' I ask.

'Better than I was when I called.'

'That's very good to hear.'

'Thank you, Jack. It was really nice talking to you. Weird, but nice.'

'You're welcome, Pia. Nice talking to you, too. And you can call again, you know. Any time between 1 p.m. and 11 p.m. – someone will be here.'

'OK, thanks. Maybe I will.'

I suddenly don't want her to hang up. I don't know why, but I just want to talk to her – to listen to her talk – for a little longer.

'Bye, then,' she says.

'Bye.'

Then the dial tone is drilling into my ear, and I'm sat here wondering why my heart seems to be beating slightly faster than usual.

CHAPTER TEN

26th February, five years ago (earlier that day)
Paris, France

The train doors open and Annie bolts down the platform as fast as her legs can carry her.

This – she thinks as she skips past a group of maddeningly slow tourists dragging wheelie suitcases – *is Absolutely Bloody Typical.*

To be on the extra-safe side, she'd booked a Eurostar that was due into Paris at 9 a.m. – two whole hours before the interview was meant to start. She'd even laughed to herself as she bought the tickets. Arriving two hours early for a trip – I'm turning into my dad!

She'd pictured herself getting to the hotel with bags of time to spare, perhaps ordering a silly little coffee and sitting out in the unseasonably warm February sun to reflect on the magnitude of what she was here to do. After three years of crappy bar work and office temping and unanswered emails to magazine editors, here she was: an actual music journalist, being sent to actual Paris to interview an actual indie band! She would sip her drink, gaze out at the Seine and enjoy this quiet moment of triumph.

But now it was all out the window – the silly little coffee, the moment of triumph, all of it. After an hour of sitting motionless outside Lille due to signal failures, her train finally sputtered into Gare Du Nord at 10.37 a.m. So now she has twenty minutes to get halfway across Paris or risk bungling her first major assignment.

She takes a deep breath and ups her speed, dodging the still-disembarking passengers and hailing an Uber as she runs. After what seems like an eternity, the car pulls up outside the station and she dives into it. She checks her phone to see she has a text from her dad – something about a doctor's appointment. Annie is halfway through scanning it when her Uber driver says something to her in French.

'Um, sorry – je suis désolée,' she replies. 'Je suis anglaise.'

'Ah, English,' the driver says. 'I was asking what you're doing here in Paris.'

She savours the words before she speaks them: 'I'm a journalist. I'm here to interview a band.'

She sees the driver's eyebrows arch in the rear-view mirror, and feels a pathetic little thrill from finally having the sort of job that can impress a total stranger. 'Who is the band?' the man asks.

'They're called The Defectors.'

His eyebrows drop back to their resting position. 'Don't know them. They are good?'

'Oh yeah, they're amazing.' Annie nods. 'They're going to be massive.'

Truthfully, she is just regurgitating what her editor told her last week when he handed her this commission. To Annie, The Defectors sound like pretty much every other bunch of scruffy middle-class white boys with guitars she's ever heard. Nothing special. Not that she would admit that out loud in the office. Maybe her editor is right, though. In a few years' time, this could be like saying she once interviewed the Foo Fighters or Arctic Monkeys.

She feels another prickle of excitement on the back of her neck. This could be HUGE. She checks her phone: 10.48 a.m.

All she has to do now is get there.

CHAPTER ELEVEN

WILL

5th March, present day
Euston Square, London

I'm still thinking about Pia's call at half seven the next evening as I stumble onto the crowded Metropolitan Line back from work.

Dev was on some training course all day, so I had the shop to myself, and we were totally dead apart from one guy who spent an hour browsing extension cables and then sloped out without buying any.

So, basically, it was just me, sat at the till, thinking about that call.

I navigate the carriage's complex obstacle course of takeaway trays and discarded *Evening Standards* and slump down into a free seat. It's weird – this used to happen all the time when I first started at Green Shoots. Every call I got would stay with me for days afterwards. I couldn't help imagining the caller's life in intricate detail, colouring in all the bits they hadn't told me. I'd picture them at work or at college or at home – putting on a brave face for friends and family, pretending everything was fine, and all the time holding this secret pain in their chest.

I'd even project the callers onto strangers; people I passed in the street. The woman who barely made eye contact as she served me in Tesco could be the same person who'd tearfully told me about their abusive husband the night before. The teenager who barged past me onto the bus might be the same frightened kid who'd confessed he was too scared to come out to his right-wing parents.

It seemed like this incredible – and incredibly strange – privilege; to see into someone's life for just a moment, to have them tell you things they wouldn't tell their closest friends. Things they wouldn't tell anyone.

Better than I was when I called. That's how Pia had said she was feeling before she put the phone down. I think about how she sounded when she said it, and for the first time in a long time, I feel . . . OK. Like I'm doing something good. Even if I'm doing it for selfish reasons. Maybe I am making some sort of difference.

Better than I was when I called. I wonder where she is right now.

The Tube driver's voice crackles through the speaker, making everyone look up, wincing, from their phones. I look up too, and as I do I catch eyes with two blokes sat opposite me. Their gazes scatter as soon as I notice them. They look at each other, lips bitten, eyebrows raised in amusement.

I feel a horrible churning in the pit of my stomach. I pick up an *Evening Standard* from the seat next to me, holding it slightly higher than necessary to mask my face, like I'm a crap spy in a crap spy movie.

I can hear them whispering over the whirr of the train. This is pathetic. I'm being ridiculous. I'm being paranoid.

But they do fit the profile *exactly* of the 0.001 per cent of people in this city that might recognise me – i.e. men, a few years younger than I am, with shoulder-length hair and wrist tattoos now half-hidden by freshly ironed office shirts. Indie kids all grown up.

The train hisses into Baker Street.

'Sorry, mate. 'Scuse me?'

I focus hard on a '60-second interview' with Paul Chuckle, and try to block out the hot thudding in my ears.

'Sorry? Mate?'

I lower the paper to see them both staring at me.

'You're not . . . Did you used to be in a band?'

My throat is dry suddenly. I attempt a smile. 'Yeah.'

'I knew it!' The first bloke slaps his knee in delight. 'I knew I recognised him!' He nudges his mate. 'Didn't I say it was him?'

His mate just shrugs. 'I've never even heard of him.'

Before everything happened, back when I was a different person, I used to daydream about what it would be like to get recognised in public by strangers. I used to pine for the attention – the furtive glances, spreading smiles, looks of embarrassed awe. Now I realise it just means people talking about you as if you weren't there – like you're a Madame Tussauds waxwork or something.

The truth is: I am the absolute worst kind of 'famous' – recognisable only to a tiny handful of people, all of whom probably think I'm an utter tit.

The first bloke turns back to me with a broad grin. 'I think I saw you lot at Bestival back in the day!'

I nod, the memory flashing into my head. That intern from Universal chopping up coke on the airbed in her tent. Powder bouncing everywhere, all of us laughing. So out of it I could barely breathe. Joe came, too. I invited him backstage. As fucked as I was, I still remember him being quieter than usual. I remember taking my shirt off on stage, swinging it around my head like the worst cliché of a rock star. It's still on YouTube, I think. The shame and the guilt heat my whole body instantly.

I need to get out of this carriage.

'Yeah, I remember it now,' says the Grown-Up Indie Kid. 'You guys were . . . all right.'

'Cheers.' That's probably as accurate a summary of our band as you'll ever hear, to be fair.

I grip the handrail, ready to stand up.

'So, what happened, then?' the GUIK asks, waving a hand at me, as if to say: *Why are you slouched on the Metropolitan Line at rush hour, rather than jet skiing with Bono and Mick Jagger in the Seychelles?*

'I just . . .' The words congeal in my mouth. Joe backstage, quieter than usual. The memory of it grips me around the throat. I can't think about this now.

I shake my head. Get to my feet. 'Sorry, this is my stop. Nice to meet you, though.' I can feel the sweat prickling on my forehead.

Why won't this fucking train *stop*?

The GUIK is up, too, his hand on my shoulder. 'No worries, man. Can I get a quick photo, though? I've got a mate who used to be really into your group – he'll think it's hilarious.'

I turn away, my head throbbing. 'Sorry, this is my stop.' I can just keep repeating that until the doors open. The train bursts out of the tunnel finally, the signs for Finchley Road flashing past in a red-blue blur.

I hear him sit back down, muttering: 'Fucking prick. Who does he think he is?'

The doors hiss open and I stagger onto the platform, gulping the dirty air. My face is boiling, the blood thundering in my ears.

Joe, backstage, quieter than usual. I never even asked him if he was all right.

I look round as the train moves off to see the GUIK holding his phone up at me. The camera flash stings my eyes through the window.

I swipe yet more *Evening Standards* off the hard, plastic bench and wait for the next train. It's not for ten minutes.

For some reason I think of Pia again. How her call had made me feel like I was OK, even if just for a few hours.

But I am not OK. I am very far from it.

CHAPTER TWELVE

ANNIE

5th March
Barbican, London

'No. Fucking. Way,' says Maya when I tell her.

We're sat in a wine bar near my office. She's squeezing me in for a quick post-work drink before her latest date – a drink she'd initially insisted she had no time for until I decided to play my trump card and tease a mention of the Defectors article. So now she's pushed her date back an hour and is sitting opposite me with saucer-sized eyes and her jaw hanging open.

'As in: actual *Will Axford* Will Axford?' she says.

I nod. 'Actual Will Axford Will Axford.'

Her eyes get wider, her jaw hangs lower. I smile. I'm quite enjoying this, to be honest. Since my life is generally quite dull, and Maya's is one long, hilarious anecdote of dating disasters, it's usually her doing the talking and me doing the gawping. It feels nice to have the spotlight for once.

'So are you gonna do it?' she asks. 'The article, I mean?'

I shrug. 'I kind of have to. Matt made it pretty clear that I'd be in danger of getting hoofed out if I didn't.'

She sips her wine and grins at me. 'This is amazing!'

'How is it amazing?' I sputter back. 'I'm going to have to contact – and possibly even meet up with – Actual Will Axford Will Axford! It's going to be horrendous, Maya.'

'Are you kidding?' she hisses. 'It's going to be great! You can finally confront him for being such a total douchelord.'

'Did you not read my article, five years ago? I already kind of did that.'

'So? This time you'll be able to do it properly. In person.'

I toy with my glass and Maya pouts at me. 'Don't tell me you're just going to act like nothing happened? After what he *did*?'

Her righteous fury drags a laugh out of me. She has literally got her hands on her hips. Maya is terrifying when she's like this, in businesswoman mode. She's Head of Marketing for a ridiculously posh handbag brand and, from what I can understand, her job mainly involves shouting at junior members of staff for several hours a day. I still can't get over how weird it is seeing her in smart suits when we spent most of our teens done up in ripped jeans and My Chemical Romance t-shirts.

'He didn't actually *do* anything, Maya,' I point out.

She rolls her eyes. 'Yes, well, that's the point, isn't it?' she says cryptically. But I know what she means. A smile flashes across her face. 'Hey, do you remember, I wrote that seriously-pissed-off email for you to send to his PR person a few days later? Calling him every name under the sun?'

'Thank God I didn't send that.' Ugh. Just the thought of their PR person makes me flinch. I can still remember her name. Jess. The girl with the fringe.

'You so should have!'

Maya and I were sharing a flat five years ago, when all this happened. I remember at the time – on the Eurostar home – making a conscious decision to not turn this into a big thing. When my friends asked what happened, I told them, and we spent a couple of weeks laughing about what an arsehole Will Axford was, and then the whole thing was pretty much forgotten. It became just a funny story. But it didn't feel funny at the time. It still doesn't. I spent most of that return Eurostar journey sobbing in the toilet. I feel a little sting of shame at the memory of it.

As ridiculous as it sounds, that day in Paris meant something to me. Even if it clearly meant sod all to Will Axford.

'Anyway,' I say. 'Enough about past, failed romance. Let's hear about future, successful romance. Who's up tonight?'

Maya laughs. She's still wearing her dark-blue work suit, but topped off with perfect hair and oodles of smoky eye make-up. She looks amazing.

'Tom, 36, a recruitment consultant,' she says. 'We've been messaging for a couple of weeks. I thought I'd make an effort as I've got a good feeling about this one.' She peers around me, at the mirror behind the bar. 'He wasn't holding a fish in his photo, for a start.'

'Is that really a thing?' I ask. 'Holding fish in photos?'

'Unfortunately, yeah. I'd say at least 30 per cent of the men you come across on the apps are holding fish in their pictures.'

'What the hell. Why?'

She shrugs. 'Apparently it's a caveman, hunter-gatherer thing. The sight of it is supposed to trigger some long-dormant thing in women; show us that they're good "providers" or whatever. At least that's what the one and only fish-holder I went on a date with told me.'

'Wait – he actually explained the logic of it to you?'

'Mm-hm. I only went out with him in the first place because I wanted to finally get to the bottom of the fish-holding thing.'

'Well, maybe it's true. Maybe it does subconsciously appeal to us.'

'Not to me, it doesn't,' Maya says. 'I don't eat fish.'

I snort into my wine glass, and she grins at me. 'If there were more men with pictures of themselves holding bags of Haribo Starmix, I might not be single.'

She glances at the clock. 'I'd better go, mate.'

I stand up with her. 'OK. Hope it's fun. Hope he's The One. Keep me posted.'

'Will do. And keep *me* posted on Will Axford Will Axford. Have you actually started trying to track him down yet?'

'Not really. I did Google him last night, actually, but . . .' I can feel Maya's eyes on me, and I tail off. 'There was nothing.'

She nods. There's no way in hell I'm telling her what actually happened last night. Me getting drunk and weepy and inexplicably deciding to call some random crisis helpline I found on Instagram.

I'm still not sure what came over me. I just wanted to talk to someone so badly, and when that number popped up it seemed like . . . not an *omen* or anything – I'm not completely crackers. But something made me call it.

Either way, speaking to Jack did actually make me feel better. It was such a strange sensation, opening up to this faceless person, *crying* to them. But it also felt . . . natural. I felt like I could tell him anything. He wasn't trying to pressure me or push his own opinions on me. I wasn't worried about scaring him or freaking him out or letting him down. He didn't come with any of the baggage that my friends and family come with. He was just . . . there. On the other end of the line. 'Listening without judgement.'

Things really did seem clearer when I ended the call. Like some of the fog in my head had evaporated. I sort of wish we'd talked longer.

CHAPTER THIRTEEN

WILL

7th March
Green Shoots office, Limehouse

Busy night. Every time I hang up the phone, it rings again.

It's quite nice, actually. No time to think between calls.

Over the past two days, that moment on the Tube has kept coming back to nag at me, like an itch I can't scratch. I spend so much energy trying *not* to think about my days in the band, and then something like that happens and it's *all* I can think about.

Last night, lying in bed, trying to sleep, I even got as far as typing 'The Defectors' into Google. I caught a glimpse of myself on the screen; mid-twenties, stupid haircut, gurning at the camera like an absolute knob. I flinched and closed my phone before the page could even load. Then I stared at the ceiling until the sun came up.

I wonder where that desire comes from – to do something that you know full well will make you feel awful? There's probably some obscure, six-syllable German word for it. I guess it's the same self-immolating emotion that drives you to hate-stalk a particularly irritating Facebook friend. Only, in this case, that irritating Facebook friend is *me*. A younger me – a different me.

A different person entirely.

I'm sure I'll end up being drawn to some cringeworthy old Defectors interview on YouTube at some point tonight. But for the moment there just hasn't been time.

The first call this evening was an immediate hang-up. Which means it was almost certainly a sex call. I know for a fact that Green Shoots – like most helplines – gets its fair share of these. But apparently our small but dedicated band of perverts don't get off on hearing a man's voice, so as soon as I say 'Hello', I get the dialling tone. From the email chains that are sent round, I know it's not the same for the female listeners, who are forced to spend roughly 10 per cent of their time in this room hanging up on literal wankers.

I initially assumed the second call was a prank or wrong number because after I said hello, there was no answer – just the murmur of a TV or radio in the background. But then a very quiet, very deep voice came through: 'I want to be a girl. I feel like a girl.'

I've had this caller before, and these two sentences are all they ever say. The first few times, I tried to probe a little: 'Tell me more about this? How long have you felt this way?' But they just repeated those same two sentences: 'I want to be a girl. I feel like a girl.'

So now, all I ever say back is, 'That's OK, that's OK.' It goes on like that for two or three minutes, and then they hang up. Same thing every time.

Am I helping that person? I have no idea. Maybe it just feels good for them to speak their truth to someone. Maybe they've spent their whole life keeping silent about it and it lightens their burden to be able to say it out loud.

I don't know. I hope I'm helping.

The third caller is Eric, whose mood tends to fluctuate wildly – especially if he's had a drink – but tonight, thankfully, he's on fine form. Listening to him when he's in this kind of fun, playful mood is a bit like experiencing your own private episode of *Gogglebox*. He'll channel surf and narrate his thoughts to me as they come. He's watching *Top of the Pops 2* this evening, which essentially means I get a running commentary on each group.

'Dear oh dear, Flock of Seagulls,' he says. 'What *was* he thinking with that hairdo?'

I laugh. Bitchy Eric is my favourite Eric. 'Why, what was it like? I don't know that band.'

'Are you in front of a computer?'

'Yeah.'

'And are you *sitting down*?' he adds melodramatically.

I laugh again. 'Yes.'

'Type "Flock of Seagulls" into Google.'

As I'm typing, the eerie similarity with what I was doing last night – Googling another forgotten band: my own – is not lost on me. But any creeping feelings of anxiety dissolve in an instant when I see the photos.

I snort with laughter, and Eric says: 'I take it you've found them, then. To think there was a brief period in about 1984 when I considered having my hair done like that.'

'You're kidding.'

'Afraid not. Ooh, the Fun Boy Three are on now, this is better,' he says. 'D'you remember them? They'll have been long before your time.'

'That was the group some of The Specials formed after The Specials split up, wasn't it?'

'Ah! I'm impressed, Jack.'

'I do my best.' Not sure how I even know this. Some of Joe's encyclopaedic musical knowledge must have seeped through by osmosis, I guess.

'I always thought Terry Hall was rather sexy, actually,' Eric says.

I laugh again. 'Very sexy.'

'I saw the Fun Boy Three's first ever gig, you know?'

'No way. Seriously?'

Eric hardly ever talks like this: about his past. It's always present with him. Over the years, I've tried probing into his early life, to see if there was anything he wanted to discuss. But he always sidestepped it, and after a while I gave up.

He carries on in this vein for a little longer, before switching channels to briefly – and hilariously – dissect Chris Packham's outfit on *Springwatch*, and then bidding me good night.

I replace the receiver and log his call on the computer, selecting 'loneliness' and 'desire for conversation' as I always do with an Eric call. The Green Shoots menu cites everything from 'physical abuse' and 'depression' to 'suicidal thoughts' and 'bereavement' as the reasons why people choose to call. But it's the 'loneliness' option I end up selecting most.

I'm about to go and make some tea, when the phone bursts into life again. I reach over to pick it up.

'Hello, Green Shoots Crisis Line?'

'Hello . . . Hi.'

A woman's voice, full of such uncertainty and trepidation that for a second my heart skips because I think it might be

'Pia' again. My thoughts have been drifting back to her pretty regularly these past few days. Wondering if and when she'll call back.

But within a second I realise this caller is not her. It's an older lady, already breathless and tearful, and I feel my neck heat up, sensing this will be a bad one.

'Hi, what's on your mind this evening?' I ask softly.

'I just can't . . . Something happened . . . I just . . .' Her breathing is jagged and frantic and she can hardly get the words out. 'I'm sorry, I'm sorry . . .'

I keep my voice as level as I can. 'Please, don't worry – just take your time. We've got all the time you need.'

'Something happened,' she repeats.

'Do you want to tell me about it?'

A pause. 'I can't . . . yet. I just need . . . This sounds silly, but I just need to breathe. Can I just breathe for a while?'

'Yes, of course, yes.'

And that's exactly what she does. For four minutes, forty-six seconds, this complete stranger just breathes down the phone at me. And with every breath, she begins to sound calmer and less manic, until finally, the hoarse, frightened gulps have completely disappeared, and she is inhaling and exhaling steadily.

I'm about to ask if I can give her another number – a specialist helpline or a professional therapist – when she says: 'Thank you so much. Good night,' and the phone goes dead.

*

I get home just after midnight.

I crawl into bed and Milligan settles on top of the duvet at my feet, purring contentedly. I usually spend the hours immediately after most of my Green Shoots shifts decompressing, unable to get one particular call out of my head, and tonight that call is The Breathing Lady. I wonder what happened to her, whether she's OK. Whether I made any difference.

I think about Pia again. Vague, formless thoughts. The cold, creeping realisation that I am fantasising about a connection I'm not sure was even there, with a faceless stranger over the phone. And yet it's the most meaningful and memorable connection I've made in months. Years, maybe.

I think about Eric. About his refusal to talk about his past. About all the connections he must have made throughout his life, and how every single one of them has fizzled out and died.

Eric is where I will end up.

Almost without realising I'm doing it, I grab my phone and do what I always do when the walls close in and the loneliness gets too suffocating. I know it's the wrong thing. I know I'll regret it. But I do it anyway.

She answers after two rings.

'Hey.' She almost has to shout over the wall of noise behind her. Sounds like she's in a crowded bar somewhere.

'Hey. Sorry to bother you, you're obviously out and about.'

'No, that's OK,' she says, her voice lowering as she moves somewhere less raucous. 'Things are winding down here anyway. So, what's up? Been a while.'

'Yeah. Sorry, I just . . .'

I hear her laugh humourlessly as I tail off. 'What is this, Will? A booty call?'

'No. It's not that, Jess. Honestly. I just wanted to see you.'

'Do you really think that's a good idea,' she says, 'after last time?' She sounds like a teacher scolding a badly behaved kid, and it makes me flush with shame.

'It won't be like last time,' I mumble.

'Hmm.' She sighs. 'I don't know, Will. If you're going to get all clingy again, that's not going to be much fun for either of us, is it?'

The shame intensifies. Hardens. 'No. I know. I won't.'

'Are you at yours?' she asks. And before I can answer she snorts: 'Well, obviously, where else would you be?'

The self-loathing starts to uncurl in my stomach and I suddenly hope more than anything that she'll say she can't come. There's a pause, filled only by the distant clamour of raised voices and clinking glasses.

'OK,' she says finally. 'I'll be over in a bit.'

I climb out of bed and start trying to make the flat look a bit more presentable. I know I'll feel worse than I already do by the time she gets here. And probably worse still by the time she leaves.

But at least I won't be alone.

CHAPTER FOURTEEN

ANNIE

8th March
Shoreditch, London

'Shit,' says Lexi. 'What's going on there, do you think?'

It's lunchtime and we're sat in one of Marker's many glass-walled meeting rooms, eating Pret wraps. On the other side of the office, we've just spotted Matt being led into another meeting room by some of the finance people. His face is pale and his head is bowed; if he weren't wearing a Chewbacca hoodie he'd look like a man being led to the gallows.

'Is he getting bollocked, do you reckon?' Lexi asks through a mouthful of parsnip crisps.

'He did mention something to me about ad revenues being way down.'

She looks at me sharply. 'Seriously?'

I immediately feel a stab of guilt. I'd been purposely avoiding telling Lexi about Marker's financial woes. She's got quite enough on her plate right now what with the whole having-a-tiny-human-inside-her thing. But she'll be OK. She's a designer – and we've only got two of those on staff. The company can't afford to lose her. Matt's already having trouble finding maternity cover for her.

I tell her as much and she shrugs. 'I hope you're right.'

'I am,' I say. 'Honestly, it's the writers who should be worried, according to Matt . . .'

A spasm of panic wriggles inside me. I have to start making some progress with this Defectors thing. I can't lose this job, I really can't.

'When did Matt tell you all this?' Lex asks.

'When he gave me this advertorial thing about this band.'

'Oh yeah.' She sweeps some sandwich crumbs off her space-hopper-like belly. 'How's that going?'

'I've tried to make a start on it, but I can't find a way to get in touch with the band,' I tell her truthfully.

Lex takes a swig of her beetroot juice – her latest extremely random pregnancy craving. 'I thought you'd already interviewed them?'

'I did, but that was five years ago. It's not like I got any of the band members' phone numbers.' This was the thought that had played on repeat in my head on the Eurostar home: *why the hell didn't I get his number?*

'Let's have a look at them, then,' Lexi says. She pops another fistful of crisps into her mouth and starts tapping at her phone. Lexi doesn't know the full story when it comes to Will Axford. I only met her when I started at Marker, three years ago, and I've never told her what happened that day. Why would I? All she knows is that I wrote a mean-spirited (though, if I do say it myself, quite funny) article about his band back in the day.

'Here we go.' She shuffles up next to me, holding her phone

out, and suddenly we're watching the first YouTube result that pops up for 'Defectors band'.

It's a clip from Bestival a few years back. The group are playing a pretty average-sounding song called 'Wet Like Water' while Will Axford prances around the stage with his shirt off. It's fair to say that he looks like he's had a couple of drinks. Despite that, the sight of his tanned, Brad-Pitt-in-*Fight-Club* abs does definitely make me feel some feelings.

We watch in silence for a bit and then Lex says: 'I'd say that "Wet Like Water" has to be the worst song title I've ever heard.'

'It isn't great,' I agree.

The song finishes and Will Axford whoops into the microphone. 'Fank you, Bestival!' he bellows. 'You lot are a seriously mental crowd, yeah?!'

Lexi scrunches her nose up. 'Is that his real accent? He sounds like a posh boy pretending to be cockney.'

I nod. 'I'm pretty sure that's exactly what he is. He told me in the interview he was from Somerset, and I was thinking: "Why do you talk like Danny Dyer, then?"' The memory makes me smile in spite of myself. I remember teasing him about it that whole day in Paris: '*As if* you really talk like that!' He just smiled innocently at me with that sexy gap-tooth grin and carried on dropping his h's. I guess the whole thing was an act. I was just stupid enough to fall for it.

'Seems like a bit of a douche,' Lex says.

'A *lot* of a douche,' I say.

'He is quite fit, though.'

I shrug. Possibly too hard. 'I guess.'

We watch him mime an air guitar as the band starts up

another song. 'He looks a bit like Jamie Dornan,' Lexi says. 'Without the beard.'

'To me he just looks sweaty and ridiculous.'

She rolls her eyes and stops the video. 'Yeah, well, you've got famously awful taste. You fancy Louis Theroux, for God's sake.'

I flick a parsnip crisp at her. 'He's sexy!'

My phone vibrates on the table in front of us. I clock the name on the screen and go to slide it into my pocket. 'I'll call her back after lunch.'

'No, don't be silly,' Lexi says. 'I'm very happy sitting here watching more videos of your hot douche singer guy.'

The phone carries on buzzing in my hand. There's no option left but to answer. 'OK, I'll just be a sec.'

I step out of the room into the corridor and take a deep breath. 'Hi, Mum.'

'Oh, Annie! Hello! I'm so glad I caught you!' The shock and excitement in her voice sends a surge of guilt through me. We haven't spoken in more than a fortnight. Which is totally my fault, of course. She's tried plenty of times, I just haven't picked up. I feel like a pitiful excuse for a daughter when I ignore her calls, but I usually end up feeling ten times worse when I answer them.

'I'm sorry, Mum, things have been so hectic lately,' I tell her. 'I've been meaning to call. How are you?'

'Oh, not so bad, can't complain!' I can tell she's trying very hard to remain bright and breezy, and it dials my guilt up even further. 'And you, love? How are you?'

'Not too bad, thanks.'

'Good. Good.' She pauses, leaving the space for me to offer more. When I don't, she adds: 'And is Dom OK?'

'Yeah, he's fine. Working hard, as always.'

'Great. Good. Lovely Dom.' Another pause. 'And what about your job? Oh, I've just done your latest quiz!' she trills. 'You'll be happy to know that I am officially 78 per cent middle-class cliché! I was rather pleased with that. They were such funny questions, love – I hope you don't mind, I sent it on to Sue and Hazel, too.'

'No, Mum, of course I don't mind. I'm so glad you liked it.'

It hurts me to hear how hard she is trying. How much effort she is putting into showing she cares. I know I should give her something back. I *want* to. But nothing will come. Ever since Dad died, it's like there's this disconnect between us. Something blocking the path. Mum and Josie have almost become closer in their grief, whereas I've just drifted further away. And the scariest thing is that I can't see a way back.

'What other news, love? Is there anything on Netflix I should be watching?'

'Let me have a think, I'm sure there's something.'

'Josie tried to turn me onto *The Kardashians*, but I hadn't the foggiest what they were talking about most of the time.'

I see Lexi collecting up her Pret debris and heading back to her desk, giving me a smile as she passes. 'I'd better be off, actually, Mum. Lunch break's pretty much over.'

'Of course, love, of course.' I hear her take a steadying breath, almost as if she's steeling herself for something. 'I was only really calling to see if you'd thought any more about coming up for a visit at some point? We'd so love to see you. You haven't been up in such a long time.'

'I know, I know.' I stare across the office to see Matt nodding gloomily at whatever the finance guys are telling him in the meeting room. It's true what she says. I haven't been home in months. Mainly because home doesn't feel like home anymore. It just feels like the place I watched Dad dwindle and die. The place where we found out how bad things were really going to get. The place where Mum and Josie *refused* to listen when I told them there were other options, other ways we could try to save him. They ignored all the research I'd done, the pages I'd printed out. They just gave up on him. They allowed him to give up on himself. Nothing's really felt like home since then.

'I'll try and get up soon, Mum,' I tell her. But I know, even before I end the call, that this is a lie. I don't think going home will solve anything. I'm pretty sure it'll just make things worse.

CHAPTER FIFTEEN

WILL

8th March
Tottenham Court Road, London

'Excuse me? Is there any chance you could turn the music down, please?'

'You what?' Dev yells across the shop floor.

'COULD YOU TURN THE MUSIC DOWN, PLEASE?'

Dev reaches past me to lower the volume of his latest wall-crumbling drum 'n' bass mix. He turns back to the thin, bespectacled, extremely-pissed-off-looking Waterstones employee stood in the MicroShop doorway.

'It's coming through the walls into our store next door,' says the bloke, whose name tag reads 'Jeremy'. 'It's putting the customers off.'

'Listen, mate,' Dev says huffily. 'This music is part of a carefully devised sales plan to attract people into this shop.'

Jeremy looks around the empty store. 'There's no one in here.'

'You're in here,' Dev shoots back. 'And tell me – why is that?'

'Well, because of the music. But—'

Dev holds his hands up smugly. 'Bingo.'

Jeremy pinches the bridge of his nose. 'Look . . . Please can you just keep the volume at a manageable level?'

He walks back into the busy bookshop next door. Dev sighs and shakes his head, turning the music off completely. 'I always knew I wouldn't be appreciated in my lifetime. I'm like Van Gogh. Or that bloke who wrote *Dragon Tattoo*.'

'I appreciate you in your lifetime, Dev,' I tell him.

He nods stoically. 'Thanks, bro. I needed that.' He twists the hi-fi dial to BBC 6 Music and claps his hands together. 'Now – whose turn is it to make tea?'

'Definitely yours,' I say. 'I unpacked that delivery of USB sticks this morning.'

'Yeah, but I dealt with the Waterstones guy.'

'Yeah, and then I told you that I appreciated you in your lifetime.'

'Shit, you're right.' Dev clicks his tongue against his teeth. 'You're lucky this shop's a democracy, William. Two sugars, then?'

'Actually can I have a coffee, please?'

He grins. 'Big night last night, was it?'

'Sort of.'

'Nice. I won't ask for details. I know you're an international man of mystery,' he says, disappearing into the kitchen. I stare out at the empty shop floor. *Big night last night*.

Jess left early this morning. It was like something out of a bad movie: as I woke up and rolled over, she was already half-dressed, preparing to sneak out of the bedroom.

She smirked when she saw the look on my face. 'Did you want me to stay and *snuggle*?'

That last word sounded wrong coated with such sarcastic venom. Especially considering our bodies had been tangled in each other just a few hours previously. I did want her to stay, though. I also couldn't wait for her to leave. The two things were directly contradictory but true nonetheless, which I suppose makes me Schrödinger's knobhead.

I watched her pull her jumper on and wondered the same thing I always wonder on these morning-afters: *why do I keep calling her? And why does she keep coming?*

She pulled her long, honey-coloured hair up into a bun and looked around the room sniffily. 'You said last time you were going to decorate a bit. Put some pictures up or something.'

'I am. I will.'

'How long have you been here now?' she asked.

'Coming up on four years.'

She gave a mocking little laugh. 'I'm sure you'll get round to it eventually.'

I sat up and rubbed my eyes. When I opened them she was still there, one hand gripping the door handle. 'We can talk if you want,' she said with a sigh. 'But some other time. I really do have to go now. I'll be late for work.'

I nodded. 'It's just that it was five years ago, last week.'

I watched her do the maths in her head. I suppose, unlike me, her entire life doesn't orbit around that particular day. 'Right, yes,' she said quietly.

'I'm really sorry, Jess,' I told her. 'For how I was back then. For how I treated you.'

'Mm'. She gripped the door handle tighter. 'Yeah, you always tell me that.'

'Do I?' I honestly couldn't remember saying it before.

'Yeah, you do.'

'Well, I am,' I said. 'Sorry.'

'Uh-huh. It's all right. I'm getting my own back now, aren't I?'

She laughed at that. I have no idea if she was joking or not. Then she grabbed her bag and looked at me. 'Will, I don't think you'll be able to be OK with what happened until you're OK with yourself. And I can't help you there. No one can. That one is all down to you.'

CHAPTER SIXTEEN

ANNIE

8th March
Ladbroke Grove, London

'Dom! Did you eat those chocolates?'

I hear his body shift on the sofa in the next room. 'No!' he calls back. And then: 'What chocolates?'

I shut the cupboard and walk out of the kitchen into the living room. 'Those posh German ones I bought yesterday. The Leibnizes or whatever they're called.'

'Oh.' He thinks for a second, then focuses his attention on the MacBook in his lap. 'No, don't think so.'

As annoyed as I am, I can't help smiling. 'You're a terrible liar. Never have an affair. I'd know straight away.'

'Haha.' He gives me a crumpled grin. 'Sorry. I thought they were up for grabs. We need to start labelling our stuff, like at uni.'

He's joking – I hope – but it still cuts a little too close to home. I spend a lot of time lately worrying that Dom and I are turning into flatmates rather than lovers. I actually can't even remember the last time we had sex. The fact that we're both usually knackered after work doesn't count. Lexi told me that she and Gavin are still doing it at least once a week – and she's nearly eight months bloody pregnant. Apparently the hormones are 'doing wonders for her libido'. I'm thrilled for her, obviously, but it does cast a slightly depressing light on my own largely sex-free relationship.

There was a long while after Dad died when nothing happened in that department, of course. I just didn't feel like it. I suppose I found it impossible to connect physically when I was still hurting so badly emotionally. What I really wanted was just to be *held* – but Dom's never been much of a one for extensive cuddling.

In the past couple of months, though, I've started to notice the desire returning. I've even felt horny again. But still . . . nothing is happening. It's not even something we've talked about. It's like we've both just accepted it. I've tried all the stupid things that *Cosmo* and *Glamour* tell you to try in these situations: 'randomly' selecting my sexiest knickers as I'm getting dressed in the morning, making sure I put them on right in front of him . . . But I can't ever seem to draw his gaze away from his iPad.

He yawns and stretches out on the sofa. He looks nice tonight – clean-shaven for once, as he had meetings today, and still wearing his crisp white work shirt with the top two buttons undone. Maybe . . . Maybe we could have sex *right now*? Maybe I could initiate it? Forget all the *Cosmo* crap – just sit down and start snogging him. We've just had a nice dinner, a couple of glasses of wine each . . . Why should it only be Lex and Gavin boffing 24-7? Why not us too?

Suddenly filled with excitement at this brilliant idea, I drop down right beside him on the couch, and rest my hand on his knee.

'Hey,' I say, kissing him softly on the mouth.

'Hey back,' he says, smiling.

Yes. This is good. This is exactly what we need.

I move my hand up onto his thigh, and go to kiss him again. But at that exact moment, he yawns again and springs to his feet, laptop in hand.

'Well, I think I'm going to head to bed, babe,' he announces.

The sting of rejection is so sharp that for one horrible second I'm worried I might cry. 'Oh . . . OK.'

'Just so knackered from work and stuff.' He yawns a third time, slightly too theatrically, then taps his laptop. 'Plus, that new *Star Wars* series has just come onto Disney+. Was thinking I might watch the first episode. And you're not interested in that, are you?'

I nail on a smile. 'Matt's been banging on about it constantly in the office. I feel like I've already seen it.'

'Oh, OK. No spoilers!' he jokes.

'It's just . . .' I swallow hard and try to keep my voice breezy and casual. 'It feels like we haven't spent any proper time together for ages.'

He sighs and reaches down to squeeze my knee. I didn't think I could feel any worse right now, but that knee squeeze proves me wrong. 'I know, sorry,' he says. 'We will. Work's just so hectic at the moment that I don't have time to think about much else.'

I nod. 'Right, yeah.'

He heads for the door. 'OK, see you up there in a bit.'

Before he can leave, I say, 'I spoke to Mum today.'

He stops in the doorway. I see his shoulders sag slightly at being yanked away from his *Star Wars* show. 'Oh, right?' He turns around. 'She OK?'

'Yeah, she's good. She was talking about me going up to visit.'

'Well, you should. Although . . .' He furrows his brow. 'Would I have to drive you? Because with work stuff, it might be diff—'

'No, don't worry. I can train it up there. I just don't know if it's a good idea. It still feels so . . . weird between us.'

'Mm-hm.' His eyes find the clock on the wall. Another sting of rejection.

'Anyway, you're tired, so . . .'

'No, we should talk about it,' he says. 'It's just . . .' He glances at the clock again. 'Maybe it's a bit late now?'

'Yeah. Of course. Don't worry. You head up.'

His face visibly brightens at being let off the hook. 'Sorry, babe. We'll talk tomorrow, I promise.'

'Yep, no probs.'

Frustration, humiliation, loneliness, horniness – all of them are pushing and shoving inside me. I wanted a physical connection – sex – but Dom was too tired. I wanted an emotional connection – to talk about Mum – but he'd rather watch *Star Wars*. Perfect.

From upstairs, I can already hear the faint sound of lightsabers swishing. Before I really know what I'm doing, I've opened my phone and started scrolling idly through the outgoing call list. And when I get to the number, I think: screw it, why not?

I dial, fully ready to hang up if I hear a voice that isn't his.

The 'engaged' tone sounds in my ear. Only when my breath rushes back out of me do I realise that I've been holding it.

Oh well. I switch the telly on and pour another glass of wine. Maybe I'll try again later.

CHAPTER SEVENTEEN

WILL

8th March
Green Shoots office, Limehouse

'OK, Jack,' Eric says. 'Your turn now. Let's see . . . how about Ryan Gosling, Idris Elba, Tom Hardy?'

I'm now four hours into my evening shift and I've gone from comforting a newly divorced father of three as he cried down the phone, to playing an extended game of 'Shag, Marry, Avoid' with a lonely pensioner.

Say what you like about this crisis line lark, but it's never boring.

Eric and I have fallen into this game because he heard someone mention it on the TV show he was watching. I've spent the past ten minutes throwing out trios of good-looking celebrities for him to categorise, and now he's decided to punt one back at me.

'You know we're not supposed to express opinions on this line, right?' I say. 'Listen without judgement and all that?'

'Oh, come on,' he scoffs. 'I'm hardly going to tell Ryan and Idris, am I?'

'All right, all right . . .' I quickly Google my three options so as to make a truly informed decision. 'OK, it's a tough one, but I'll go for . . . marry Idris, shag Tom, avoid Gosling.'

Eric explodes in derision. 'Avoid Gosling? Avoid *Ryan Gosling*?'

'He's not all that. He looks like a skinnier, non-bald Phil Mitchell.'

Laughter floods the phone. 'God almighty, Jack, you've terrible taste in men. It's a bloody good thing you're straight.'

I laugh back, mock-offended. 'How do *you* know I'm straight?'

'Oh, it's all in the voice. You've a very heterosexual voice.'

'I don't know why, but I'm quite offended by that.'

He chuckles. 'I have to say, that's one of the few things that cheers me up when I feel low – the way your generation seems far more open and accepting about things like sexual preference than mine was.' He sighs: 'Still is.'

'Again, Eric – how exactly do you know which generation I'm from?'

'As I said, Jack, you can tell a lot about someone by their voice.'

'Oh, OK. So what can you tell about me, then – other than my apparently glaringly obvious straightness?'

I hear him mute the TV, which has been rumbling in the background. He's obviously having fun, coming out of himself a little, and I feel a little boost at the thought I'm making this lonely man's day marginally better.

'I'd say you're in your . . . early thirties?' he offers.

'Mmm,' I reply neutrally.

'And I bet you've got an interesting job doing something

creative. A lovely girlfriend – perhaps even a wife. Maybe even a young child?'

I make more neutral noises, but I'm very much hoping he'll leave it there. I don't exactly relish being reminded of the kind of life I could have had if things hadn't turned out the way they did. To me, what Eric has just described represents that moment on a game show when a losing contestant is shoved in front of a conveyor belt of glittering prizes: 'Here's what you *could* have won . . .'

For a brief second, I imagine correcting him: 'No, actually, Eric, you're way off the mark there, mate: I work in a failing electronics store and live alone with a cat. And as for the "lovely girlfriend or wife", I'm not sure exactly how you'd categorise my toxic entanglement with Jess, but there's definitely nothing "lovely" about it.' How would he react, I wonder, if I just started talking – about the band, about Joe, about the rut I'm not sure I'll ever manage to climb out of.

The irony is, I spend all my time at Green Shoots telling callers how healthy it is to talk about their problems, but when it comes to talking about my own . . . I don't know. It's never helped. Or maybe I've never found the right listener. After everything fell apart, Mum and Dad packed me off to a couple of therapists, hoping it would help me process what had happened. But I couldn't be fully honest with them. I could never find the courage to shine the light on the darkest corners of that day, five years ago. The cold, hard, irredeemable fact that it was all my fault.

Still, hearing Eric so perky manages to cheer me up. He's had a few wobbles over the past couple of months – occasionally he's sounded very down indeed. He never goes into detail about why exactly he's feeling low. But he has mentioned he's on medication – anti-depressants, pills for anxiety, that sort of thing.

'I can neither confirm nor deny,' I say to his extremely inaccurate guess about what my life looks like.

'I thought that might be the case,' he laughs. 'Still – we've made some progress tonight. I know a tiny bit more about you. Mainly the fact that you have shocking taste in male celebrities.'

'Oi. Throw me three more and I'll prove you wrong, if you like.'

'No, no. I'd better let you go,' he says. 'Other people waiting to get through and all that. I don't want to hog the line.'

'Well, it's been great talking to you, Eric. As always.'

'You too, Jack. Speak to you soon.'

I put the phone down to log the call on the computer. Almost immediately, it starts ringing again.

'Hello, Green Shoots?'

'Oh . . . Hello,' a female voice says. 'Is that Jack again?'

CHAPTER EIGHTEEN

ANNIE

8th March
Ladbroke Grove, London

There's a second's silence and I wonder if I've got it wrong. It's not him after all. But then:

'Yes, hi, this is Jack.'

'Oh, hi.' My heart is thudding at the realisation I've actually got through to him. They must have other volunteers on this line. What were the chances of it being him again tonight? 'It's, erm, "Pia" here,' I add.

He clears his throat: 'Oh right. Yes. Hello.'

A slight sting of disappointment. He clearly doesn't remember me. But I pull myself together. He might get twenty or thirty calls a day: why would he remember mine?

'We actually spoke a few days ago,' I say. 'You very kindly assured me that I wasn't a dick?'

He laughs – a proper full-throated chuckle. 'Yes, of course, I remember.'

'Don't worry. I'm sure you get lots of calls.'

'No, not at all. Well, yes. But I remember you. Of course. It's nice to hear you again. Hear *from* you. I mean . . . it's . . .' He breaks off and takes a breath. 'I'm glad you called.'

He sounds oddly flustered. Like he's doing an impression of Hugh Grant in pretty much every Richard Curtis film – all posh, bumbling awkwardness. It's sort of . . . sweet.

'So, how are you?' he asks. 'Are you doing any better than you were the last time we talked?'

'A bit, thanks. I don't really know why I'm calling back. Just had a weird day, and last time, talking to you helped me get things straight in my head. I hope that's OK.'

'Of course,' he says. 'That's what this line's for.'

'Thank you. I still feel bad, though. Like I'm using you or something. For free therapy.'

'Use away. Free therapist, phone Beefeater – whatever you need.'

I laugh again. 'So you *do* remember.'

'Of course.' I can hear the smile in his voice and it makes the back of my neck tingle.

'So, how are you doing?' I ask. 'Has it been a busy night?'

'Yeah, sort of.'

'How many calls do you get, on average?'

He coughs. 'Actually, I'm not really supposed to talk about anything relating to myself or to this line. No opinions or what have you. This call is about you. We're just here to listen.'

'Right, of course.' I remember a phrase he used last time. '"Listen without judgement"?'

'That's the one,' he says. 'I think lots of people find it odd at first – having a one-sided conversation, where the other person doesn't really talk back.'

I shuffle my feet underneath me to sit cross-legged. 'Oh, I'm used to it. My boyfriend is an excellent one-sided conversationalist.'

'Oh, haha, right.'

I feel a spasm of guilt at that. What am I doing, slagging Dom off to a total stranger while he's sat upstairs? A little too quickly, I add: 'No, he's great, actually. Really great. He's just very busy. Tons of work on at the moment.'

'Mm-hm.'

Now I'm outlining his workload to a total stranger. What the bloody hell is wrong with me? 'I just wanted to talk to him about something that happened today, but he was a bit too tired. So, that's why I called you.'

'That's great,' Jack says. 'Do you want to tell me about what happened?'

I take a breath. I can still hear Dom's TV show rattling away upstairs. 'I got a call from my mum,' I say slowly. 'She wants me to come and visit, because I haven't in a while. But I just . . . I don't know . . .' I tail off, unable to find the right words. I can never find the right words.

'Sorry,' I mutter. 'Not very eloquent tonight.'

'Don't worry,' Jack says softly. 'Take your time. We've got all the time you need.'

I take another sip of wine. 'It's to do with my dad, you see. He, erm . . .' I drift into silence again and Jack finishes the sentence for me.

'He passed away, I remember you said.'

He says it so gently. I feel my eyelids start to prickle. I blink hard, take another sip of wine and keep talking.

'Yes. It was a while ago, but things have been off between

my mum and me ever since. My sister, too. Because she always takes Mum's side . . .' Guilt stabs at me again. 'Ugh, sorry, I feel bad talking about them like this. Behind their backs.'

'Pia,' Jack says firmly. 'You don't need to feel bad. I don't know you. You don't know me. You can tell me anything: there's no judgement here. Sometimes it's easier to talk to someone you don't know, someone you can't see.'

The simplicity of the statement dissolves the guilt in an instant. *You can tell me anything. There's no judgement here.* My God, it is freeing.

'I guess it all just got really messy towards the end,' I say. 'Dad had been through three chemo treatments by that point, and nothing was working. It was like he had given up. And I felt like it was our job – as his family – to not let him. To try absolutely everything we could do to save him.'

'Mm-hm.'

'But Mum and Josie, they just wouldn't listen. I spent so many hours researching new kinds of treatment, different drugs, but they wouldn't even look at the options I'd found. They just kept saying we needed to "respect Dad's wishes". I couldn't believe it. It was like they were just going to . . .' The words 'let him die' are on the tip of my tongue, but I can't quite say them out loud. I swallow thickly. My neck feels hot suddenly and I reach up to scratch it. 'Now he's gone. And I know Mum needs me, I know they're both grieving too, but I can't get past what happened. They just *let* him give up. And now there's just this . . . blockage between us. Or an even bigger blockage than there was before.'

'How do you mean?' Jack asks.

'It's just that, ever since I was a kid, I always felt like there was this split in my family. My mum and sister are so similar and it's always seemed like they are this little team. And Dad and I were another team. And obviously I love Josie and Mum, so much, but . . . it's like I've lost my teammate.' My voice cracks and I realise I'm crying. I press a hand to my eyes but the tears slip through my fingers.

'Sorry,' I gulp. 'I don't know why I'm telling you this.'

'It's OK, it's good,' is all he says.

He doesn't feel the need to fill up the silence. He stays quiet; gives me time to get myself together.

'I talk to him sometimes,' I say finally. 'My dad.'

'Mm. And what do you say?'

'It's not a prayer thing or anything. I don't believe he can hear me. It's just nice sometimes to have someone to direct your thoughts at. If I've read a book or seen something on telly that I know he would've liked, I'll sort of . . . imagine talking to him about it. Even say it out loud sometimes.' I shake my head. 'It sounds stupid.'

'Not at all,' he says softly.

I wipe my eyes. I've never told Dom that. I've never told anyone that. I listen to Jack's quiet breathing on the other end of the line. *I don't know you. You don't know me.* I wonder what he looks like. What kind of person he is. I dry my face and blow my nose, then wince as I imagine the snotty cacophony on the other end of the phone.

'Sorry. Not a very pleasant noise for you there.'

'S'all right,' he chuckles. 'I've heard worse, believe me. You're actually one of the less offensive nose-blowers I've encountered. We get some proper honking, trombone ones on this line, trust me.'

I laugh snottily. After a pause, he adds: 'Are you OK?'

I take a deep breath. 'I don't know. I thought I was coping. I thought I was . . .' I let out a laugh-sob as the thought crosses my mind: 'I was going to say I thought I was "over it", but I don't think you ever get over losing someone you love.'

'I don't think so either,' he says.

'Babe?'

I look up with a start to see Dom standing in the doorway in his pyjama bottoms. 'Who you talking to?' he mouths.

'Maya, I'd better go,' I blurt. 'Speak to you later.' And then I hang up the phone.

CHAPTER NINETEEN

26th February, five years ago
Paris, France

'Let's meet in the hotel lobby.'

That's what the email had said. It had failed to specify, however, that this particular hotel lobby was the size of a small airport.

Breathless and perspiring, Annie glances wildly around the vast, marble-slathered waiting area. It's just gone 11 a.m. in Paris. The interview should technically already have started. All around her are clumps of slickly dressed business people, baseball-cap-wearing tourists and uniform-clad staff, but no one resembling the person she's supposed to be meeting – The Defectors' press agent, Jessica.

Annie fires off an email to Jessica, announcing her arrival (why the hell didn't she ask for a phone number?) before heading straight for the nearest bathroom. Inside, she finds yet more cream-coloured marble, and her own sweaty, dishevelled reflection staring back at her in the mirror.

She pats her damp hairline with some paper towels and tries to fix her blotchy eyeliner. The traffic was so bad in central Paris that she had to duck out of her Uber early and sprint the final four streets to the hotel. As a result, she looks not like a super-cool professional music journalist, but rather a panda that's stepped off a treadmill.

She gives up on the eyeliner, splashes her face with some deliciously cold water, and checks her email. No reply from Jessica. She resurfaces into the lobby, her eyes peeled, and narrowly avoids crashing into a pretty woman with a very severe fringe.

'Shit! Sorry,' Annie gasps. 'I mean – excusez-moi!'

'That's OK,' says the girl with the fringe. English. English accent.

'You're not . . . Are you Jessica, by any chance?' Annie asks.

The girl smooths her fringe with her fingertips. 'Yes. Call me Jess. And I'm guessing you're Annie? From UKmusic.com?'

'Yes! Hello! I'm so sorry I'm late. Nightmare journey.'

Jess looks Annie up and down, raising an eyebrow. 'Did you swim here?' she asks.

'No! No – I came on the Eurostar,' says Annie, unnecessarily.

'Right. I was joking?'

'Oh. Ha. Nice one!' Annie dabs at her damp forehead with her shirt-sleeve.

'Uh-huh,' says Jess. 'Well, I'll take you up if you're ready. We've got a room booked for the interview, and the boys are already raring to go.'

The lift ride to the tenth floor is excruciating. There are mirrors on the walls, ceilings and doors – each one apparently intent on highlighting the glaring differences between Jess (sleek, calm, beautiful) and Annie (a quite literal hot mess).

They pad down the soft, carpeted corridor towards the room. Annie is too nervous to even bother making small talk: not that Jess seems like she'd have much time for it anyway. Definitely not a small-talk person, Jess. They come to a halt outside the door, and she slaps a keycard onto the monitor.

'Here we go, then . . .'

Inside the room, three scruffy boys in their mid- to late-twenties lie sprawled across the sofas and bed. The air is heavy with the scent of stale alcohol and fried food. The smell of hangovers.

'That's Sim, that's Al, that's Mike,' says Jess, pointing a finger at each in turn. 'This is Annie, from UKmusic.com.'

'What's up, Annie from UKmusic.com?' Horizontal on the couch, Sim grins at her woozily. He holds up a sticky polystyrene box. 'Do you want a chip?'

'Um, no, I'm good, thanks!' Annie says brightly. 'Great to meet you all!'

Jess glances round the room, her brow wrinkled. 'And where's . . .'

A door opens on the other side of the room to reveal a tall, lean, good-looking boy with shaggy brown hair. He swaggers in, clutching several gin miniatures in his fists. 'I've just found another fucking mini bar!' he barks.

Jess shakes her head in mock dismay. But she's smiling at him. Annie realises it's the first time she's actually seen Jess smile.

'And this reprobate,' Jess says, 'is Will.'

CHAPTER TWENTY

WILL

14th March, present day
Harrow, Middlesex

I knew she had a boyfriend.

I mean, she mentioned him within the first few minutes of the first call. And then, during the second call, she talked about how she'd wanted to speak to him earlier that night but he'd been too tired. So she'd called Green Shoots instead. It seemed like she was insinuating that things weren't that great between them. Or maybe I'm reading way too much into one throwaway comment. Anyway, the important thing is: I knew there was a boyfriend in the picture.

So I'm not sure why it felt so jarring to actually *hear* him. Because that must have been him. A male voice in the background, calling out: 'Babe?' It had to be.

Even more jarring, though, was how Pia responded to him. *Maya, I'd better go. Speak to you later.*

I guess it's not surprising that she pretended to be talking to someone else. I'd bet that at least three-quarters of Green Shoots callers probably phone us without their partners or children or friends knowing it. That's why they're calling, right – because they've got no one else to talk to. Phoning a crisis line isn't exactly something you shout about from the rooftops.

I exhale and run my fingers through my hair. Why the *hell* am I thinking about this so much? About her? I don't do this with the other callers. At least, not to this extent. What is it about Pia that I just can't shake? A cynical voice in my head answers that one straight away: *you've got no connections in the real world, so you're imagining one with this total stranger.*

As usual, the cynical voice is probably bang on the money. I certainly can't think of a decent rebuttal to that suggestion, and there's no one else here to defend me. No one except Milligan, that is, who pads into the bedroom from the living room and gently swats my ankle with his paw, reminding me that I'm late with his mid-morning Dreamies delivery.

I reach down and scratch the back of his neck. 'You're right, sorry, mate. Come on, let's get you some food.'

He follows me through to the kitchen, where I empty a generous pile of biscuits into his bowl before topping up his water. 'Best stay in here today,' I tell him as he plunges nose-first into the grub. 'The bedroom's a bit of a tip.'

This is an understatement. Waking up this morning, with the thought of a long, empty day off ahead of me and absolutely nothing to fill it with, I'd suddenly remembered Jess' comments about what a state my flat was in. I decided then and there I would spend the day finally cleaning up a bit.

Since moving in, the corner of my bedroom has played home to a wobbly tower of battered cardboard boxes that had previously been festering in my parents' attic. I decided my first job would be to sort through these and see if there was anything worth keeping, before dumping the rest in the recycling. Hence why my bedroom floor is currently a labyrinth of tatty papers and dusty boxes.

I opened a few of them this morning and had a brief flick through, but there was nothing I either needed or wanted. It was mostly folders from school and university, long-out-of-date tenants' agreements for old flats and flyers for early Defectors gigs. I couldn't be bothered to trawl through every single item, so I just made the executive decision to bin the lot.

I grab the first box and head out of the bedroom. As I'm making my way through the living room, though, Milligan darts in and zig-zags through my legs.

I teeter and swerve to avoid him, and the ancient gaffer tape holding the box together chooses that precise moment to split open. A sea of detritus comes spilling out all across the living room carpet.

'Bloody hell, Milligan. Thank you for that.'

I drop to my knees to start clearing up. And that's when I see it.

When I see him.

In among all the folders and papers is a dog-eared yellow Snappy Snaps packet, its contents spread evenly across the floor. They are photos I can't even remember taking – from so long ago that people still printed actual copies of photos, and Snappy Snaps was a thing. They must be fifteen years old.

In nearly all these photos, there's the same face looking back at me. The same shock of messy blond hair, the same piercing, cloud-grey eyes, the same shy, crumpled smile.

Joe.

CHAPTER TWENTY-ONE

ANNIE

14th March
Shoreditch, London

The email I've been dreading finally arrives just as I'm about to leave the office.

Hey Annie

What's the latest with the Defectors thing? Have you made any progress? Be good to get it up and running asap.

Matt

My heart sinks as I read the words. Matt's been so busy for the last week that he hasn't even mentioned the Defectors advertorial piece. I was half-hoping he might have forgotten all about it, or that he'd hit on some other scheme to boost the site's cashflow. But clearly not.

My fingers hover over the keyboard. I'm not sure what to type back. Despite Maya's pep talk about how 'amazing' it would be to confront Will Axford, there is nothing I'd want to do less. I think Maya assumes it would be this ultra-feminist, girlbossy moment where I get to tell him what I really think of him and walk off triumphantly into the sunset. But it wouldn't be that. It would just be cringe and embarrassing. He probably wouldn't even remember who I was.

I start tapping out a reply to Matt. 'I've managed to track down the band's drummer,' I write truthfully. Simon McGillan – on whose Instagram page I found that number for the helpline.

Thinking about Green Shoots causes my mind to drift automatically to that last call with Jack. It felt so good to speak about that stuff – about missing Dad and about my anger towards Mum and Josie. Just being able to talk it all through, out loud, felt like this huge, visceral release.

The way the call ended, though . . . I can't stop thinking about that. The way I panicked when Dom came in. It was almost as if talking to Jack so frankly, so openly, felt like . . . a betrayal. Like I was going behind Dom's back.

I wonder what Jack thought.

Lexi comes over and squeezes my shoulder. 'I'm off, you coming with? It's after six.'

'I've just got to reply to this email from Matt,' I tell her. 'What are you up to tonight?'

'Same thing I'm always up to,' she says, buttoning her coat around her enormous belly. 'Lying on the sofa, watching *Dawson's Creek* and farting.'

'Slightly TMI there, mate.'

'What are you up to on Saturday night, though?' she asks. 'We could go to the cinema or something, if you fancy it?'

'Ah, I'd love to, but we're having Maya and Dom's friend

Oliver over on Saturday. Oliver just split up with his girlfriend, and when I showed Maya a picture of him, she was like, "He looks like Henry Cavill's hotter brother, you *need* to introduce me".'

Lexi laughs. 'Oh my God, amazing. I love a meet-cute. All right, well, see you tomorrow then, babe.' She kisses me on the cheek and leaves.

I turn back to the computer to stare at what I've written so far to Matt. It translates as: 'In the ten days since you gave me this assignment, I have managed to successfully locate the drummer's Instagram page.' What Matt said about redundancies comes flooding back to me. I need to show him I am actually working on this. I need to make some sort of progress.

I open Simon McGillan's Instagram and send him a DM, telling him I'm writing an article about The Defectors and asking if he'd agree to an interview. I provide my email address and phone number, but the fact he hasn't posted on here in about four years doesn't exactly fill me with hope for a reply.

An idea suddenly hits me. My old Gmail account: the one I was using five years ago, when I wrote that article. I think I still remember the password . . .

I log in to the account and type 'Jessica' into the search box. And there she is. Three emails, all dated roughly five years ago. Jessica Michaelides. Stupid sexy Jessica with her stupid sexy fringe. She probably won't remember me. She probably doesn't even still check this email address.

I google her quickly. She's on Instagram, but her profile is locked. I find her on LinkedIn, though, and it says she still works as a freelance music publicist. It's worth a go.

I open a new email and start typing.

Hello, Jessica,

I hope you're well. You probably won't remember me – my name's Annie Lucas, we met about five years ago in Paris. I was (still am!) a journalist and was there to interview The Defectors, who you were doing the PR for.

Anyway, this is quite a random question but – are you still in touch with any members of the band? I'm looking to write a piece about what they are up to now for Marker Media.

Thanks so much,

Annie

I sit back in my chair and re-read the words I've just written. It's a perfectly normal, perfectly polite email.

But I'm still not quite sure I have the guts to send it.

CHAPTER TWENTY-TWO

WILL

14th March
Harrow, Middlesex

I can't remember a time when I didn't know him.

That's what I think as I stare down at the photos scattered across the living room floor. He was always there. And even when he wasn't, I don't think a day ever went by that I didn't think about him. Worry about him.

I lower myself to the floor and sit cross-legged among the pictures. A vice begins to tighten in my chest. I haven't seen Joe's face in years. I've never been able to bring myself to look at photos of him.

Milligan hops into my lap. I place one hand on his soft, purring back and reach slowly for the picture nearest to me. The effect is visceral. My stomach clenches like I've been hit. The photo is from sixth form college. We must have been 17. We're sat on desks in the music room, holding up acoustic guitars and gurning stupidly at the camera – eyes closed, tongues out, classic 'rock star' poses. Tears blur my vision as I reach for the next one.

The reason I can't remember a time when I didn't know Joe is because there wasn't one. His mum, Chrissie, met my mum in NCT class. They became close, and when Joe was born – just a few weeks after I was – we were the first people that came to visit. My parents still have a photo of it somewhere. Mum and Chrissie, both looking knackered but ecstatically happy, cradling tiny me and tiny Joe in their arms. From then on, we were inseparable.

I realise my hands are shaking now as I pick up another photo. A blurry picture of us soundchecking in the school hall. This must have been taken just a few hours before our first gig.

It had been my idea to start a band. Joe was always shyer than me, and I thought it would be a good way to bring him out of his shell. I roped him in, along with two other guys from our year, and we christened ourselves 'About Time'. Once we'd learned to proficiently murder a few tracks by The Ramones and The Specials, I secretly signed us up for the college band night. Joe was furious. He begged me to let him back out. But I just told him not to worry. Everything would be OK.

I stare at the photo, my heart thumping at the memory of that night. We'd all been drinking to loosen our nerves, but as soon as we got on stage, Joe did what he always did in social situations: clammed up. He started sweating, staring at the floor, shaking so hard that his fingers kept slipping on the frets.

People in the crowd began laughing and heckling – even booing – and our drummer got pissed off and chucked his sticks at them. The plugs were yanked out and our music teacher ushered us off stage. I was off my face by that point, and just remember finding the whole thing funny. But Joe vanished without even helping us pack up the gear.

I knew exactly where he'd be. There was a Burger King on the high street – midway between his house and college – and during one bored Saturday night as 14-year-olds we'd discovered a fire escape that lead straight up to its roof. Since then, that roof was where we'd come to drink and smoke and listen to music.

I climbed the rickety metal stairs and saw him sat there, his long legs dangling over the edge of the roof. He was just staring into the middle distance, head slumped onto his chest, arms splayed at his side. He looked like a puppet with its strings cut. It was a look I would become all too familiar with over the next few years, but this was the first time I'd seen him like that. You wouldn't even say he looked sad or depressed, really: he just looked . . . empty. Like the cable connecting him to life had been pulled out.

I stumbled drunkenly towards him, wrapping my arms around his neck from behind. 'Remember tonight, Joseph,' I announced, 'because it'll form the basis of the introduction in our first ever *NME* cover piece.' I adopted the nasal, know-it-all tone we often used when impersonating music journalists: '"When About Time played their first ever gig, a shambolic affair at their college band night, they could never have suspected they would one day be headlining the legendary Glastonbury Festival . . ."'

Joe shrugged me off, and I sat down next to him, our legs dangling together. 'Sorry, man,' he said quietly. 'I really screwed up.'

'*You* screwed up?' I said. 'Dave threw his fucking drumsticks at the audience! I'm pretty sure they hit Mr Markowska. He'll be in detention till Christmas.'

I couldn't get a smile out of him. 'I told you I couldn't do this,' he muttered, staring out at the row of bookies and chain bakery stores opposite.

'Mate. Shut up. Of course you can do this.'

'I just . . .' He held his hands up and examined them. 'There's something wrong with me, Will. I get so nervous and anxious. I can't control it. I've been telling you for weeks I wouldn't be any good on stage.'

'You don't need to be good on stage! You've got me, haven't you? I'm fucking *great* on stage.'

I knew that acting the big-headed twat was the best way to coax a grin out of my best friend. So I wasn't surprised as I saw the ghost of a smile emerging.

'First gigs are *supposed* to be terrible,' I continued. 'Remember what you told me about The Velvet Underground? Didn't they play some suburban high school in New Jersey and half the parents and students walked out after the third song?'

That ghost-of-a-smile got stronger. 'Probably wasn't the right venue to debut a tune called "Heroin".'

I leaned into him and laughed. 'Exactly. Shit first gig. And they turned out all right, didn't they?'

'We're not exactly The Velvet Underground, Will.'

'No – we'll be way better than them.'

He laughed into the back of his hand. 'I wish I had your optimism.'

'You don't need to – I've got enough optimism for both of us. I always have. All you need to do is keeping writing fucking brilliant tunes. And maybe let someone else apart from me hear them.'

He shook his head. 'They're not fucking brilliant.'

'Shut up, knobhead, they are.' This was my technique back then whenever Joe fell into one of his moody spirals: just refuse to engage. Bombard him with sweary praise until he cracked and smiled and came back to earth.

He swung his legs in the air, his heels bouncing off the first 'G' in the Burger King sign.

'Let's get some practice in for that *NME* interview, then,' I said, re-adopting the nasal tone. 'So I'm here with Joe from About Time, the hottest new band in the UK right now. Joe: what was going through your mind after that horrendous first gig?'

I held my balled fist under his chin, like a microphone. He leaned forward and spoke into it. 'What was going through my mind was that I wanted to throw myself off the roof of Burger King.'

That's really what he said. I thought nothing of it then. I think I even laughed.

I continued the mock interview. 'But luckily you didn't throw yourself off, and am I right in thinking that your lead singer, and best pal, William Axford, gave you an incredible pep talk on that same fast-food restaurant roof, which turned your whole outlook around?'

His mouth tugged upwards at the side, as if snagged by an invisible fish hook. 'You're right in thinking that William Axford followed me up there and started pissing me off by conducting a fake interview, yes.'

'Hm. Fascinating. And, tell me, what do you think about

this rumour that William Axford is currently in a polyamorous sexual relationship with Megan Fox, Alicia Keys and Mila Kunis? Any truth to it?'

He snorted with laughter and I slung my arm around him triumphantly. 'One day, Joseph,' I said, swinging my hand out grandly in front of us, 'one day, all this will be ours.'

'What, Ladbrokes and Greggs?' he scoffed.

'No, you twat. Fame and fortune and polyamorous sexual relationships with the world's hottest women. We're gonna make it, Joe. Me and you. I can just feel it.'

His eyes met mine finally, a smile stretched wide and bright across his face. 'If you say so, Will,' he said.

CHAPTER TWENTY-THREE

ANNIE

16th March
Ladbroke Grove, London

'I just can't get on board with dating apps,' Oliver says. 'Swiping through tons of photos, making a snap judgement about whether you want to get to know someone based on one picture of their face. It just feels a bit . . . dystopian.'

Maya leans forward over the table to accentuate her boobs. 'I *totally* know what you mean.'

I glance at Dom and he raises his eyebrows woozily. We are two bottles of merlot deep into our mini-dinner party, and maybe it's the fact that I'm more than a little tipsy, but everything seems to be going swimmingly. Everyone is wolfing down my spaghetti amatriciana à la Nigella, and Maya and Oliver are getting on like a house on fire – flirting outrageously as they compare dating-app war stories. Even Dom is being charm personified. It's been so long since I saw him with other people that I've forgotten what he's like when he makes an effort. When he's actually *trying*, rather than slumped on the sofa squinting at his laptop. It reminds me of when we first got together.

I watch him fondly for a moment longer, then turn my attention back to the conversation. Oliver is talking about his lack of success on Hinge since his break-up, and Maya is gazing at him swoonily as she fiddles with her hair. There is absolutely no doubt in my mind that these two will be having Very Good Sex at some point in the not-too-distant future. Possibly even tonight.

Who knows, maybe Dom and I will end up doing the same thing . . .

'I've got any dating-app horror story beat,' Maya announces. 'No one can top it. I've got the Steak Weighing Man.'

I dissolve into laughter. 'Oh God. Not the Steak Weighing Man.'

'Annie's heard the Steak Weighing Man story *many* times,' Maya says.

Oliver's smile widens. He is totally under Maya's spell. 'Can someone please explain who the Steak Weighing Man is?'

I start to refill all our glasses. 'We're all going to need another glass of wine for this story . . .'

Everyone laughs and Maya launches into it. 'I went on a date about a year ago with this guy. He took me to this super-posh restaurant, and as we sat down, he made this remark about how he'd been here once before and he was sure they were skimping on the size of their steaks. I thought, "OK, bit random, but whatever." Then, when our food arrived,' she allows herself a dramatic pause, 'he produced a set of *hand-held electronic scales*, and proceeded to weigh his ribeye to prove it was nowhere near the 10 oz the menu had promised.'

Dom erupts into laughter. Oliver covers his mouth with his hand. 'You are fucking kidding?' he says through his fingers.

'Swear to God,' says Maya. 'I went straight to the loo and called Annie.'

'I mean . . . why?' Oliver cackles. 'Did he think it would impress you?'

'That's exactly what I asked Annie!' Maya shrieks back. 'I said, "Does he think it makes him seem assertive and financially astute? Why did he even bring me to a restaurant that he suspects is gipping its customers?!"'

'I was unable to answer these questions because I was laughing too hysterically,' I point out.

Maya raises her glass triumphantly. 'So, there you go. No matter how bad a date is, it *can't* be as bad as the Steak Weighing Man.'

We all take a moment to recover from this anecdote as Dom gets up to serve second helpings of spaghetti. 'It does make you think, though, doesn't it?' Oliver says as Dom settles back down next to him. 'Sometimes it feels like life is just work, work, work and watching TV and swiping through the dating apps. Sometimes I wish I could just sack it all off. Quit my job and go and live by the sea. Become a surf instructor or something.'

'Mate, you can't even stand up on the board,' Dom laughs through a mouthful of pasta.

'I know what you mean,' Maya tells Oliver. 'Sometimes I wonder, "Is this all there is?" I've actually been seriously thinking I should go to Peru and do one of those ayahuasca retreats to help me figure out what I really want from life.'

'*What* retreats?' Oliver asks.

'Ayahuasca,' Maya says. 'It's this South American psychoactive drug that you drink and it gives you hallucinations and visions and you have this epiphany about who you really are and what you really want.'

I can't help grinning. I love Maya in moments like this. She's always been this kind of person: totally brave and ever-so-slightly bonkers. She gets an idea in her head, and she'll just do it. After university, she went travelling through South-East Asia all on her own. She's utterly fearless. She does things I would *never* have the nerve to do.

Oliver takes a forkful of pasta and chews thoughtfully. 'So, what, you go to Peru and drink this stuff and suddenly your whole outlook changes?'

Maya nods. 'It helps you look at things from a different angle, I guess. I'm thinking about doing it this summer.'

Dom pulls a face. 'Seriously?'

Maya looks at him, defiant. 'Yeah. Why?'

He shrugs and pours more wine. 'No, I just . . . From what I've read about these retreats, it just sounds like something for rich hipster dickheads who've got more money than sense.'

There's a moment's silence filled only by the sound of forks hitting plates. I feel my cheeks flush. 'Dom,' I say quietly.

He holds his hands up and laughs. 'Sorry. All I mean is, it just sounds like kind of a stupid fad.'

Maya puts her fork down and fixes him with a steely frown. 'It's not a *fad*, Dom. Indigenous people have been drinking ayahuasca for centuries.'

'Yeah, fair play to the indigenous people, I'm not criticising them. They're making a killing off dumb westerners who fly all the way to Peru to stay in a hut and drink some weird tea. Good luck to them.'

He and Oliver burst into hysterics at this, and I feel such a sudden, intense ripple of dislike for Dom that it actually shocks me. More than once in the past, he has described Maya to me as 'a bit much' – but he's never actually been rude to her, to her face.

I don't know what to say, I feel beyond embarrassed. But luckily Maya seems to be taking it all in her stride. 'Well, lucky for me I don't need your approval then, Dominic, isn't it?'

'It is,' he agrees. He goes to top up my glass but I hold my hand over it. We catch eyes for a second before he looks away. I suddenly feel like I've drunk too much and I can't tell if this moment is as awkward for everyone else as it is for me.

Oliver clears his throat and changes the subject. 'So, Annie, I haven't really asked about your job. You're a journalist, right?'

Dom laughs into his glass. I look at him, feeling suddenly *so* ready for a fight.

He holds his hands up again. 'Sorry, babe. It's just . . . "journalist"'. He makes finger quotes around the word. 'It's not like you work for the *New York Times*. It's more, like, lists and quizzes and stuff.'

I look over at Maya. Her narrowed eyes are trained on Dom. She is radiating disapproval.

'It's cool, though,' Dom says hurriedly. 'Marker is a really fun site.'

Oliver nods. 'Yeah, I read Marker all the time at work. What are you working on right now?'

Before I can answer, the scrape of Dom's chair rings around the room as he stands up suddenly. 'Right,' he says, clapping his hands together. 'Anyone for pudding?'

*

Later, as I'm washing up the plates and feeling the beginnings of tomorrow's hangover creep into my temples, I sense Dom enter the kitchen behind me.

I glance round to see him pretending to read something on the calendar by the fridge. He's wearing pyjama bottoms and his old Bruce Springsteen t-shirt, his lips pouted in faux-concentration.

'I thought you'd gone to bed,' I mutter.

He grunts, still squinting at the calendar. 'Fun night.'

'Yep.'

'I reckon Olly and Maya got on well.'

'Definitely.'

After a moment, I feel his arms wrap around my waist and his breath on the back of my neck. 'Sorry,' he whispers.

'For what?' I ask, squeezing more Fairy liquid onto the sponge. 'Belittling my job or taking the piss out of my best friend?'

His arms unclasp from around me. 'Oh, come on, Annie. I was just a bit drunk! I was only joking. Maya knew that.'

'Right. So, you were being serious about my job, then?'

'No, I just . . .' I dry my hands and turn to face him. He pinches the bridge of his nose and sighs. 'You used to talk about wanting to write properly, that's all. I thought you were getting sick of Marker.'

'Maybe I am. It doesn't mean you get to take the piss out of me in front of our friends.' His rolls his eyes, and I feel furious suddenly. 'I like my job! It's not my dream job, but I'm good at it.'

'I know! All right. I'm sorry.' He exhales through his nose, like a teenager bored of being shouted at.

I turn back to the sink. I'm expecting to hear him stomp upstairs, so I'm more than a little shocked when I feel his hands on my bum. It's been so long since he touched me like this, my anger actually fades for a second. He leans in and kisses me softly on the cheek. 'Why don't you leave the washing-up and come upstairs?'

I'm half tempted – if only to prove that we're OK, that we're a normal couple.

But I shrug away from him. 'You can't just insult my job and then try and have sex with me, Dom.'

Another exasperated sigh as he lets go of me. 'Fine. I'm sorry. Just trying to be nice.'

And with that, he stomps back upstairs.

CHAPTER TWENTY-FOUR

WILL

17th March
Green Shoots office, Limehouse

All Saturday night I wandered aimlessly up and down Harrow High Street so as not to be stuck at home next to the leaning tower of boxes and the photos inside them.

Saturday night is usually a Green Shoots night for me, but someone else had signed up for that shift this week. So, instead, after a few broken hours of sleep, here I am on the Sunday-afternoon shift – using phone calls from anonymous strangers to try and take my mind off Joe. The only problem is: no one's calling.

It's been ridiculously quiet so far – just one quick check-in each from Eric and Sandra, and a very apologetic man who'd mistaken Green Shoots for a garden centre in Tamworth. I was so desperate to talk to somebody I even asked if there was anything on his mind he'd like to discuss. But he said he just needed to buy some weed-killer quite urgently and he had to go.

Three hours in, though, everything changes. I'm in the

kitchen making a tea, when I hear the phone sing out in the office. I put the mug down and sprint back down the corridor, grabbing the receiver before it can cut out.

'Hello, Green Shoots?'

'Oh hi! Is that Jack?'

Her voice is like a shot of pure adrenaline. 'Pia! Hello!'

'Hi!'

I settle down into the chair, my heart thumping. 'How are you?'

'I'm good! Is this a . . .' She breaks off and laughs. 'God, I was about to ask if this is a "bad time". My natural British instincts kicking straight in there.'

'Oh, there's never a bad time to call this line. That's the Green Shoots motto. Well, unofficial motto.'

'OK. Good. I thought you weren't going to answer, actually. I was about to hang up.'

'I know, sorry. I was just in the kitchen, making tea. But when I heard the phone I ran straight back to pick it up. That's my level of dedication, Pia. There is a cup of tea going cold as we speak because I am *such* a professional.'

'You're a hero, Jack. A martyr, really.'

'Thank you, thank you. I know.'

'But seriously. Go and get your tea. I can hold on.'

'Really? I'll be twenty seconds.'

'I'll be timing you.'

I sprint back to the kitchen to grab my mug, feeling almost giddy with excitement about being on the brink of a new conversation with her.

'Back!' I say, dropping into the office chair.

'That was twenty-one seconds,' she says.

'OK. A solid effort. You might say a . . . *So-Solid* effort.'

She groans. 'Oh my God. Jack. Did you really just make that joke?'

'I did, yes. I'm sorry. I wasn't thinking.'

'I think that was the first single my sister bought. I remember her playing it on repeat in our room for the whole of summer 2001.'

'It's a tune.'

'It is *not* a tune.'

'It totally is.'

'I thought you weren't allowed to express opinions on this line?'

'That's not an opinion, Pia. It's a fact.'

Her laughter mingles with mine as I lean forward to take a sip from my mug. The anxiety in my stomach begins to unknot as I settle into that strange, and now familiar, sensation that we *know* each other. That we've known each other for ages.

'How's the tea, then?' she asks. 'Worth going back for?'

'Definitely. I make a mean cuppa.'

'Me too. It's a vital life skill. I remember my dad telling me, "Never marry anyone who can't make a decent cup of tea".'

'Ha.' It's possibly the roundabout reference to me being a good potential husband – or more likely, the mention of her dad – but the frantic pace of our conversation dies out suddenly. I hear her exhale slowly. 'Anyway . . .'

'So. How are you?' I ask.

'I'm OK, thanks. I'm sorry to keep calling. I hope you don't think it's weird.'

'Of course not! I'm really glad to hear from you.' Too much information, there – but it's the truth.

'Oh. Well, that's nice.' I can picture her blushing as she says it and it makes me grin. 'I tried calling earlier, but you were engaged.'

'Well, I'm glad you tried again. It ended a bit abruptly, our last call.'

I wince. That comment just slipped out, and it's a step beyond too much information – it's totally inappropriate. Bringing up a previous call, trying to push a caller in the direction of something they may not want to talk about: both major no-no's in the Green Shoots rulebook. Pia's silence in response just makes me feel even worse. 'I'm really sorry, Pia,' I say. 'I just meant—'

'No, it's OK,' she cuts in. 'I know what you meant. My boyfriend walked in and I suppose I didn't want him to know I was talking to you. To a crisis line, I mean.'

'Mm-hm.'

'I've been trying to imagine what he'd say if he knew I was calling you.'

'And what do you think he'd say?'

She sighs down the line. 'I don't know. I think he'd just be . . . confused. *I* don't really know why I'm calling you, so I don't suppose he'd have the faintest idea either. I'm not sure we're communicating very well at the moment, to be honest.'

I sense she has more to say so I stay quiet, giving her the time she needs to process her thoughts.

'We had a dinner party last night,' she says finally, 'and he got drunk and was a bit . . . off with me. And my best friend.'

'Mm-hm. Right.' I let the silence settle again, hoping she will say more.

'I just feel that he's changed, somehow,' she continues. 'Maybe it was when my dad was ill. I was so focused on that,

I didn't notice anything else. I probably wasn't the greatest girlfriend.'

'Right, but you were going through an unbelievably difficult time, weren't you?' Not expressing opinions is one thing, but I find I cannot let that one pass without comment.

'Yeah, I was,' she agrees. 'But now that I'm starting to come out the other side of that grief, which was so intense, everything feels different between us.'

'But maybe it's . . .' I break off. I have so much I want to say to her right now; this conversation is sparking thoughts that have been reeling around my own head, unsaid, for years. But I manage to hold myself back this time.

'What were you going to say?'

'No, nothing. I shouldn't be giving my personal opinion. Green Shoots rules, and all that.'

'I don't mind, if that's what's worrying you,' she says softly. 'I'd really like to hear what you were going to say.'

I stare out of the window at the purple-pink sun beginning to set behind the tower blocks. I wish, more than anything, that I could talk to her. *Properly* talk. Not just listen. But the rules are there for a reason. Callers phone this line to make sense of their own issues, not have my problems fired back at them. *But what if our problems interlink? What if she's going through something I've been through? Wouldn't it mean more to hear that, rather than a constant wall of 'mm-hms'?*

I clear my throat. 'I just think going through something like that – the death of someone close to us – changes us,' I say slowly. 'Maybe it makes us different, rather than the people around us. I don't think you can come through something like that and still be the same person as you were.'

'So, maybe it's not Dom who's changed, but me?'

'Maybe.'

She's quiet for so long I wonder if she's still there. 'Pia?'

'Sorry. Yes. I'm just thinking about what you said.'

'Mm-hm.'

'So, have you . . . Do you have experience in this . . . area, too, then?'

I have to swallow hard before I can answer. 'I probably shouldn't . . . This call is about you.'

'Of course. I'm sorry, Jack.'

I'm not sure if that 'sorry' is for overstepping the mark or an expression of condolence for the experience I have in this area. Either way, it's a few seconds before I can speak again. I have to move the phone away to take a steadying breath.

I think of Jess suddenly. How different talking to Pia feels to talking to her. How tired and wretched and worn down I always feel in Jess' company, as opposed to how light and free I feel with Pia. Without missing a beat, a cynical little voice in my head pipes up: *That's because Pia doesn't know you. She doesn't know what you're really like.*

'Jack?'

I realise I've spaced out completely. I clamp the receiver back to my ear.

'Sorry, Pia. I missed that?'

'I was just asking if you're usually on the line at this time? Sunday afternoons?'

'Yep, this is always me,' I say without thinking. 'Sunday afternoons.'

'Oh, OK. That's good to know. I'd better be going now, but maybe I'll give you a call next week, then.'

'Next week.' I try to keep my voice steady as my heart doubles its beat. 'That'd be great.' I make a mental note to sign up for every Sunday-afternoon shift from now until the end of time.

'Cool. It's a date, then.'

'It's a date.'

'Have a good week. And thank you, Jack. Thanks for listening.'

CHAPTER TWENTY-FIVE

26th February, five years ago
Paris, France

'So, go on then Annie, fire away . . .'

Annie perches on the stiff-backed hotel chair, facing all four members of The Defectors, who are squashed shoulder-to-shoulder on the cream-coloured sofa. It feels a little like a job interview suddenly.

Annie feels her cheeks redden at the four pairs of eyes on her. She digs into her rucksack for her Dictaphone, but when she looks up again, they're all still goggling at her and grinning. Especially the lead singer, Will Axford. He makes a big show of cracking open a gin miniature and then wincing as he takes a swig. It's not even midday. Will is clearly an absolute knob, but Annie is still finding it very difficult to stop looking at him. The sleeves of his t-shirt have been hiked up to display the full extent of his tanned, lightly muscled arms, and as she catches his eye his smile widens, revealing a weirdly attractive gap between his front teeth. She takes a breath and tries to gather herself.

She's nervous – and it's not helping that Jess the publicist is still in the room, overseeing proceedings. Tapping away frantically at her phone, Jess hovers in the corner, right at the edge of Annie's peripheral vision, like a mosquito in a leopard-print blouse.

Annie clears her throat and fiddles with the Dictaphone. 'Just checking it's working. I always get paranoid that I've forgotten to switch it on!'

Will snatches it off the coffee table and holds it to his mouth: 'Check one, check one-two,' he booms. 'Testing, testing!'

It's a pretty feeble attempt at humour, but Will's bandmates all convulse with laughter as if it's the greatest joke they've ever heard. In the corner Jess offers a soft chuckle and shake of the head, before going back to her phone.

Will grins as he replaces the Dictaphone on the table between them. 'Seems to be working. The red light's on, anyway.'

Annie swallows. 'OK, cool. Um, so . . .' She had prepared a carefully written A4 sheet of questions for this interview, but it now feels amateurish and silly to pull it out. She'd look like a kid who'd won a competition rather than a proper music journalist. She'll just have to freestyle.

'So, this gig tonight is your first time playing in France,' she says. 'What have you guys been getting up to here?'

In the corner, Jess coughs lightly. The other Defectors all glance at Will. Clearly, he is the alpha male in charge here. He yawns, cat-like, and stretches his tanned arms behind his head. 'We've been getting into trouble, mainly,' he says.

The other three snigger with schoolboyish laughter at this. Annie smiles politely. 'What sort of trouble?'

'Wouldn't you like to know?' Will shoots back, with a wink.

He actually winks at her. Annie is starting to feel a bit sorry for the poor boy – he's shooting for Keith Richards but landing on David Brent.

'Well, yes, that's why I asked,' she fires back, feeling more confident now she knows Will is a douche rather than an intimidating rock god. The other three band members must mistake this response for flirtation because they chorus 'Oooooh!' simultaneously. Out of the corner of her eye, Annie sees Jess has looked up from her phone and is frowning at her. She gets a little frisson of pleasure from that.

Will laughs and takes another hit from his tiny gin bottle. 'Look, Paris is a wicked city and we've been having a good time here, that's all,' he says. 'I think a lot of the good, old-fashioned fun has disappeared from rock 'n' roll, you see.' His bandmates nod their heads solemnly at this. 'You've got bands like fucking Coldplay and the fucking Mumfords – they're all vegan and tee-total and boring as fuck, basically. For me, rock 'n' roll should be about tearing it up. You know? Living life to the fullest.' He holds up his empty gin miniature as proof that he's doing this. 'We're really living that life, and we're one of the only groups out here who are.'

'Amen,' says the drummer through a mouthful of chips.

Annie nods and smiles. Will is clearly a ridiculous human being, but he's also proving to be a pleasingly lively interviewee. That slagging-off-Coldplay stuff is sure to get clicks galore, and her editor will be chuffed with her. 'OK, cool,' she says. 'And how about the new album? What can you tell me about it? Will it be a shift in musical direction from your debut?'

Will yawns, apparently uninterested in this question, and glances over at Mike, the guitarist. Mike picks the baton up enthusiastically, launching into a long monologue about how The Defectors want to use their sophomore record to 'blend Sixties garage rock with, like, Kraftwerk-type shit'. Annie continues to nod along politely, aware that Will is still watching her closely, a smile playing on his lips.

A text message alert sings out suddenly and Will removes his phone from his trouser pocket. He glances at the screen and for a moment, his smug grin dissolves. His face is unreadable as he stands up. 'What is it?' Mike asks.

'I'll just be one second,' Will says. 'Gotta go downstairs. Joe's arrived.'

CHAPTER TWENTY-SIX

ANNIE

20th March, present day
Vauxhall, London

'This place is absolutely ridiculous.' Dom frowns as he squints around us. 'How long is this going to take?'

I yank a shopping trolley out of the rack and wheel it towards him. 'Shouldn't be long, I only need to get a few things.'

He sighs and pulls out his phone. 'OK. Well, be as quick as possible. I'm getting a migraine from just being in here.'

He remains glued to his phone as we venture into the main part of the store. To be fair, it *is* a bit much. It's a huge warehouse just outside Vauxhall station called 'The Pink Party Palace'. Its website was the first result that came up when I googled 'Where to buy baby shower stuff central London' before leaving the office an hour ago. I'm pretty behind on sorting Lexi's shower, so my aim was to bulk-buy everything I'd need for this Saturday right here and now. Since Dom's office is in Vauxhall, I'd suggested us meeting here and then heading home together. I had the fleeting idea that it might be fun; an excuse to go on a silly, random little excursion, just the two of us. But maybe I misjudged it slightly. He just seems pissed off that I've made him come.

Since The Pink Party Palace apparently caters for everything from hen dos to wedding anniversaries to kids' birthdays, around us are miles upon miles of fluffy cushions, tiaras, balloons, teddies, dresses, Baby-gros, all of them in retina-scorching pink and emblazoned with slogans like 'Mummy's Lil Princess', 'Shopaholic' and '#BeKind'.

'God, this place is like IKEA,' I say, gazing around the endless flamingo-coloured landscape in search of a baby-shower section.

'I was thinking more Dante's Inferno,' Dom murmurs. He looks up from his phone and wrinkles his nose. 'I mean, I thought you were into feminism and stuff?'

Irritation flashes through me. 'I am into "feminism and stuff".'

'And yet . . .' He reaches over to the shelf we are passing and pulls off an apron bearing the slogan 'MAMA NEEDS MORE GIN!'

He shoots me a smug, 'point-proved' grin as he flaps the apron about. If Maya had reached for the same item to make the same point, I'd probably be laughing. But with Dom it feels preachy and annoying. My hackles are up – but I can't exactly start a fight when it was my suggestion for him to come here with me.

'I don't see what's particularly "un-feminist" about being a functioning alcoholic,' I say, putting the apron back on the shelf, next to many other gin-themed accessories.

'You know what I mean, Annie,' he says. 'It's a bit . . . lame, all this stuff, isn't it? A bit corny?'

'Well, I've never organised a baby shower before,' I shoot back. 'I didn't know where else to go.'

He's scrolling on his phone again now. 'I was telling Clare you were organising this thing, and she couldn't believe it. She was like: "Do people still *have* baby showers? Aren't they just a bit cringe?"'

Ugh. Posh Clare from Dom's weekly quiz team. I grit my teeth. 'Well, lucky for Clare she's not coming, then.'

'I guess.'

'Look, it's not really my thing,' I tell him. 'But Lexi can do what she wants – and to be honest I'm quite touched she asked me to organise hers.'

Dom nods. 'You wouldn't want one, then?'

'What, a baby shower?'

'Yeah.'

'Well, I . . .' I glance over at him. He's still staring at his phone. 'No, probably not.'

'Mm-hm.'

We walk in silence for a bit. The only sound is the squeak of the trolley's wheels and the tinny rendition of 'Girls Just Want To Have Fun' echoing over the store stereo. I'm trying to figure out whether that was just a throwaway question or a way of trying to talk about something more serious. Was it Dom's way of asking me if I want kids? It's crazy, but in nearly three years together, this is probably the closest we've ever got to having that conversation. For our first year together we were still getting to know each other – and more importantly, still in our twenties – so the issue never really came up. And then Dad got sick, and everything became about that.

I look over at Dom again. He is still engrossed in his phone.

Maybe I should say something. Make it clear that, although I don't want a baby shower, I do want a baby?

Or at least, I think I do. Maybe.

I wonder what *he* wants.

I reach for his hand. 'Sorry for dragging you here. I thought it might be fun. I thought we could take the mickey out of it together.'

'I *was* taking the mickey out of it,' he huffs. 'But apparently not in the way you wanted.'

'OK, sorry, you're right. That apron was dumb. And not very feminist.'

He sighs and lets go of my hand. 'Seriously, Annie, can we just get what you need and leave? We still have to go to Tesco to get stuff for dinner, too.'

'We can get stuff for dinner here.' Since we're passing through the 'hen do' aisle, I pull a sack of penis-shaped penne off a shelf and dump it in the trolley. I'm quite pleased with this joke, but Dom just rolls his eyes at me.

'Very funny.'

'Are you seriously telling me you wouldn't eat that pasta just because it's shaped like willies?'

'No. I wouldn't eat that pasta because it's probably not very good quality.'

I laugh. 'Right. So if it was handmade from 100 per cent durum wheat, but shaped like willies, you wouldn't have a problem?'

He takes the pasta out of the trolley and puts it back on the shelf. 'Can we just *not* right now? I'm not in the mood. I'm knackered and hungry.'

'OK, OK . . .'

I start scanning for the baby-shower section again, but my phone pings in my bag. It's a Twitter DM. From Mike Drury. The guitarist for The Defectors. I scan the message and my stomach flips – a mixture of nervousness and relief.

'Everything OK?' Dom says.

'Yeah. Just a work thing. An interview that's come through.'

By way of proving to Matt that I really was on the case with the Defectors piece, I contacted Mike the guitarist yesterday. I've still had no reply from Simon the drummer on Instagram, so I googled the other band members, Mike and Al. I found Mike on Twitter straight away, and messaged to ask if he'd be willing to speak to me for the article. I made the executive decision *not* to mention that I was the same Annie Lucas who'd written a brutally hostile hit-piece about his ex-band five years ago. He must have either forgiven me for it or forgotten my name, because here he is now in my DMs, saying that he'd 'love to speak to me' but he's currently away on holiday. He wants to set up an interview for next week.

I slip my phone back in my bag. At least this will get Matt off my back. And maybe this interview with Mike will be enough. Maybe I won't even have to speak to Will Axford.

'Look, let's get her to help us,' Dom says impatiently. A Pink Party Palace shop assistant is breezing towards us, wearing a flamingo-coloured polo shirt and a baseball cap with a tiara on the front.

'Hi guys! I'm Carla. Is there anything I can help you with today?'

'Yeah, we're looking for baby stuff,' Dom says.

'Oh amazing!' Carla beams at me. 'When is the little one due?'

'Oh no, I . . .'

I feel my cheeks flush. Dom forces a loud laugh through a rictus grin. 'Ha. No, not us! Not our baby.'

Carla clears her throat. 'Oh, I'm so sorry.'

She genuinely looks mortified, so I rush to let her know it's OK. 'No, please don't worry! It's my friend's baby shower. I'm just trying to get some stuff for it. Do you have any suggestions for games or activities? This is my first time organising a shower.'

Carla visibly brightens, back on solid ground. 'Oh yes! Well, a really fun and very popular activity is "Pooey nappy" – you buy a pack of nappies and a big tub of chocolate mousse, and everyone at the shower gets a nappy full of "poo" each to tuck into!'

Dom winces. 'I'm gonna go to Tesco, OK, babe? I don't think we both need to be here.'

'Yeah, of course. I'll meet you outside.'

'Or we can just meet at home?' he suggests. 'You might take longer than me, that's all.'

'Yep, we can do that.'

'Do you know the sex of the baby yet?' Carla asks as I watch Dom walk off.

'Yes – he's a boy.'

'Oh lovely. The boys' stuff is just over here.'

I follow her, responding politely to all her questions about the shower. But all I can think of is how forced Dom's laugh was when he said, 'Not us. Not our baby.'

CHAPTER TWENTY-SEVEN

WILL

22nd March
Tottenham Court Road, London

Through the crack under the bathroom door, I can see the laces on Dev's fluorescent trainers whipping back and forth as he paces outside.

'Will? You all right in there, man? You've not fallen in, have you?'

I take a deep breath and try to pull myself together. 'Sorry, Dev. I'll be out in one second.'

'It's cool, it's cool, I wouldn't normally rush you,' he calls through the door. 'I mean, don't get me wrong, I know how important a man's morning toilet time is. You wanna sit down, relax, gather your thoughts, maybe do Wordle, check Insta. All that stuff. It's arguably the best part of the working day.' More pacing. 'But it's just that the delivery van has just arrived, so I need you to man the till while I make sure nothing's been nicked or broken.'

My eyes find the clock in the corner of my phone screen. Without realising it, I've been sitting in this cubicle, staring at this email, for the best part of half an hour. I shake my head and stand up. 'Yeah, of course, sorry, Dev. I'm coming right out. Just feeling a bit . . . peaky.'

This is the mother of all understatements. In fact, as I glance down at the email again, my entire body feels positively alive with panic. My skin is prickling, my head is swimming, my heart is pounding. I reach up to wipe my forehead and my fingers come back damp. 'A bit peaky' doesn't quite cover it.

'OK, man. Whenever you're ready . . .' I hear Dev's footsteps retreating as he returns to the shop floor.

Hey up, Will,

Very long time no speak! Really hope you're doing OK man. We should catch up properly soon – are you still in London? I'm just writing to see if that journo has been in touch with you too, about this Defectors article? I'm away at the moment but I said I could do an interview when I'm back – just wanted to make sure you were cool with it first . . .

Let me know, dude,

Mike x

Still clutching the phone, I unlock the door and exit the cubicle. I haven't heard from Mike Drury in nearly four years. We spent most of a decade in each other's pockets, yet right now I can't even remember the last time I saw him.

The email had arrived half an hour ago as I was helping Dev yank up the MicroShop shutters and open the store for the day. I'd stared at the words blankly for a few seconds, unable to properly process them. And after nearly thirty more minutes of blank staring, I'm not sure I've come any closer to doing so.

It just doesn't make sense. *This Defectors article . . .* What Defectors article? Why the hell would anyone want to write about The Defectors? We released one album and a handful of singles more than half a decade ago. Even at the peak of our popularity, our number of Twitter followers wasn't even into five figures. It barely even registered in the music press when we broke up. So why would anyone still be interested in us now? There *is* no 'us' now.

I spin the rusty tap faucets and try to let the sound of rushing water soothe the clattering anxiety in my chest. Who is this journalist? And why would Mike need to check if I was 'cool with it' before he spoke to them? What exactly is he going to be speaking about? Is he going to tell them about Paris? Is he going to tell them about Joe?

I feel nauseous suddenly. I actually have to grip the side of the sink to steady myself. The idea of everything coming out in the open. The idea of having to dredge that stuff up again, to relive those moments I've spent five years trying to erase . . .

'Will?'

Dev's muffled voice comes through the bathroom door again. His tone is soft, and weirdly it has a far more soothing effect on me than the violently churning water. I turn off the taps and stare at myself in the grimy mirror. I don't have to relive anything. I don't have to dredge anything up. I can just do what I've been doing since it happened: nothing. I can slam the door, I can shut it all out.

'Sorry, Dev, I'm coming out right now.'

I dry my hands, delete the email and slip the phone back into my pocket.

CHAPTER TWENTY-EIGHT

ANNIE

23rd March
Ladbroke Grove, London

The balloons have been inflated, the Baby-gro bunting is up, and the definitely-non-vagina-shaped cake is laid out on the coffee table.

So far, I have to say, this baby shower is going great. It may be too soon to judge, though, since the person having the baby hasn't actually arrived yet.

Lexi has just texted to say she's going to be late – *the bump kept me up all night, kicking* – so right now I'm hosting six of her best mates from school, plus Maya, who's become close with Lex through me. I'm currently flapping about in the kitchen, making cups of tea for everyone, as well as trying to find some sort of child-friendly drink for the two toddlers belonging to Lexi's friends Tibbs and Vicki.

Dom helped me put up the decorations – slightly grudgingly – but he's long gone now, having evacuated the flat more than an hour before 'all the excitable women' turned up. As

I pour the tea, I hear Maya's voice float through from the living room, followed by the tinkle of laughter. Maya is amazing at these kinds of things. She's fun and gung-ho and fluent in small talk – plus, she's single, which is apparently a thrilling novelty for Lex's exclusively married or engaged friendship group.

They crowded around her as soon as they arrived, asking in quiet awe about apps and ghosting, telling her how much they missed 'the freedom of being single', all while probably thinking, 'Thank God that's not me.' The Steak Weighing Man story has already been rolled out, to much delighted and horrified squealing.

'GULLIVER, NO! THAT'S NAUGHTY!'

A loud crash from down the hallway tells me that one of the toddlers has wriggled loose and broken something. I rush into the living room just in time to see Tibbs' son Gulliver casually stepping over the shattered remains of one of our good John Lewis plates, managing to kick cake crumbs all across the floor in the process.

'I'm *so* sorry, Annie,' says Tibbs. 'He saw the cake and just went for it! Gully really has an exploratory nature, so we try to nurture that and not hem him in, you know?'

'Of course,' I say as Gully's exploratory nature leads him in the direction of Dom's brand new iPad.

'You've got to let them roam,' agrees Vicki. 'You've got to let them learn to make their own mistakes.'

'Mm,' I say, wondering how many John Lewis plates I am going to have to sacrifice today to further Gulliver's education.

From the armchair, another girl – Allegra – looks up from breastfeeding her tiny baby to chime in: 'My Cressida's three now and Tim insists on letting her break anything she wants to. He thinks if she gets it out of her system now, it'll pay off in the long run.'

'I'm so bad at being strict whenever I have to look after my nieces,' Maya says. 'I let them get away with anything because they're just so damn cute.'

'Do you want kids of your own?' Vicki asks her.

'Yes,' Maya nods. 'One day, I hope.'

'Aw. You'll get there,' says Allegra, stroking her son's head.

Vicki glances in my direction, and for a second I'm worried she's about to fire the same question at me. Asking a single person if they want kids isn't exactly great social etiquette, but at least it's obvious why Maya hasn't got round to having them. If she asks me, though, there's sure to be an embarrassed silence while the entire room wonders why Dom and I haven't.

'I'll nip and get the dustpan and brush,' I say quickly, nodding at the broken plate.

Before I can leave, though, Tibbs says: 'So, what's on the schedule for today, Annie? What have you got planned in terms of games and activities?'

The six of them look straight at me and I feel myself flush. All of these women have extreme Head Girl energy, and I suddenly feel like I'm back in sixth form.

'Erm, well, I was thinking we'd play "How Old Was She?"' I say cheerily. 'I got a load of photos of Lex as a baby from her mum, and I thought it'd be fun to guess what age she was in each one!'

'Oh. Cute,' says Allegra, tucking her breast away and radiating disappointment.

'That sounds awesome, Annie,' Maya says brightly. I couldn't love her more.

Tibbs pulls a face. 'No "Pooey Nappy"?'

'What the hell is "Pooey Nappy"?' asks Maya.

'There's *always* "Pooey Nappy" at a shower,' Vicki declares.

'Well, the lady in the shop told me about that, but it sounded a bit . . . gross?' I say meekly.

This is greeted by hoots of disapproval from all six. 'Annie, no! It's fun! It was the absolute highlight of my shower!' Tibbs digs into a Waitrose bag for life at her feet. 'Don't worry – I actually brought some chocolate mousse with me because I know how much Lex loves it. We can use that as the poo.'

'Right, OK,' I say. 'Though I don't have any nappies, I'm afraid.'

'We've got that covered, too, don't worry,' Vicki laughs, as she and two others pull stacks of Pampers out of their handbags.

'OK. Great. Good.' I smile. I'm getting the definite sense that my baby shower is in the process of being politely hijacked. But oh well. If Lexi has fun, that's all that counts. 'I'll go and get that dustpan,' I say.

Back in the kitchen, I disconnect my charging phone to see that I've got a new message. From Mum.

Hope the shower goes well today, sweetheart. I bet you've done a brilliant job. Lots of love to Alexie!

Speak soon, Mum XXXX

All the noise in the other room seems to fade away as I stare at the screen. I can't even remember telling Mum about the shower. But I must have done. And she must have remembered. An image flashes into my head of the calendar she keeps above the landline in the kitchen. I picture today's date with 'Alexie's baby shower' written in her small, neat handwriting underneath it. The days or weeks passing, with Mum waiting patiently for today, for an excuse to text me, to let me know she's thinking of me. I feel tears begin to gather as I am hit full in the chest by how much I miss her. The force of it shocks me – as strong and sudden as the grief for Dad that creeps up out of nowhere.

But something else hits straight away. The memory of Mum pushing those papers I'd printed out, about clinical trials and new treatments, straight back into my hand, not even bothering to look at them. Not even listening to the options. Maybe if they'd listened to me – or let *him* listen to me – he might still be here. I feel my throat tighten as I think about how to reply to the message.

And then the doorbell rings.

From the down the hall, I hear shrieks of excitement from the living room. 'Lexi's here! Lexi's here!'

I take a deep breath and wipe my hand across my eyes. I can think about this later. Right now is all about Lex. I put my phone in my pocket and summon my brightest smile as I go to let her in.

*

'So . . . "Pooey Nappy",' Lexi says. 'Was that your idea?'

I snort into my cup of tea. 'It was not, mate, no.'

Lex nods. 'I guessed as much. Sorry. Tibbs can be quite . . . forceful. She likes to be in charge of things.'

'Don't be silly. It was fun. You had fun, right?'

'I had *so* much fun.'

'It was a fucking great shower,' Maya declares from next to her. 'Ten out of ten, Annie. No notes.'

We clink our tea mugs together. It's four hours later.

Photos have been taken, presents have been unwrapped and a substantial amount of chocolate mousse has been eaten out of nappies. The sun is going down through the living room window, and most of the party has left. It's just Maya, me and the mum-to-be sprawled on the sofa with our feet up, nursing strong cups of tea.

Lexi's baby shower has officially been a resounding success. I am so pleased – and so relieved – about that fact. But still, all afternoon, that text from Mum was nagging at me. I had to make a concerted effort at times not to be dragged off into my own thoughts. The twin emotions of missing her and not being able to forgive her battling it out inside of me. I can't go on like this, just avoiding her. Avoiding home. I have to do something. I just don't know what.

As if reading my mind, Lexi suddenly asks: 'You weren't annoyed, were you, babe? About Tibbs taking the lead on the games stuff? I noticed you were a bit quiet at certain points?'

'Of course not, no,' I say. 'Tibbs is definitely way more qualified than me on the games front. I've been wondering, actually, why you didn't ask her or Vicki to organise the shower? Don't get me wrong – I loved doing it, and I love that you asked me. But they seem like the more . . . obvious choices.'

We all laugh. Then Lexi surprises me by leaning forward to grab my hand. 'Annie, I've known those girls all my life,' she says. 'And I know sometimes they can be a bit cringe, but I grew up with them and they mean a lot to me. But I asked you because I wanted you to know that you mean a lot to me, too. We've only been mates three years or whatever it is, but I love you, babe. I really do.'

'Awww.' Maya jabs both of us in turn with her big toe. 'I'm gonna cry now.'

Lexi flaps a hand in front of her face. 'I actually am. Hormones are mental right now. I cry at everything. Sorry.'

'Mate, don't apologise!' I pull her into a hug. 'I love you, too. So much. Thank you for asking me. Really. It means so much to me as well.'

Her bump is pressed right into my belly, and suddenly I feel a tiny kick through my jumper.

'Baby's moving,' Lex whispers. 'Can you feel him?'

'Yeah,' I whisper back. 'He's showing his support for the hug. He's a strong advocate of female friendship.'

'Either that or he's like, "Oi, get your hands off my mum",' Maya says.

Lexi laughs. 'To be honest, I think he's just hiccupping from the metric tonne of chocolate mousse I've eaten.'

We break away and smile at each other. I glance down at her humongous stomach. 'I still can't believe it. You're going to be a mum.'

She puts a hand on her belly and sighs. 'I know. It is quite mental, isn't it? I'm shit scared, to be honest with you.'

'You'll be amazing, Lex. I know you will.'

'You absolutely will,' Maya adds firmly.

'Thank you.'

Without thinking, I reach for my phone on the coffee table.

'You expecting Dom to call?' Lexi asks.

'No, just thinking about my mum, actually. She messaged earlier.'

'Ah, right . . .'

Lex and Maya know all about my issues with my mum and

sister. They've seen me through God knows how many rough patches with my family since Dad died.

'Everything OK?' Maya asks.

'Yeah. It wasn't a big deal – just her texting to say good luck for the shower. It's just feels so hard, missing someone and still being angry with them at the same time.'

They both nod and Lexi gives my hand a squeeze. 'Have you tried telling her what you feel?' she says. 'Why you're so angry at her?'

I shrug. 'I just feel like if we were to have a proper heart-to-heart about everything – about Dad – then all these awful things would come spilling out. I'd say things I didn't mean – or even worse, that I *did* mean – and there would be no coming back from that.'

Lexi rubs my hand. 'What did you text her back?'

'I just said, *Thanks, all went well, speak soon*. But I can't just keep treading water like this, you know? I can't keep avoiding the issue.'

There's a second's silence. Then Maya asks: 'What does Dom think about it?'

'Oh, he . . .' I think about the last time I tried to talk to Dom about any of this. 'He's been quite busy lately with work stuff.'

I'm not certain, but I think I see Lexi and Maya exchange a very brief glance at that. I'm even about to ask them what's up.

But then we hear Dom's key in the front door, and the chance is gone.

CHAPTER TWENTY-NINE

WILL

24th March
Green Shoots office, Limehouse

'What's the weather like where you are, Jack?'

'Pretty grim. Cloudy and windy. How about where you are?'

'Not half bad. The sun's just come out. I should be out in it, really.'

'What's stopping you?'

'Well, there are these kids outside in the street. Being rather . . . loud.'

It's just after 3 p.m. on Sunday, midway through the afternoon shift, and I'm fifteen minutes into an Eric call. He's been on great form the last few weeks, but today he seems pretty down. I'm determined to cheer him up – and it will require all my training, experience, compassion and tact to do so. It's more than a little distracting, then, that the same annoying thought keeps buzzing through my head: *If Pia calls and it's engaged . . . will she call back?*

A spasm of shame. I squeeze the bridge of my nose and expel

the question from my mind. What's wrong with me? Eric needs my full attention right now.

'How loud are we talking, then?' I ask, trying to keep my voice as bright and breezy as possible. 'Are they letting off fireworks? Playing heavy metal with the amps up to eleven?'

He gives a polite, forced laugh. 'No, just skateboarding and shouting.'

'Right.'

He sighs. 'I didn't used to be like this, you know. Cooped up at home all day, too frightened to even go outside. I mean, they're just kids having fun, for God's sake.' I get the impression he's trying to convince himself more than me. When he speaks again, his voice is smaller. 'I don't know what's happened to me.'

'We all get anxious sometimes, Eric. The world can be a pretty daunting place.'

'Not for everyone else. Not for you, I imagine, Jack.'

'I'm usually too busy skateboarding and shouting to notice.'

There's nothing forced about his laugh this time. 'Very good.'

I smile, hearing him brighten. But then he sighs again: 'I should be out there, really, doing something. Rather than sitting here like a lemon, with the curtains closed.'

'What would you like to be doing?' I ask.

'I used to love travelling . . .' His voice tails off. I hear him take a swig of something.

'Where was the best place you ever went?' I persist.

He takes a second to answer. 'I loved Berlin. Have you ever been?'

'No, never.'

'Oh, it's a fabulous place. The architecture, the clubs, the people. I first went with some friends, just after university. We were staying in one of those dreadful youth hostels. You know the type: bunk beds, thirty people to a room.' He takes another sip and laughs. 'I remember one night, we got back to the room about four in the morning, and everyone else was fast asleep. So we're creeping around in the dark, not wanting to wake anyone. My friend Michael didn't want to get woken up by the daylight, so he's scrabbling around the bunk to find his eye-mask from the plane. He finally finds it, puts it on, and we go to sleep. Anyway, a few hours later, he wakes up to find the very beautiful Brazilian girl from the bunk above standing over him, looking extremely pissed off. And that's when he realises - it's not his eye mask he's wearing . . . It's her *pants*.' He explodes into snuffling giggles. 'He's picked up a pair of her knickers by mistake, draped it over his face and fallen asleep.'

'Oh my God . . .'

Eric is spluttering with laughter now. So am I. 'He went bright red!' he giggles. 'He was stammering to apologise to the girl, trying to explain that he was gay and it was a mistake and he wasn't particularly interested in her pants – all while the rest of the room glared at us like we were a bunch of awful perverts.'

'That is incredible. So what did you do?'

'Oh, we just packed our bags and got out of there. Went straight to find another hostel.'

He bursts out laughing again. As good as it is to hear him back on form, I'm suddenly desperate to know what happened to these friends. Why aren't they still in touch? How did Eric go from a sociable, jet-setting adventurer to someone whose only connection to the world is this crisis line?

He settles down, and I hear the clink of glass as he takes

another sip of his drink. 'I haven't thought about that trip in years.'

'Sounds like a lot of fun.'

'It was, it was.'

I glance out of the office window. 'Well. Still no sign of the sun this end.'

'It's in full force over here,' Eric laughs. 'Maybe I will go out for a quick wander. Just to get some air.'

'I think that's a great idea.'

'Thank you, Jack. As always, speaking to you has brightened my day up no end.'

A glimmer of satisfaction swims through me. 'It's an absolute pleasure as always, Eric.'

'Really, I mean it: thank you. Speak to you soon.'

I put the phone down and start logging the call on the computer. The glimmer becomes a glow that spreads evenly through my whole body. Inside this office, I am good. I am useful. I am helping. I am in control.

I walk through to the tiny kitchen and boil the kettle. I made Eric feel better. At least, I hope I did. And if I happened to make myself feel better, too, where's the problem in that?

The kettle clicks off. I make the tea and head back to the office. As I sit down, I find my thoughts drifting naturally back to Pia. It's nice, having something else to think about. But it would be nicer to actually speak to her.

I sip my tea and try to distract myself from the silent phone by browsing *The Guardian* website. But three-thirty becomes four becomes four-thirty, and still it doesn't ring. It hadn't even occurred to me that she might not call. She'd sounded so definite: *It's a date*.

But maybe she was just saying it to be nice. Saying it for something to say. Four forty-five. Of course she won't call. It's a Sunday. She's a normal person – she's out having fun, seeing friends. Five now. An hour before I have to lock up and leave. I'd have to wait another week to speak to her. But what if she doesn't even call *next* Sunday? What if she doesn't ever—

The phone bursts into life and I nearly jump out of my skin.

'Hello, Green Shoots?'

'Oh, hello . . . I just needed someone to talk to?'

A male voice. One I've not heard before. I work hard to banish all traces of disappointment from my voice. 'Of course. What's on your mind today?'

CHAPTER THIRTY

ANNIE

24th March
Ladbroke Grove, London

'I'm just off out,' I say.

Dom's attention stays focused on his iPad. 'Oh. Where to?'

'Just . . . for a walk.'

He finally looks up. 'Are you OK?'

'Yeah. Just wanted to get some air. It's so nice outside.'

We both glance out the living room window at the leaden grey sky. I clear my throat awkwardly.

'Right . . .' Dom says. 'Do you want me to come with?'

'Erm . . . No, it's OK. Thanks. I was just going to try to dredge up some work ideas. We've got a big brainstorm tomorrow.'

'OK, fair enough.' Dom turns his attention back to the football match he's watching. 'Can you pick up some milk while you're out?'

I grab my coat and scarf from the hall and open the front door. It doesn't feel great, this. Lying to my boyfriend about why I'm leaving the flat on a Sunday afternoon. There is no big brainstorm tomorrow. It is definitely not 'nice outside'. But how could I possibly tell him the truth?

I step out onto the street, huddled up in my coat, as the chilly wind whips my hair back. I pull out my phone and scroll down the recent calls list. This feels wrong. It feels like . . . cheating, almost. Ridiculous as that sounds.

I press the phone to my ear and listen to it ring. My guilt is not helped by the flutter of excitement in my chest as I hear his voice.

'Hello, Green Shoots?'

'Oh, hello Jack!'

'Pia!' He sounds genuinely pleased to hear from me, and it makes my grin spread wider. 'I was beginning to think you wouldn't call.'

'Don't worry – I'm a woman of my word. Sorry, though, it's a bit later than I would have liked. I've spent most of today clearing up after yesterday.'

'What was yesterday?' he asks.

'Baby shower.'

'Ah, right. Unless I've missed something pretty major during our previous calls, I'm assuming not yours?'

'Correct,' I laugh. 'My friend's. But I was organising it.'

I cross the street and start walking in the direction of the little park opposite the Tube station. 'So, how did it go?' Jack asks.

'It was good, thanks. My friend had a great time.'

'Cool, glad to hear it.'

'Yeah, it was really good. Really, really good.'

'Right . . .' Jack chuckles. 'You've said that a few times now, Pia. Which leads me to think there's more to say about it than *just* that.'

I wave a 'thank you' at the car that's stopped for me at the zebra crossing, and reflect on how weird it is that this total stranger seems able to read between the lines of my words. Pick up on signals I wasn't even sure I was giving. When Dom asked me how the shower went yesterday, he picked up on nothing of the sort. But then, maybe I'm showing more of myself to Jack than I do to him. Which is weird as hell in itself.

'Once again, Jack, your intuition is spot on,' I tell him.

'You're not dealing with an amateur here, Pia. I've been doing this for years. So, come on: out with it.'

I push open the rusty park gate and find an empty bench. In front of me are two young mums, probably only a year or two older than I am, laughing as they push their toddlers on the swings.

'I guess the whole thing just made me think about stuff with my boyfriend. You know, next steps: marriage, kids . . .'

'Right, yes.'

'We went shopping together earlier this week, to get stuff for the shower, and the shop assistant assumed it was us having a baby. And Dom made this face, like . . .' I break off, trying to think how to describe it.

'Are you making the face right now?' Jack says. 'You are aware I can't see you, right?'

I laugh. 'It was a . . . panicky, almost frightened face.'

'Mm-hm.'

'We're in our early thirties, and we've never really talked about this stuff. Which is weird, right? Obviously everything with my dad kind of . . . knocked me sideways for a while. But now I feel like maybe these are questions we need to start asking. Otherwise . . . what are we doing together?'

'So how would you have felt if he'd made a happy, excited face?' Jack asks.

'I'm not sure. Maybe I would have been equally freaked out.'

'Have you thought about just coming out and asking him whether he wants kids?'

I exhale through my nose. 'I should be able to do that, shouldn't I? After we've been together nearly three years. But I still have this weird . . . *thing* about it. As women, we've been programmed to see talking about kids as the big red nuclear button – one whiff of a conversation about it will scare a man off.'

He gives a soft laugh. 'Why do you think that is?'

'Maybe because it's so final. If I ask him, and he says "no", then . . . where do we go from there?'

For a moment, the idea of life without Dom flashes in front of me. I've already lost Dad. I'm barely speaking to the rest of my family. Lexi's about to disappear into motherhood, and Maya is way too amazing to remain single for much longer. If Dom and I broke up, I would be really, truly *alone*.

On the other end of the phone, Jack stays silent. I can hear him breathing, allowing me the time I need to collect my thoughts. I watch the two mums in front of me, who are now posing for selfies with their toddlers. 'Anyway, for Dom and I to have kids, we'd have to have sex, and there's no danger of that at the moment.'

I give an involuntary laugh – possibly out of sheer surprise that I've just said something to Jack that I'm not sure I could even say to my best friends. He coughs quietly, though, and I immediately sense I've overstepped the mark. I feel my face heat up.

'Sorry, Jack. Way too much info there. You didn't need to know that.'

'Don't worry, erm, it's fine . . . We can talk about whatever you want.'

'Thanks, but I think sex is probably a bridge too far.'

'No, honestly – I'm happy to listen . . .'

He tails off, so I finish the sentence for him. 'To me talking about sex?'

That's the third time I've said 'sex' in under a minute. I should probably stop saying 'sex' so much.

'Yeah, OK, maybe it would be a bit weird,' Jack says, and we both laugh. Not for the first time, I try to imagine what he looks like. For some reason I'm thinking brown hair and green eyes. Tall. A kind smile. I wonder if he's sexy. He definitely *sounds* sexy.

My cheeks flush. God, what the hell is *wrong* with me today?

I clear my throat. 'Anyway. I guess with kids it's hard to know if you want them because you *really* want them or because they're what everyone else wants; because you'll be judged or pitied if you don't have them.'

'I know what you mean,' Jack says.

The mums are now concentrating on strapping the toddlers into their pushchairs. 'Getting engaged, having kids . . . they're such obvious next steps for all my friends. But for me . . . I don't know.'

'What about marriage, then?' Jack asks. 'Do you want to get married?'

The simplicity of the question knocks me sideways. No one has ever asked me that before. Why would they? Mum, Lexi, Maya, my sister: they'd all just assume the answer was 'yes'.

'I like the idea of being married, but not *getting* married,' I say. 'I hate the thought of a massive wedding. Not a fan of being the centre of attention all day. I can barely handle those awful two minutes when the whole office sings "Happy birthday".'

Jack laughs. 'I'm the same.'

'I think—' I begin, but Jack cuts me off.

'Dammit, sorry Pia, I'm really sorry to interrupt, but I just realised that it's two minutes to six now, which means it's the end of my shift and someone else will be taking over the line.'

'Oh, right.' A thud of disappointment hits, but I try not to let him hear it. 'Of course – I've been rattling away for far too long anyway. Sorry!'

'No, I'm sorry,' he says. 'Genuinely, I really don't want to end this conversation. I'd keep talking to you for hours if I could. But the listener who's doing the evening shift is doing it from home, so I have to transfer over to the remote line and that's always a bit of a faff.'

'No worries, Jack, of course.'

'If you want to keep talking, you can just call straight back after we've hung up, and you'll be connected to the new listener.'

I watch the two mums leave the park, their kids wriggling in the pushchairs. 'That's OK, Jack,' I say. 'I only really want to talk to you.'

My cheeks flush again at the sound of his laugh. 'Well. That's . . . a really nice thing to hear, Pia. I'd been looking forward to you calling as well.'

'Next Sunday, then?'

'Next Sunday,' he says. 'Can't wait.'

CHAPTER THIRTY-ONE

26th February, five years ago
Paris, France

Annie nods and tries to focus on what Mike is saying, but her eyes keep drifting back to the hotel door.

It's been ten minutes now since Will left to go and meet Joe, whoever Joe is. Since then, Annie has got precisely sod all in the way of interesting interview material. It's mainly been Mike the guitarist wittering on about Krautrock, and Annie's fairly sure her editor will not be happy if she turns in 2,000 words on 1970s German prog.

The problem is that Will is so clearly the main draw of this band – the lead singer, the songwriter, the best-looking member, the only one giving out anything in the way of decent quotes – and without him present, the whole interview is turning into a bit of a damp squib.

So, Annie sits there, nodding and smiling and praying for him to come back before too much more of her allotted time has melted away.

Finally, as Sim the drummer is launching into an anecdote about the new brand of hi-hat he is now using, Annie hears the zip of a keycard in the lock, and the door opens to reveal Will. 'Thank God,' she thinks – though she notices straight away that there's a different energy about him now. The roguish smirk and swagger are gone, and he seems shifty and uncomfortable, shoulders hunched, mouth turned down in a frown.

Someone else follows him in through the door. This, presumably, is Joe. Dressed in a slightly-too-large Adidas hoodie, his face is obscured by a mop of dirty blond hair. He's as tall as Will and looks about the same age, but his awkward, stooped posture and overly baggy clothes give him the air of a lost little boy. He lingers behind Will, tugging the sleeve of his tatty jumper and staring down at the carpet. Without even seeing his face properly, Annie can tell this is someone who is deeply uncomfortable in their own skin.

The other members of the band greet Joe with unenthusiastic grunts. Jess gives him a brief glance before turning her attention back to her phone. Since Will doesn't bother to introduce him, Annie stands up and smiles, offering the boy her hand.

'Hello! I'm Annie.'

Joe seems to draw even further into himself, his head ducking lower and his hands finding his pockets. Annie immediately regrets saying anything – he clearly does not enjoy being the centre of attention. But then the boy steps forward, takes her hand limply and shakes.

'Hey. I'm Joe.'

He looks up and for a second she meets his eyes through the curtain of blond hair. He's handsome. Or, no, maybe 'handsome' is the wrong word. Will is handsome – this boy is . . . pretty. Delicate features and cloudy grey-blue eyes. Annie notices faint traces of acne scarring across his sharp cheekbones. He smiles, but to Annie it looks more like a wince. Something that expresses pain rather than happiness. She smiles back, trying not to stare at the dark circles under his eyes.

'Nice to meet you,' she says.

'You too.' Joe lets go of her hand and looks back down at the carpet.

Will turns to him. 'Cool, so listen, man, we've still got a bit more of this interview to do. Maybe you can just hang back in the other room for a sec? Jess, can you get Joe set up in there?'

Jess looks up from her phone, irritated. Her expression says: 'Seriously?'

But Will tilts his head at her, puppy dog-style, and she softens. Standing up, she gestures for Joe to follow her. 'Of course. Come on, Joe, it's just through here.'

Will watches her as she goes. Annie watches him watch her. She wonders if perhaps there is something more between the two of them – if their relationship goes beyond just PR and 'talent'.

With Jess and Joe out of the room, Will bounds back over to the sofa and squeezes in between Sim and Mike. Instantly, he comes back to life – he is very much the cocky, preening rock star again.

'So.' He smirks at Annie. 'Where were we?'

'Well, I was talking about my new hi-hat . . .' Sim says, but Annie cuts him off. No more messing about now. This is her first proper interview. She wants it to be good.

'I wanted to ask a few of our quick-fire questions,' she says. 'We've got a list that we always ask everyone we speak to on the site – they're kind of silly, but hopefully fun, too.' She looks directly at Will. 'So, first up: what was the first single you bought?'

The band all chuckle and nudge each other. 'Oh God, this is gonna get embarrassing . . .' says Mike.

'Not for me,' Will says. 'Mine was Manic Street Preachers – "The Masses Against The Classes".'

Sim snorts. 'Fucking as if it was.'

'It was!'

'He's just trying to sound cool,' Sim tells Annie.

'I don't need to *sound* cool, my friend,' Will counters. 'I *am* cool.'

The rest of the band hoot in derision. Annie laughs – this is exactly what she's after – funny banter and entertaining quotes, not long, dreary speeches about what sort of equipment they use. On the sofa, Will is getting jostled from all sides by his bandmates. He catches Annie's eye, raises his eyebrows and smiles. She likes this side of him – goofy and silly. Not taking himself too seriously. She likes his smile, too: it gives him one dimple, the shape of a teardrop, right in the centre of his left cheek.

'No one's first single is cool,' Sim scoffs. 'That's the rule of first singles. Mine was fucking "Fill Me In" by Craig David. And I'm man enough to admit it.'

Everyone laughs. The bass player, Al, raises his hand. '"Buggin" by Dane Bowers. I'm not proud of it.'

'Ouch,' says Will, wincing.

'These are surprisingly UK Garage-themed answers for an indie band,' Annie says. 'You lot would get on with my sister – she was obsessed with "21 Seconds" by the So-Solid Crew.'

'Well your sister's got wicked taste,' Will says. 'That one's actually a banger.'

'It really isn't,' Annie shoots back.

Will smiles his teardrop-dimple smile at her again. Ugh, she thinks, he really is handsome.

'Seriously, Will, what was yours?' Sim asks. 'No bullshit this time.'

Will shrugs. 'I told you – Manic Street Preachers.'

Annie leads forward to speak into the Dictaphone. 'Let the record show that Will Axford paused before answering.'

The rest of the band laugh. Will leans forward, too. 'Let the record show that Annie from UKmusic.com is chatting nonsense – it was a shrug, not a pause.'

Grinning at each other over the Dictaphone, Annie is suddenly very aware that her face is just inches away from Will's. She feels her cheeks flush. As she leans back again, she's sure she sees Will's gaze land on her chest for just a moment.

'Well, if you're not going to tell the truth, then . . .'

'What you on about?' he protests. 'I am tellin' the truth!'

'Whatever.'

Feeling emboldened by the dimply smiles Will keeps giving her, Annie decides to poke at him a little further.

'Where are you from, by the way, Will?' she asks. 'Where did you grow up?'

'Like . . . down Somerset way,' Will replies hesitantly. 'Why?'

'No, nothing. Just I thought you might be from Walthamstow or something. Your accent is almost . . . cockney?'

Sim snort-laughs at that, and Annie is certain she sees Will's cheeks go pink. But he doesn't seem angry or annoyed: the smile is still there, brighter than ever. Annie gets the impression that he rather enjoys being teased by her. A good thing, as she rather enjoys teasing him.

'Nah, man. That's just how I talk,' he says, sounding more Danny Dyer-ish than ever.

'Mm-hm.' Annie nods. 'Sure it is . . .'

The other band members laugh again, but Annie can't focus on anything but Will and his sexy teardrop dimple. She suddenly wishes it were just the two of them in the room.

'OK, so, next question,' she begins – but Will cuts her off.

'All right, all right . . . You want the truth?' He holds his hands up. 'Can you *handle* the truth?'

Annie laughs. 'Go on . . .'

He takes a deep breath. '"Dancing In The Moonlight" by Toploader. That's the first single I ever bought.'

His three bandmates buckle in hysterics next to him. Annie actually has to shout over them as she replies, quite truthfully: 'Oh my God – that was mine, too!'

This makes Sim, Mike and Al laugh even harder. Will just smiles and nods, as if he was expecting her to say this. He leans forward and holds his fist out. She leans forward and gently bumps it with hers.

Then he ducks his head to speak into the Dictaphone again. 'Let the record show that I do NOT want this information turning up in your article.'

She ducks her head down with him. 'Let the record show that this will be the HEADLINE of my article.'

'Let the record show that you two should get a fucking room,' Sim giggles.

Annie feels her own cheeks redden this time. But Will just

shrugs and holds her gaze. 'We've already got a room, to be fair . . .'

He gestures around as if to prove it – but as he does he notices Jess, who has just stepped back in from the other room. His grin dissolves instantly and the other boys stop laughing.

'All getting very rowdy in here!' Jess says through clenched teeth. 'Everything OK?'

Will nods. 'Yep. All good. We're just doing some funny, quick-fire questions, that's all.'

'Right. How fun.' She smiles at Annie, eyes flashing under her fringe. 'Well, I just came in to say you've got time for a couple more questions, Annie, then we'll have to wrap up. OK?'

'Oh, right. OK, thanks.'

Annie takes a breath and gets herself together. Just as her editor doesn't want 2,000 words about cymbal brands, he probably also doesn't want 2,000 words of flirtation between her and the lead singer – as enjoyable as that would be to produce. She tries to focus, remembering her original brief for the interview, and rattles off a few more quick-fire questions, before touching briefly on their hopes of being signed to a major label, and the rumours that they are set to tour North America next year with The Strokes.

And the whole time, Will continues to hold her gaze, that smile still on his lips.

When Jess finally calls time a few minutes later, the other boys thank Annie and scatter to various corners of the room to check their phones. But Will stands up to face her.

'Well, thanks, Annie from UKmusic.com. That was really fun.'

'I'm glad,' she says. 'I had fun, too.'

Imagine if it was just the two of us, she thinks, alone in the room. What would I do?

Let's face it: she probably wouldn't have the nerve to do anything.

'Well . . . See you around, I guess,' Will says. 'Look forward to reading your piece.'

'"Defectors singer in Toploader shame" – it's gonna be quite the scoop.'

Quite the scoop? She winces. She sounds like her mum. But Will laughs and digs his hands into his pockets. Annie is suddenly very aware of Jess' eyes on her.

'OK. Well, thanks again. See you later.'

'See you,' he says.

She grabs her Dictaphone and heads for the door. Jess walks with her. As the door opens, Annie turns around for a last look at Will. But he's halfway into the other room, speaking to Joe.

'I'm sure you can see yourself out,' Jess says. It sounds more like a threat than a suggestion.

'Of course. Thanks so much, Jess.'

In the lift down to the lobby, Annie feels regret nagging at her. But why? What, realistically, could she have done differently? It's not like she could have just asked him out, right there. Granted, he did seem to be flirting with her – but then Will Axford is probably the kind of boy who flirts with everyone. She imagines telling her flatmate, Maya, that she felt there was a connection between them. Maya, the cynic, would laugh in her face. 'You were interviewing him, mate!' she'd chide. 'Of course he's gonna be nice to you – he wants you to write nice things!'

She steps out of the revolving doors of the hotel into the sunshine. The clouds have all disappeared now, the sky is clear blue and it's a beautiful, crisp, bright day. That nagging sense of regret fades: she's here in Paris with almost nine hours to kill until her Eurostar home. She will not let fancying some random boy ruin her day out.

She sets off towards the river. Her first stop will be that house her dad told her about – she'll take a picture outside and send it to him as a surprise. She suddenly remembers that text from him – something about seeing a doctor. She's about to reach for her phone to re-read it when she hears the slap of shoes behind her. She turns round to see Will Axford running towards her, grinning. Her heart leaps into her throat.

'Sorry, Annie, I just wondered . . .' Will slows to a stop, puffing, out of breath.

'Wondered what?' she asks.

'I just wondered what you were up to for the rest of the day?'

CHAPTER THIRTY-TWO

WILL

27th March, present day
Green Shoots office, Limehouse

I am greeted with something of a surprise as I walk into the office for my Wednesday-evening shift.

I'd checked the rota earlier and seen that the afternoon shift was being covered remotely by another listener. So I'd assumed I'd have the office all to myself. But as I walk in, ten minutes early, I find another person sat at the desk. Tanvi.

She swivels round in the chair and beams at me, the phone clamped to her ear.

She mouths 'Hello!' and I perform an elaborate mime – palms raised, apologetic grimace, tapping of invisible watch – which is supposed to convey: *Sorry, I'm a bit early, I'll wait outside.* But she wags her finger and beckons me inside.

'Mm . . . Yeah . . . Yes . . . I know what you mean . . .' she murmurs into the phone. On the desk in front of her is a phone charger, a couple of apple cores neatly stationed on wads of kitchen roll, and a well-thumbed Penelope Fitzgerald paperback, splayed open by the mousepad.

It's strange seeing someone else in this space. Hearing someone else listening.

I stand in the corner while she continues the phone call, racking my brains for small-talk topics. This is why I usually lurk outside: conducting a normal conversation like a normal human being is something that requires maximum effort for me. Ideally, I need at least two hours to prepare.

'Yes, well, why don't you tell me what it was, and I'll see if I can shed any light on it . . .' The expression on Tanvi's face suggests this is a pretty serious call, so it's fair to say I'm more than a little taken aback when the next thing she says is: '"Stick it on her" . . . No, that one's less rude than it sounds. It just means "flirt", I think. "I'm gonna stick it on her" is like, "I'm going to give her my best chat-up lines" . . . Yeah . . .'

She holds the receiver away from her mouth and looks at me. 'I'm translating *Love Island* for Eric,' she whispers, and I have to bite my lip to stop laughing.

'Mm-hm . . . Mm-hm . . .' She twirls the phone cable around her forefinger, chuckling as she speaks. 'I'm not an *expert*, Eric – my eldest watches it, that's all. Which means some of these ridiculous phrases seep into my brain against my will. Go on, what's the other one you didn't understand . . .? "Moving mad"?'

She turns to me with a shrug, pulling a pantomime 'panicked' face. I do actually know that one – purely because Dev uses it regularly to describe the actions of his on-again-off-again girlfriend, Thea. I grab a Post-It and jot the meaning down, holding it up to Tanvi.

She squints at the paper and mouths 'Thank you!' Into the phone, she says: 'It means, "Acting in an unusual or uncharacteristic manner . . ." Yes, exactly . . . So Piers Morgan, for instance, would be "moving mad" if he didn't make a total arse of himself on Twitter.'

I can hear Eric's laughter crackling in the handset. Tanvi glances at the clock. 'Anyway, Eric, you know the drill, love – I'm going to have to slope off now, because it's time for the shift to switch over. Yeah . . . You too . . . Take care of yourself. Don't go moving mad, all right? Bye, then.'

She hangs up the phone and shakes her head. 'Honestly: explaining ITV2 reality-show lingo to a pensioner. I do love this job sometimes.'

I laugh. 'How was he?'

'Oh, on sparkling form.'

'Ah, good. He's been a bit up and down when I've had him lately.'

'I know, he can get a bit glum from time to time. But today he was chuckling away like nobody's business. Which is more than can be said for Sandra . . .' She rolls her eyes.

'Oh no. Is she off her meds again?' Our other regular caller – Sandra – is coping with long-term physical and mental illness, and as vital as I know it is for her to speak to another human being every day, it can be something of a chore listening to her.

'I'm not sure,' Tanvi says, glancing at the logbook, 'but she was on for *forty-eighty minutes* with me today. Thank God for Eric and his newfound obsession with watching reruns of *Love Island*.'

'I do love Eric.'

'Oh, he's my absolute favourite,' she grins. 'He's such a dude.'

Something occurs to me from the conversation I've just overheard. 'So you tell him that you've got kids, then?'

'Yeah.'

'It's just that Marie's always banging on about "no personal information" and what have you . . .'

Tanvi rolls her eyes again. Marie is the director of Green Shoots; a woman I've only met once, very briefly, but whose aggressive earnestness and total lack of humour very much come across in her regular emails about the importance of listeners withholding anything about their own lives from callers.

'I honestly don't see what the harm is,' Tanvi says. 'Why does it matter if Eric knows I have kids? It's nice for him to feel like he's talking to an actual human being, rather than a bloody answering machine. I wouldn't tell a first-time caller, or a total stranger, anything personal. I don't think I'd even tell Sandra. You've got to use your best judgement, though. And with Eric . . . I feel almost like I know him.'

'Me too.'

She shrugs. 'I can't see what's wrong with divulging the odd thing about yourself, as long as you're comfortable with it, and the caller's comfortable with it.'

'Yeah, totally.' I say, thinking of Pia. 'I feel the same way.'

Tanvi stands up and begins collecting her bits from the desk. 'Right-o. Back to the madhouse. Have a good shift, Will.' She stops gathering for a second and looks at me. 'It was really nice to see you. To talk properly.'

'Yeah, it was great,' I say, surprising myself that I actually mean it.

'Stop by early again next time, if you fancy. Best part of this whole gig is having a brew and a gossip.'

'Sounds good.'

She smiles and heads off. Normally in this situation, I would be breathing a silent sigh of relief, grateful that the interaction was over and I was on my own again. But right now, I actually wish Tanvi had stayed longer. I was so busy enjoying our chat that I forgot to feel anxious about it.

I go to the kitchen to make a cup of tea before settling down into the rickety chair and logging in to the computer. As I wait for the phone to ring, I think about what Tanvi said.

I can't see what's wrong with divulging the odd thing about yourself, as long you're comfortable with it, and the caller's comfortable with it.

There have been a few occasions now when Pia has put a personal question to me or asked for my honest opinion on something. She's obviously comfortable with me opening up to her, showing her something of myself.

The question is: am I?

CHAPTER THIRTY-THREE

ANNIE

28th March
Shoreditch, London

Towards the end of a dreary Thursday-afternoon team meeting, Matt drops a bombshell.

Lexi, cup of mint tea balanced precariously on her humongous belly, has just asked if her maternity cover has been sorted out yet, as she'll need to get a handover email ready. Matt coughs, tugs his goatee and replies: 'We won't be getting any maternity cover.'

There are ten of us sat in the meeting room. We've spent most of the last half-hour yawning and secretly checking our phones under the table. But now all eyes are on Matt. He coughs again.

'Seriously?' Lexi says.

'Yeah. It's cool, though. No big deal.' He juggles his Sharpie casually, as if to show just how cool and not-a-big-deal it is. 'Money's a bit tight at the moment, so we'll just have to scrape by until you're back.'

Marker's head designer, Jermaine, clears his throat. 'But

Matt, Lex is the only other designer we've got. And we're already stretched as it is with just the two of us. So, if it'll just be me for nine months, then . . .'

'Jermaine. Mate!' Matt holds his hands up, rictus grin stapled across his beard. 'You'll be fine. We'll be fine. If we really need it, we can bring a freelancer in whenever things get too hectic.'

'But we're—'

Matt cuts him off with a tap of his Apple watch. 'Sorry, guys, I've got another meeting with the finance bods upstairs. But don't worry. Everything's going to be coolio. We'll talk again soon.'

We all stand up and eye each other nervously. Things definitely don't feel particularly 'coolio'.

'Annie, can you hang back a sec?' Matt asks as I'm heading for the door with the others.

'Sure . . .'

I sit back down and Lexi gives me a look as she leaves, closing the door behind her.

Matt's rictus grin has gone, replaced by an anxious frown. He looks genuinely worried now: he's not even hiding it. My first thought is that I'm about to be fired, and a wave of panic shoots through me.

'So. The Defectors thing,' Matt says. 'What's happening?'

I breathe out, feel the panic dissolve. 'Right, well, I reached out to the guitarist, Mike, and—'

Matt nods impatiently. 'Yep, you told me that last week. And?'

'He said he'd be up for an interview this week, but I emailed again a couple of days ago and he still hasn't got back to me.'

Matt's frown lines deepen. He tugs so hard at his goatee that I'm worried it might actually come off. 'Look, Annie, as you can probably tell, the numbers aren't great on the site at the moment. We seriously need to get this advertorial feature up and running so we can get a bit of a cash injection. Right?'

'Totally, I get it,' I say. I've been rehearsing this speech in my head for the past fortnight, so I launch straight into it. 'I just wonder if maybe this Defectors thing is a bit of a dead end? I've really tried to get in touch with them – all of them . . .' I feel myself blush at the lie, but I press on. 'But clearly they're not up for talking. I've actually made a list of other bands that might work for the "Whatever Happened To . . ." section: The Ting Tings, Klaxons, Reverend and the Makers . . .'

Matt holds a hand up to stop me. 'Annie. I pitched the Defectors idea to the ad guys and the people at the jeans brand who are sponsoring the feature. They loved it. If I have to go back to them now and say, "We've tried, and it's not gonna work", that's not going to fill them with confidence for the rest of the series, is it?'

'I guess not . . .'

'We can't fall at the very first hurdle, it'll make us look like amateurs.' He sighs. 'Look, if you're not up for this, that's fine. But you need to let me know, because this Defectors thing *needs* to happen. So, I'll give it to Zara instead, OK?'

That wave of panic hits again. If Marker can't even afford mat cover for Lexi, then surely they'll be looking to make redundancies before long. There are four of us writers on the staff – and each of us knows the site could easily get along with three. This Defectors article: this is how I make myself indispensable. This is how I make sure I'm not first out of the door. I need to do it. Even if I have to swallow my pride and meet up with Will Bloody Axford.

'Matt, please, I can do this,' I say firmly. 'Sorry I've been so slow until now. But I'm on it. I'll make it happen. I promise.'

He nods. 'OK. I want this to go live on the site within the next fortnight, so you really need to start making headway.'

'I will, I will.'

Back out on the office floor, I ignore Lex's inquisitive glances over the top of her monitor and dive straight into my inbox. After that first Twitter DM, we'd switched to email to communicate, and there was definitely a mobile number in Mike Drury's signature. I find it, jab it into my phone and duck straight out into the corridor. Before I can lose my nerve, I press 'call'.

He answers after three rings. 'Hello?'

'Oh hi! Is that Mike?'

'Yeah. Who's this?'

'Hi Mike, this is Annie Lucas, from Marker Media. We were in touch over email, and—'

He cuts in abruptly. 'Yeah, hi, Annie. Sorry I haven't got back to you. Things have been pretty hectic.'

'No worries! Look, I'm sorry to chase you over the phone, it's just that my editor is keen to get the article up on the site as soon as possible, so I was wondering if you'd still be up for a quick interview this week?'

There's a long pause. 'Mike?'

'Yeah', he says. 'Look, Annie, I'll level with you. I was totally up for talking to you. I still am. But I got in touch with Will, our singer, to check if it was cool with him, and I haven't heard back, so . . .' He tails off.

'Oh. OK. Why would you need to check with Will?'

Another pause. 'I just don't feel comfortable talking about this stuff until I know Will is on board.'

'What "stuff" is there to talk about?' I ask. 'This would just be a fun, light-hearted nostalgia piece about why you guys decided to call it quits, and what you've all been up to since.'

He laughs humourlessly. 'Look, if Will gets back to me and says it's cool, I'll call you straight back. OK?'

I clear my throat. Try to sound casual. 'You wouldn't have an email or a number for Will, would you? Maybe I could drop him a line myself?'

The longest pause yet. 'No, I wouldn't feel OK about giving that out. Sorry.'

'Please, Mike, if we could just meet for a quick coffee or something, then—'

'I'm really sorry, Annie.'

The line goes dead. Dammit. There's only one thing for it.

I walk straight back to my desk, still ignoring Lexi's glances, which have now upgraded from 'inquisitive' to 'downright indignant'. I click into my 'drafts' folder, and before I have time for second thoughts, I hit 'send' on the email to Jessica.

CHAPTER THIRTY-FOUR

WILL

30th March
Harrow, Middlesex

'I can't stay long.'

That's the first thing she says as she sweeps through the door of my flat on this unseasonably warm Saturday morning. Right behind her is that familiar scent of her flowery perfume, which instantly takes me back five, six, seven years, to a different life.

'Oh. OK.' I close the door behind her. 'No worries.'

She stands in the centre of the living room and grimaces down at Milligan, who is gamely attempting to nuzzle her ankle. 'Got a friend's birthday thing in Kilburn,' she says. 'Not too far from here, so I thought I might as well come by first.'

'It was really nice to hear from you,' I say.

I honestly can't remember the last time Jess texted me first. The past five years have been a near-constant cycle of me feeling down, sending her a desperate, pleading message, and then her coming over and making me feel even worse. Repeat *ad infinitum*. Yesterday, though, as I was locking up the shop with Dev, she texted out of the blue, asking if she could drop by this morning.

It's strange, her being in my flat without me having begged her to come. I have no clue what she's doing here and it makes me feel anxious and excited at the same time.

She brushes some invisible dust off my sofa and sits down, clutching her handbag to her chest, seemingly concerned that a rat might scurry off with it.

'So, whose birthday is it?' I ask, sitting down on the rickety wicker chair opposite her. I suddenly imagine a parallel universe in which Jess might invite me to the birthday thing. In which I would spend this Saturday in the way most normal people spend their Saturdays – talking, laughing, drinking with other human beings.

'It's no one you know,' Jess says. She takes a packet of cigarettes out of her bag. 'Do you mind if I smoke?'

Without waiting for an answer, she lights up and inhales. 'So, look, the reason I came round. I got an email from this journalist, wanting to do a piece about The Defectors.'

Panic seizes me by the throat. 'What?'

Jess raises her eyebrows at whatever expression I'm currently making. 'You got an email, too?'

'No. Mike did.' My stomach squirms. I take a breath to compose myself, but it comes out ragged and shaky.

'Mike Drury?' Jess wrinkles her nose. 'I didn't know you two were still in touch.'

'We're not. It's the first time I've heard from him in years.' I cough. The cigarette smoke is clogging my throat, making the anxiety churn harder. 'Anyway, what does he want, this journalist?'

'She,' Jess says. 'It's a her. Funnily enough, it's . . .' She pauses and bites her lip, as if making up her mind about what to say next.

'What?' I ask.

She takes a drag on her cigarette and smiles at me through the smoke. 'Nothing.'

'So, what does she want?' I'm not even bothering to try and sound casual. My heartbeat is thundering, and that calm smile on Jess' face is shifting the creeping sense of dread up a gear.

She shrugs and crosses her legs. 'I don't know. She just said she wanted to interview you. To write a feature about why the band broke up and what you were all up to now.'

'I don't understand. Why would anyone care about that?'

'No idea,' Jess agrees, taking another drag on her Marlboro Light. 'It's not like you guys were ever that big of a deal.'

I nod and stare down at the carpet. My cheeks are burning. I need to calm down. I don't want Jess to see me like this. She's used to seeing me lonely and gloomy and needy – but she's never seen me fall to bits right in front of her.

'I'm guessing you wouldn't want to speak to this woman,' she says. 'To go back over all that stuff? To relive it. I'm guessing that would be really painful.'

I scan her face for any sign that she's twisting the knife on purpose – intentionally trying to make me feel bad. She must know I would never, in a million years, want to 'go back over all that stuff'. But she's unreadable. She always has been.

Before I can answer, she carries on: 'But maybe . . . Maybe it would be a good thing to do? A positive thing. You weren't exactly the nicest person back in those days – to me or to anyone. It might be healthy to face up to that. To talk about it and explore it. Like a confession, almost.' She gives a quiet laugh. 'You might even feel better after talking to her.'

I close my eyes. But that photo of Joe and me, at school, sears itself onto the backs of my eyelids. Even in the darkness, his grinning face is all I can see. 'Please, Jess . . .' I whisper.

'So, shall I tell her you'll meet her?' she says breezily. 'When would be good?'

'Please . . .' I bite the inside of my cheek hard to try and regain a hold on myself. 'I just can't,' I murmur. 'I just don't want to think about it all.'

She drops her cigarette stub in an empty coffee mug and pats the sofa next to her. 'Come here.'

Automatically, I go and sit beside her. My hands clasp in my lap, and I stare down into the carpet again. I feel her body shift closer to mine. She runs a hand through my hair and my whole body flinches at the novelty of being touched so gently.

'Oh, Will,' she sighs. 'What are we going to do with you? You're so lost, aren't you?'

My throat is dry and my head is pounding suddenly. I press the heels of my palms into my eyes. 'I don't want to think about it,' is all I can say.

'Look at me,' she says. I turn to face her. She's wearing a short-sleeved black jumpsuit and silver hooped earrings. Her long hair, usually piled into a messy top-knot, has been curled today and it bounces at her shoulders. Even through my confused, self-loathing fug I am aware she looks spectacular. 'My therapist says I have this thing,' she announces suddenly. 'This, like, "caring instinct". Something in me seeks out people who are broken, who need looking after. It's just in my nature.'

I don't even know what to say to that. It conjures the deep, dark, pit-of-my-stomach sensation that Jess is still punishing me for the person I used to be; keeping me trapped in this cycle of neediness and self-loathing as some sort of weird power-play. Keeping me broken so that she can pretend to fix me. And I go along with it all, willingly, because feeling bad is better than feeling nothing at all.

She sighs again and gently strokes my beard. 'I like you better clean shaven.'

'I like myself better clean shaven.' She smiles at that. I don't tell her that the only reason I keep the beard is that I get recognised less when I've got it. I look less like the baby-faced lead singer of failed indie band The Defectors.

'I'll tell her that you're not interested, shall I?' she says softly. 'The journalist: I'll get rid of her?'

My body quivers with relief. 'Oh my God, Jess. Thank you. Yes. Thank you.'

I reach forward and wrap my arms around her in a clumsy hug, still muttering 'thank you'. I just want to be held. As pathetic as it sounds, that's what I want. I want to be told I'm OK. That everything will be OK. But instead, Jess leans back and kisses me hard on the lips. My body responds instantly.

'This doesn't mean anything, OK?' she says as I cover her mouth with mine again. 'This is just a bit of fun.'

'OK. OK . . .'

She starts unbuttoning my shirt and lifts her chin to let me kiss her neck.

'It doesn't mean anything,' she whispers again between kisses. And I don't want it to. I don't want to think about what it means. I don't want to think about *anything*, just for a while. I want to lose myself completely. I just want to feel something other than this constant, bone-deep loneliness. She unbuckles my belt as I reach behind her, undoing the buttons on the back of her jumpsuit. I kiss her again, close my eyes and let the smell of her perfume engulf me. It's five, six, seven years ago. I'm somewhere else. I'm someone else.

CHAPTER THIRTY-FIVE

ANNIE

31st March
Waterloo, London

I'm not sure why I'm so nervous.

I'm not sure why I spent nearly an hour choosing my outfit and faffing about with my hair. I'm not sure why I got here twenty minutes early. I'm not sure why I just went to the loo to touch up my make-up. I'm also not sure why I ordered this double-shot cappuccino. It's definitely not helping my jitteriness.

I take another sip anyway. I'm sat in the window seat of the café Jessica suggested – a little hipstery place just outside Waterloo station. She replied to my email yesterday afternoon. There were no 'Hey-how-are-yous' – all she said was: 'Are you free for a quick coffee tomorrow to discuss?' I didn't even think about the fact that Dom and I had already made vague plans to go for a roast today – I just wrote straight back to say 'yes'. Part of me was even relieved at being able to wriggle out of the pub, as it meant I could make my Sunday-afternoon call to Jack later without having to think of an excuse.

Not that Dom seemed particularly bothered I was dropping out. He just mumbled something about seeing if one of his mates was up for it instead, before turning his attention back to *Match of the Day*.

My phone rings and my stomach flips as I reach for it. But it's not Jessica. It's my sister, Josie. I haven't even spoken to her in weeks. I slip my phone back into my bag. I can call her back later.

'Annie.'

I've just taken a large sip of coffee, and my attempt to look up, swallow and say hi at the same time results in me spluttering unattractively into my napkin.

'Hey! Jessica! Sorry!' I say, frantically wiping froth from my mouth.

'It's Jess,' she says, sitting down opposite me, and frowning at the soggy napkin.

'Right, Jess. Long time no see!'

'Mm-hm.' She's wearing a long black trenchcoat and a chunky, blood-red scarf that matches her lipstick perfectly. The sexy fringe is gone – her hair is longer now, pulled up into a tight topknot. But she has barely aged a day since I last saw her. There's no getting around it: she is still significantly thinner and prettier than I am. And unfortunately, no amount of hair faffing and make-up re-touching on my part is going to change that.

'How are you?' I ask, pocketing my damp napkin.

'Good, thanks.' She picks up a menu and peruses it. 'You?'

'Yeah, great. Thanks so much for agreeing to meet.'

'No worries.'

The waiter, a willowy young man with a pencil moustache,

comes over. His eyes light up as he takes Jess in. 'What can I get you?'

'Do you have lemon verbena tea?' she asks.

'Yes, we do.'

She nods at him. 'One of those, thanks.'

'Coming right up!' he beams.

'So.' She shuts the menu and looks at me. 'I was quite surprised to get your email.'

'I know. Sorry. Quite random! My editor is keen to do a "Where are they now?" piece on The Defectors, and I remembered I had your email from that trip to Paris. Are you still in touch with the band?'

'I'm in touch with Will,' she says.

'Right.' I take another sip of coffee. 'How's he doing?'

She unwraps her scarf and folds it carefully over the back of her chair. 'He's fine.'

'Do you think he'd be up for a quick interview with me for this article?'

Jess smiles at me. 'After what you wrote about him in your *last* article?'

I blush and force out a laugh. 'Ah. Yes, sorry. I hope he's not still annoyed about that?'

'I don't think he even noticed,' she says coolly. 'But since I was on press duties, I got a fair bit of shit about it from my boss.'

'Oh no.' Is this why she wanted to meet up? So she could yell at me for something I wrote five years ago? 'I'm really sorry, Jess.'

'It's fine.'

'One lemon verbena tea!' Our waiter lays the cup gently down in front of Jess, his grin now teetering into 'leer' territory.

'Thank you.' She rewards him with a small smile as he walks away.

'Do you think there's any way you could put me in touch with Will?' I ask. 'As well as the interview, I'd like to apologise for writing that piece a few years ago. It wasn't very professional.'

'I've already told him about this new article you want to do,' she says, stirring her tea. 'And he said he wasn't keen.'

'Oh. Really?' The disappointment stings. Hard. It takes me a second to realise why. It's not only that I'm worried about letting Matt down and jeopardising my job. It's also that Will Axford apparently has zero interest in seeing me again.

'Did you . . . mention my name at all?'

The question is out there before I can take it back. I wince and Jess gives me a tight smile. 'Are you sure he'd remember you?' she asks sweetly. 'They got interviewed by lots of people back then.'

Another sting – although I notice she didn't actually answer my question. 'No, of course,' I say. 'It's just that we ended up kind of . . . hanging out that day.'

Jess' smile tightens further. She gives no indication of whether or not she already knew this fact. I find myself hoping very much that she didn't. Pathetic as it is, I feel like I've scored a point against her.

She blows the steam off her tea and takes a sip. 'I don't mean to be rude,' she says – a surefire indication that's she about to be – 'But Will "hung out" with a lot of girls in those days. I'm sure they all think they had this "special" moment with him, but . . .' She rolls her eyes and laughs. 'You know what I mean?'

'Ha. Yes.' I nod, feeling like she's just scored ten points in return.

She examines me evenly as she takes another sip of tea. 'I get that you want to be put back in touch with him. But I'm not sure he feels the same way, so . . .'

'No,' I say, rushing to correct her. 'It's not like that at all! Honestly. I've got a boyfriend!'

It comes out slightly too high-pitched, and Jess rewards me with a patronising, *well-done-you* head tilt. 'It's just for this article,' I add. 'My boss was a big Defectors fan, you see, and—'

She cuts me off with a wave of her hand. 'Will's been through a lot, OK? He doesn't want to dredge it all up again for some article. I'm sorry.'

Dredge *what* up? She's reminding me of Mike Drury now, with his insistence that he had to check with Will first before he could speak to me. 'I'm not looking to dredge anything up,' I say. 'It would just be a light-hearted piece about what Will's up to now.'

Jess gives a shrill laugh. 'Nothing light-hearted about that. He's working in one of those dreary electronics shops on Tottenham Court Road.'

I pause to let the weight of that information settle. Even in the brief time I spent with him, it seemed absolutely obvious that Will Axford was destined for success. Clearly, The Defectors never really took off, but I always assumed he went on to some other bright, shiny career – maybe music production or songwriting or management. He seemed like the kind of person who couldn't fail. So, working in a 'dreary electronics shop' doesn't quite square up.

And then something else hits me. Jess has just pretty much told me where to find him. If I want to make myself look *really* desperate.

Jess takes another sip of tea and reaches for her scarf. I get the sudden impression this meeting is already coming to an end.

'Look, if you just had an email address for him, then I could get in touch directly—' I start.

'I already told you.' She says it slowly, as if speaking to a child. 'He's not interested in talking to any journalists. And even if he was, it probably wouldn't be one who's already slagged him off in a previous article.'

'Jess, I'm sorry if—'

'There's nothing to be sorry about, Annie,' she says casually. 'I just thought I'd do you the courtesy of telling you, face to face, that it's not going to happen.' Just for a moment, as she places her cup back on the table, the polite smile she's been wearing dissolves.

'There are plenty of other failed bands and musicians you can write about,' she says. 'Just leave Will alone.'

CHAPTER THIRTY-SIX

WILL

31st March
Green Shoots office, Limehouse

'Pia!'

'Hey, Jack. How are you?'

'I can barely hear you. Where are you?'

'Sorry, I'm . . .'

The sound of traffic wipes her voice out. I press the phone to my ear. 'Pia?'

After a few more seconds of blaring and honking, the traffic noise dies away. 'There we go,' she says. 'Just ducked down an alley.'

'Had you wandered into a Formula One race or something?'

Not exactly my best gag ever – but she still laughs. 'No. I was on that big roundabout near Waterloo station. Which is apparently the noisiest road on Earth.'

'Ha, right.'

She's in London. I never realised that. Because of her accent

I guess I always assumed she was up north somewhere. But no. At this very moment, she is just a Tube ride away from me.

'How are you doing?' she asks.

'Good, thanks. And you?'

'Yeah, good,' she says. And then: 'Actually, not that good. I just remembered that you're the one person I don't have to lie to when I answer that question.'

'Well, that's a nice thing to hear,' I laugh. 'But less nice to hear that you're not doing well. What's up?'

'Oh, just had a very weird work thing. A meeting that took a pretty insane U-turn.'

It strikes me that I have no idea what she does for a living. She's never really spoken about that.

'Do you want to talk about it?' I ask.

She hesitates. 'No, I don't think so. It would take a long time to explain.'

'I'm happy to listen.'

'No, it's OK. The upshot is just that my boss is going to be very pissed off with me tomorrow.'

'Oh, man. I'm sorry.'

'Ah, that's all right, I can handle him.' She sighs. 'So. What's going on with you, Jack? What's new in your world?'

'Well . . .'

I think about my chat with Tanvi earlier this week. How she'd argued there was nothing wrong with letting the caller know the odd personal thing about you, from time to time. Truthfully, I'd love to tell Pia what's going on with me. I'd do anything to have someone to talk to about what happened yesterday. To untangle why it is I can't even hear the name of my old band without turning into a gibbering wreck. To get to the bottom of why Jess is the only person I can turn to when I'm lonely, yet being with her makes me feel more alone than ever.

I try to imagine, just for a second, what Pia's reaction would be if all that came spilling out of me. If she knew the first thing about me – about what I've done – she'd never call again.

'Ah, you know – same old, same old,' I tell her.

She laughs. 'Keeping your cards close to your chest as always, Jack.'

'What about you?' I say. 'Anything else on your mind, apart from this work thing?'

'Well . . . There was something else that happened today.'

'Right?'

'I got a missed call from my sister, who I hadn't spoken to in weeks. I just called her back and . . . I don't know. It was weird.'

'Weird how?'

'It's hard to explain. It was mainly just small talk, about how we hadn't been in touch for a while, what she's been up to, how her husband is. And then out of nowhere she mentions this text that Mum sent me last week, to say good luck for that baby shower.'

'Mm-hm.'

'She didn't explicitly say anything, but I just got the sense she was insinuating I should make more of an effort with Mum. Which of course I should. I know I should. But . . .'

She takes a breath. I can tell she wants to say more. I keep quiet; leave her the space she needs.

'I understand why they're angry at me,' she says finally. 'But I want them to understand why *I'm* angry at *them*. When they'd both given up and accepted the worst, I was the only one still looking for ways to save him. And I could have found something if they'd just let me try. But they didn't. And whenever

I miss them, whenever I feel guilty for pushing them away, that thought instantly comes rushing back and gets in the way.'

'Mm-hm. How do you think your mum and sister would react if you told them all that?'

She laughs. 'I have no idea. They're quite different from me. My mum, in particular. I know she means well and she wants to be supportive, but her way of being supportive usually has the exact opposite effect.'

'How do you mean?'

'Well . . .' I hear her take a breath as she considers this. 'For instance, whenever the subject of me wanting to be a writer ever came up, she would say things like, "I'll be first in the queue at your book signing, darling" or "When you win the Booker Prize, I hope you'll thank your poor mother in the speech". She doesn't seem to realise that her particular brand of encouragement just amounts to heaping on massive amounts of pressure. I know she doesn't mean any harm. But the problem is, her definition of "success" is different from mine. For Mum, something's only worth doing if it leads to money or fame or – ideally – both. But Dad always understood that it's enough just to *write*. That it doesn't necessarily matter whether you make any money out of it or not.' She stops and gives a short laugh. 'Sorry, went off on a bit of a tangent there.'

'That's fine. That's good,' I say. 'You've never mentioned wanting to be an author before.'

'Yup.' She sighs again. 'Not that I'm doing much about it, of course.'

'Why not?'

'I don't know. There's a whole folder on my laptop called "Book Stuff". Quite misleading, really, because you couldn't call it a "book" – it's more a collection of jumbled thoughts that I've been trying to paste together for the past four years. But I haven't looked at them for ages. I haven't really written anything since Dad died.'

'Why do you think that is?'

'Maybe because – at times – it felt like I was writing stories for *him*. And now he's gone, it's like . . . why would I bother writing, if here's not here to read it?'

I hear her swallow thickly. She sounds like she's about to cry. My immediate instinct is to tell her she's OK. That everything will be OK. Then I realise that's exactly what I wanted Jess to tell me yesterday. And what would it have changed if she had?

So instead I ask: 'Was your dad a writer?'

Pia swallows again. 'He never made a living out of it – but yes, he loved to write. He spent his whole twenties submitting funny, weird sci-fi stories to all these pulpy Seventies magazines. He got a few things published, too, but when he realised he probably wasn't going to be the new Stephen King, he knuckled down and got a "proper" job, working for the council.'

'Mm-hm.'

'I've never directly asked her about it, but I'm pretty sure that was down to my mum. They got together about a year before his last story was published and, knowing Mum, she would have made it *abundantly* clear that a struggling author was not her idea of serious husband and father material.'

'Right. So he stopped writing altogether after that?' I ask.

'I think so. But he never stopped reading. And when I started to show an interest in both in my teens, he was over the moon. He was always plying me with books and bottomless encouragement. It's like all my memories of reading and writing are linked to him.'

She sniffs and takes another shaky breath. I know for certain now that she's crying. It makes me wince. I hate hearing her like this.

'I'm sorry, Pia. Let's talk about something else.'

'No, it's actually nice.' She laughs suddenly, sounding almost surprised by the fact. 'It's nice to remember the good things. I just miss him. So much. That's why it's so hard with my mum and my sister. I know I should go up and see them. Get it all out in the open. But I'm such a wuss. I need to be braver.'

'I know what you mean,' I say. 'I do too.'

She laughs again. 'Oh yeah? What do you need to be brave about?'

'Oh, there are too many things to pick just one, Pia.'

'Not that you'd tell me even if you did.'

'No, exactly: Phone Beefeater Code.'

'Ah, yes, the PBC.'

We both laugh this time. And then Pia says: 'Hey. I tell you what, Jack. Why don't we say that, this week, we both have to do something brave. We have to take one step each outside of our comfort zones, no matter how small or insignificant it might seem.'

'Ha. OK . . .' That familiar combination of anxiety and excitement races through me – though it doesn't take long for excitement to win out. 'That sounds good.'

'And then we report back next Sunday. And no invoking the PBC!' she says mock sternly. 'If I'm telling you mine, you need to tell me yours.'

My heartbeat thumps and my grin stretches wider.

'OK, Pia,' I say. 'You've got a deal.'

CHAPTER THIRTY-SEVEN

26th February, five years ago
Paris, France

'This isn't weird, is it? Me tagging along with you? You can just tell me if it's weird. Honestly, I won't mind. Is it weird?'

Annie laughs. 'No, Will, for the thousandth time: it is not weird.'

They are walking over the Pont Alexandre III, heading to the north side of the city. The sunlight bounces off the Seine, and Annie sneaks a glimpse at Will as he strides along next to her. She feels a little light-headed. Because, truth be told, this *is* a bit weird.

The very hot lead singer of a sort-of-famous indie band has just run down the street after her and shoehorned himself into her day. And rather than acting all arrogant and swaggering, like he was in the hotel, he now seems sort of sweet and nervous. This is the kind of thing that happens in Richard Curtis films, not in real life. Annie wishes she could have five minutes to call Maya and formulate some kind of plan.

'Good to get out of that hotel room,' Will says as they pause to admire the view of the Eiffel Tower across the river. 'It was just getting a bit . . .' In lieu of an adjective, he puffs out his cheeks.

'Right, yeah.' Annie is very interested to know what exactly it was in that room he was so eager to escape. Maybe Jess? But she keeps the question to herself for the time being.

'So.' Will transfers his gaze from the tower to Annie. 'Shall we get a drink or something?'

Annie hesitates. As delighted as she is about the Richard Curtis-esque U-turn this day has taken, there is something she'd been planning to do here in Paris. A funny little surprise for her dad. But it's going to sound extremely uncool and weird when she explains it to Will.

Oh, get a grip, she tells herself. After all, who means more to her: her father or some random hot boy?

'OK, this is going to sound strange . . .' she starts.

'Strange is good.' Will grins. 'I like strange.'

'So, my dad is a big fan of this French writer from the early 1900s, Alphonse Carnet . . .'

'Ah, Alphonse Carnet!' Will cries. 'I love his work.'

'I'm assuming this is sarcasm?'

'It is. Never heard of the guy.'

Annie laughs. 'Right. Well, when I told my dad which part of Paris we were doing the interview in, he mentioned that Alphonse Carnet had lived really near here. So I looked up his address, and I was thinking I'd go and visit his house to take a picture for my dad.' She pauses, concerned about sounding geeky and odd. But Will is still grinning so she continues. 'See, he lived in quite a weird apartment block. My dad was telling me about it – the landlord tried to increase his profit by building another floor in between the third and fourth floors. The third-and-a-half floor. Because Alphonse Carnet was quite short – about five foot – he could just about stand up in his apartment, but all his other visitors would have to stoop about with their heads bent.'

Will laughs. 'Like in *Being John Malkovich*?'

'Exactly! This place could have been the inspiration for *Being John Malkovich*. But I totally understand if you're not up for it. It is quite random. We could just have a coffee and then I could go by myself.'

'Are you kidding? I'm well up for it!' Will genuinely seems delighted by the idea of this excursion. Annie feels her smile stretching. 'Really?'

'Yeah! Let's do it,' he says. 'We'll check out the Malkovich place, and then maybe we can get some food afterwards.'

'Don't you have to soundcheck before the gig?'

'Yeah, but not till seven-ish. We've got ages.'

Ages. She feels a jolt in her stomach. How long is he planning to spend with her?

*

They wander in silence for a moment, as Annie finds the best route on Google Maps.

Will's phone rings. He takes it out, glances at it and slips it back in his pocket without answering.

'So, who's Joe?' Annie asks, thinking suddenly of the boy with the mop of blond hair and the sad eyes.

'He's my, er . . .' Will squints into the sunlight as if searching for the right word. 'I grew up with him. He's my best mate, I suppose.'

'Cool. And he's come over to see the gig?'

'Yeah. He kind of . . . just showed up. I didn't even know he was coming till late last night.'

'Oh, right.'

'He's like that, Joe. I love him, but he can be a bit unpredictable. You know those friends where it's great when it's just the two of you, but as soon as there are other people around, it doesn't . . . work?'

'Mm,' Annie says, even though she's not quite sure what he means. 'So you didn't want to hang out with him today?'

As soon as she says it, she thinks: *shut up, you idiot! Are you trying to get rid of him?!*

But Will just shrugs. 'Well, yeah. But he just told me he'd rather have a wander around on his own. That's what I mean – he comes all the way here and then he wants to be alone. I can't figure him out sometimes. It's weird. It's like, I know him so well and I also don't really know him at all.'

'You can speak to him if you want to,' Annie says. 'Don't mind me.'

Will looks at her, not understanding. 'That phone call you just got,' she explains.

'Ah no,' he says breezily. 'That was just Jess.'

Annie nods, a thrill of victory tingling through her as she imagines how Jess will react when she finds out Will has come sprinting after her. She desperately wants to find out if there is anything going on between the two of them. She's not particularly keen on Jess, but still – it wouldn't feel right running around Paris with someone else's boyfriend.

They reach the end of the road and come upon a fairly nondescript, yet typically Parisian, apartment block – all high windows and wrought-iron balconies. Annie looks down at her phone, then back up at the building. 'This is it. Twenty-five rue Jarry.'

Will examines it. 'No blue plaque. Sucks to be Alphonse.'

Annie laughs. 'He isn't very well known. My dad is into quite obscure writers.' She hands Will her phone. 'Can you take a photo of me?'

'Photo of us, surely?' Will says, grinning his sexy, gap-toothed grin. 'Your dad's definitely going to want me in it, too.'

Oh God, Annie thinks, I really do fancy this boy. 'Don't take this the wrong way, but my dad is not the biggest Defectors fan.'

Will sighs. 'Philistine.'

'I know.'

'OK. You ready?'

He steps back. Annie smiles and Will takes the photo of her. Then he comes to stand next to her. 'Cheeky selfie?'

He flips the screen, and suddenly both their faces are on it. Annie winces the second she sees herself, wishing she'd put on more make-up. But when Will hands the phone back to her, a miracle has clearly occurred, because she looks good in the photo. Really good. She makes a mental note to favourite it later.

'OK. Mission accomplished,' she says. 'Where shall we go now?'

'Aren't we going inside?' Will says. 'I want to see the mad little Malkovich floor!'

'We can't go in. We don't know anyone who lives here.'

'No problem.' Will reaches past her and presses a random doorbell.

'What are you doing?' Annie laughs.

A voice crackles through the intercom. Will clears his throat. 'Oui, bonjour, c'est le . . .' He turns to Annie and whispers: 'What's "postman" in French?'

Annie shrugs, her hand pressed to her mouth to keep the laughter in.

'C'est le . . . homme de poste?' Will says into the intercom.

Incredibly, the buzzer sounds and the lock unclicks. 'No way!' Annie hisses.

Will smirks and opens the door for her. 'After you.'

They step inside and climb the creaky wooden staircase. When they pass the third floor, they both have to clutch the bannister in startled delight. Because it's still here: the third-and-a-half floor.

Midway up the stairs, the wall has been broken and a whole new corridor has been haphazardly constructed. The ceiling can't be more than five feet high.

'Oh my God,' Annie whispers. 'I can't believe this!'

She ducks her head and steps into the tiny hallway. Will, a good ten inches taller than her, has to crane his neck so dramatically that his head is almost at a right angle to his body.

They stand in the surreal corridor, holding their surreal poses, laughing at each other.

'I feel like we're in *Lord of the Rings*,' Will says.

Behind him, one of the apartment doors opens and a little old lady emerges, dragging a wheeled shopping cart. The top of her hat just about grazes the ceiling. If she is particularly fazed by seeing two crooked-necked tourists giggling in her hallway, she doesn't show it.

'Bonjour,' she says brightly.

'Bonjour, madame!' Will chimes. 'Er . . . Sorry, mon français n'est pas bon. Mais, nous sommes ici pour Alphonse Carnet?'

The old lady's eyes light up. 'Oui! Oui! Il vivait dans mon appartement!' She points into her apartment. 'Here! He lived here!'

'What?!' Annie stares at Will, dumbfounded. 'This is insane.'

'He wrote books here,' the lady says.

Will points at Annie. 'Son père est un grand fan d'Alphonse Carnet.'

'Ah oui?' the lady says. 'Allez, entrez, entrez!'

She ushers them into her home. They look around, dazed, still unable to remove the grins from their faces. Annie tries to shake her amazement at what is happening and imagine Monsieur Carnet, more than a century ago, pottering around the very floor she is now standing on, writing books that her father still reads today. A strange kind of time travel.

'This is incredible,' Annie tells the woman. 'C'est incroyable!'

The old lady beams up at her.

'Hey, give me your phone,' Will says.

'Why?'

'To take a photo! For your dad.'

'Oh, right!'

She hands him her phone. Will turns to the old lady and mimes taking a photo. 'C'est OK?' he asks.

'Oui, bien sûr!' The old lady looks delighted.

Annie is so overwhelmed by the whole experience that she doesn't even think about how she looks as Will takes the picture. She just grins like an idiot, with her ear pressed against the ceiling.

'Great snap,' Will says, examining the phone.

'Merci, madame, merci, merci beaucoup,' Annie gabbles, shaking the old lady's hand.

They all leave together, Will carrying the lady's shopping cart down the stairs for her, before bidding her goodbye on the street outside.

'I cannot believe that just happened,' Annie says. 'I need to send this picture to my dad.'

'Cool.' Will takes out his own phone. 'You send the picture, I'll work out what we do next.'

Annie exhales, still feeling giddy. 'Whatever we do, I'm not sure it's going to top that, to be honest.'

Will smiles at her. 'Well, let's give it a try anyway.'

CHAPTER THIRTY-EIGHT

WILL

3rd April, present day
Harrow, Middlesex

The phone rings as I'm feeding Milligan – a 'special treat' breakfast that consists of a half-can of Waitrose tuna (not that I imagine he can tell the difference from the Lidl stuff) surrounded by Dreamies biscuits. Even if I can't find much to celebrate today, I figure there's no reason my cat shouldn't enjoy himself. Celebrating vicariously through a household pet: this is potentially a new low. Milligan is nuzzling his furry head between my fingers to get to the grub just as I hear my phone sing out on the kitchen counter.

For a moment, I wonder if a miracle has occurred and Jess has remembered. But no – of the 742 contacts in my phone, there was only number it was ever likely to be. And right now I can't think of anyone I'd rather speak to. I smile as I pick the phone up.

'Hello? Dad?'

'Oh Will! Hello! So glad we caught you!' he cries. 'I'm just plugging your mother in, too. We'll just get the headphones in here, so we can both hear you. Wonders of modern technology and all that. Now then . . .'

I listen to the various muffled bumps, scratches and murmurs that represent my parents trying to manifest a three-way telephone call. I've tried, many times, to explain the concept of the 'loudspeaker' setting to them, but Mum says it sounds too tinny – 'like listening to ham radio'. A powerful rush of affection for both of them runs through me. 'There we go,' Dad says finally. 'That's better – can you hear us both now?'

'I think so. Hi Mum, are you there?'

Mum's voice crackles into my ear. 'Oh hello, darling! Yes, I've got you loud and clear. Happy birthday!'

'Happy birthday,' Dad echoes.

'Thanks. Thank you.'

'I hope our card arrived?' Mum says. 'You know how useless the snail mail is down here.'

'No, it did, it arrived yesterday. Thank you.'

I look over at the card – a beautiful Turner painting with Mum and Dad's scribbled wishes inside. It looks slightly pathetic, sat there on my knackered IKEA coffee table, nestling not among dozens of other cheery birthday greetings, but between my half-empty cereal bowl and various stained coffee mugs.

'So, how are you?' Dad asks. 'Have you got anything nice planned for today?'

'I think it'll just be a quiet one, really,' I tell them. 'I'm off to work in a mo, and then . . . I'm not sure, to be honest.'

'Oh. Right-o . . .' The disappointment seeps through the handset, and I force out a lie. 'But maybe I'll go for a drink with a couple of people after work.'

'Oh, that'll be *lovely*, I'm so glad.' I can hear the sun bursting through the clouds in Mum's voice, and it breaks my heart.

'We were thinking it's been so long since we've seen you, Will. You must come down for a weekend soon, if you fancy it?'

'Yeah, I will do.' It's been ages since I last saw them – yet the first thing that pops into my head is that 'coming down for a weekend' would mean missing a Pia call.

'How's work?' Mum chimes in.

'Fine, thanks. Busy. But good. How are you both?'

They strike up a familiar duet – Mum improvising on the theme of 'Oh you know, can't complain', and Dad riffing freely on 'Not much to report, really.'

'Good, good,' I say.

There's a pause, and then I hear Mum take a steadying breath. 'It's so lovely to hear you, Will. But you are . . . *OK*, aren't you, love? I just . . . hope you're OK?'

She can't hide the desperation and concern in her tone, and it makes the sentence sound more like a plea than a question. I stare at the birthday card and try to picture the two of them right at this moment, sat side by side on the sofa, earphones split between them, cradling over the phone to speak to their only child. The image hits so hard that it takes me a second to find my voice.

'I'm OK, Mum,' I say. 'I promise.'

'OK, love.'

I can tell she wants to probe further, but she doesn't. I imagine Dad touching her arm gently, mouthing 'Not now'. Milligan slinks between my legs and paws at my ankles. 'I should probably get going for work, though. It was great to speak to you.'

'Of course, son, you too. Have a fab birthday.'

'I will, Dad, cheers.'

'Lots of love from us.'

'And from me to you, Mum. Bye.'

'Bye-bye, love.'

*

Throughout the entire Tube journey to work, my head stays full of them.

Being my parents, they are the reason I am here, of course. But they're also the reason I'm *still* here. There is no way I would have made it through what happened without them. I don't remember much of that day itself, nor the days and weeks after, but I do know they were the only constant: always there, refusing to give up on me. When my thoughts were at their darkest, and all I wanted to do was stop existing, their love was the only thing that kept me from trying to do so. They hugged me, talked to me, listened to me, cooked for me, sat with me in police stations, doctors' surgeries and therapists' offices. I even moved back in with them for six months or so while I attempted to get back on my feet.

I keep thinking about that thing Pia said during our last call: how she feels her mum is constantly putting pressure on her to succeed. My parents never did that. Never. They were supportive – always – but they never made me feel like I'd be a failure if I didn't become some rock 'n' roll megastar. In the end, it was only me who felt that. They were never anything other than fully in my corner.

The thing they were always most concerned about was whether I was OK. I remember Christmases back at home, right when the band was at its biggest – when we were on the cusp of being signed to a major label. I would get pissed and arrogant and start spouting off to Mum, Dad and their friends about how The Defectors were going to be huge and they'd be seeing me on the cover of every magazine pretty soon. At the time, I remember being frustrated that they didn't seem more impressed by it all. Looking back now, though, all I can remember is my parents' anxious glances at each other as I poured myself yet another glass of wine.

I used to feel embarrassed for them. Having to bump into people in our little village – parents of people I went to school with – asking, 'How's Will's big music career going?' I'd picture them shuffling their feet, staring down at the pavement while they mumbled, 'Well, it didn't quite happen for him in the end . . .' I used to imagine that I'd let them down because the band had failed, and I'd gone from being the next Alex Turner to being a total nobody.

But I see now the only disappointment they felt is that I wasn't happy. And they feel it now, today, more than ever. I wish I could change that. But unfortunately, I think being truly happy is the one thing I'm not capable of any more.

CHAPTER THIRTY-NINE

ANNIE

3rd April
Tottenham Court Road, London

Am I really going to do this?

I stand rooted to the spot on what is possibly the busiest junction in London – the corner of Oxford Street and Tottenham Court Road. Office workers tut and mutter darkly as they barge past me, in search of their lunchtime sandwiches.

Before I left the Marker office, I emailed Matt to tell him I was taking a long lunch break. He responded by asking for a Defectors update as soon as I got back. So, this is it. My last chance at making this article work. My last chance at delivering something that could potentially save my job. And I don't even know if I'll have the guts to go through with it.

I haven't told Matt about meeting up with Jess. How would I even begin to explain that half-hour of unbridled awkwardness when I don't really understand it myself? Luckily, Matt has had other things on his plate this week. Lex went off on maternity leave last Friday, and Matt has spent most of the past two days fending off desperate requests for freelance support from Jermaine. But this afternoon, he will want to know, once and for all, whether I can make this piece work. And the answer to that question will depend on what happens in the next few minutes.

I smooth my hair down, and button the top tog on my duffel coat. The mild spring weather we've been having has turned today, and central London is blustery as hell. The clouds above look bruised and moody: ready to burst at any second.

God, I thought I was nervous before meeting Jess. But this is something else. My stomach is churning. My legs feel like jelly. All this for a boy who probably doesn't even remember me. Ridiculous. What was it Jess said last Sunday?

Will 'hung out' with a lot of girls in those days. I'm sure they all think they had this 'special' moment with him . . .

I take a deep breath and start walking north, up Tottenham Court Road.

I haven't even planned what I'll say to him in the event that I find him. Jess has already told him about the article, so I know full well that he doesn't want any part of it. There is no good reason for me to be here. It's bordering on creepy. I could play it off as coincidence – 'Hey, Will, remember me? What are the chances!' – but Jess would eventually tell him that she'd let slip where he worked, and I'd end up looking even more pathetic and stalker-ish.

Part of me doesn't even care. Part of me just wants to see him again.

On the Tube ride over here, I suddenly remembered that photo we took together on that day in Paris. It's the only photo I've got of us. A selfie outside Alphonse Carnet's strange little apartment block, just after Will had come running after me. I look quite nice in it: my eyes half-closed against the sun, smiling brightly with Will Axford's arm slinked around my shoulder. Will looks annoyingly fit in the photo, too: grinning that sexy gap-toothed grin, his swaggering confidence burning right through the phone screen.

I keep walking, my heart still thumping like a drum. My eyes are tick-tocking from one side of the road to another, searching for anything that could possibly be described as a 'dreary electronics shop'. But so far there's nothing that even comes close. I spot a Games Workshop, a Habitat, way more Starbucks than one strip of pavement could possibly need – but nothing that fits the description of the kind of store Jess mentioned.

Until, a few blocks from Goodge Street Tube station, I see it. A sign on the other side of the road that reads: 'MicroShop'. Through the grimy glass of the store window, I can see all manner of hi-fi equipment, cables and TV screens, jumbled together in a haphazard promotional display.

The shop is empty except for a man behind the counter. Before my stomach has time to lurch, though, I realise it's not Will. Definitely not. I'm not sure if I feel disappointment or relief.

Still, just because he's not there this second, doesn't mean this isn't the shop Jess was referring to. I cross the street and dawdle outside, wondering if I should go in. Just walk up to the counter and ask, 'Excuse me, does Will Axford work here?' But something holds me back. Possibly the thought of him emerging from out the back, looking at me blankly and saying, 'Sorry, who are you?'

On the other hand, though, what if he does remember me? What if his eyes light up and he starts stammering in amazement, saying, 'Oh my God, Annie! I'm so sorry, I fucked up, but there hasn't been a single day in the past five years that I haven't thought about you!'

Bloody hell. I catch sight of myself in the Starbucks window and shake my head. I need to get a grip. Why can't this just be no big deal?

My stomach is still churning and my heart is still pounding and I still can't decide what to do. *Stop being a chicken*, I tell myself firmly. *Be brave.* The word makes me smile. My 'brave thing'. This could very well be it. I try to imagine telling Jack about it on Sunday. It would take a hell of a lot of explaining, but I'm sure he'd be willing to listen.

I take a deep breath and check my reflection one more time. But just as I'm about to head for the MicroShop door, I feel my phone buzz in my bag. I take it out to see a text from Lexi. *Water's just broken!* it reads. *BABY COMING!!!*

CHAPTER FORTY

WILL

3rd April
Tottenham Court Road, London

At work, things are easier.

A big delivery arrives first thing, so I spend most of the morning and early afternoon back in the stockroom, labelling and unpacking while Dev mans the shop front.

After lunch, Dev is mysteriously AWOL – muttering on the phone in the stockroom, then rushing out just before lunch without offering any explanation for when he'll be back.

Left alone in the store, I stand behind the counter and watch central London ebb and flow through the windows. I find my mind floating to Pia, as it does so often these days. I wonder idly what she's doing right now: if she's done her 'brave thing' yet.

I have absolutely no clue what mine will be. And I can't invoke the 'Phone Beefeater Code' this time – we agreed on that. The thought occurs that I could just make a 'brave thing' up – but lying to Pia wouldn't feel great.

I look up as the door clatters open. It's not a customer

– only Dev, perspiring freely through his hoodie and cradling a plastic M&S bag.

'Would you believe that the nearest Marks and Sparks is *35 minutes'* walk?' he puffs indignantly. From out of the carrier bag, he produces a chocolate Colin the Caterpillar cake. 'The Tesco and Sainsbury's ones don't even come *close* to Colin,' he says with a grin. 'See, that's the kind of boss I am, William. I go the extra mile. Quite literally in this case.'

I stare at the cake, nonplussed for a second, until the penny drops. I feel my face get hot. Dev wrinkles his brow. 'I wasn't planning on singing,' he says. 'I mean I *can* sing, but . . . Do you want me to sing?'

I think of Pia again – her comment a week or so back about cringing when the whole office sings 'Happy Birthday' – and it makes me smile. 'Definitely not, no. No singing.'

'Thank God for that,' Dev says. 'Anyway, happy birthday, mate.'

'Thanks. How did you . . .?'

'Well, I've got your details, haven't I? You filled out all those employee forms when you started. I know it all, man: date of birth, national insurance number, middle names, I've got all the dirt on you . . . William *Frederick Martin* Axford.'

I don't know what to say. In situations like this I wish I had a bit more recent experience in acting-like-a-normal-human-being. My small-talk game is truly pitiful. Plus, I am genuinely knocked back at being on the end of such a generous gesture. 'Well . . . cheers, Dev,' I offer eventually. 'You shouldn't have. Thank you.'

He grabs a knife from the kitchen and sets about clumsily dissecting Colin, chopping out two doorstop-sized chunks of his torso. He hands one to me on a bit of kitchen roll.

'So, how old are you, then?' he asks through a mouthful of chocolate icing. 'I mean, I could check your employee form, but it's less creepy to just ask.'

'Thirty-three today,' I say.

'You don't look a day over 32.' He swallows with some difficulty. 'What you up to later, then? Got any big plans?'

Luckily, the house-brick-sized bite of cake I've just pushed into my mouth gives me time to prepare a believable answer to this. As I chew, I begin mentally constructing an elaborate lie about a huge birthday dinner in Soho with a bunch of mates. But by the time I've swallowed, I find I don't have it in me to deliver it.

'Not much, really. I think I'll just have a quiet one.'

Dev nods. 'Yeah, I hate birthdays too. I mean, I hate *my* birthday. I quite like other people's.'

He puts the cake down and looks around the empty shop. 'And with that in mind, since we've got zero traffic in here right now, I was thinking maybe we should close up early and celebrate.'

I start to protest, but Dev waves Colin's disembodied head at me. 'It's not for you, Will. It's for me – like I said, I love other people's birthdays. So, come on, man: humour me. I'm taking you out for one birthday drink, or else . . .' He tails off.

'Or else what?'

'Or else . . . you're fired,' he says weakly.

I laugh through my second mouthful of cake. I'm about to make something up – tell him, actually, I've just remembered,

I do have plans. But then I hear Pia's voice in my head, clear as a bell.

This week, we both have to do something brave. We have to take one step each outside of our comfort zones, no matter how small or insignificant it might seem.

Going out for a drink with a colleague on your birthday is about as small and insignificant as it gets in the courageous stakes. But, for me, it definitely qualifies as something brave. I flash forward to next Sunday, in the Green Shoots office: I imagine Pia's reaction as I tell her – truthfully – that I stuck to our deal. I did my 'brave thing'.

'OK', I tell Dev. 'What did you have in mind?'

He dusts his chocolatey hands off. 'Let's see . . . D'you like golf?'

*

Twenty minutes later, we are about six streets away from the shop, and approximately two hundred miles from my comfort zone.

We're stood in the dimly lit waiting area of 'Caddystack' – a pancake house-cum-crazy golf emporium that opened recently on Goodge Street. I've walked past this place every day for the last few months, wondering what kind of person would actually come in here. And apparently, the answer is me.

As we queue for our clubs and balls, I am straining to act like this is no big deal. My stomach is roiling and my head is throbbing as I try hard to remember the last time I was out for an informal social engagement with another human being. The fact that I've even used the phrase 'informal social engagement' suggests it's been a while. My heartbeat is gaining speed now, and with every new thump another anxious thought cuts through me. What if I get recognised while we're out? Or what if Dev starts asking personal questions? What if he wants to know about my life before MicroShop? What if he's somehow found out about the band? What if he knows about Joe? What if this is all an elaborate ploy to ask me what really happened that night? The sweat begins to prickle on my forehead. I remember an old technique from one of the therapists Mum and Dad set me up with: *breathe in for four, out for six.*

This is ridiculous. I'm being pathetic. I'm being paranoid. I do another in-for-four-out-for-six and think of Pia.

Next to me, Dev is staring around at the Caddystack decor, which resembles a Fifties American diner designed by someone who's pathologically obsessed with Tiger Woods.

'I wonder who started this hipster trend of opening bars and restaurants where you can also play a random sport?' he asks. 'They've done it with table tennis, table football, darts – and now mini golf, too.'

'Ha. Yeah.' I nod. Try to laugh. Try to forcibly eject the anxious thoughts from my brain. Try to be normal. 'Basically, all you have to do is work out a crappy pun combining a sport and a food or drink, and you've got yourself a successful start-up,' I say.

Dev grins at me. 'Maybe we should sack off MicroShop and launch "Orange Squash": a juice bar in the middle of a squash court?'

This time I don't have to try to laugh: it comes naturally. 'Yeah . . . Or "Pie-kwondo"? You do some martial arts and then have a chicken and leek pasty?'

'Beautiful,' Dev replies. 'How about "Quarter-Rounders"? Quick hamburger before your game of softball?'

By the time we've collected our clubs and descended the black-lit staircase towards the first hole, we're still brainstorming terrible hipster pop-up puns, and my heartbeat has returned to something resembling its regular speed. Maybe the key to getting through this is to stop focusing on things like heartbeat speed. Just relax. In for four, out for six.

The Caddystack course is unlike any other mini golf course I've ever been to, in that it's not within touching distance of the British seaside. Instead it's housed inside a neon-lit basement whose exposed brick walls are currently reverberating to ear-splitting hard techno. And rather than the usual crazy-golf clientele of bored-looking families on holiday, Caddystack's customers all seem to be young, good-looking and achingly hip.

'Go on,' Dev says. 'You're the birthday boy so you can tee off.'

I lay my ball down in front of the first hole, which is located inside a gigantic luminous stack of pancakes. As I do, I glance at a group of teenagers who are currently thrashing away at the hole in front of us. 'Those lot are definitely bunking off school,' I say.

'Yeah,' Dev says. 'I wonder what they think we're doing here at half four on a Wednesday afternoon?'

I pull my club back and get ready to whack the ball. 'They might think it's a quirky first date?'

Dev nods. 'Mm. Or a very disappointing stag do.'

Unfortunately, he says this just as I'm taking my swing, and the sudden bark of laughter it provokes causes me to slice my shot right off the first green and ricochet off the wall next to the teenagers.

They spin around in unison to give us a death stare, and we both manage to suppress our smiles as we wave apologetically at them. 'Sorry,' Dev shouts, pointing to me. 'First time!'

Dev places his ball down and gives it a gentle thwack. It trundles up the stack of pancakes, teeters for a second on the edge of the hole and then dribbles all the way down again, landing back at our feet.

'OK,' he says. 'We're clearly going to be here a while, so I'll get the drinks in. What you having? It's on me. Well, it's on the MicroShop petty cash.'

'I'll have a lager, please. Whatever they've got. Cheers.'

'Right. I'm getting a gin and slimline. Don't judge me – I'm trying to lose this.' He grabs his belly and gives me a grin before heading off to the bar.

I picture how I thought I'd be spending my thirty-third birthday when I woke up this morning. That lie I told Mum about going for a drink with a colleague: I've turned that into the truth. That feels good. As small as it is, I'm doing my 'brave thing'. That feels good, too. I watch Dev ordering at the bar and suddenly feel overwhelmingly grateful.

Not just to him, but to Pia as well.

CHAPTER FORTY-ONE

ANNIE

6th April
Balham, London

'I just don't understand why we *both* had to come?' says Dom for about the hundredth time this morning. 'Don't you think Lexi would rather see you on your own?'

I sigh as we turn the corner into Lexi and Gavin's south London street. Dom has been whinging like a sulky teenager the entire train journey over here. To the point where I now am starting to wish I *had* come by myself.

'Well, she invited both of us,' I point out. 'And Gav will be there, too, obviously.'

He shoves his hands into his coat pockets. 'But that's my point. It's just so awkward: I'll be left with Gavin at some point, and I don't really know the guy. Plus, he's just had a baby – the last thing he'll want to do is make small talk.'

I push open their front gate. 'He's not had the baby, Lexi has.'

'Yes, but he'll still be knackered, won't he?' Dom follows

me into the front garden. 'He'll just be thinking, "Why has Annie brought her boyfriend along, too?" And he'll be right.'

He pulls his phone out as we get to the doorstep, and glowers down at it moodily. Honestly, why are men like this? I'm never particularly thrilled whenever I get left alone with one of Dom's mates' wives at some party or wedding or other. I don't exactly cherish the idea of spending an hour swapping platitudes about clothes and boxsets with a near-stranger. But I would never complain about it, or use it as a reason not to go. I even make an effort with annoying Posh Clare, for God's sake. And she is *seriously* hard work.

'Look, can you just be normal?' I ask, trying to hide the exasperation I'm feeling. 'I'm meeting my friend's baby for the first time. This is quite a big deal.'

Dom puffs his cheeks out and rolls his eyes. 'OK. I'm just saying, if I was in their position, I don't think I'd really want to be entertaining visitors and making small talk.'

I ring the doorbell. As Dom turns his attention back to his phone, I try to remind myself that I *do* love him. I think back to our very first dates. Dom was working in hospitality PR at the time, and he'd get us into one ultra-swish restaurant after the other. The food was unbelievable, but I liked that Dom wasn't show-offy about it: he seemed almost apologetic about the five-star treatment we kept getting. He was funny and self-deprecating and the way he looked at me . . . There were never any awkward moments or gaps in conversation. He made me feel fun and interesting and sexy.

He can still be like that. I know he can. I just haven't seen it for a long time.

'Hey, guys.'

Lexi's husband, Gavin, opens the front door with a crumpled grin. In fact, it's not just his grin that's crumpled. His shirt, his trousers, his hair: everything about him gives the impression of frantic disorder and very little sleep. But through his soft, sunken features, his eyes shine brighter than I've ever seen them. He looks *so* happy.

'Gav! Congratulations!' I step forward to hug him as he ushers us inside.

'Cheers, Annie.'

Dom beams at him as we step into the living room. 'Congrats, mate!' he says, pumping his hand. 'Such awesome news!'

The moody, whinging teenager has disappeared suddenly, replaced by a warm, bright, infectiously enthusiastic man. Almost that same man who took me on those first dates. I am constantly amazed by Dom's ability to transform like this whenever there are other people around. It's partly the reason that Lexi and Maya never fully get it when I complain about him being moody: he's never let them see it. He doesn't let anyone see it but me.

'Come on through and meet the big man,' Gavin says. 'Sorry the place is such a bombsite.'

'Are you kidding? Don't worry.'

Their living room, normally so spick and span, is a jungle of scattered clothes, muslins, cushions, plates of half-eaten toast and cups of half-drunk tea. On the sofa, Lexi sits with her legs tucked underneath her, cradling a tiny blanket-swaddled bundle.

'Oh, Lex . . .' I whisper it gently as I sit down next to her. She rests her head against mine and gives a soft laugh as we both stare down at the perfect little sleeping face in the blanket. 'He's so beautiful.'

I've already seen dozens of pictures, of course, but they really don't do him justice. In the flesh, he's beyond adorable – tiny wrinkled fingers, wispy brown hair and that warm, milky smell.

'What a cutie,' Dom says. 'Congrats, Lex.'

'Thanks, Dom.'

'He looks so serene,' I say.

'For now, maybe . . .' sighs Gav, and Dom laughs.

Gav nods towards the kitchen. 'I'll make some teas, shall I?'

'I'll give you a hand,' says Dom. He shoots me a brief oh-God-here-comes-the-small-talk glance before switching his smile back on for Gavin. They leave the room, and I wrap Lexi into a gentle hug.

'Lex. I can't believe it.'

'Neither can I.' She has that same air of utterly knackered joy that Gavin has, and it makes her look even more beautiful than usual.

'I'm sorry it was so bad,' I say, and she nods grimly. As well as the dozens of photos, I also received a nine-minute-long voice note direct from the hospital bed the morning after, laying bare every gruelling detail of the fourteen-hour labour. Forceps, stitches, haemorrhoids: just hearing about it all made me wince. I can't even imagine what it must have been like to endure.

'It's so shit that you went through that, mate,' I say. 'But *look* at him.'

'I know.' She smiles. 'He was worth it.'

'Any names yet?'

'We still haven't decided. Gav's taken to calling him "The Unit" because he's so big.'

I laugh softly. 'Maybe leave that for a middle name.'

The Unit stirs and lets out a little strangled cry. 'What is it, bubba?' Lexi whispers. 'Are you hungry?'

She eases him onto her nipple and he starts feeding. I watch Lexi smiling down at him, wondering what it must feel like. Wondering whether I'll ever get the chance to do it.

'So. What's going on with you?' she asks.

'Lexi. You do not have to be polite. Nothing that's going on with me is as interesting as this guy.'

I point to the suckling baby and she laughs. 'Please. I've spent the last three days thinking exclusively about this guy. I'd genuinely like to hear about something else. How's work?'

'Not great,' I tell her truthfully. 'I am missing you massively. Jermaine is stressing because you're gone and there's no cover. And Matt is constantly telling us how screwed the site is, financially.'

She frowns, and switches the baby to her other breast. 'What about that advertorial thing you're on with that band? Wasn't that supposed to be the cash cow that saved us?'

'Ah, yes. Well . . .'

With Lexi currently breastfeeding her three-day-old baby, now is probably not the best time to launch into the full backstory of what has gone on between Will Axford and me. Now is not the time to tell her that I attempted to stalk him at what may or may not have been his place of work. And that, ultimately, I couldn't even summon the nerve to go in and check.

Instead, I tell her a more concise version of the truth. 'I spoke to the band's guitarist and their PR person, and both told me they're not up for it.'

'What about the fit singer?' Lex asks.

'He's not up for it either, according to the PR girl.'

'Shit.'

'Yup. I told Matt a couple of days ago that the piece wasn't going to happen.'

'How did he react?'

'He almost looked like he was expecting it. I could tell he was disappointed, though. He said he'd ask Zara or Nick to pitch a few ideas for the series instead.'

Lexi raises her eyebrows as she strokes the baby's head. 'Right . . . You didn't want to pitch anything else yourself?'

'I don't know,' I say. 'I realise that getting my foot in the door of this advertorial thing is probably the best way to ensure I've still got a job when the inevitable cutbacks start happening. But . . .'

'But what?' Lex says.

'I just . . . Maybe I'm not even that bothered about keeping my job, in the end. Maybe losing it would light a fire under me to do something else.'

Lex wrinkles her brow. 'As in . . . leave Marker?'

I shrug. It's odd: ever since that last talk with Jack, I've been thinking more and more about my writing. My *real* writing – the writing I came to London to do. Fiction, short stories, maybe even a book someday. None of that writing has felt right ever since Dad died, but speaking to Jack about it made me remember how much enjoyment I used to get from it. It made me want to try again.

Yesterday, I saw something on Twitter – an advert for a 'New Writers' Event' happening next week in a pub near the office. One of those things where people can read their works-in-progress out loud, get feedback, meet other writers, meet agents, that sort of thing. It's the kind of the event I would never in a million years have even considered attending a few weeks ago. But for some reason, yesterday, I wondered if maybe I should go. I even made a note of the date.

Lex is still frowning at me, though, so I say: 'I don't know. Maybe I'm being stupid.'

The Unit stops suckling, and Lexi gently eases him off her nipple, slipping her boob back into her nightie. Dom and Gavin come back from the kitchen, bearing four steaming mugs of tea. Dom shoots me another look designed to ensure I realise just how much he would rather not be here. I take the tea off him and remind myself once again that I do love him. I do need him.

After all, there's a good chance I might soon be 31 and unemployed. I'm not sure I could face being 31 and single, too.

CHAPTER FORTY-TWO

WILL

7th April
Green Shoots office, Limehouse

It's one of those dead Sunday-afternoon shifts where the phone barely rings and every second seems to drag.

I'm three hours in and not even Eric or Sandra has called yet. All I've had is two immediate hang-ups and a wrong number. Pre-Pia, I would have spent the past few hours wondering why I even signed up to waste my afternoon in this way. But not now.

Now, even as the final hour approaches, the butterflies in my stomach are still flapping wildly. Because I know she'll call.

I take a sip of tea and my heart skips when I hear the chime of a phone. But it's not the Green Shoots landline: it's my mobile. A text from Dev. It reads:

JU-DONUTS. You do some martial arts in your pyjamas and then have a Krispy Kreme.

I chuckle to myself and send him back a 'chef's kiss' emoji. Ever since my impromptu birthday trip to Caddystack on Wednesday, we have been messaging each other whenever we come up with a new terrible pun name for a sport-themed hipster restaurant. After locking up the shop on Friday, I even took Dev up on his regular offer of a quick drink after work. The look of shock on his face made me laugh out loud. Two pints of lager with another human being in one week: I'm basically Keith Richards.

It's strange how strongly these toe-dips back into normality affect me. The occasional cup of tea with Tanvi before a shift, and now the odd pint and silly text exchange with Dev: they are like cracks of sunlight breaking through a long-boarded-up window.

The landline rings. I reach across, grinning before I even pick up the receiver. Somehow, I just know it will be her.

'Hello, Green Shoots?'

'Hey, Jack!'

'Pia! I thought it might be you.'

'Oh, OK. Phone Beefeater *and* psychic now, are you?'

'That's right. How are you doing?'

'Good, thanks. You?'

'Good! Really good. All ready to spill the beans about my pathetically small "brave thing".'

She hesitates. 'Ah, yes, the "brave things" . . .'

'Pia . . . Tell me you did yours? Because I've sure as hell done mine.'

'Jack. I'm sorry. I fluffed it.'

I let out a mock-theatrical gasp. 'I'm not angry, Pia. I'm just disappointed.'

She laughs. 'I was this close to doing it, and then . . . Well, it would take too long to explain. Anyway, my friend had her baby this week, too, so that's knocked any brave-thinging off track slightly.'

'Ah, amazing,' I say. 'Are she and the baby doing OK?'

'They're both great,' she says. 'Went to see them yesterday.'

'Nice. Well, you can always try the "brave thing" again this week.'

She sighs. 'No, I think that particular ship has sailed. It was a work thing, and now my boss has given the work thing to someone else.'

I lean forward to take a sip of tea. 'Yeah, I remember last time we spoke you said you were in trouble with your boss or something. Is everything OK?'

'Yeah. It will be.' Something in her voice tells me she's not sure about this. But before I can probe further, she says: 'Anyway, go on, then: tell me yours. Your "brave thing".'

I clear my throat. 'OK. You ready for this?'

'I'm sitting down. I've got a strong cup of tea.'

'Good. Right, so, this week . . . I went for a drink with a work colleague.'

A pause. 'Is . . . that the end of the story?'

I laugh. 'I know, it sounds very small and lame. But if you knew me, Pia, you would understand that it definitely counts as a "brave thing".'

'I feel like I do know you, Jack. A little bit, anyway.'

I can hear the smile in her voice as she says it. But I also know for certain that she means it. I have to swallow hard before I can respond. 'I feel like I know you, too. A little bit.'

A moment passes in silence. A moment in which the realisation hits home that I will probably never meet this person in real life. I will never *really* know her. One day, she will stop calling and I will never speak to her again.

In this moment, the thought of it is almost too much to bear.

'Well, congratulations,' she says finally. 'If you say it was a "brave thing", I believe you.'

I take a breath and try to compose myself. 'It definitely made me feel good,' I tell her. 'And the "brave things" were your idea, so I have you to thank for that. Thank you, Pia. Seriously.'

'You're welcome.'

What if I just came out and told her? What if I just said, 'Look, Pia, I know this is weird and extremely unprofessional, but I feel like we have some kind of connection here, and I was wondering if you wanted to meet up, face to face?' I'd be banned from Green Shoots for life if anyone ever found out, of course – but what would that matter if it meant I got to meet Pia?

But then who's to say I even would get to meet her? What if her reaction to this outpouring was – quite understandably – to slam the phone down and never, ever call back? I'd lose Pia for good – and if she ever decided to complain about me asking to meet up, I would lose Green Shoots, too. And without both of them . . . Well, I don't even want to think about that.

So, instead I ask: 'What else is new with you? Do you want to talk about this work thing at all?'

She exhales into the phone. 'No, there's not much to say. Except I think I might have made myself a prime candidate for a sacking fairly soon.'

'Right. Shit.'

'Yeah. But the weird thing is . . . I don't know how much I even care,' she says. 'I need the money, obviously, but . . . part of me wonders whether getting sacked might be the kick up the arse I need to have a go at what I've always really wanted to do.'

'Writing?'

'Yeah.' I hear her take a sip of her drink. 'After getting back from seeing my friend and her baby last night, I looked through all these short stories I'd written a few years back. I hadn't even opened the file since Dad died. It was hard, at first, because it reminded me so much of him.'

'Mm-hm.'

'Anyway, mostly the stories were quite cringe and not very good, but one stuck out. It was something I started writing around the time he got really ill. I even started tinkering with it last night, editing and making changes, adding new bits. It felt good.'

'That's brilliant.'

'I guess. But then I opened it again about an hour ago, and suddenly it feels cringe and rubbish again.' She laughs. 'It's just so hard to judge, you know? I saw an advert on Twitter for this "New Writers' Event" happening next week – you go along and read stuff out and people give you feedback. I was thinking maybe I should go.'

'Definitely,' I say. 'That sounds amazing.'

She sighs. 'It also sounds pretty terrifying. I'm crap at public speaking at the best of times, so the idea of reading one of my own stories out loud in front of a room full of strangers . . .'

'I know what you mean.'

'I've never read my stuff to *anyone*, so to go from that straight to this event feels like a pretty big leap.'

'Mm.' The computer fades into screensaver mode and my reflection stares back at me from the black screen. An idea suddenly occurs. 'Well, you could always practise now?'

'What do you mean?' she asks.

'I mean – correct me if I'm wrong, Pia – but you still owe me a "brave thing", don't you?'

She laughs. 'I do.'

'So . . . wouldn't that be a "brave thing"?' I say. 'To read me the story now?'

CHAPTER FORTY-THREE

ANNIE

7th April
Ladbroke Grove, London

'What?'

I hear him clear his throat over the line. 'Well, you know the Green Shoots motto, Pia: "Listen without judgement",' he says. 'You can read me something you've written – whatever you like – and I am literally not allowed to give an opinion. It's against company policy.'

I shift on the sofa, feeling a squirm of anxiety in my stomach. 'So, even if you think it's horrendous, you can't tell me it's horrendous?'

'Exactly. It could be the worst piece of crap ever committed to paper, and I wouldn't be able to say a thing.'

'Not exactly doing wonders for my confidence here.'

His laughter crackles in my ear. 'Come on – I think it could be good. You get to practise reading your stuff out loud – sharing it with another person – in the safest safe space in existence. Phone Beefeater Code, remember?'

'You've been playing fast and loose with that code tonight, Jack.'

'True. All I'm saying is: if you want to get over that first hurdle of just showing your work to someone else, then . . . maybe I could be a good candidate?'

I stare at the laptop on the coffee table in front of me. He's right, of course. I can't think of anyone else I'd even consider reading my stuff to. Not Maya or Lex. Certainly not Dom, who only reads ex-footballers' biographies, and once told me he agreed with Noel Gallagher that fiction is 'a waste of fucking time'. But this story, in particular, is *so* private. It would be like showing Jack a side of my character that I barely even acknowledge myself.

But then, what's the point of writing these things if I'll never show them to anyone? And Jack's right: he might be a good person to start with.

'Pia?' I've obviously been silent for long enough that Jack feels compelled to check if I'm still on the line.

'Sorry, yes, I'm here.'

'No, I'm sorry,' he says. 'Maybe I overstepped the mark. Of course you don't have to read it to me if you don't want. I'm sorry for suggesting it.'

'It's fine,' I tell him. 'It's just . . . It's a big deal for me.'

'I know it is,' he says softly. And something about the gear shift in his voice makes me lean forward automatically and reach for my computer. With a click I open the document.

The story is a jumble of things: funny, sad, a bit surreal in a hopefully-not-too-wanky way. It's about a girl whose dad is dying (write what you know, and all that) – a kind of imagined version of what I would have liked my final conversation with him to be. With a bit of weird magical realism chucked in for good measure.

I re-scan the first few lines. Am I actually going to do this? I feel genuinely nervous now, my throat sticky and dry.

'OK,' I say. 'I'll read it to you.'

'Only if you want to. No pressure.'

'I want to. No judgement?'

'No judgement,' he promises.

And with that, I start reading.

It feels beyond strange hearing the words out loud for the first time. But I take it slow and steady, remembering to breathe after every full stop. And the more I read, the easier it gets. The more enjoyable it gets.

I can't help wondering how Jack looks as he's listening to me. What kind of expression is on his face. After the parts that are meant to be funny, I hear him laugh softly. But other than that, he stays quiet.

It's not a long story – it takes me just over five minutes to read. When I reach the end, Jack remains silent. The squirming in my stomach has melted now, and I feel a pleasant, tingly exhilaration. The story is good – I know it is – and reading it aloud, I could tell more easily which parts worked and which didn't. I feel an immediate urge to go back and tinker with it – make it better.

'So . . . that's the end,' I say dumbly.

'Ah, OK.' He leaves a pause that seems to last approximately five years, and then adds: 'So, how did it feel reading it out loud?'

'I'm not sure I like this no-judgement thing, actually.'

He laughs. 'Look, I said I wouldn't tell you if I thought it was bad, so I can't tell you if I thought it was good either.'

'Right. But . . . if I put a gun to your head: good or not good?'

He sighs, humouring me. 'For what it's worth, Pia, I thought it was brilliant. Genuinely, properly *brilliant*.'

My whole body reacts to the compliment – a rush of warmth and gratitude that lights me up from inside.

'But it doesn't matter what I think,' he adds. 'It matters how you felt about letting someone else hear it.'

I'm sat up straight on the couch now, one arm hugging my knees, still reeling from the fact that he liked it. 'It felt good,' I tell him. 'It was like I was seeing it from a bird's-eye view. I could see which bits I liked, but also which bits I thought could be improved.'

'That's great.'

'Yeah. Thanks, Jack. Seriously. That was a big thing for me.'

'Not just a big thing. A "brave thing".'

I smile. 'It was.'

'So, there you go, Pia,' he says. 'You've read someone else your stuff, and they thought it was brilliant. I bet that if you read it at this event everyone else will think it's brilliant, too.'

'Ha. Maybe. I'm still not sure if I'll have the guts to read, but I do think it'd be good for me to go along,' I say. 'Just a first step on the road to putting my stuff out there.'

'When is it?' he asks.

'This coming Wednesday, at half seven.'

'Well, I'll be sending you bottomless good vibes on Wednesday at half seven, then.'

'Thank you. Hey – you could always come along if you fancy. It's at a pub called the Lamb & Flag in Clerkenwell.'

Silence.

A silence long enough for me to wither as I realise what an

utterly batshit bonkers thing that was to say. Where did it come from? Why did I tell him that? I feel hot suddenly. Mortified. Is this my subconscious trying to somehow arrange a meeting with him in real life? If so, I need to have a pretty urgent discussion with my subconscious about the concept of subtlety. I don't even know if he's in London. I've basically just asked him out. Or at least, told him exactly where I'll be next Wednesday evening.

After what feels like a decade-long wait, he says: 'Oh, right. OK.'

'Bit too much information there, sorry!' I force out a sing-song laugh.

'No, I . . .' I hear him clear his throat. 'I'd love to come along. If you really wanted me to.'

'Oh. Well . . . Yeah. If you wanted to.' Fuck. What am I doing? My heart is battering against my ribcage now. Is this a good idea? 'Are you in London, then?' I ask before I can stop myself.

'I am, yeah.'

'Right. OK. Well. It could be nice. To see you. In real life. After all our chats.' I'm talking in staccato. Why am I talking in staccato? I sound like Christopher Walken.

Jack gives a shaky laugh. He sounds as nervous as I am. Maybe more so. 'Yeah. Definitely. It would be really nice.'

'How will we recognise each other?' I wonder aloud. I almost feel like I've floated out of my body and am now watching this scene unfold from above. This insane scenario in which I am essentially arranging a blind date with a total stranger.

But he's *not* a total stranger. He's Jack.

'Red carnation in our buttonholes?' he says, forcing a laugh. 'Or, no . . . I've got a red jumper. I could wear a red jumper?'

'Yes. OK. I've got a red jumper, too. Shall I wear that? Or will it be weird if we're both wearing red jumpers? That would be weird, wouldn't it? How about I wear a green jumper?'

He laughs at my gabbling – a warm, kind, affectionate laugh that has a strangely calming effect on me. 'I'll wear the green,' I say.

'Sounds good.'

I press a hand to the back of my neck: it's boiling. I swallow hard and try to steady myself.

'So. You'll be in the red jumper, I'll be in the green jumper,' I say.

'Copy that.'

For a moment, we're both quiet. All I can hear is the kick-drum thump of my heart. And then, without even meaning to, I blurt: 'Fuck. This is weird.'

It's like opening a relief valve: all the tension and awkwardness that's been building up comes rushing out and suddenly we're both laughing like drains at the madness of what's happening. I feel a mixture of exhilaration, relief and nervous excitement charge through me.

'I know,' Jack says after we've regained composure. 'It's really weird. Pia, seriously: if this is too soon or too inappropriate, then just say. I promise you I won't come.'

'No, I want you to come. I'd really like to meet you.' As the words come out of my mouth I realise it's something I've been wanting for a while now.

'I'd like to meet you too,' he says.

'So, then.'

'So. See you Wednesday, Pia.'

'Yep. See you Wednesday, Jack.'

CHAPTER FORTY-FOUR

26th February, five years ago
Paris, France

'My dad can't believe we were actually in his apartment,' Annie says. 'He's going crazy.'

She holds her phone up to show Will the chain of exclamation-mark-heavy texts her father has sent in response to that photo in Alphonse Carnet's living room.

'Haha!' Will grins. 'Nice one.'

They are walking east now, along the river, towards a restaurant that Will knows. Annie is still feeling light-headed from the experience of being inside that surreally tiny flat – and her dad's exuberant reaction to the photo is only cranking her excitement levels higher.

Another text comes through: *The third-and-a-half floor is STILL THERE!!! I'm freaking out here, love!! xxx*

She chuckles to herself. Then she remembers that message he sent her earlier this morning. *Hey, so what's this doctor's appointment about?* she writes. *Is everything OK?*

It'll be fine, love, he replies. *I'm sure it's nothing major. Anyway – I'm off to get that photo framed!!! Love you xxx*

She laughs again. There's a good chance he's being serious about that. She glances over at Will, walking along next to her, and realises this would never have happened without him.

'Thanks so much,' she says suddenly.

He looks at her. 'For what?'

'For getting us into the building. I would never have had the guts to try and go inside on my own. It really has blown my dad's mind. He's so happy.'

Will shrugs. 'Of course!'

Will Axford is the sort of person, Annie thinks, in whose company anything seems possible. When he's looking back at his phone again, she finds that selfie he took of the two of them outside the apartment block. She sends it to Maya, along with several 'shocked face' emojis.

'So, where is this place again?' she asks, slipping her phone back in her bag.

Will squints down at his Google Maps. 'It should be just around this corner here. It's called Le Relais de l'Entrecôte. My manager told us about it – the food's supposed to be amazing.' He looks up from the phone. 'You're not veggie, are you?'

'No.'

'Phew. They only do one dish – steak, chips and salad. Apparently it's so good they don't need to serve anything else. The steak's got this special, secret sauce, and—'

Will breaks off as they turn the corner into a smaller street. There is a queue in front of them snaking nearly halfway down the road. There must be sixty people in it.

'Shit,' Will says.

They wander to the front of the line, where a cartoonishly stereotypical French maître d' sneers at them over his moustache.

'Oui?'

'All right, mate!' Will says chirpily. 'Bonjour. Erm . . . How long do you reckon the wait will be?'

The maître d' gives a supremely Gallic shrug. 'Maybe ninety minutes. This is our busiest time.'

'We've been waiting over an hour,' snaps a middle-aged American woman at the head of the queue.

Annie smiles at Will. 'It's OK. We can just go somewhere else.'

Will purses his lips for a moment in thought. Then he leans in to whisper to her. 'Is it OK if I hold your hand for a second?'

Annie is so taken aback by the question that she almost forgets to respond. 'Erm, yes, sure, I guess?'

Will takes her hand and turns back to the maître d'. 'It's just that it's our honeymoon, you see,' he says. 'We were married yesterday, and I've been telling my wife here for years how amazing your restaurant is. It's part of the reason we chose Paris for our honeymoon destination!'

The maître d' frowns at Will. Annie senses the American lady and her friends bristle. She has to bite hard on her lip to stop herself laughing.

'We have a boat tour on the Seine booked in an hour,' Will says. 'I wonder if there's any chance you'd have pity on a couple of newlyweds and possibly allow us to sneak in now for a very quick lunch? It would mean the world to both of us. It would really make our honeymoon!' He adopts the same puppy-dog expression he had turned on Jess earlier, when he asked her to look after Joe. The Americans have now gone from bristling to muttering. Annie is having serious trouble keeping a straight face.

The maître d's steely frown seems to melt a little in the tractor beam of Will's big brown eyes and gap-toothed grin. He clears his throat. 'Let me check,' he says, disappearing into the restaurant.

Will squeezes Annie's hand and gives her a hopeful smile. She feels her pulse skip.

'So. You're just married, are you?' The American lady is observing them through narrowed eyes.

'That's right,' Will says. 'Big wedding in England yesterday.'

'I notice neither of you are wearing rings.'

'No, we don't believe in all that,' Will shoots back. 'Our love forms a stronger bond than any precious metal.'

Annie almost breaks at that, but manages to pass it off as a cough. The maître d' reappears. 'OK, quickly,' he says, beckoning them inside.

Will pulls Annie through the door, just as she hears the American lady's voice ring out sharply in complaint.

They are shown to a little table in the centre of the restaurant. The decor only exacerbates Annie's feeling of light-headedness: it's all crushed red velvet, gold furnishings and low candlelight in here. 'I cannot believe that worked,' she whispers as they sit down.

Will chuckles. 'Any time we see that guy, we need to act like we're married, OK?'

Annie nods. What does 'act like we're married' mean? Do they have to kiss? Please God, she thinks, let us have to kiss.

'This is very much not how I was expecting this day to go,' she says.

Will grins at her. 'Is it going better or worse than you expected?'

'Better,' she says. She feels his knee gently brush hers under the table. Was that by accident or on purpose? Should she knee-brush him back? She's always been crap at flirting. She wishes she could duck outside and phone Maya for some tips.

Will picks up the menu in front of him. 'Weird that they even have menus. I thought they only served one thing.'

'They're for wine, I guess?' Annie says.

Will nods, scanning the list. 'I know fuck all about wine.' He claps the menu shut again. 'Let's just get a bottle of house red? Or do you want a cocktail first or something?'

'Er . . . Well, it's only half twelve?' Annie winces internally the moment she says it, annoyed at sounding so uncool.

'We're in Paris!' Will cries. 'We've got to have a nice bottle of red with our steak frites!'

He smiles at her woozily. She suddenly remembers the two gin miniatures he downed during the interview. Paranoia jabs her hard in the ribs. The way he's been acting all day – running after her, pushing that random doorbell, making up that lie about their honeymoon – maybe it's not because he's a roguish romantic with a helpless crush on her. Maybe it's just because he's drunk.

'Is this part of the "rock star" thing, then,' she says. 'Being pissed the whole time?' She intended it to sound flirty and teasing, but it comes out thorny and sarcastic.

Will raises an eyebrow. 'I'm not pissed. I'm just enjoying myself. Trying to show you a good time.'

Another jab of paranoia. Does he think this is still part of the interview? Is all this just 'colour' for her article? She feels foolish suddenly. Like a competition winner who's convinced herself she's the lead singer's girlfriend.

'Right. It's just that you drank those bottles of gin during the interview, too, so . . .'

Will snorts and pinches his finger with his thumb. 'They were about this fucking big!'

She forces out a laugh. Why does she always do this – overthink things, make things awkward? Why can't she just be light and fun? The waiter approaches, notepad in hand. Light and fun, she tells herself. From now on, I'm going to be light and fun.

'Bonjour, messieurs dames,' says the waiter in a bored voice. 'How would you like your steak cooked?'

'Medium rare for me, mate,' Will says.

'Well done, please,' Annie says.

The waiter scribbles on his pad. 'And to drink?'

'A large glass of house red,' Will says, not looking at Annie.

'I'll just have a Diet Coke, please,' she says.

Will hands the menus to the waiter. 'Merci.'

There's a moment's uncomfortable silence as he leaves. Annie stares at the tablecloth, thinking: light and fun, light and fun. She looks up, catching Will's eye and they both smile.

'Our first fight as a married couple,' she says solemnly.

Will bursts out laughing at that, and suddenly she doesn't feel so foolish. The way he's looking at her now – the way he's been looking at her all morning . . . This is not just about colour for the article.

'Our first fight,' he says. 'And we survived it.'

She nods. 'Maybe this marriage is going to work after all.'

'Maybe.'

Another waiter passes, plonking a basket of bread between them.

'Cheers, geez,' Will says.

Annie laughs, imitating his mockney twang. '"Cheers, geez".'

Will smiles. 'What?'

'Seriously, why do you talk like that?'

'Like what?'

'Like Danny Dyer playing one of the Kray twins.' He cracks up laughing again. 'You just told me you're from Somerset,' she adds.

'What can I say,' he shrugs. 'This is how people from Somerset talk.'

'Oh, come on,' she chides him. 'You grew up with Joe, right? How come he doesn't talk like that?'

Will's grin fizzles out. 'Yeah, well . . .' He stares into the candlelight for a moment, apparently lost in thought.

'Sorry . . .' Annie says, though she's not quite sure what she's apologising for.

Will shakes his head, snaps out of it. 'No, I was just thinking about Joe. Hope he's OK.' He smiles. 'He's always on at me about drinking too much, too.'

Annie nods. 'He cares about you.'

'Yup.' He's staring at the table again.

'Seriously, Will,' Annie says. 'If you want to call him – to go and hang out with him instead, I really don't mind.'

He looks up at her, his deep-brown eyes coloured copper by the candlelight. 'To be honest, Annie, I'm quite enjoying hanging out with you.'

His knee nudges hers under the table. Her neck feels hot suddenly. She's quite glad that the waiter chooses this moment to lay their drinks and two plates of green salad down in front of them. As Will thanks the waiter, Annie checks her phone. Maya has replied to the photo she sent. The message reads: *Wait . . . Is that the hot singer? IS SOMETHING HAPPENING??*

Annie smiles as she puts the phone back. It feels like something might be.

CHAPTER FORTY-FIVE

WILL

8th April, present day
Green Shoots office, Limehouse

'I just had the Breathing Lady,' Tanvi says. 'Have you ever had her?'

It's five to six on a drizzly Monday, and we're having a quick cup of tea between shifts. Tanvi has just done the afternoon, and I'm on for the evening.

'Yes, I think so,' I say, taking a sip from my mug. 'You mean the lady who says she just needs to breathe?'

Tanvi smiles. 'That would be the Breathing Lady, yes.'

'I had her a few weeks back. I thought she was just a one-off caller.'

'No, I've had her a few times now,' Tanvi says. 'It's funny. Calls like that really make me think: we *are* doing something good here. I have no idea what that poor woman is going through but she does seem lighter by the time she says goodbye.'

'Definitely.' I think back to the night I heard her. I couldn't get the call out of my head. It had sparked such a wave of melancholy and loneliness that I'd ended up calling Jess. Which, as always, had made me feel worse. 'It affected me a lot when I spoke to her,' I tell Tanvi. 'I felt like I needed to decompress afterwards.'

Tanvi nods. 'That's why you should come to Partage, Will. When was the last time you went?'

'God, it's been ages,' I say. 'Years.'

'Partage' is the informal name for Green Shoots' monthly debrief: a meeting where listeners are encouraged to gather and share concerns they might have, discuss difficult calls they've taken, and give each other advice on how to deal with particular situations. Support each other, basically. When I first signed up for the line, nearly five years ago, I went to one or two Partages, just out of politeness, really. But they seemed more about establishing a community within the listenership than anything else – and making friends was not the reason I joined Green Shoots. So I stopped going.

'We've got one this Wednesday evening,' Tanvi says. 'Linda's hosting – and her coffee-and-walnut cake is infamous. You should come if you're free. It'll be fun.'

'Wednesday evening . . .' My stomach swoops just speaking the words out loud. 'Actually, I've kind of got plans Wednesday evening.'

'Oh yeah?' Tanvi raises an eyebrow at me as she takes a sip of tea. 'Hot date, is it?'

'Ha. No.'

Her eyes light up. 'It is!'

'It's not.'

'How come you're blushing then, William?' She jabs a finger at me. 'Explain the blushing!'

I laugh despite myself. 'It's not a *date*, it's just . . .'

How the hell can I possibly explain it? There's no way I can tell Tanvi the truth: namely that – unless my nerves fail me – I am going to be spending Wednesday evening meeting one of this helpline's anonymous callers *in person*. A meeting that will not only be morally questionable, but also possibly illegal.

That moment yesterday – when Pia told me about the writers' event and said 'Come along if you fancy it!' – it freaked me out beyond words. I'd spent most of the call up to that point thinking about how much I wanted to meet this person, how devastated I'd be if she stopped calling. And then – out of nowhere – she came out with that invitation. I was so shocked I could barely answer.

And even when I did answer, it was excruciating. As soon as I told her I'd love to come, I felt every sinew in my body cringing at once. Because surely she didn't mean it? It was probably just one of those things you say to be polite – you don't think the person will genuinely take you up on it. Especially if said person is speaking to you under a pseudonym on a crisis line, for God's sake.

But then . . . as we kept talking, it really did seem like we were on the same page. As much as my brain kept trying to convince me otherwise, something in her voice sounded so real when she said, 'I'd really like to meet you.'

She's all I've thought about these past few weeks. I've fantasised constantly about meeting her in person. But the idea of it actually happening . . . The fear is *so* strong. Not that she won't live up to my idea of her, but that I won't live up to hers of me. She doesn't know who I really am. What I've done. She wouldn't have agreed to meet me if she did. Meeting her in real life would only make losing whatever connection we have more painful. So, why torture myself? Maybe it's better to keep her as a voice over the phone. An imaginary person I can pin my daydreams onto.

Tanvi's smile dissolves as she watches my sentence peter out. 'Sorry, Will, I'm being nosy. You don't have to talk about it if you don't want to.'

'No, I actually would like to talk about it,' I say. Truth be told, I'm *desperate* to talk about it.

She gives me a kind smile. 'OK, so . . . who is this person?'

'Well, I don't really know her, to be honest.'

Tanvi nods. 'So, it's a blind date?'

'I guess. We've chatted a fair bit already, but we've never met.'

'Mm-hm. Over one of those apps, was it?'

I take a sip of tea. 'Erm . . . Yeah. One of those apps.'

'Well, what are you worried about? You're not a bad-looking boy, and actually quite good company once you get a few cups of tea down you.'

I laugh. 'Thanks. I just . . .' I exhale shakily, suddenly nervous about exposing too much of myself. But Tanvi nods, urging me to go on. 'I just get quite anxious about these kinds of things. I'm not even sure I'll go, in the end.'

She tilts her head at me and frowns. 'Will,' she says firmly. 'If you stand this poor girl up, you and I are going to fall out.'

That makes me laugh again. 'She's probably having this exact same conversation with one of her friends right now,' Tanvi adds. 'She's probably just as nervous as you are.'

'That . . . might be true, actually.'

'Of course it's true,' she snaps. 'So stop moping about like a knob, comb your hair, put on a nice shirt and go and meet her.'

'Maybe.'

'Not maybe. Yes.' She scooches forward on her chair, looking me straight in the eye. 'Things don't happen without a bit of effort, Will. Things happen because you *make* them happen. You know?'

I nod, letting the words sink in. 'You're right.'

She rolls her eyes and makes a *yes-obviously-I'm-right* gesture. A grin spreads across my face. 'Are you like this with the callers, too? Telling them to stop moping about and make things happen?'

She smiles back at me. 'No. They're strangers. We're friends.'

I let those words sink in, too. They make me feel better than I have in a very long time.

Tanvi finishes her tea and glances up at the clock. 'Right, I'd better let you get on. Eric will be wanting his evening natter, I'm sure.'

She stands up and starts gathering her things. 'Thanks, Tanvi,' I say suddenly. 'It was really great to chat. I really appreciate it.'

'Any time.' She gives my shoulder a squeeze. 'I'll be thinking of you Wednesday night. Let me know how it goes.'

CHAPTER FORTY-SIX

ANNIE

9th April
Shoreditch, London

Inside the glass walls of the main Marker meeting room, Matt looks the happiest I've seen him look in months.

He's been in there nearly an hour now, talking excitedly to two finance guys and Zara – our junior writer and the new person in charge of the 'Whatever Happened To . . .' advertorial series.

I knew Matt had passed the feature onto her after I came back from my fruitless Will Axford stalking mission last week. I told him, once and for all, that the Defectors thing wasn't going to happen. He pursed his lips and nodded, giving big *I'm-not-angry-just-disappointed* energy, and then went straight across to Zara's desk. Zara suggested some rapper who used to be massive a decade ago, and within three days she'd already tracked him down and conducted an anecdote-packed two-hour Zoom with him. The piece is set to go live on the site tomorrow, and it looks like they're discussing the next one right now in the meeting room.

Through the glass, I see Zara talking now – maybe pitching an idea for the second instalment. Matt and the finance guys are all nodding enthusiastically, broad grins spread across their faces.

So, there it is. I've blown my chance to make myself indispensible. Now I am very much . . . dispensible.

I glance across the office at Lex's empty desk. God, I miss her. It's really not the same here without her. Behind her monitor, I can see Jermaine – our head (and now only) designer – doing very little to mask the constant look of over-worked frenzy on his face. I don't know why, but it feels like things are coming to a head here. Something's going to happen – I can sense it. Whether I want it to or not.

And yet, all I can think about is tomorrow night.

I sigh and take a sip of coffee. I wish I had someone to talk to about it. Someone who could tell me whether I'm out of my mind even *thinking* about going to this event now. But let's face it: there's no one I can confide in about this particular situation.

The only person I could discuss it with is the person I've arranged to meet.

*

Back at home that night, I don't even hear Dom's key in the lock as he comes in from work.

I'm sat in our tiny box-room office, hunched over my computer, so engrossed in what I'm writing that the world around me seems to have dissolved. The idea came on the bus home – a new short story, this one about a boy and a girl who connect over a helpline, and then, finally, make plans to meet in real life. Even as I'm writing, I imagine Jack reading it. Or me reading it *to* him, over the phone. I could even tell him about it tomorrow . . .

'Babe?'

Dom taps on the door and I flinch with shock.

'God, sorry, you frightened me.'

'Oh-kay,' he says, confused. 'Just wondering, shall I take that chilli out of the freezer? We could have it tomorrow night?'

I shut the laptop and turn to face him. 'Erm . . . Actually, I'm going to be out tomorrow night.'

'Oh yeah?'

'Yeah. Meeting Maya for drinks.'

'Oh, OK.'

I panic suddenly that Dom can tell I'm lying. I've never been very good at it, and I certainly don't enjoy it. I'm not sure why I even feel so guilty. Nothing's happened between Jack and me, and nothing *will* happen tomorrow, either. I'm sure of that. It doesn't matter what Jack looks like, or what I feel when I see him: I've never cheated on anyone, and I'm not about to start now.

But there's also that nagging thought in the back of my mind: what if I *like* the way he looks? What if I feel *something* when I see him? I live with my long-term boyfriend, for God's sake. What the hell am I going to do then?

I just need to see him. That's all. Things will be clearer once I've met him in real life. Everything else can wait.

Dom nods at my closed laptop. 'Are you working?'

'No. Well, kind of. Had an idea for a short story.'

'Oh.' He wrinkles his nose. 'Right.'

Irritation prickles the back of my neck. 'What's that face for?'

'What face?'

'You did a pissed-off face.'

He laughs. 'Not pissed off. I just thought you were done with that stuff, that's all.'

'I never said I was done with it,' I say sharply. 'I just haven't done it for a while, that's all.'

'OK, OK.' He holds his hands up, miming *calm down*. It makes the irritation flare even harder.

'This – fiction writing – was what I always wanted to do,' I tell him. 'I'm not going to be working at Marker my whole life.'

He frowns. 'I thought you liked Marker? You got pretty fucked off with me at that dinner with Maya and Oliver when I said it wasn't proper journalism.'

'I was fucked off at you belittling my job! It doesn't mean I *like* my job.' I'm aware I'm not being entirely rational now. But Dom just seems to have a knack of saying the wrong thing lately – or at least the thing that will annoy me most.

As if reading my mind, he sighs and says: 'Look, I don't want to fight about it. Feels like we're constantly getting at each other at the moment.'

'You're right.' I grit my teeth and try to compose myself. 'I'm sorry.'

'That's OK,' he says. But then, rather than apologising too, he adds: 'Have you eaten?'

'Not yet.'

'OK'. He raps the doorframe with his knuckle, a sign that the conversation is over. 'I'll do us some pasta or something.'

'That would be great, thanks.'

'I'll let you get on and finish your story.'

I listen to the clump of his footsteps down the stairs. But I don't bother to re-open my laptop. I can't finish the story yet. I won't know until tomorrow how it ends.

CHAPTER FORTY-SEVEN

WILL

10th April
Tottenham Court Road, London

'Dev?'

'Yeah?'

'Would you say this jumper is red?'

He turns to look at my sweatshirt as we yank the rusty MicroShop shutters down. 'I guess so. Why?'

'No, nothing.'

He slips the padlock through the metal hoop and takes another look at me. 'I mean: it's reddy-purple, isn't it?' he says.

'What?'

'It's not *red*-red. It's like . . . terracotta.'

'Right . . .' I run a hand through my hair. I really do not need another thing to worry about right now.

Half an hour ago, I was checking my reflection in the shop bathroom for about the zillionth time today when I suddenly panicked over the true redness of my red jumper. I'm being ridiculous. I know I am. Maybe my brain is creating stupid, made-up problems to distract me from the very real, very terrifying thing I am about to do.

'Terracotta is just a wanky way of saying "red", though, isn't it?' I ask.

Dev shrugs. 'I guess.'

I point to my chest. 'When push comes to shove, would you describe this as a "red jumper"?'

He sighs. 'I don't know, Will. Probably. What is this? Are you going to try and sue Primark for false advertising or something?'

'No. Sorry, it's . . . nothing.'

He wrinkles his brow. 'Are you all right, William? You've been jittery all day.'

'Have I? Yeah, no, I'm fine.'

'Do you want a quick pint and a chat?'

'I can't tonight,' I say. 'Maybe tomorrow, though?'

'Sounds good.' He thumps me on the shoulder. 'All right, man, have a good night.'

'You too.'

I watch him pull his enormous headphones out of his jacket pocket and head off towards the Tube station. I take a few deep breaths and try to gather myself. And then I walk to the bus stop.

Over the past few days, I've been working up a nice little daydream about how tonight might go. It currently looks something like this: I walk into the Lamb & Flag and spot Pia at exactly the same moment she spots me. In that moment, all the anxiety and terror dissolves: we smile at each other, and I instantly know that meeting her was the right thing to do. Shegets up on stage to read her story, it goes down a storm, and then we spend the rest of the evening lost in conversation, barely even aware of the hours flying by until the barman calls 'time'.

The bus arrives and I clamber on board. I head straight for the top deck and find a free double seat near the back.

It's a nice daydream. The problem is: it's just that. A dream. I have no idea what's really about to happen. No idea what she'll think of me. And even if a miracle occurs and my daydream comes true . . . what happens next? I know she has a boyfriend. And even if she didn't – would she really want to know me if she found out the full story? If she found out about the band? If she found out about Joe?

I grip the seat tight and stare out of the window at London flashing past below me. All day I've been repeating Tanvi's words in my head: 'Things don't happen without a bit of effort, Will. Things happen because you *make* them happen.' All day, I've been mentally repeating those sentences like a mantra, reassuring myself that going to this event tonight is the right decision. But right now that mantra is failing me. Right now, I can feel something inside me screaming to get off this bus and go home. To just take the daydream and run, because this will all end badly. I gulp some more air, and try to focus on something else. Anything else.

I latch on to a conversation behind me – a middle-aged couple bickering about what to have for dinner. Should they go to Tesco or Aldi? But their words keep slipping through my grasp. All I can think about is Pia.

I pull out my phone and check the time. Seven fifteen. The bus is nearly at Clerkenwell station now.

In a quarter of an hour, I will see her.

CHAPTER FORTY-EIGHT

ANNIE

10th April
Clerkenwell, London

I hear the pub door open and my head swivels so fast I'm surprised I don't get whiplash.

But no – it's three men, probably all in their late fifties, and not a red jumper in sight. I reach for my glass of Diet Coke, chomping down three ice cubes in a futile attempt to try and calm my bubbling stomach.

Why the hell did I arrive early? This is so much worse. Watching the door like a hawk from the corner table, jumping out of my skin every time I see a vaguely reddish item of clothing. I wish to God we hadn't gone with this stupid bloody red-and-green-jumper idea, anyway. It's making the whole thing even more stressful than it already is.

Plus, my chunky green & Other Stories woolly jumper is not, in hindsight, what I would have chosen to wear for . . . whatever tonight is. Not a first date, obviously. But a first . . . something. I bought this jumper purely for slouching around in at home. It's not exactly flattering. Why didn't I just say 'blue'? I've got a really nice blue merino sweater from M&S. But no, I had to randomly blurt out 'green' instead. Clearly, my subconscious hates me.

I take another swig of Coke. God, I'm so nervous. My eyes flick back to the door, even though no one has come through it. Sat at a tiny table next to the door is the organiser of tonight's event – a suitably bookish-looking man in a black polo neck and wire-rimmed glasses. As I came in, he asked if I wanted to put my name down to read this evening. I told him no. Quite frankly, the thought of having to spill my soul in public *and* meet Jack in person on the same night is just a tad too much to deal with. There's another event next month. Maybe I'll feel up to it then. Right now, I can't think much beyond the next ten minutes.

I scan the crowd as my stomach continues to swoop and whirl. The pub is pretty packed already, and the thought suddenly hits me that Jack might already be in here. What if he's ditched the red jumper thing and worn something else?

I fiddle with the sleeves of my stupid bulky sweater as I try to pinpoint any men in here that could feasibly be Jack. But it's a minefield because I don't really know anything about him. I've gabbled on and on at him over the past few weeks, telling him pretty much everything about my life. But his Phone Beefeater Code means he's revealed very little about himself. I've always imagined him roughly the same age as me – but I can't know for sure.

There's a man at the bar in a red crewneck - probably in his mid-forties. But he's sat with four other men. And he certainly doesn't have the air of someone scanning the room for a girl in a green jumper.

God, this is a nightmare. I'm busting for a wee now, probably shouldn't have downed my Coke in record time. But if I get up I'll lose the table. Screw it. I stand up and head for the loo, praying they've got a decent mirror in there.

Maybe Jack will have arrived by the time I come back.

CHAPTER FORTY-NINE

WILL

10th April
Clerkenwell, London

The chalkboard outside the pub reads: 'TONIGHT AT THE LAMB & FLAG! NEW VOICES IN FICTION: A WRITERS' EVENT.'

This is definitely the place. A part of me was secretly hoping there might be two Lamb & Flags in Clerkenwell, and I would go to the wrong one. A simple mistake that I could easily explain to Pia over the phone on Sunday. But no.

I check my phone. 7.33 p.m. My heart is beating so hard it feels like my whole body is vibrating.

A group of people walk past me and push through the pub doors, allowing me a second's glimpse of the crowd inside. My gut, my heart, my head: all of them are screaming at me – *just go. Leave now.*

I close my eyes for a moment and try to tune into Tanvi's voice again: 'She's probably just as nervous as you are.'

The gentle thud of music emanates from the pub, interspersed with laughter and the clinking of glasses. I glance at my reflection in the window behind the chalkboard. And then I walk inside.

Directly to the left of the entrance is a tiny, rickety-looking table. Sat at it is a thin bloke in a polo neck who smiles and asks if I'm planning on reading anything tonight. I shake my head and keep walking, heading straight for the bar, hoping my legs don't completely turn to jelly before I get there.

As soon as I reach the bar, I scan the pub. And as soon as I scan the pub, I see her. Not Pia. But . . .

She's standing at the opposite end of the bar. She has her head bowed, checking her phone. But it's her. It's definitely her.

It's Annie.

Annie from five years ago. From Paris. From that day.

An invisible vice fixes itself to my chest and starts turning. It *can't* be her. But it is.

I haven't thought about her in . . . I can't even remember how long. I'm not sure why. I guess I've spent the past five years doing everything I can – consciously and unconsciously – to wipe that day entirely from my memory. And that meant wiping Annie, too.

She's still scrolling on her phone. In my brain, it's like the floodgates have burst open, and these snapshots from that day in Paris come rushing back. The mental equivalent of me spilling that box full of photos of Joe. Memories I've kept locked up tightly for years all coming crashing through at once. I can't deal with this. This is too strange, too random. Pia can wait. I have to get out of here before Annie sees me.

But my legs won't move. My whole body has frozen, like a broken computer. I have to physically push myself away from the bar to start moving. But before I can, she glances up from her phone and looks right at me.

It's only then I realise. She's wearing a green jumper.

CHAPTER FIFTY

ANNIE

10th April
Clerkenwell, London

The man standing at the other end of the bar is a little older – and a little more bearded – than the boy I met five years ago in Paris. But there's no doubt about it.

That is Will Axford. That is Will Axford in a red jumper.

It's like I can actually feel the gears clunking and whirring in my brain as I try to comprehend what I'm seeing. He doesn't move a muscle. He just stares at me: eyes wide, his mouth open slightly, revealing that tiny gap between his two front teeth. This can't really be happening, can it? All this time, when I've been speaking to Jack . . .

Before I'm even aware of what I'm doing I start moving round the bar towards him. His gaze follows me as I go. But still he doesn't move. My heart is thundering. I suddenly remember the night of my first Green Shoots call. I'd found the number on The Defectors' drummer's Instagram. It never occurred to me he might be promoting the line because Will worked there.

All this time . . .

Suddenly, he's right in front of me. Still not moving. Still not speaking. He looks like he's having serious trouble processing this moment, too.

'Will?' I let out a shaky breath. '*Jack*?'

He runs a hand over his beard before glancing around the pub and back to me. 'What . . . What is this?' he says. 'What's going on?'

That stupid mockney accent he spoke with in Paris has disappeared. His voice is softer now. Posher. It's Jack's voice. Jack's voice coming out of Will Axford's mouth.

I can't help myself. I don't know why, but I start laughing.

'This is just . . . *mad*,' I say. I can't take my eyes off him. How different he is. The beard, the voice, the way he carries himself. There's none of that silly adolescent swagger about him now. He doesn't just look different. He looks *better*.

Why the hell can't I stop laughing? Will isn't laughing. He's not even smiling. He's just staring at me in what appears to be total disbelief.

'It's mad,' I repeat stupidly. 'I found that number – the Green Shoots number – on Simon's Instagram when I was just starting on that article about you, and then—'

'Article?' Will says. Something in his face hardens.

My head is still spinning so fast I can barely get the words out. 'Yeah, I was supposed to be writing this article. About your old band. For the site I work for. And I was trying to track you down for an interview, but first I found Simon McGillan's Instagram page, and it had . . .'

I tail off, my words withering under Will's stone-like stare. His eyes flicker left and right, as if trying to compute what he's hearing. And then he blinks and swallows. 'That article,' he says. 'That was you?'

I nod. 'Yeah. I assumed Jess had told you. I met up with her – she said you were still in touch?'

Will goes to say something, but the words seem to dissolve on his lips. He closes his eyes and squeezes the bridge of his nose. 'Wait . . .' he mutters. 'Is that what this – us, our conversations – has all been about?'

I shake my head, nonplussed. 'What do you mean?'

'You knew I didn't want to do the interview, so, what . . .? You used the Green Shoots line to try and *trick* me into it?'

'*What*?' The idea is so ridiculous it almost makes me laugh again. 'No. Of course not! I mean: I wanted to speak to you, obviously, to find out what happened with the band, but—'

Will flinches. He isn't listening. He just keeps talking – more to himself than to me. It's like a story is unspooling in his head, and I can't interject to tell him it's the *wrong* story.

'All this time, asking me questions about myself, trying to get me to open up, it was just for this fucking *article*?' He says the last word with such venom that I actually wince. He looks broken. I can see the hurt shining in his eyes when they meet mine. The urge to laugh has evaporated now, and I find I'm actually having to try very hard not to cry. For a moment I think I can see tears forming in Will's eyes too. But he scrubs a hand across them and keeps talking.

'That line is for people who need help,' he hisses. 'It's not for journalists, scavenging for a fucking story.'

'Will, please—'

'What were you hoping? That you could get me to trust you,

and then sooner or later, I'd start spilling my guts about the band and about everything that happened?'

'No, Will – it's not like that!' It comes out loud enough to cause several heads at the bar to turn towards us. But I can't let him think this. I just can't. 'I didn't know, Will, honestly. I didn't!'

Finally, he moves. Without saying another word, he turns and goes to walk away.

Instinctively, I reach out to grab his shoulder. I can't let him leave like this. I need to make him understand. But he shakes my hand away.

'Annie.' He looks me straight in the eye. This time I see the tears form and settle before he has time to wipe them away. 'I don't want to do the interview,' he says. 'I don't want to speak to you. Don't ever call the line again.'

CHAPTER FIFTY-ONE

26th February, five years ago
Paris, France

'Are we seriously going to the Eiffel Tower?'

Will says it with such cartoonish disdain that Annie can't help laughing. 'Too cool for the Eiffel Tower, are you?'

He shrugs. 'It's just a bit . . . basic, isn't it?'

Annie rolls her eyes. 'You're such a hipster. This is the first time I've ever been to Paris, and I'd like to see the Eiffel Tower. If that makes me basic, then yes: I'm basic.'

Will grins and leans into her as they walk. 'You're not basic, Annie. You're complex. I can tell.'

She rolls her eyes again. Annie is not a fool – she knows a stupid, cheesy line when she hears one. The problem is, when that stupid, cheesy line is delivered by an extremely hot lead singer with a weirdly sexy teardrop dimple, it's hard not to be affected by it.

Full up on steak frites, Annie and Will are heading back west now, along the river. Over the wrought-iron roofs of central Paris, the spire of the Eiffel Tower soars above them.

It's getting colder now, but the sky is still clear blue, and Annie has the sudden desire to take another photo. Maybe she could even suggest another selfie, of the two of them. But she decides against it. She doesn't want Will to think she's even more 'basic' than he apparently already does.

'Do you mind if I give Joe a quick bell?' Will asks. 'Just to check if he's all right.'

'Of course. Tell him to come and hang out with us at the Eiffel Tower. I bet he'd be less of a dick about it than you.'

Will chuckles, holding the phone to his ear. After a few seconds he takes it away. 'Not picking up.'

As he pockets his phone, Annie asks: 'So, have you really known him since you were kids?'

'Before that, even. Our mums met in NCT class.'

'Ha. That's amazing. So cool that you've stayed close all this time. Especially because – and I know I only met him for a second – but he seems quite . . . different to you.'

Will nods. 'He is. I mean: he wasn't always. His dad left when we were about ten, and his mum kind of lost it for a while. It was almost like she took it out on Joe. She became so critical – he just couldn't do anything right. He definitely became quieter after that. More drawn into himself.'

'Right.'

'And then she remarried soon afterwards and had another kid, and suddenly all her focus was on that. It was like she forgot about Joe completely.'

'That's awful,' Annie says.

'Yeah. I sort of took it upon myself to look after him from then on. We'd been so close as kids, you know? But then, when we got to secondary school, I got into football and being in plays and going to parties and whatever – but Joe just got more and more introverted. I'd be constantly bugging him to come out and socialise, but he'd just stay in his room listening to music.'

They cross the street, heading for the base of the Tower. 'He had such wicked taste,' Will continues. 'The Fall, Kate Bush, Joy Division, Mogwai: he got me into all of them. Every mix CD he made me was immense – and he made me a lot of mix CDs.' He smiles at the memory. 'I even roped him into starting a band when we were about sixteen. But he just couldn't hack being on stage, being in front of people.'

Annie nods. 'He didn't seem like someone who'd relish being the centre of attention.'

'No,' Will agrees. 'I just wanted him to come out of his shell, you know? I still do. He's such a fucking amazing, funny, super-clever dude. But he never lets anyone see it.'

'Except you,' Annie points out.

Will scratches the back of his neck. 'Except me.' He turns to her suddenly. 'Have you got brothers and sisters?'

'I've got a sister.'

He nods. 'I'm an only child, but I always felt like Joe is what it must be like to have a little brother. Sometimes you're embarrassed by them, or you kind of resent them for holding you back. But when it comes down it, you'd do anything for them. Anything.'

'Mm-hm,' Annie says softly.

'I know he gets a bit down sometimes,' Will says. 'Sometimes I feel he wants to talk to me about it all, but I just don't know what to say. I don't know anything about this stuff, so what am I supposed to tell him? Except for, "Ah cheer up, mate, look on the bright side"?'

'Maybe you don't have to tell him anything,' Annie says. 'Maybe you just have to listen.'

Will bites his lip. 'Maybe. Sorry. It's stupid to be droning on about all this.'

'Not at all.'

She means it. Truthfully, she likes him better in these moments. As much as the swagger and the dimple and the cheesy lines make her blush, it's at times like these she realises she doesn't just fancy Will Axford: she actually likes him, too. She can tell there is someone else there beneath the silly pop-star bluster. She'd like to get to know that person.

But then they turn a corner and that person disappears – replaced instantly by the swaggering lead singer. 'Here we go, then,' Will says, clapping his hands as they step into the shadow of the Tower. 'Look at the size of that fucker!'

Annie stares up at the gigantic iron monument, squinting to see the top. In front of them, in the open space between the Tower's four huge feet, is an ice rink. Surrounded by speakers pumping Europop, it's bustling with tourists, all laughing as they try to stay on their feet.

Annie points it out to Will. 'Look – they've got a skating rink!'

'No, no, no.' Will holds his hand up. 'We're already at the Eiffel Tower. That's basic enough. We can't throw ice-skating into the mix.'

She grins at him. 'You do realise we're going on it?'

'You do realise we're definitely not,' he says. 'My street cred would disappear like that.' He snaps his fingers.

'Your street cred disappeared the minute you used the phrase "street cred".'

He laughs. 'Fuck's sake. Come on, then.'

They hire skates and slide out onto the ice. Will flails immediately, his arms windmilling, and Annie has to hold him steady. Through his jacket, she feels the muscles in his arm tighten as she grabs him.

'Can't bloody believe I'm doing this,' he says, gripping the edge of the rink. 'I must really like you.'

'Ha.' Annie pushes off, her back turned so he won't see her cheeks flushing. Why does he keep saying things like that? Does he actually really like her?

At that moment, through the speakers, a familiar piano ditty rings out. Annie spins around, and Will is already staring at her with his mouth open.

'No fucking way,' he says.

'Oh honey!' Annie puts a hand to her chest, adopting a gooey American accent. 'They're playing our song!'

The first verse of Toploader's 'Dancing In The Moonlight' kicks in, and the two of them just stand there, laughing and laughing.

'Come on, Will, don't be shy,' she says, skating back towards him. 'I know you know the words.'

Will covers his face with his hand. She sees his grin stretching either side of it. 'I'd ask you to dance,' he says, 'but I think I'd fall over.'

'Well, we can't just stand here by the edge all afternoon,' she tells him. 'We've paid eight bloody Euros for this. Here . . .'

She holds out her hand. He smiles at her and takes it. Gently, she pushes off and Will glides away with her towards the centre of the rink.

CHAPTER FIFTY-TWO

WILL

10th April, present day
Clerkenwell, London

'Jess. It's Will. Call me back as soon as you get this. I really need to speak to you.'

I hang up and shove the phone back into my pocket. I've called her probably ten times since walking out of that pub half an hour ago, and she's still not picking up. She'll think I've gone crazy when she finally checks her phone. I definitely sounded nuts leaving that message: my voice jagged and raspy and furious. Maybe I *have* gone crazy.

Even as I walk now – storming through the streets, head bowed against the wind, not knowing where the hell I'm heading – I can feel people giving me dirty looks as I barge past. I don't even care. I just keep walking.

What the *fuck* just happened?

The moment I realised the truth – that Pia was Annie – it was like something snapped inside me. Anger, confusion, humiliation, despair – all of them came crashing down at once, drenching me, flooding my brain so that I couldn't even speak or think straight. I just had to get the fuck out of there as quickly as possible.

I've spent the past month believing there was a connection between Pia and me – harbouring this ridiculous fantasy that this could be the start of something. But all this time, she was just trying to weasel information out of me for her fucking article. How much did Jess and Mike tell her? Does she know about Joe? Is that what she was working up to asking me about during all those phone calls?

'Oi! Watch where you're fucking going!'

I spin round to see a big bloke with a shaved head glaring at me. I didn't even realise I'd bumped into him. I just turn and keep walking as he fires more verbal vitriol at my back. I'm so angry I'm half-hoping he follows me and tries to start something. I want somebody to take this out on. I want to punch and kick and rip, even if I get punched, kicked and ripped in return.

All this time. All this time it was Annie. How did I not know? How could I not tell?

Snapshots of the day in Paris are rushing back now. Arriving jumbled up, out of order, in my head. I remember ice-skating at the Eiffel Tower. That weird little apartment with the low ceiling. Telling people we were married so we could skip the queue at that steak restaurant. All of it was wiped out by what happened later that night. But now it's starting to come back to me.

That whole day I was wondering if I should try to kiss her. Wanting to *so* badly. Clumsily flirting with her in the hope that she might kiss me first. That clichéd (but totally accurate) butterflies-in-the-stomach feeling when you realise you're starting to *really* like someone. It doesn't even feel like it was me that experienced all this now. I suppose it wasn't. When I woke up the next day, I was someone else. A completely different person.

I remember fretting all afternoon about whether or not I should invite her to the gig. I didn't in the end: I was worried about Jess finding out, and assuming something was going on. Jess and I weren't *together*-together then – we were never really *together*-together – but she still would have kicked up a fuss. Even though I now know she was shagging around behind my back by that point, too.

So, instead I—

I stop dead in the middle of the street as the realisation hits me. I told Annie we'd meet again later that night. We were stood on that bridge, the sun was going down, and I told her: *I'll meet you back here. Right on this spot. After the gig.*

And then . . . And then.

I start walking again, my heart still going like the clappers. After all this time, it turns out she is Pia. I can't believe it. I just can't.

I feel my phone buzzing against my leg. My hand goes straight to my pocket.

'Jess?'

'Will? What the fuck? Are you OK?'

'Why didn't you tell me?'

'What are you talking about? Tell you what?'

'That journalist!' I snap. 'The one that wanted to interview me about the band. Why didn't you tell me it was Annie, from Paris?'

I hear her swallow. 'I thought . . . I don't know. I didn't think you'd even remember her. I didn't think it was important.'

'You didn't think . . .' I scrub a hand across my face. 'I spent all day with her, Jess! All of *that* fucking day. You didn't think maybe that was worth mentioning?'

'Look, I'm sorry, OK?' she says. 'I didn't want to worry you. I knew it would freak you out to think about that day. So I just thought it was best to get rid of her without telling you. Which is what I thought I did.'

'Well, you didn't do a very good job because she's managed to find me, hasn't she?'

'OK, Will. Calm down.' She says it like she's talking to a child, and it just makes me angrier. 'She must have got your details through someone else. Sim or Al, maybe. How did she get in touch with you? Email?'

'No, she—' I break off abruptly. I've never told Jess that I volunteer at Green Shoots. No one knows I do it. Except, apparently, Annie. Who said she found it on Sim's Instagram. But I never told Sim either . . .

'It doesn't matter,' I mumble into the phone. I feel light-headed again suddenly. 'You just should have told me it was her.'

'Like I said, I didn't want you to freak out.'

'I don't think that was it.'

'What do you mean?' she says sharply.

I take a shaky breath, still marching forward, not looking where I'm going. 'I think you liked having something over me,' I say. 'A weird sense of control. Having power over me.'

She gives a shrill laugh. 'You're fucking nuts, Will. You're paranoid.'

My head is really spinning now. Maybe she's right. Maybe

I am paranoid. I never told Sim that I volunteered at Green Shoots. So how could Annie have found out through him? Unless I got it wrong. Unless she was telling the truth. She really *didn't* know I was Jack . . .

Jess' voice brings me back to earth. 'Will? Are you still there?'

'Yeah . . .'

'Your voice sounds weird. Where are you?'

I blink and look around me. I have no idea where I am. I've just been staggering blindly for the past half an hour, lost in my thoughts. I'm in a dark, nondescript street somewhere. The noise in my head clears and I realise how quiet it is. I take a breath.

'Why do you still do this, Jess?' I ask. My voice sounds steadier now. Calmer.

'Do what?'

'Punish me. For who I was before that day in Paris. I'll always be sorry for the way I treated you. But you treated me like shit, too. You went behind my back. All the time.'

Silence. 'Only because you went behind my back first.'

I shake my head. 'I know. I'm sorry. I was an arsehole. I feel like we made such a mess of each other. And whatever there is between us now . . . it's not good. For either of us.'

'Are you fucking kidding?' she hisses. 'You're the one who keeps crawling back to *me,* Will. Whenever you realise how much of a fucking wreck your life is, I'm the one you call. I'm the one that comes to comfort you. I'm all you've got.'

The truth of it hits me with a dull thud. I did have Pia. But Pia is gone. Annie is Pia. But how did Annie know I was Jack? In the pub, it seemed so obvious what had happened. That rush of fury when I figured out she'd been using Green Shoots to get information from me about the band and Joe. But now that I think about it . . .

You're fucking nuts, Will. You're paranoid.

I squeeze the bridge of my nose. I can't focus. I can't think straight. My brain is just whirring and stalling, whirring and stalling.

'I'm all you've got,' Jess repeats quietly.

'You don't even like me,' I say.

She just sighs. She doesn't deny it. 'Look, I don't know what the hell's gotten into you. But it's pathetic. I'm sure you'll wake up tomorrow, feel fucking stupid and call me apologising and begging me to come over again.'

I'm walking more slowly now. But as I round the corner, I see what is definitely the soft glow of a pub sign at the end of the street. I speed up.

'You're right,' I tell Jess. 'It is pathetic. And I'm sorry. It will never happen again.'

'Will—'

I hang up the phone and head for the pub, aiming to drink myself into oblivion.

CHAPTER FIFTY-THREE

ANNIE

10th April
Ladbroke Grove, London

Dom is sat on the couch when I get home, watching something on his laptop.

He's in his pyjama bottoms and a hoodie, feet up on the coffee table, squinting at the screen. He barely looks up as I enter the living room.

'I thought you were out with Maya tonight?'

I throw my keys into the bowl on the dresser. 'Yeah. I was. She had to go early.'

Dom raises his eyebrows. 'Hot Hinge date?'

'Something like that.'

He pauses his show and nods to the kitchen. 'There's chilli left if you want it.'

'I'm OK, thanks. Do we have any wine?'

'I think so, in the fridge.'

I walk into the kitchen. As I pour myself a large glass of chardonnay I check my reflection in the mirror. I look normal.

At least, I think I do. On the bus home, I was terrified I might break down and just start sobbing at any moment. I could feel the tears gathering behind my eyes, like a dam was about to burst inside me. But it didn't. And now I just feel numb. Like the whole thing didn't even happen to me. Like I'm on autopilot.

'Do you want a glass?' I call through to Dom.

'No, I'm cool.'

I go back into the living room and sit down on the smaller sofa opposite him. I was sat right here, in this exact spot, when I first called Green Shoots. When I first spoke to Jack.

Will.

'What are you watching?' I ask Dom.

'Just this new Marvel thing on Disney+.'

'Mm-hm.' The wine has a cheap, metallic taste. But I take another large sip anyway. 'Any good?'

'Yeah, it's OK.' He shuts his laptop and wrinkles his brow. 'Are you all right, babe?'

I take another big gulp of wine. I'm not sure *what* I am at the moment. But it's definitely not 'all right'.

That look on Will's face before he walked out. I can't stop thinking about it. I couldn't do anything to stop him leaving. I just stood there, frozen to the floor of the pub, watching him push his way out through the crowd. I let him go. I let him think that I'd abused his trust – that all this time I'd been calling Green Shoots just to get information on him for the article.

I don't want to speak to you. Don't ever call the line again.

As I watched him go, I thought about everything else that I've lost. I lost Dad. It feels like I've lost Mum and Josie, too. Or, at least, I will if I don't do something soon. I'm almost certainly going to lose my job soon.

And now I've lost Jack. Will. Seeing him in the flesh – that insane moment when I realised he and Jack were the same person – it was like a light coming on. *Oh, it's you!* Ridiculously, I couldn't help fixating on how good he looked. And the fact that he was Jack, too – this person I'd grown so close to over the past few weeks, this person who'd made me think differently, who I'd told things I'd never told anyone before.

I can't bear the idea that he thinks I was just using him. The idea of never speaking to him again . . .

'Babe?' Dom is still staring at me with an anxious look on his face.

I don't know why, but at that moment the dam finally breaks.

'Annie? What the—'

I bury my head in my hands. 'I'm sorry. I'm sorry.'

I'm crying so hard that my whole body is heaving. I hear Dom rush up from the sofa and feel him drop down next to me. The warmth of his hand on my back. 'What happened? What is it?'

The tears are streaking down my face. I can hardly get the words out. 'Everything,' I gulp. 'I've made a mess of everything. I don't know what I'm doing.'

'What are you on about? What's brought this on?'

'I just feel so . . . lost.'

He pats my back. I hear him sigh. 'I don't know what's going on with you lately.'

'I don't know what's going on with you either,' I say into my hands.

'What do you mean?'

‘We don’t really talk anymore. And if we do talk, we just argue.’

I feel his hand leave my back. ‘That’s not true,’ he says stiffly.

‘It is, Dom.’

A voice inside me is shrieking: *what are you doing? Shut the fuck up!* Do I really want to get into this conversation right now? I’ve just been through the mental checklist of everything else I’ve lost. Dom is all I’ve got left. The one thing keeping me anchored, the one thing keeping me from falling so far behind everyone else that I can’t catch up. I can’t lose him, too. I just can’t.

I press my fingertips into my damp eyelids. I’m scared of being on my own. But that’s no reason to stay in a relationship. Plus, I know what I felt when I saw Will. When I realised he was Jack. You shouldn’t be feeling those feelings when you’re with someone else.

I wipe my eyes and look up. Dom is just staring into space next to me, scratching the back of his neck. The weight of that lie I told – that I was meeting Maya for drinks – suddenly seems too much to bear.

‘I sort of met someone . . .’ The words are out there before I can stop them.

Dom turns to look at me, his face hardening. That voice inside me gets louder: *Shut the fuck up NOW!*

‘Nothing happened,’ I tell him. ‘I swear to you on my life. I would never do that. But I felt something . . . Maybe I still do.’ I put my head back in my hands. ‘I’m sorry. I don’t even know what I’m saying.’

He says nothing. Just lets me keep crying quietly. And

then I hear him exhale through his nose. 'OK. Well, I guess it makes me feel less bad.'

'Bad about what?'

'Annie, I'm sorry. I've been trying to figure out how to tell you.' I look up at him, about to say, 'Tell me what?' But the look on his face tells me before he does.

'I slept with someone else.'

CHAPTER FIFTY-FOUR

26th February, five years ago
Paris, France

The rest of the afternoon passes far too quickly.

After half an hour of stumbling about in fits of giggles on the Eiffel Tower ice rink, Annie and Will decide to take the Metro into the centre of Paris. Emerging into the surreally narrow streets of the Marais, they drop in on vintage clothes stores, attempting to outdo each other by trying on the stupidest items they can find.

Later, as they meander back west along the river, they pass the vast monumental hall of the Musée d'Orsay. They've been walking and talking for hours now, so they decide to stop for a coffee. Sipping their cappuccinos, they watch the crowds moving back and forth along the banks of the Seine, picking out people at random, inventing stories about their lives.

Will's phone rings as he asks the waiter for the bill. He glances at the screen and slips it back in his pocket. It can't be Joe, Annie thinks, because surely Will would answer if it was? Maybe it's Jess.

She doesn't know. And right now she doesn't particularly care. She can feel the gig looming now: their time together is coming to an end. These past few hours have been like living in a strange little bubble. Just the two of them – as if no one else really existed. But now reality wants them back.

'Shall we head?' Will says, standing up.

They keep walking. Annie is not sure where they're going now. She doesn't even want to ask. She just wants to keep walking around this city with this boy, just for a little bit longer.

She checks her phone, which is full of messages from her dad – still enthusing about the Alphonse Carnet photos – and Maya – begging for information about this kind-of-date Annie seems to be on. But there's nothing really to tell yet. Annie has no idea how it will end.

'Did Joe get back to you?' she wonders aloud.

'Nah,' Will says. 'It's cool, though. I'll see him after the gig.'

She sets her jaw and looks straight ahead. It's the first time in hours that the gig has been mentioned. Truthfully, Annie would like to come and see it. But she's not going to stoop to asking Will if she can. That would be way too pathetic. So, either he invites her or . . . the day is over, she supposes. And who knows if they'll see each other again.

'You looking forward to the gig?' she asks as they pass a group of students playing pétanque in the Invalides gardens.

Will just shrugs. 'They all blur into each other, to be honest.'

He seems apprehensive, too – but Annie can't work out if it's just nerves ahead of the concert or . . . something else. Not for the first time today, she wonders what he's thinking.

Will veers right, onto the Pont Alexandre III – the same bridge they'd crossed together six hours previously. Amazing, Annie thinks, what can happen in six hours. To the west is the Eiffel Tower, to the east the Place de la Concorde, and as the sun starts to set, colouring the Seine a deep red-gold, it's like they've stepped into a postcard. For a moment, she feels almost breathless with regret that this is it.

They stop for a moment to admire the view. And then Will turns to Annie and smiles sadly.

'So,' he says.

'So,' she replies.

There's no getting past it. It's time.

CHAPTER FIFTY-FIVE

WILL

12th April, present day
Green Shoots office, Limehouse

Even in my wild old rock 'n' roll days I don't think I was ever unfortunate enough to suffer a two-day hangover.

But that's exactly what I'm staring down the barrel of right now. I wince into the mirror of the tiny Green Shoots bathroom, trying not to look too closely at my crumpled, ruined reflection. I shake out another Nurofen and chase it down with a glug of water from the tap.

I can't even remember how I got home two nights ago. After hanging up on Jess, I'd walked into that pub, ordered a pint and a shot, and kept going from there. The last thing I remember was stumbling into an offie, long past closing time, and paying for six cans and a bottle of vodka. The next thing I knew I was sprawled out on my sofa, my head screaming in agony, and the sun was streaming in through the curtains. In the corner of the room, Milligan sat watching me with what I swear was a look of frightened concern on his little face.

I'd phoned Dev straight away to tell him I had a stomach bug and wouldn't be coming in. And then I'd spent the next twenty-four hours trying – and failing – to sleep.

I head to the kitchen, pour myself a pint of tap water and walk back into the office. I've been on the afternoon shift for four hours now, and the phone has barely rung once. I haven't even had Eric. I very nearly didn't come in for this shift – the urge to stay curled up in the foetal position with my duvet over my head was still extremely strong at midday today. But something dragged me here. Something drove me the entire length of the Metropolitan Line to sit in this chair, waiting.

The thought that Annie might call.

But then: why would she? I told her never to phone Green Shoots again. Of all the jagged, blurry memories that flashed into my throbbing head yesterday morning, that one was the most painful. It still is.

Maybe Jess was right. *You're paranoid*, she'd said. And it's true that even the slightest mention of the band tends to send 300 volts of sheer panic right through me. If I get the inkling I've been recognised – or that someone might know The Defectors, and ask what happened, why we split up – it's like all logic flies out the window. My brain just shuts down and all I can think is: *how do I get out of this situation?*

I'd been so certain about what Annie seemed to be admitting: that she'd been calling Green Shoots to try and get something out of me for her interview. But in the cold light of day . . . Why would she admit that? And how would she even know I volunteered here when I never told Sim? I never told anyone. My *parents* don't even know.

Then the paranoia creeps back in. Another voice in my head

starts whispering: she was there with you, in Paris, on *that* day. Why else would she be writing this article unless she knew? She could easily have found out what happened. Maybe she's always known. Why would anyone want to write an article about The Defectors otherwise? We certainly weren't much cop musically.

I take a swig of water and rub my aching temples. I wish I understood.

There's also the fact that, against the backdrop of this blistering migraine, other memories have been floating back, too. That whole afternoon with Annie. We must have spent five or six hours together. I'd blocked it out so completely, stuffed it into the darkest corner of my subconscious. But now fragments are coming back. Walking through the city with her, talking, joking: I'd felt the lightest, the happiest, the most like myself I'd felt in years. It all came crashing down, of course, with what happened later that night. But still: those memories are real. That was how she made me feel.

The phone bursts into life next to me. The ghost of my headache is violently reanimated and I wince in pain. I take a deep breath before I lift the receiver. Please let it be her. Please.

'Hello, Green Shoots?'

'Oh . . . hello, Jack.'

Eric. Disappointment – followed by a rush of relief. I haven't spoken to him once during my last three shifts, and I've noticed from the log book that he seems to be calling less and less lately. Despite everything else that's been going on, I've been worried about him.

'Eric!' I say as brightly as I can. 'Great to hear you. How's things? It's been a while.'

He clears his throat noisily. 'Yes . . . Not brilliant today, as it goes.' His voice is thick and slurred. I know instantly that he's been drinking.

'Oh I'm sorry to hear that,' I say. 'Well, you're in good company. I'm down in the dumps, too.'

He forces a laugh. 'Oh dear, Jack. What have you got to be down about?'

'Various things. Everything seems a bit bleak at the moment.'

'I know the feeling.'

I catch a glimpse of my reflection in the window. What the hell am I doing? People call this line to talk about their own concerns, not to have someone else's emotional baggage flung on top of them. I take another swig of water and push Annie and everything else out of my head. Eric will leave this call feeling better. That's my job.

'So, what's up?' I say. 'Let's talk it through?'

'Nothing to talk through. Not even sure why I'm calling. Just feeling a bit hopeless, Jack. A lot hopeless. Haven't slept for a few nights now.'

'Mm-hm. I'm sorry.'

'Thinking about . . . stuff. The past. I'm just so tired, Jack.'

'Mm-hm.' I can't see a route in to try and make him feel better. But that's OK. Just let him talk. Just listen.

'Spent most of today staring at the ceiling, trying to will myself to sleep,' he says. 'No joy. So I've . . . taken some pills.'

'Mm-hm.'

The 'verbal nod' slips out automatically. It takes me a second to process what he's just said. 'What do you mean, "some pills", Eric?'

I hear him take a swig of something. He doesn't answer.

'Eric?' I hold the phone closer to my mouth. 'You took a sleeping pill? Or you took . . . several sleeping pills?'

He starts mumbling incoherently. I can only make out the occasional word. He's not all there, and my body is now alive with fear. I glance up at the pinboard next to me, which is full of emergency numbers and helplines that deal with more serious cases than we are trained for.

I try to keep any sense of anxiety out of my voice. 'Eric, listen to me. Are you OK? Do you need help?'

'Sometimes, I just get so low.' He's slurring his words now and my heartbeat doubles its speed. 'I think . . . no one would miss me.'

'Eric . . .' All my instincts are screeching at me to tell him – quite forcefully – that of course someone would miss him. That lots of people would miss him. But the truth is: I don't know that. I don't know him. And if I say it, and he asks me who, I won't be able to answer. And then I will have confirmed his worst fears, and I can't bear to think how that might make him feel. Or what it would make him do.

I clear my throat and say: 'I'm here for you right now, Eric, and I care very deeply what happens to you. I promise you that.'

I hear the sharp clink of glass hitting a table. 'You're a good lad, Jack, you really are.'

'Eric, please . . .' I can't keep the anxiety out of my voice now. It's bleeding in, whether I like it or not. Because fuck it: fuck the Green Shoots rules. I would miss him. I really would. Why can't I say it if it's true?

'I would miss you, Eric. I would miss you.' The words stick in my throat.

Eric just laughs. A high-pitched, croaked chuckle. I'm not sure if he even heard me.

'I'm sorry,' he says. 'I can't bear feeling so lonely. All the time. It's *all the time*.'

I clasp the phone so tightly my knuckles turn white: 'Eric, you need to let me know *right now* if you're OK. Do you need me to call an ambulance? Tell me your address!'

'You're a good lad, Jack,' he repeats, the words melting into one another.

I don't know why, but I suddenly blurt: 'My name isn't Jack! It's Will. Will Axford.' I'm shouting now. I can't help it. 'Eric – seriously – you need to let me know that you're OK!'

'Will,' he says. 'Will Axford. That's—'

At that moment, the line goes dead, and all I'm left with is the dial tone drilling in my ear and panic screaming in my chest.

CHAPTER FIFTY-SIX

ANNIE

12th April
Peak District, Derbyshire

'This 1415 TransPennine Express service to Sheffield will shortly be arriving in Derby. Derby, our next stop.'

The train wheezes to a halt at the station. Through the window I watch people spill out onto the platform, dragging their wheelie suitcases behind them. The waiting crowds part for them, and then flock into the train themselves. I squeeze up closer to the window as a man with a bulky backpack sits down next to me.

The little café by the ticket machine is gone. It was called something ridiculous like 'FastGrub' or 'QuickSnack'. I had a meal in there once. The train had broken down here and we had to get off and wait for the next one coming through to Sheffield. It must have been two or three months before Dad died. I was eating my lukewarm chicken wrap as the replacement service rumbled in, and I remember very clearly thinking, *I could just stay here.* Stay in this café, miss the train, pretend all this wasn't happening. That way I wouldn't have to see him. I wouldn't have to come face to face with how much thinner he had become, how much balder; how much more life had ebbed out of him since my last visit.

The café is gone now. There's a shiny new Costa in its place. I spot other little changes at the station, too. It's to be expected, I guess. It's been almost a year since I last made this journey.

The train pulls out with a hiss. As we rumble off towards Chesterfield, I flip my phone over on the table. A text from Maya. It just says: *Love you.*

I text her straight back: *Love you too. Thank you x*

Still nothing from Dom. Not a single word since I walked out of the flat the night before last.

The minute he told me, I had this strange feeling that I'd known all along. That the information had already been there in my brain, hiding, waiting to be unlocked as an explanation for why everything had been so weird between us lately. But it took me breaking down to actually force the confession out of him. If I hadn't been so knocked sideways by what happened with Will, then who knows – maybe Dom would never have told me.

Posh Clare. His ex-colleague. It happened one evening, he said, a few months back, after their weekly pub quiz. I knew which evening straight away: Dom hadn't got back until about 1 a.m. He'd texted me to say the Tube was fucked. When he finally arrived home, he'd climbed into bed next to me, like nothing had happened.

He told me it had only been that one time. That he'd been drunk. That he'd been feeling lonely and isolated because I'd been shutting him out since Dad died. I didn't say anything. There was nothing *to* say. He was right, I probably had.

He told me the secret had been killing him, but he just didn't know how to tell me. He told me he loved me and he was so sorry and he knew – just knew – that we could work this all out.

I packed some things and told him I was going to Maya's. He was crying by this point, begging me not to go. It freaked me out how calm I was as I walked out of the flat. Here I was, torpedoing the one solid thing left in my life, and I just felt . . . tired. I just wanted to sleep.

Obviously I was shaken by Dom's confession. But the truth is: I was more shaken by what happened with Will. What I felt when I saw him.

Yesterday morning, Maya had stood over me at breakfast and ordered me to stay home. She'd even offered to take the day off to keep me company. But I felt OK. I went to work.

It was only last night, as I was brushing my teeth at the tiny sink in her spare bedroom, that the cracks finally appeared. The instant I saw Mum's name flashing on my phone screen, I could feel the tears coming. As soon as I answered, they had arrived.

I don't think I even made any sense. I was just sobbing and gabbling at her about how Dom and I were taking a break, telling her I'd made such a mess of things and I didn't know what I was doing.

She just listened quietly. Let me sob myself out. And then she said: 'Annie, love, why don't you come home?'

CHAPTER FIFTY-SEVEN

WILL

12th April
Green Shoots office, Limehouse

'Will?'

'Tanvi!'

'Hey! Nice to hear from you. I've been wanting to text you to see how your hot date went, but I thought I'd wait and—'

'Tanvi, sorry, listen to me,' I cut in sharply. 'Something really bad has happened.'

The breeziness is sucked from her voice. 'What?'

I'm pacing back and forth inside the tiny office, my phone clamped to my ear, my heart thundering in my chest. 'I just had Eric on the phone,' I tell her. 'He sounded worse than I've ever heard him. And he said he'd taken some pills. Sleeping pills. He was woozy, slurring his words. And then the line just went dead. Tanvi, fuck, I don't know what to do. What should I do?'

I'm trying to catch my breath but it's like there's something blocking my airway. I take a shaky gulp of water and suck in a lungful of air.

'Tanvi?'

'I'm thinking,' she says.

'Can we track the number? Surely we must be able to do that in these situations?'

'No, the calls come through anonymously,' she says. 'That's why the callers trust us – we have no way of finding out who they are, even if we wanted to.'

I collapse into the rickety office chair. My head is pounding again. I feel like I'm having a panic attack. 'I can't let this happen, Tanvi,' I gasp. 'I just can't. There has to be something we can do.'

More silence. I squeeze my eyes shut, rub my throbbing temples and pray that she can think of something.

'Are you still in the office?' she says finally.

'Yeah.'

'OK. Wait there. I'm leaving work now. I'm coming to pick you up.'

'What, why?'

'I think I know where Eric lives.'

*

Twenty minutes later, I'm jumping into the passenger seat of Tanvi's Citroën Saxo as it pulls up outside the Green Shoots office. 'So, are you going to tell me what the hell's going on?' I ask.

'Put your seatbelt on,' she orders.

I do so, and she pulls away from the kerb fast. Her phone is up on the dashboard, showing Google Maps. The line we're following points east, out of London.

‘Where are we going?’

‘OK, so, I had a call with Eric last year,’ she says, shifting the car into third gear. ‘He mentioned there was a bit of kerfuffle in the street outside because of a parade that was happening that day. You know how he gets about people making noise outside his house?’

I nod as she zooms off the roundabout and onto a dual carriageway. ‘Well, I asked him about it, and he told me: “Oh, it’s a summer street-party thing: the Kirkmond-on-Crouch Parade. They do it here every year.”’

I glance again at her phone. The final destination reads: *Kirkmond-on-Crouch, Essex. Arrival in 46 minutes.*

‘I probably would have forgotten all about it if Eric hadn’t made a point of picking up on it,’ she adds. ‘He said: “Oops, too much information, there! You know where I live now . . .”’ She glances at me quickly and then back at the road. ‘It was such a random name for a place that it stuck in my head.’

For the first time since the line went dead half an hour ago, that queasy sense of despair in my stomach is permeated by a thin beam of hope. ‘So, did he tell you his address?’ I ask.

She overtakes a lorry, and shakes her head. ‘No. But I googled Kirkmond-on-Crouch. It’s a tiny hamlet in Essex. Population: 831.’

The beam of hope dissolves and the queasiness floods back. ‘So, what . . . We’re just going to go to this little village and ask everyone we meet, “Do you know an old man called Eric?” We don’t even know his second name!’

She keeps her voice level and her eyes on the road. ‘If you’ve got a better suggestion,’ she says, ‘let’s hear it.’

CHAPTER FIFTY-EIGHT

ANNIE

12th April
Loxley, Sheffield

'Hello, love.'

As Mum opens the door to me I have to try very hard to hide my shock. I've only seen her over Zoom these past few months – her face always rendered smudgy and out-of-focus by this house's painfully weak Wi-Fi connection. So I never got the impression that she'd changed.

But here, in the flesh . . . it's like I'm looking at a different person. She's got so much thinner. She's wearing the navy-blue Boden cardigan I bought her a couple of Christmases back, but it's baggier on her now. It makes her seem smaller. Her hair – usually full and flowing around her shoulders – is scraped up into a messy bun.

She gives me a crumpled smile and holds her hands out. 'It's so good to see you.'

I step forward and put my arms around her. She feels brittle. Scarily fragile. Like she would break if I held her too tightly.

For a moment, the guilt that surges through me is too much to bear. I know instantly, in this moment, that I'm the one in the wrong. That I should have come back more, made more of an effort.

In my head, it was always easy to justify keeping away. Josie lives in the next village over with her husband, so it's not like Mum's on her own. Plus, she's got tons of friends in the area. What difference would it make if I was here or not?

Right now, though, as I hold her, I realise I was kidding myself. It has made a difference. I can feel the difference it's made. 'It's good to see you, too,' I whisper. 'I'm so sorry it's been so long.'

'Not to worry.' Mum breaks away from the hug and holds me at arm's length. 'Right. You put your case upstairs and I'll get the kettle on. Then you can tell me everything.'

It makes me smile. Mum can't do anything – particularly not a major heart-to-heart – without a strong cup of tea. It's something I've definitely inherited from her.

'OK, I'll just be a sec.'

I carry my case upstairs as she heads through to the kitchen. But as I walk up, the feeling of painful guilt is replaced by a stab of righteous indignation. The staircase is decorated all the way up with framed photos of our family, most of them featuring Dad. Looking into his smiling green eyes again and again, I remember quite clearly why I've not been able to come back here. Why I'm still angry.

She just let him give up. If she'd listened to me – if Josie had listened to me – he might still be here.

I wheel my suitcase along the soft carpet of the upstairs corridor. Everywhere you turn, the house reminds you that he's not in it. Every room has a hole at its centre: an empty space where he should be.

At the end of the corridor is what used to be my and Josie's childhood bedroom. I walk in and look around, my stomach lurching at the Blu Tack stains on the walls from long-torn-down posters, and the glow-in-the-dark stars still stuck to the ceiling. This is where I stayed in those final, awful weeks, when it became clear the third bout of chemo wasn't working and Dad's condition took a drastic downhill plummet. I'd spend all day at the hospital and all night in here. Unable to sleep, I would lie staring at the ceiling, the pillow hot and damp from my tears, as I tried to pick out the constellation shapes Dad had laid out for us as kids – the Big Dipper, Orion, Andromeda.

In the kitchen downstairs, I can hear the clink and rustle of Mum making tea. Memories flood back of Dad cooking us breakfast there when we were growing up. He still wanted to do it, right up until the very end. Josie and I would have to wrestle the pan off him. 'What's the point?' he'd say grumpily as we sat him down. 'What's the point, if I can't even make my own daughters pancakes?'

It was hard to see the point of anything at that time.

I leave my suitcase by the door, and walk back down the landing towards Mum and Dad's bedroom. *Mum's* bedroom. With its half-lived-in bed: one side of the duvet rumpled, the other untouched. I notice that Mum still lays two pillows out on Dad's side, as if he might just come back and slide under the covers next to her, like nothing ever happened.

The nightstand on Dad's side, which used to be a chaotic, overgrown jungle of dog-eared books, magazines and papers, is now completely bare.

Two doors down is Dad's study. A little box room at the back of the house, this is where he would retreat to fire off letters to *Private Eye* about local council skulduggery, or even – he'd once told me after a couple of drinks – where he'd still occasionally dabble with his own fiction writing.

This was his room. And it's the strangest of the lot because it's *exactly* the same.

He's been gone more than a year now, and Mum hasn't touched it. It's like she's not even been in here. The wonky shelves lined with his books – Ray Bradbury and Shirley Jackson and Ursula Le Guin – the knackered old iMac on the desk, the huge metal filing cabinet, filled with decades-old bank statements. It's like some sort of weird shrine to him.

But then, what's the alternative? Clear all this stuff away and chuck it in a skip? Stick everything in boxes and head to the charity shop? That would be sad and strange and unacceptable, too.

That's the problem when someone dies: there are no right answers. Every option is the wrong one.

'Oh, here you are.'

I turn to see Mum in the doorway, holding two mugs of tea.

She looks around the study like she'd forgotten it was a room in her own house. 'I thought you were unpacking your stuff in the bedroom?'

'Thanks,' I say, taking one of the cups from her. 'There's not much to unpack, really.'

'Are you only up for the weekend, then?' She frowns. 'I thought you might stay longer?'

'You might regret that offer when Maya boots me out and I have to come and live with you permanently.'

'Oh, sweetheart,' she says, cupping the mug in both hands. 'Tell me what happened, then. With Dom?'

I sit down in Dad's office chair. 'Well, we—'

'Not in here,' Mum says quickly. 'Let's go downstairs. Talk properly.'

'Why can't we talk in here?'

She glances around at Dad's books. 'It's just not the proper place for a chat, Annie.'

The words spark a sense memory. In the hospital, towards the very end. I'd been up all night, looking into clinical trials for new cancer drugs – I'd even found a private clinic in Greece that had availability immediately. Dad was in that half-asleep-half-awake limbo state and I was desperately trying to talk to Mum about the clinic, make her see that there was still hope. But she just sat there clasping his hand, shaking her head and muttering: *This isn't the proper place to talk about this, Annie.*

In that moment, it all comes rushing back. The frustration. The fear. The fury at her . . . *passivity.* How could she just sit there and let it happen, when there were other options? I'd *found* other options.

'It's never the proper place or the proper time, is it?'

The comment comes out sharper than I intended and shame stabs me in the stomach again. Mum sighs and looks down at the carpet. 'Please, Annie,' she says quietly. 'Can we not?'

I stay rooted to the chair, suddenly fully ready for a fight. 'Not what?'

'You're not the only one that lost him,' she mutters. 'You're not the only one that misses him.'

I try to keep my voice calm and measured. 'It felt like I was the only one who was losing him at the time, Mum. You and Josie just . . .'

She looks up from the carpet and meets my gaze. Her eyes are hard and shining. 'We just what?'

'You just wouldn't *listen* to me.' I can feel the tears coming already. The pressure building behind my eyes. 'I felt like I was the only one fighting for him when you'd both given up.'

She doesn't react with anger, as I was afraid she might. She just squeezes her eyes shut and shakes her head. She looks tired. 'Is that really what you think happened?'

'Well, what *did* happen?'

Her eyes are open again, burning into me. 'That clinic in Greece . . . Every doctor in the hospital was telling us it was too late, there was nothing to be done.'

'But how did they *know*? Why wouldn't you even let us *try*?' I swipe at my eyes with my sleeve. The tears are coming now. My hands balling into fists. God, I *knew* this would happen. This was why I was afraid of coming back here. I knew I wouldn't be able to stop it all spilling out of me.

Mum puts a hand to the doorframe to steady herself. She can't even step into the room. *His* room. 'Annie, I don't want to get into all this again,' she mutters. 'I just can't.'

Anger pulses through me – tinged with guilt at the sight of her frail body in the doorway. Anger and guilt. That's all I ever feel in this house now: anger and guilt. That's why I don't come back. 'You didn't want to get into it at the time, either.'

'Well, can you blame me?' she says, letting go of the frame. 'My husband was dying and you wanted to tell me a load of nonsense.'

In that moment, the guilt dissolves. The anger wins.

'*Nonsense*?' I hiss. 'It wasn't *nonsense*, Mum. It was a way to save his life!'

She shakes her head sadly. 'You were the only one that ever believed that, love.'

'Maybe because I was the only one who actually gave a shit!'

She stares at me, open-mouthed, eyes blazing. 'How dare you say that?'

I don't really know *what* I'm saying. I know I should take it back, but I don't. 'See, this is why I was afraid to come back,' I tell her. 'Because I knew I'd say something I regretted.'

Before I can decide what to do or say next, my body makes the decision for me.

'Where are you going?' Mum demands, moving aside as I stomp past her.

'This was a mistake. I'm sorry.'

'Annie!'

Without another word, I walk down the stairs, past all the framed photos of my smiling father, and straight out of the house.

CHAPTER FIFTY-NINE

WILL

12th April
Kirkmond-on-Crouch, Essex

By the time Tanvi's phone instructs her to come off at the next exit for Kirkmond-on-Crouch, my fingernails have all been bitten right down to the skin.

We've spent most of the journey zooming along the motorway in silence – a silence punctuated only occasionally by Tanvi fielding calls from her husband about what to cook the kids for dinner, or muttering something vaguely optimistic at me, along the lines of: 'Don't worry, Will,' or 'We'll find him, I'm sure.'

I am less sure. The way I see it, the only reason Eric calls Green Shoots is that he has zero interaction with the outside world. He doesn't seem to know anybody, and nobody seems to know him. It doesn't matter how tiny this town's population is if he never leaves the house.

But as Tanvi pointed out, I don't have any better suggestions. So, here we are.

It's coming up to six now and the sun is beginning to dip

in the clear blue sky as we pass a sign that reads, 'You are now entering Kirkmond-on-Crouch'. I feel my chest tighten. The chances of us leaving this place with good news suddenly seem horribly, impossibly slim. If we don't find Eric – the most likely outcome – then I'll spend the next few weeks and months waiting desperately for him to call. And if he doesn't call, then this queasy dread – this not-knowing – may well be with me forever.

On the other hand, what if we do find him and it's already too late? I'm not sure I would be able to survive that either.

Tanvi slows down as we enter what appears to be the town's main road – row after row of identical terraced houses, interspersed with the odd mini market. 'What do we do?' I wonder aloud. 'Just start asking people?'

Tanvi pulls over by the side of the road and turns to me. 'I guess there's no other option.'

She winds her window down as a young mum walks past with her two kids in tow. 'Excuse me, love,' Tanvi says with a smile. 'Sorry to bother you. We're looking for a man who lives in this village. His name's Eric, he's probably in his sixties. Do you know him?'

The woman shakes her head. 'Afraid I don't, sorry.'

Tanvi winds her window back up as the woman walks away.

'We could just start knocking on doors?' I suggest.

'We'll be here all night,' she mutters. 'Let's go a little further.' She starts the car and we keep driving. Turning left at a little stone war memorial by a pub, there's a Post Office. A man is stood outside, with his back to us, locking the doors.

'Worth a shot?' Tanvi says.

'Definitely.'

She pulls up outside the Post Office and we both get out. 'Excuse me?' Tanvi waves at the man, who smiles brightly at us. 'We were just wondering if you could help us?'

'What is it you're after?' he says, coming towards us.

'We're looking for a man we think lives in this village. A chap called Eric.'

'Eric, Eric . . .' The postman wrinkles his nose in thought. 'You've not got a surname?'

'Afraid not. He'd be in his late sixties, I think?'

The postman exhales through his mouth.

'If there's anything you can do to help us, it would be massively appreciated,' I tell him.

He scratches his grey-tinted beard and eyes me cautiously. 'Well . . . I'm not sure I could tell you, even if I did know this bloke. I can't go around giving out addresses willy-nilly.'

I nod. 'Of course. We totally understand. Thanks a lot.'

I turn back towards the car. But Tanvi stays put.

'I'm sorry, but . . . We've come from London because we're really, really worried about this man. There's a chance that something bad has happened to him, there's a chance his life is in danger, and we know for a fact that he doesn't have any friends or family.'

The postman examines her, the creases in his forehead deepening. 'What are you two, then, if you're not friends or family?'

I glance at Tanvi, but she keeps her gaze firmly on the postman. 'We volunteer for a charity. A crisis helpline called Green Shoots. Eric is a regular caller, and something happened on a call earlier today that gives us reason to believe he might be in danger. He mentioned taking several sleeping pills. We've been speaking to Eric for years. We really care about him. We just need to know that he's OK. He doesn't have anyone else.'

The postman looks at her, then at me, his jaw clenching and unclenching. 'I'm sorry. I am. But I can't give out people's addresses.'

Tanvi nods. 'I understand.' She turns to me. 'OK, Will, let's start knocking on doors.'

She starts the engine as we get back in the car. 'We'll take a door each,' she tells me. 'Starting from the top of that main road.'

'OK.'

Before she can pull away, there's a knock on the window. The postman's face is there, wrinkled with concern. 'You seem like decent people,' he says slowly. 'I hope I'm not making a mistake here.' It's like he's talking more to himself than to us.

'I promise you,' Tanvi says softly. 'We just want to know if he's all right.'

The postman nods and swallows. 'You can probably guess by the size of the village that my post round is not the biggest. So, you do tend to remember names. There's the odd letter comes through for a "Mr E. Sinclair". They usually look like bills. I don't know if it's this Eric chap you're after, but I suppose it might be. He's at 38 Galton Road. I can show you if you like?'

He climbs into the seat behind Tanvi, and she pulls away from the kerb. My breathing is ragged again suddenly. I have to wind the window down to gulp the air coming through. For a second I think I might be sick. Tanvi glances at me as she drives. 'You all right, Will?'

I nod.

'Just here,' the postman says.

Tanvi brings the car to a standstill outside one of the terraced houses. It looks identical to every other house we've passed in Kirkmond-on-Crouch: so nondescript as to resemble a child's drawing of a house. Two floors, four front windows, a red slate roof with a little chimney poking out of the top. The curtains are all closed. There's no visible sign of life.

The door pushed open, with a body behind it.

My stomach knots and pulses. I can't do this. I can't see this.

But I'm getting out of the car with them. I'm following them through the rusty front gate and up to the mustard-yellow front door.

'OK,' says Tanvi. 'So . . .'

She ends the sentence there, letting it hang in the air unfinished, and just continues to stare at the door. Then she looks at me and nods. I watch as my arm reaches out and presses the doorbell.

For a few seconds, there's nothing: only the sound of my heart galloping.

'Eric?' Tanvi shouts. 'Eric, it's Tanv—' She breaks off and turns to me. 'What's your safe name?'

'Jack.'

'It's Sita and Jack,' she yells through the door. 'From Green Shoots! We're just checking you're OK.'

We wait. Nothing.

'It might not even be him,' the postman says quietly.

Tanvi thumps the door with her fist. 'Eric!'

Still nothing. I hear the postman shift on the gravel path behind me. 'He may not be home.'

My stomach lurches again. What if he *is* home and he's not answering? That would only mean one thing . . .

I have to know if he's OK. I have to. The not-knowing would kill me. If there's any chance we can help him, I have to take it.

Tanvi steps back from the door and sighs. I glance at the ground. There are several large stones the size of dinner plates marking out the border of the path. They look heavy.

'I'm sorry,' I hear myself say to the postman. 'I'll pay for this.'

Before he can ask what I'm on about, I reach down to pick up a stone. It is heavy. I need both hands as I lug it towards the window beside the front door.

'Will, what—' is as far as Tanvi gets before the splash of shattered glass drowns her out.

For a second there is just stunned silence. I look down at my hands, sparkling with flecks of glass, barely able to believe what I've just done. Judging by the looks on the faces of Tanvi and the postman, they can't quite fathom it either.

Finally, the postman finds his voice. 'I'm calling the police!' he shouts, fumbling for his phone.

I hear doors opening on the houses around us, see heads poking out, staring at me. I lurch forward, no longer really in control of what I'm doing. I pick up the stone from the windowsill and use it to swipe the glass from the edges of the frame. And then I clamber through.

The room is dark and smells like it hasn't been aired in weeks. I can hear the postman talking to the police outside. I fumble for a light switch and as soon as I find it, I open the front door. I'm staring at Tanvi, but she's looking behind me, into the room.

'Eric!'

She tears past me and falls onto a figure slumped on the sofa.

The door pushed open, with a body behind it.

'Eric! Can you hear me?' Tanvi is shaking the figure now. I still can't quite see his face. I can see his arm, dangling limply from the edge of the sofa, the fingers brushing the top of an empty pill bottle. The handset of a landline phone lies next to it on the floor.

I have to grab the mantelpiece to hold myself steady. The postman steps into the room, open-mouthed, his phone still pressed to his ear.

'Ambulance!' Tanvi yells at him. 'Get a fucking ambulance!'

'Yes . . . Yes,' he sputters. His face is ghostly white. Into the phone he says: 'Ambulance, we need an ambulance. Now. 38 Galton Road.'

'Eric!' Tanvi screams. She turns to look at me, her face alive with terror. 'Will! Come here! Help me!'

But I can't come. I can't help. I'm not even here. I'm in Paris, five years ago, stood in the doorway of a hotel room, watching my best friend die.

CHAPTER SIXTY

ANNIE

12th April
Loxley, Sheffield

I'm not even sure where I'm walking.

Since storming out of the house, I've just been turning street corners at random, my head pounding and the blood thundering in my ears.

Nonsense.

That was actually what she called it. The minute the doctors told us there was 'nothing more to be done', I had spent every waking hour on the internet, trying to prove them wrong. Trying to show everyone that there *was* still hope. It took me all day, calling various specialists at that Greek clinic, having the same stilted conversations in broken English as I explained Dad's situation over and over again. And then printing out all those pages from their site because I knew Mum would never look at it all on a phone screen. I knew it was a long shot. Of course it was. Wasn't it worth at least considering, though? But no one even listened to me. They all just shrugged and dismissed it. *Nonsense.*

I turn the corner, scrubbing away the tears that are still falling down my cheeks. When is this going to be over? When am I going to stop feeling like this – so angry, all the time? I feel it in my *bones*.

I should have got more time with him. He should still be here.

The pain is only exacerbated by the fact that everything in this tiny town reminds me of him. Every street, every tree, every shop conjures some memory of a time with Dad.

I realise with a jolt that the road I'm walking down will take me straight to the high street. I'm bound to bump into someone I know there, and to be honest I'm not overly keen on the idea of making small talk with an old primary school acquaintance while tears stream down my face. So, instead, I take a left turn down a smaller side street that leads under the railway bridge, not even thinking about where it comes out.

Which is why, when I spot the park on the other side, the nostalgia is so sudden, so strong that it actually stops me in my tracks. The black iron railings, the graffitied benches, the huge beech tree right in the centre. This place was the site of so many picnics and birthday parties throughout my childhood. But what really stands out is the treasure hunt.

It was one dreary weekend, decades back – Josie and I must have been about eight and ten – and Mum and Dad decided out of nowhere to conjure us up an adventure. They worked up an elaborately detailed map of Loxley, featuring clues and crosses and pathways, and then Dad ran all over town, hiding little toys and sweets and presents where the X's were.

It was *so* much fun. The four of us racing through the village: Josie and I squealing with delight whenever we cracked a clue or found a piece of 'treasure'. But the best bit came right at the very end of the day. The final 'X' marked the exact spot I'm now standing on, directly underneath the huge beech tree. I sit down, resting my back against the gnarled trunk, and touch the grass either side of me.

Josie and I dug away at this spot with our garishly coloured beach spades – searching for what we later learned were two bags of Haribo. After a while, though, we'd still not found anything, and Dad grabbed another spade, muttering: 'I know I buried those ruddy things *somewhere* around here . . .'

As it turned out, he'd not marked his burial site clearly enough, and despite digging countless holes under this tree, we simply couldn't find the sweets. Far from being disappointing, it was easily the best, funniest part of the whole afternoon. Mum eventually joined in, too, and the four of us sat laughing and digging in the shade of the hanging branches, spinning stories about how future civilisations would uncover two mysterious bags here in a thousand years' time, and wonder what on earth their ancestors used these 'Tangfastics' for.

Just before we gave up and headed home – Haribo-less yet happy – we asked a passer-by to take a photo of us. It must still be in the house somewhere, though I haven't seen it in years. Josie and me are at the front, pointing in mock-despair at all the fruitless holes we've dug, with Mum and Dad behind us, squeezing hands, looking not at the camera but at each other. The last time I saw the photo, it was that look between them – the smile they were sharing – that stuck out. There was this quiet triumph to it: the joy at having created this brilliant day together for their kids. They looked like such a . . . *team*.

I feel a sudden spasm of shame as I think about what I said

to Mum back in Dad's study. The look on her face when I told her I was the only one that cared about him. Of course I wasn't.

I hear the squeal of the park gate, and before I even turn around I know it will be her.

She walks towards me slowly, her eyes red and a little damp, hands thrust deep into the pockets of her coat. 'Looking for those Haribos?' she says. 'Any luck?'

'Nope.'

'That was a fun day, wasn't it?'

'Yeah, it was.'

'Do you mind if I join you down there?'

She places one hand on the tree trunk, and automatically I take her other one, helping her to the ground. As she settles beside me on the grass, she squeezes my fingers gently before she puts her hand back in her pocket.

'How did you know I'd come here?'

'I didn't,' she says. 'I bumped into Jane Collier while I was looking for you, and she said she'd just seen you heading under the railway bridge.'

An involuntary laugh escapes me. 'Impossible to hide in this bloody town.'

'It is that.'

We sit in silence for a moment as I try to assemble the right words for the apology I owe her. But before I can, she turns to me: 'I'm sorry for what I said, love. It wasn't nonsense, that clinic. I apologise for saying that, I didn't mean it.'

I nod. 'Thank you. I'm sorry for saying you didn't care. That was stupid and wrong and I didn't mean it either.'

She pats my knee softly. 'I appreciate that. And for what it's worth, you're wrong about me not listening to you, not taking the clinic stuff seriously. I did take it seriously. I asked every doctor in the hospital, and they all told me the same thing: it would cost us hundreds of thousands of pounds and it *wouldn't work*.'

I cover my face with my hands. I remember her telling me all this at the time. But I was so blinded by rage at the injustice of what was happening to Dad . . . It was like I couldn't process anything. It was like I had blinkers on. All I heard was her telling me to give up on him.

'You think your dad was well enough to get on a *plane* at that point, Annie?' she adds. 'Have you forgotten what he was like in those last few weeks? In so much pain he could barely sleep . . .' I shut my eyes against the image those words conjure – those nightmarish final days. 'You wanted it to work so badly,' she says, 'you lost sight of whether it actually would.'

'I just didn't want to lose him,' I whisper through my hands.

'And what about your father? What do you think he wanted?'

I blink and look up at her. 'What do you mean?'

'You think he wanted to go on like that? Chemo after chemo after chemo, getting thinner and weaker, gradually losing more of himself every time. He didn't want to live like that, Annie.'

I watch my tears fall onto the knees of my jeans. Tiny drops that bloom and spread as they hit the denim.

I hear Mum swallow hard. When she speaks again, her voice is gentler. 'He couldn't take any more of it, love. He told me, so many times, towards the end. And I didn't want him to go through any more of it either. I wanted him to have some peace. The hospitals, the chemo, the pills . . . I just wanted all that horrible *fucking shit* to be over for him.'

The words make me physically flinch. I don't think I've

ever heard Mum swear. She once grounded Josie when we were kids for saying 'boobs' at the dinner table. Her teeth are gritted now. She's wearing a look of raw anger I've not seen on her face before.

'You think I don't miss him?' she says with a strangled sob. 'You think I don't wake up every morning wondering how I'll get through the day without him?'

'Mum . . . I'm sorry.' The sight of her crying is almost too much to bear. 'I was just so angry. So angry that it was happening to him. I still am. I knew it would break me if he died. And it has broken me, Mum. It's like I can't . . .'

I don't get the chance to finish my sentence. Mum pulls me into her, folds her arms around me. It's a *real* hug, this time – not the clumsy, awkward embrace we had at the front door earlier. Wrapped in her arms, I am suddenly ten years old again. My mum. Oh my God, I've missed her.

'I'm sorry, Mum, I'm so, so sorry.' I repeat the words over and over into her shoulder.

'I'm sorry, too, love,' she sniffs. 'I should have made you feel listened to. Everything you did, I know you only did it because you were terrified of losing him. I was, too. So was Josie. We just had different ways of showing it, I suppose. Josie's like me, and you're like your father. You always have been.'

We stay like that a little longer, our arms around each other, sobbing softly under the beech tree. Until finally the sobs run out. I feel exhausted – emotionally drained – but for the first time in a long time, I don't feel angry. That tight knot of rage that's lived for so long in my chest seems to have loosened now. I pull back and for a moment we both smile at each other in silence.

Mum takes out a tissue and blows her nose. 'I hate going in that room,' she says suddenly. 'His little office. It reminds me too much of him. I know I should do something – sort through all that stuff – but I just can't face it.'

I nod. 'I get that.'

She sniffs and puts the tissue back in her pocket. 'So, are you going to tell me, then?' she asks. 'About Dom?'

I shrug. I suddenly don't feel I have the energy to get into Posh Clare and all the rest of it. 'There's not much to tell. It just wasn't working. It hasn't been for a long time.'

She wrinkles her forehead. 'Are you OK, though, love?'

'I think so,' I tell her. 'It's funny – it's not even the thought of losing him that I'm really sad about. It's more the terror of being on my own. I'm 31 and single and living in my best friend's spare room.' I close my eyes and press my fingers gently into my eyelids. 'I just feel like I had a plan for where my life was going, and now it's fallen to pieces.'

'Well, that's OK,' Mum says softly. 'I certainly didn't have a plan when I was your age.'

'Really? It always seemed to me like you did. Get married, get Dad to stop mucking about with his writing and find a proper job, then—'

She interrupts me with a raised index finger. 'Excuse me. I didn't "get" your father to stop writing. That was his idea.'

'It was?'

'Yes. I rather liked him writing, truth be told. But we both knew we wanted a family, and we weren't sure our respective passions could fund that. So we had to be realistic. And your father was very happy in his job. It didn't stop him reading and writing and doing everything else he loved in his spare time, and it also meant we could give you and Josie a decent childhood.'

I kick at the turf with my foot. This is a lot of new information to take in. 'You said your "respective passions". What was your passion?'

Mum bristles slightly. 'If you must know, I always fancied myself as a painter.'

I blink at her. 'Mum, you've literally never mentioned painting once.'

She looks mortally offended. 'I never missed *Watercolour Challenge*!'

'So? I never miss *Married at First Sight*, doesn't mean I want to shag a total stranger.'

She snorts with laughter at that. 'God, it's good to have you home, love.'

'It's good to be home. I'm sorry it's taken so long.'

She nudges my knee with hers. 'I've started giving it a go, actually – the painting lark. I've even started taking life drawing classes!'

'Seriously? Mum, that's brilliant.'

'Yes, it is rather fun.' She drops her voice to a whisper, even though we're the only people in the park. 'Although, it's slightly embarrassing, too. Turns out our nude model is Geoff Hobbes from the butcher's in town. I don't know where to look now when I go in for my chops.'

'Wow. That is really not an image I wanted in my head.'

'No,' says Mum, laughing. 'Let's go home, shall we?'

I nod. I stand first, and then help her up.

'You'll be OK, love,' Mum tells me, brushing the back of her trousers off. 'You know that, don't you? This thing with Dom. You'll be OK.'

'I hope so,' I say. 'But it's funny – even as we were breaking up, I could hear this little voice in my head telling me to shut up. Saying, "If you let this relationship go, you'll always be on your own".'

'Annie . . .' She places her hands on my shoulders and kisses me gently on the forehead. 'You're not on your own.'

CHAPTER SIXTY-ONE

WILL

12th April
Kirkmond-on-Crouch, Essex

'It's OK, Will. It's going to be OK.'

I don't think Tanvi is even aware she's saying it. She's just murmuring it to herself over and over, like a mantra, her hands clamped to the steering wheel, her eyes fixed on the road ahead.

In front of us, the ambulance tears down the dual carriageway, siren on, blue lights flashing, carrying Eric.

Eric's body.

I flinch in the passenger seat. Can't think like that.

It's OK, Will. It's going to be OK.

Since I put that stone through the window, it's like everything has been happening in stop motion. One minute I was slumped against the wall in Eric's front room, waiting for the ambulance, too scared to go and look at him. The next, the postman was helping me into Tanvi's car, telling me he'd deal with the broken window. And now: pulling into the hospital car park, following the stretcher down a strip-lit hallway, trying to keep the memories from flooding my brain.

I still haven't seen Eric's face. I have no idea what he looks like.

Finally we reach a door we can't follow him through. As he is led into an operating room, a nurse with a kind smile sits Tanvi and me down on a hard, plastic bench in the corridor. 'We're going to pump his stomach,' she says.

We just nod dumbly.

'We'll let you know his condition as soon as we can.'

'Thank you,' Tanvi croaks.

The nurse gestures further down the corridor. 'There's a more comfortable waiting area just through there if you'd rather?'

'I think we're OK here,' Tanvi says. 'Thank you again.'

The nurse smiles and leaves us.

We sit in silence for a few seconds, listening to the sound of distant footsteps and the beep of invisible machines.

'I'm sorry,' I mutter. 'I should have been more help back there.'

Tanvi shakes her head. 'What are you on about, Will? You were *amazing*. If you hadn't smashed that window, we might have been too late.'

We might still be too late. The thought hangs in the air between us – unspoken. There's another thought, too. One I'd also rather leave unsaid. But I can't. I have to know.

'Tanvi?'

'Yeah?'

'How did you know?'

She looks at me. 'How did I know what?'

I swallow. My voice feels thick in my throat. 'How did you know that calls to Green Shoots come in anonymously? That we can't track them?'

She blinks and rubs her forehead. 'Because I've had cases before where callers have sounded suicidal and I've asked Marie about tracing the numbers. But she said it wasn't possible. Why?'

I cover my face with my hands. 'I can't let this happen, Tanvi. I can't let this happen again.'

Silence. Even though I can't see her, I can feel her eyes on me. 'What do you mean "again"?' she says.

'I never told you why I volunteer at Green Shoots, did I?'

'No.'

I rub my eyes and turn to look at her. 'My friend used to call the line. My best friend.'

She is watching me carefully. 'OK . . .'

'I never knew. I only found out after he died.'

It's like saying the words out loud has poleaxed me. Suddenly I'm shaking, jagged sobs coming out of my mouth.

'Oh God, Will . . .' Tanvi pulls me into her, wrapping an arm tightly around my shoulder. 'I'm so sorry. What was his name?' she whispers.

'Joe.'

I hear her breath catch in her throat. Her grip on my shoulder tightens. 'He'd have been about your age? Same sort of accent?'

I nod. She pulls away, staring at me. She looks almost frightened.

'I spoke to him, Will. It must have been him.'

A strange, strangled sound escapes me. It's as if my body is being pulled apart from all angles.

'Funny boy?' Tanvi says. 'Quite shy? Really into his music?'

I press both hands to my boiling face.

Tanvi is crying now, too, I think. 'Oh God, Will, I didn't know. He was such a lovely lad. I used to look forward to his calls. He was a regular for years, just like Eric. But one day he stopped calling, and . . .'

As her voice breaks, mine returns. The words come spilling out of me, breathless and ragged. 'We were in Paris. I was in a band and he'd come over to see us play. I knew he'd been a bit down lately, so I tried to cheer him up – get him to come out and explore the city with me. But he didn't want to. He just said he'd rather be alone. I tried calling him and he didn't pick up. But I should have *kept* calling: I should have tried harder. I never should have left him on his own. I didn't know how serious it was, he'd never told me . . .'

I'm shaking harder now, struggling to go on. Tanvi grabs my hand. 'It's OK, Will. You don't have to talk about this if you don't want to.'

I shake my head violently. I *do* want to. It's painful, but I can feel that I need it. It's like cutting out a growth: something that's been gnawing inside me, poisoning me, for years.

'He never answered the phone,' I tell her. 'And then, that night, he didn't show up to the gig either. I was freaking out afterwards, we just couldn't get hold of him. We tried knocking on his hotel room, but there was no answer. So we got someone from the hotel to open it, and . . .'

The door pushed open, a body behind it.

'It's OK, it's OK,' Tanvi whispers as I dissolve in her arms. Joe's body, behind the door. My memory goes blank after that moment. It's like it's been wiped. But I keep talking. I tell

Tanvi that the next thing I remember is being at the hospital. I can't even remember if Jess or Sim or the others were there, too. They must have been, surely? The French doctor told me there was no way of knowing whether it was intentional. Joe was on so many pills – prescription drugs, anti-depressants, sleeping tablets – that mixing them even with a small amount of alcohol, not to mention the anti-pain medicine he was secretly taking, could have triggered the heart failure.

But what if he knew that? What if that's *why* he did it?

Tanvi squeezes me tighter as the tears keep coming. 'And then a few weeks later,' I gasp, 'I was helping his mum cancel all his bank stuff and his phone bill, and I noticed he'd been calling this one number over and over again, for years.'

'Green Shoots,' she murmurs.

I nod. 'I wasn't there for him. I let him down. But I thought maybe, if I signed up for the helpline he used to call, I could be there for others like him.' I draw in a painful, jagged breath. 'But it doesn't change the fact that it's my fault. He's dead because of me.'

Tanvi sighs deeply and pulls away from the hug. My gaze drops automatically to the floor. 'Will. You can't say that. It's just not true.'

I shrug. I just feel numb now. Like I've cried myself empty. 'I could have saved him.'

'Maybe. Maybe not.' She places her hand over mine. 'But think of all the others you've saved since.'

CHAPTER SIXTY-TWO

ANNIE

12th April
Loxley, Sheffield

'I'm not sure about this, girls,' Mum says. 'I'm having second thoughts suddenly.'

My sister Josie looks up from the box of tattered paperbacks she's sorting through. 'Mum, we've started now, so we might as well finish.'

'I feel silly, that's all,' Mum sighs. 'I don't need my own "art studio", do I? Who do we think I am: Picasso?'

I catch Josie's eye, and we both grin. 'I actually see you more as Loxley's answer to Andy Warhol,' I tell Mum. 'And this room,' I gesture around Dad's study, 'will be your Factory.'

Mum chuckles and shakes her head, apparently satisfied by this, and the three of us get back to work.

This whole thing had been my idea. After learning about Mum's secret passion for painting – and finding out that Josie had also been on at her to do something about Dad's study – the thought occured to me: this room had been Dad's writing nook, why couldn't we turn it into Mum's art studio?

It would be a two-birds-with-one-stone project: we'd finally sort through all Dad's stuff properly – safely store the important bits, clean out the not-so-important bits – and then convert this space from a stale, sombre relic of the past to a clean, bright portal to the future.

Mum liked the concept – or maybe she just liked the idea of the three of us doing something together – so now Josie's here, and the Lucas family are in full *Grand Designs* mode.

As soon as Josie arrived, two hours ago, I think she could sense something was different. As we opened the door, I saw her eyes go to Mum first. And Mum smiled back at her – an unspoken signal that things had been said, and everything was clearer. Brighter. I didn't speak either – I just stepped forward and pulled Josie into a hug. I could feel her shock – her body stiffening as I wrapped my arms around her. It had been so long since we'd really hugged like this. But after a moment I felt her relax and she hugged me back even harder.

She was eager to ask about Dom, find out exactly what happened. But I just told her what I told Mum: that I was OK, and I didn't really want to talk about it. Not right now, anyway. So, we all went through to the kitchen, drank wine and ate pasta. And then the idea about transforming Dad's study into Mum's studio hit me, and we took our plates and glasses and migrated up here.

'He was such a hoarder, honestly,' Josie laughs as she grabs yet another dusty cardboard box from the top of the bookshelf. 'Who keeps cinema ticket stubs from twenty-odd years ago?'

'He was like that, your dad,' Mum says fondly.

Josie pulls out a ticket at random. 'I don't know why, but I can't picture him going to see *Judge Dredd*.'

Mum peers at the date on the stub. 'You were both screaming toddlers at the time: I imagine he just wanted to get out of the house.'

I'm sat cross-legged on the floor across from them, rifling through another box. 'I can't believe he kept all these postcards I sent you on my gap year,' I say, holding up a bunch of them. 'One from every city me and Maya visited.'

Josie tuts at me. 'You're such a swot, I can't believe you sent *postcards* on your gap year. You were supposed be getting drunk and copping off with random Swedish boys.'

'Oh, I did that, too.'

'Annie Pia Lucas,' Mum says mock-sternly. Hearing my middle name immediately makes me think of Will. I'm half-wondering if maybe I should tell them about him, when Josie holds up her box and shrieks: 'Oh God. I've found his airplane sick-bag collection.'

This causes the three of us to convulse into hysterics. Josie spreads out the thirty or forty crinkled (and thankfully unused) paper sick bags on the floor, all bearing the names of different airlines.

'I'd forgotten all about that,' I say. 'Every time you got a flight anywhere, you had to make sure you brought him back a sick bag.'

'Seriously, Mum,' Josie asks. 'How and why did he start doing this?'

Mum wipes her eyes, her smile wider than I've seen it in so, so long. 'We went on a plane for the first time together – to Italy, must've been '78 or '79. We were both so excited about it that your father kept everything as a memento, from the luggage tickets to the bloody sick bag. I thought it was so funny, so sweet. The next time I went on a plane, I brought him back another sick bag, as a joke, and it went from there.'

'Well, we're definitely not throwing these away,' I say, looking down at the ridiculous collection – a visual representation of my brilliant Dad's eccentricity, laid out for all to see.

'I'm not sure I want to throw any of it away,' Mum says.

I squeeze her shoulder. 'We don't have to. We can keep it all if you like – even the *Judge Dredd* ticket stubs. But it'll feel better to organise it properly into boxes, and put them up in the attic. Clear a bit of space in here for your Andy Warhol Factory.'

Mum and Josie laugh, and I leap up to my feet, suddenly feeling full of inspiration. 'We can move the desk and computer out, and you can have an easel there, by the window, Mum.'

Josie jumps up next to me. 'Yeah – and we'll paint the walls! Yellow, maybe, or something brighter than this dreary grey.'

'A big bunch of flowers on the table over there, a mixture of your and Dad's favourite books on the shelves.' I smile at Mum. 'It's going to be brilliant – I can see it now.'

I really can, too. Mum beams up at us from the carpet, which is covered with papers, letters, photos and books, as well as our three empty pasta plates and wine glasses: remnants of our evening in here, laughing and reminiscing.

It's the first time I can remember the three of us being in this room together. It's the first time in a long time I can remember having *fun* in this house.

'I think Dad would have liked this idea,' I say.

'I do too,' says Josie.

I point to a blank spot of wall above the computer. 'And

there,' I say to Mum, 'we can hang the *pièce de résistance*: your life-sized watercolour of a naked Geoff from the butcher's.'

Mum bursts out laughing and Josie groans: 'Oh God, don't.'

'I've got a better idea, actually,' Mum says. She's been sorting through one of Dad's shoeboxes full of photos, and she hauls herself up from the floor, holding one in her hand.

'I was thinking I might get this picture blown up and framed.'

She holds the photo against the wall so we can see it. And there it is: Josie and me beneath that huge beech tree, pointing in mock-despair at dozens of shallow holes in the ground. Mum and Dad behind us, squeezing hands, sharing a quietly triumphant smile. The memory slams up against me again – but it's not just sadness that swells in my chest this time. There is light in there, too.

Josie leans into me and I put my arm around her waist.

'Perfect,' I say, and Mum's smile stretches even wider.

For some reason, I think of Will again. I remember telling him, maybe the first or second time we spoke, that I've always felt like there was an unspoken divide in our family: Mum and Josie on one side, me and Dad on the other.

But now, as Mum comes across to pull both of us into another tight hug, it really feels like we're all on the same team.

CHAPTER SIXTY-THREE

WILL

12th April
Southend-on-Sea, Essex

The corridor is still empty. The machines beep softly behind the closed doors either side of me. Around the corner, I can hear Tanvi's voice. She's calling her husband, explaining everything, telling him she'll be home late.

I look up at the large white clock on the wall. It's nearly 9 p.m. now. Just over four hours since I took that call from Eric. It feels a lot longer. As for me, I don't really know *what* I feel right now. Exhausted, mainly.

It was so freeing to finally say those things out loud. To tell the truth about what happened to Joe. But it also brought it all rushing back in high definition: the guilt, the terror, the anger. I don't suppose I'll ever stop feeling responsible for what happened. And now I'm sat here, in another hospital, waiting to find out if it's happened again.

The soft pad of footsteps from the end of the corridor tells me Tanvi is coming back. As she rounds the corner, a door opens and the nurse with the kind smile re-emerges. She's still wearing that kind smile. Surely she wouldn't be smiling unless . . .

'He's stable,' she tells us. 'Very frail. But stable.'

'Oh my God.' Relief buckles me. I slump forward in my seat, pressing the heels of my hands into my eyes.

'Thank you,' I hear Tanvi tell the nurse. 'Thank you so much.'

'Would you like to see him?' she responds.

I look up, meeting Tanvi's gaze. I know we're thinking the same thing: how exactly will a 'very frail' old man react to the news that two supposedly anonymous helpline volunteers have tracked him down in real life?

'Does he know we're here?' Tanvi asks the nurse.

'Yes. We told him the people that found him are still waiting.' She smiles at us. 'The people that saved his life.'

Tanvi looks at me. I nod, and she offers me her hand. I take it.

We follow the nurse through the door. The electronic bleat of machines is louder now. The squeak of my shoes on the plastic floor. My legs feel rubbery, like they might give way any second.

'Here we are, Mr Sinclair. Some visitors for you.'

The nurse ushers us into the room. And finally I see his face.

In all these years of speaking to Eric on the phone, I realise I've unconsciously built an avatar of him in my head: an imagined version of what he looks like. I've always pictured him as willowy, debonair, tufty-haired – like John Waters with a midlands accent. And the man lying in bed, surrounded by beeping screens, fits that description almost exactly. The only real difference is that he's older than I imagined – or at least he looks it. His forehead is tiger-striped with deep, wide creases, and there are dark, shadowy bags under his eyes.

But he's here. He's alive, he's OK, and the relief is overwhelming.

He looks from Tanvi to me and back again. His face is a mask of shock and exhaustion. 'I don't know what to say,' he murmurs. 'Except: thank you.' His voice is rougher than usual. Croakier. But it's Eric's voice. I'd know it anywhere. 'I don't know who you are or how you got in, but . . . thank you.'

Tanvi glances at me and takes a step towards the bed. 'I'm Tanvi, Eric. And that's Will. But you'll know us as Sita and Jack. From Green Shoots.'

'Green Sh . . .' Eric's mouth hangs open and his eyes widen. They twitch back and forth between us, as if his gaze can't decide who to settle on. After a moment, it settles on me. He takes a shaky breath.

'Jack?' he whispers.

I nod. 'I hope we haven't overstepped the mark, Eric. I was so scared after that last call with you – the line went dead just after you told me you'd taken those pills. We had to do something. We had to come and find you.'

He's still staring at me, dumbfounded, not even blinking.

'You mentioned the Kirkmond-on-Crouch parade that time, remember?' Tanvi says. 'And so . . . here we are.'

'Sita and Jack,' Eric repeats. His hands are over his face now. He is crying, his whole body trembling. 'I can't believe it.'

Tanvi and I exchange a panicked look. 'I'm so sorry, Eric,' I say.

'"Sorry".' His voice comes out muffled between his fingers. 'You saved my life. I just . . . can't believe this. I can't believe you're here.'

'We just couldn't let anything happen to you,' Tanvi says. 'You gave us quite a scare.'

'I'm sorry,' he sobs. 'I'm so sorry. I'm an old fool. Everything just seemed so bleak. It's very hard to keep going sometimes when you've not got a single person in the world that cares about you.'

Tanvi walks across to the bed and sits down next to it. She covers Eric's hand with hers.

'Eric,' she says. 'What do you think we're doing here?'

*

For the next hour, over cups of lukewarm vending-machine tea, Eric ends up telling us the story of his life.

It's odd: how often I've spoken to him on the phone, and yet I knew nothing at all about his past. He only ever seemed to want small talk when he phoned Green Shoots – silly, gossipy chat about what he'd seen on TV or what he'd had for dinner. I had no clue that the whole time I was nattering about *Bake Off* or *Top of the Pops*, I was talking to someone who'd lived the most *incredible* life.

He tells us about growing up in Coventry in the Sixties, and being kicked out of the house at 19 after coming out to his parents. 'My father wasn't the most liberal bloke on the planet,' he says drily. He goes into the complicated relationship he had with his mother, who never truly accepted him for who he was, and even point-blank refused to meet his long-term partner, Graham. Even so, Eric still uprooted his entire life to come here and care for her when she got ill.

'The dementia was the strangest thing,' he tells us. 'She

remembered me right up until the very end – she knew I was her son – but she couldn't remember that I was gay. That piece of information had slipped through the cracks. So she treated me like she did when I was 16. It was bizarre. Feeling loved by her – *really* loved – for the first time in decades, but knowing it was only because she'd forgotten this key part of who I am. Even during her very last days, I never had the heart to tell her all over again.'

He tells us how he'd moved around throughout his twenties and thirties – living in Morocco, Barcelona and Berlin. Most amazing of all, though, are the stories he tells us about his days as an activist in London in the Eighties. He was a member of ACT UP – a radical protest group that worked to improve the lives of people with AIDS and challenge prejudices about the disease.

He tells us about sit-in demonstrations at pharmaceutical companies; lying drenched in fake blood outside the offices of a tabloid newspaper that was spreading lies about AIDS sufferers and gay people. He and some mates even catapulted condoms over the wall of HM Prison Pentonville, in protest at the inmates not being allowed them.

'Eric, this is incredible,' I tell him. 'You should write this stuff down.'

He shrugs. 'I'm not sure anyone would be interested in it, Jack.'

'Trust me, Eric,' Tanvi says. 'Netflix would be all over you, mate.'

Eric rocks with laughter at that. The thrill of seeing him happy – or something close to it – is worth more than I can possibly explain.

'So, how long have you been in Kirkmond-on-Crouch?' I ask.

He sighs. 'Coming up on ten years now. I moved here because it was close to my mother's nursing home. After she got ill, I wanted to be near enough to visit every day. Graham had just passed on, so I was already at rather a low point. It was probably a mistake to move all the way out here to the middle of nowhere where I didn't know anyone. I completely isolated myself, really. Mum died, eight years ago, and since then it's as if time's stood still and flown by at the same time. I've sort of allowed everything to drop by the wayside – friendships and the few relatives I've got left. I've let myself go rather stale here.'

I nod dumbly. I know how that feels. *It's as if time's stood still and flown by at the same time*: the line so perfectly captures my own predicament that I can't quite find the words to comfort him.

'But you must go out occasionally?' Tanvi asks. 'Do you know anybody in the village?'

'I order most of my groceries online so I don't have much reason to go out and about,' Eric says. 'There are times when I don't leave the house for weeks.' He breaks off and tries to conjure a smile. 'Sorry – I'm doing what I always do when I talk to you two: complaining.' He shakes his head. 'I still can't believe you're here. I really can't.'

Tanvi pats his hand and grins.

'Why did you never tell us any of this stuff over the phone?' I ask him. 'Don't get me wrong – I'm a big fan of listening to you do a *Gogglebox*-style commentary over whatever TV show you're watching—'

'Oh, me too,' Tanvi cuts in.

'But I don't understand why we never talked about any of

this other stuff. I've tried to ask you about your earlier life over the years, but you never seemed to want to speak about it.'

He smiles sadly. 'I suppose I thought that it would just make me more maudlin if I talked about it – the bad stuff would depress me, and the good stuff would remind me of what I'd lost. But with you here – in person – it feels different. I'm not sure why.'

The nurse pops her head in to say that perhaps Eric should get some rest.

'Of course,' Tanvi says. She stoops down to give Eric a hug. 'It was lovely to finally meet you.'

He's crying again now – but smiling this time as the tears flow. Laughing, even. 'Lovely to meet you, Sita.'

I go in for a hug, too. I feel his frail body trembling as I hold him. As I break away, he takes a deep breath and wipes his eyes with a tissue. 'I don't know how I can ever thank you both for what you've done.'

'I do,' Tanvi says. 'You can give Green Shoots a call. As soon as you're out of this place.'

He nods. 'I will.'

'I mean it, Eric.' She gives him a stern look. 'You promise?'

'I promise.'

'OK. I don't want to have to send Will round to put your windows through again.'

That makes all three of us snort with laughter. 'Bloody hell, Eric – I do owe you for that window,' I say. 'Let me give you some cash.'

That just makes him laugh harder. 'I think we can probably call it even, Jack, seeing as you saved my life.'

'Come on, you two,' the nurse says gently. 'You'd best be off – he really does need to get some rest.'

Tanvi nods. 'OK. Eric – speak soon, love, all right?'

I grin at him. 'Rest up and get better.'

'Thank you both again,' he says. 'So much. Not just for today. But these past few years, too.' He blots his damp eyes with the sleeve of his shirt and smiles at us. 'Honestly, I don't know what I would have done without you.'

CHAPTER SIXTY-FOUR

26th February, five years ago
Paris, France

Annie stands on the Pont Alexandre III, staring down into the dark water, feeling like such a fool.

It's half past eleven now. Half an hour after Will said they would meet, right back here on this bridge. And yet he's nowhere to be seen. They didn't even exchange numbers. She has no way of getting in contact with him.

Except perhaps by emailing Jess. But she'd sooner dive headfirst into the Seine than do that.

She knows Will is OK. She knows nothing has happened to him. She's spent the past few hours sitting in various bars and brasseries in the Champs-Élysées, scrolling Twitter. There are plenty of posts about the Defectors gig, which obviously went off without a hitch. There are plenty of photos of Will jumping about on stage. There's no good reason for him not to be here. Except that he apparently doesn't want to be. Maybe he found someone he'd rather hang out with at the aftershow party.

Annie flushes with humiliation. What a *fucking wanker.*

She checks her phone, ignoring the million-odd new texts from Maya, demanding information about the 'date'. It's 11.40 p.m. now. The last Eurostar is long gone. Whether she likes it or not, Annie is staying the night in Paris. Alone.

She has one more feeble, hopeful glance down the length of the bridge. Maybe this is a funny, romantic prank: Will is hiding behind one of the ornate lampposts, ready to jump out and surprise her. She catches herself smiling at the thought and the humiliation burns deeper. *Stop being so pathetic*, she tells herself. He's not coming. He probably never intended to.

She walks back to the Left Bank, anger and shame seething in her stomach. She spots the neon-lit sign of an Ibis hotel and heads for the entrance.

She asks for a room for the night, gritting her teeth as she passes over her debit card to pay the extortionate last-minute fee. There's no way she can claim this back from her editor. Same goes for the brand-new Eurostar ticket she'll have to purchase tomorrow morning. This is her fuck-up; she has to pay for it.

It will be a lesson. A very expensive lesson never to trust stupid sexy lead singers with teardrop dimples and gaps between their front teeth.

Up in the room, she switches the light on and finds her reflection looking back at her in the corridor mirror. She is alarmed to see that she's crying. Because it's not the humiliation that stings now: it's the disappointment. She really liked this boy. She really thought something might happen. But he's stood her up in the middle of the night, in the middle of a strange city, not giving one single solitary shit about her feelings or even her safety.

She throws her rucksack onto the bed. Screw him.

She opens the minibar and takes out an eye-wateringly expensive bottle of white wine. It makes her think of those gin miniatures Will was swigging when they started the interview. It's a reassuringly unlikeable image: Will as the preposterous, preening wannabe rock star. She focuses on that version of him.

Downing half the mini bottle in one go, she opens her laptop. She's way too wired to sleep, so she might as well make a start on her article.

The wine is already rushing to her head. She takes out her Dictaphone and starts spooling through the interview recording, searching for the most stupid, pretentious, cringeworthy things Will said. She feels the venom and the humiliation seeping back in. This is good. This is what she needs. She starts typing.

God, she hopes that he reads this. She wants it to really hurt.

CHAPTER SIXTY-FIVE

WILL

23rd April, present day
Tottenham Court Road, London

'So, have you spoken to Eric lately?'

'Yeah, he called during my shift two days ago,' Tanvi says. 'He was back home. Taking the piss out of *Love Island* reruns. He seemed good.'

I take a swig of lemonade and stretch out on the grass. 'That's good to hear. I've seen his name in the log book so I knew he'd called, but I haven't actually had him myself yet. Seems like he's calling less often than before.'

'Well, that's the idea, isn't it?' Tanvi shrugs. 'If our callers no longer need to call then we're doing our job right. In an ideal world, Green Shoots wouldn't exist. No crises, no crisis helplines.'

I scratch my stubble. I've never thought of it like that. 'I guess you're right.'

It's a gloriously bright Tuesday, and we're sat in the little park near MicroShop, having a picnic-style late lunch. Tanvi's office is based around here too, and when she found out how close we worked, she suggested a middle-of-the-day hangout in the sun. We've just polished our M&S sandwiches off, and are currently ploughing our way through a large bag of Percy Pigs.

It's been over a week since that insane trip to Kirkmond-on-Crouch, and only now do I feel the dust is finally starting to settle. So much happened in such a short space of time that it's taken a good few days to process it all. There was the fact that I finally told someone about Joe, about what happened that day in Paris, and the guilt I've been carrying ever since. And then there was the whole smashing a window, breaking into a house and saving a man's life thing. The entire evening was just . . . a lot.

I've felt physically exhausted ever since, like my body was working through the shock of it all. But in the last day or so, things have started to get calmer and clearer. I'm coming out the other side and I feel . . . lighter. Like my vision is sharper, my brain less muggy. There's no getting around it: with Jess out of my life – and people like Tanvi and Dev and Eric in it – I feel happier than I have in a long time.

And yet still – despite all this calm and clarity and lightness – I can't stop thinking about her.

Annie.

She appears to have taken what I said in that pub to heart. I've certainly not spoken to her on the Green Shoots line, and I've seen no record of anyone that could be her in the log book. She has stopped calling, just like I told her to.

But now that some of the fog in my head has dissipated, now that the very thought of Paris doesn't send me spiralling blindly into panic mode, I'm starting to realise . . . she *can't* have known that I volunteered at Green Shoots. She can't have been using the line to try to get information out of me for the article. At least, I'm pretty sure she can't. Either way: I can't get around the fact that my mind drifts to her constantly. As strange as it is to admit . . . I miss her.

Tanvi nudges the Percy Pigs in my direction. 'Let's finish these up. I'd better get back.'

I nod. 'Me too. Dev's out this afternoon, so I'm manning the shop on my own.'

Tanvi drains her lemonade and looks at me. 'On that subject, I had something I wanted to run past you, actually.'

'Oh yeah?'

'Yeah. I was wondering how wedded you are to your job?'

'My job? At MicroShop?' I pop a Percy Pig in my mouth. 'I guess I'm not particularly wedded to it. It pays the bills, and Dev is really great. But apart from that it's just . . . a job.'

Tanvi nods. 'Right. See, I've got this cousin who works at the British Library. She's an oral historian.'

'Uh-huh.' I immediately decide it will be too embarrassing to admit that I don't know what an oral historian is. Instead I feign comprehension and nod: 'Cool. That's cool.'

'Yeah, it's a really fascinating job,' she says. 'It's all about interviewing people and creating an oral record of stories and events and movements that probably wouldn't ever get written down otherwise. Really interesting, not-very-well-known pockets of history that might completely disappear unless people like my cousin recorded them.'

'OK?' I'm not entirely sure where she's going with this.

She reaches for the Percys bag and pulls out a handful. 'Anyway, I was telling her about our trip to find Eric, and you asking him about all that ACT UP stuff he was involved in during the Eighties. She thought it could make a really interesting oral history project.'

'Right, yeah. That sounds amazing. Someone should definitely do that.'

'Yeah,' she says. 'You.'

I look at her blankly. 'How d'you mean?'

'I mean, do it properly: go back and interview Eric about the whole story, record it, and then do some research and try to find other people who were involved in that movement as well. My cousin Swetha says there are openings in her department at the British Library. You'd obviously be on a starting salary, but who knows – might be a more interesting way to make a living?'

'Ha. Maybe.' I reach for the bag of sweets, ready to change the subject. But Tanvi is staring at me, stony-faced.

'Will. I'm serious.'

'What?'

'This could be a great opportunity. It could be something you might actually enjoy. That might actually fulfil you. Why wouldn't you want to at least give it a go?'

'I don't know. Because . . .' I exhale, trying to find the right words. I loved talking to Eric about his ACT UP years, delving into these brilliant old stories. But getting *paid* to do that: that's a fantasy, surely? And after what happened with the band, I came to terms with the fact that I would never actually enjoy a job again.

Tanvi seems to read my mind. Still staring at me, she says: 'Because . . . what? You don't deserve to be happy?'

I shrug, and avoid her gaze.

After a pause, she says: 'You know, this past week I've been thinking a lot about what you told me. About Joe.'

Hearing her say his name makes me wince. But then – she spoke to him. She *knew* him, like I know Eric.

'I've been trying to piece together some of our conversations,' she continues. 'On my last shift, I even dug through the old log books to jog my memory. I remember we talked mainly about his childhood: his fucking arsehole of a father. His mum – how Joe felt she just abandoned him after she remarried. How worthless it made him feel. That was why he started on the anti-depressants.'

I swallow hard as I take in what she's saying. 'He never told me any of that. He tried so many times over the years to talk to me about how he was feeling. I just never knew what to say. I knew he got down from time to time, but I didn't know he was taking *pills* for it. I didn't know things were so serious. If I'd known, I would never have let him go off on his own that day. Never . . .'

I can feel the tears gathering again now. I'm not worried about crying in front of Tanvi – she's already seen me fall to bits – but we're not in an empty hospital now, we're in a busy park. I can't lose control here. I bite the inside of my cheek and try to gather myself.

Tanvi reaches across and gives my hand a squeeze. Instantly, I feel calmer.

'Joe never talked to me much about the present,' she says. 'But he *did* talk occasionally about a friend he grew up with, a friend he'd known all his life. His best friend.' I close my eyes and feel those last three words wash over me. 'I promise you, Will: I never heard him say anything but good things about this best friend. He talked about how much this person meant to him, how close they were. You said last week that you let him down, but I think he felt he was letting you down, too. He felt you were slipping away from him, drinking too much, going off the rails. He was worried about you.'

I close my eyes and inhale sharply. The pain is physical: hearing these words is like having him back and then losing him all over again.

'He was . . . a damaged soul, Will,' Tanvi says. 'He didn't deserve to be, but he was. In all my years speaking to him, though, I didn't ever hear him talk about ending his own life. I honestly didn't. Like the doctor told you: there's no way of knowing whether what he did was intentional. It's easy, with hindsight, to think we should have done things differently. But you're not to blame, you hear me? You didn't know the gravity of his situation. You said yourself: you tried to be with him that day, but he wanted to be alone.'

The tears are coming now: I can't stop them. I don't even care that people are looking over. *You're not to blame*. The words echo in my head. I'm not sure I even believe them. But hearing them is still like a weight being lifted, if only for a moment.

Tanvi squeezes my hand again, harder. 'So, what do you want to do, Will?' she says softly. 'You want to spend the rest of your life punishing yourself? Do you really think that's what Joe would have wanted?'

CHAPTER SIXTY-SIX

ANNIE

29th April
Shoreditch, London

I'm in the middle of editing a 'Which *White Lotus* Character Are You?' quiz written by one of our interns (I'm Armond, apparently – quite pleased with that) when my phone pings on the desk. I flip it over and check the message:

I miss you. I'm sorry. I love you xxx

Even a week ago, a text like this would have had me questioning whether I was being too hasty – whether I should give him another chance. But now it just sparks a flash of irritation. If you 'love' me so much, why the hell did you shag Posh Clare?

I scroll up through Dom's previous messages. The tone of them has changed significantly over the past two weeks. In the days immediately after I walked out, they were intense, passionate, panicked: *Why won't you pick up the fucking phone???* or *Please Annie please don't do this!!* Now, though, his words have mellowed. He tends to send me one message a day along the same lines of the one I've just received: a short, sharp reminder that he's still hurting and he still loves me.

I haven't even been back to the flat yet. We've spoken on the phone a few times – long, tearful, late-night conversations in which Dom tells me the same things he's been telling me in the texts: that he misses me, that's he's sorry, that he's sure we can work it all out. Sometimes, in the middle of the night, as I toss and turn on Maya's rickety sofa bed, I miss him too. Or maybe I just miss having *somebody*. I don't know. But by the time morning comes, I'm always sure that I'm making the right decision by ending things. I know how hard it will be; I know the hard part hasn't even really started yet. The hard part will be going back to the flat, packing up all my stuff, giving Dom back the keys. The hard part will be the weeks and months that follow, when I finally have to 'put myself out there' again, diving back into the apps, spending my evenings and weekends recycling the same small talk in pubs, hoping that this total stranger turns out to be The One. There is part of me that wishes I could just swallow my pride and go back to Dom. Just because it would be easier. Safer. But deep down, I *know*. I know we shouldn't be together.

I know because I get can't Will Axford out of my head.

It was Sunday yesterday. A long, lonely, rainy Sunday in which the hours seemed to drag and drag. Maya was out on a daytime date, and by about half four in the afternoon, I was *this* close to calling Green Shoots. I wonder if Will still volunteers there on Sundays. I wonder if he misses talking to me as much as I miss talking to him.

In the end, I managed to resist the temptation to pick up the phone. I went back to doing what I've been doing constantly since coming back from Sheffield – reading. Or *re*-reading, actually: delving back into old favourites and comfort reads from my teens and twenties: Leonora Carrington, Elizabeth Taylor, Flann O'Brien, Stephen King – even Dad's old favourite, Alphonse Carnet. And when I'm not devouring other people's stuff, I'm writing my own. I have no idea if the stories I'm churning out are any good – but they keep coming. I definitely feel good while I'm writing them, so that must mean something.

Yesterday, after digging back into Monsieur Carnet, I started work on a new story set in Paris. About a girl and a boy who spend the day together there. They arrange to meet later that night, but the boy doesn't show. The girl is left alone on the bridge. Write what you know, and all that.

That memory of standing on the bridge, of Will not turning up, is the one thing I keep clinging to when the knowledge that I might never speak to him again gnaws at me. I can't deny how I felt when I saw him in that pub. But he's still the same person that left me stranded in the middle of a foreign city, in the middle of the night, with nowhere to stay. Even if some of the pop-star arrogance has dissolved and he's dropped the silly mockney accent – he still stood me up. He still lied. I try to keep that thought front and centre, telling myself it's probably for the best that nothing ever happened between us.

But it doesn't stop me longing to see him one more time.

My phone beeps again – but it's not Dom. It's Mum, on the group chat with Josie. For months this group has been totally dormant, but in the fortnight since I got back from Sheffield it's been pinging away like mad. I smile as I read

Mum's message; she's in B&Q, sending us photos of paint samples for her new art studio. I'm in the middle of typing out my reply when I see Matt marching over to my desk.

'Annie? Can I have a quick word?'

'Yeah, of course.'

I follow him into one of the meeting rooms and we sit. He looks knackered – bags under his eyes and worry lines set deep into his forehead. Even his goatee seems to be sporting a few more grey hairs than it used to.

'OK, listen, Annie,' he says. 'Obviously you know things aren't going great for us at the moment. Page impressions are down, advertising's non-existent. All charts are pointing arsewards.'

'What about Zara's advertorial?' I ask. She's now on the fourth instalment of the 'Whatever Happened To . . .' series, and each one has been better than the last. I was worried I might feel bitter about how great her articles have been – after all, she was only given a shot at the series after my Defectors piece fell apart. But I genuinely don't. I'm chuffed for her. It's possibly a sign that my passion for this job isn't quite what it once was.

Matt tugs at his beard and looks at me. 'Zara's stuff has been excellent, and it's definitely helping us to get out of the red. But there's *so much* fucking red, Annie, that's the problem.' He pinches his nose and sighs. 'Between you and me, I'm going to have to ask a few people to take voluntary redundancy.'

'OK. Shit. Wow.'

He nods grimly. 'So, what I'm asking is: do you want that? It'll be eight months' salary, and you might not even have to work your notice.'

I blink and take this information in. Just a few weeks ago,

I was living in absolute terror of a conversation like this. Unemployed at 31, back on the scrapheap. But now, for some reason, it doesn't seem like a setback: it seems like an opportunity. Eight months to regroup, eight months to figure out what I really want to do. I've been treading water for years, waiting for something to push me. And now that something has finally arrived.

'I understand if you need some time to think about it,' Matt says.

I shake my head. 'I don't, actually. I'll take it. I'll take the redundancy.'

CHAPTER SIXTY-SEVEN

WILL

10th May
Kings Cross, London

I am sat in a squashed corner office on the third floor of the British Library, listening to a dead man talk about the 1972 miners' strike.

This is not an incredibly niche séance. It's a job interview. Tanvi's cousin, Swetha – the oral historian – is sat across from me, her laptop between us on her desk. From its speakers, the voice of a now-deceased Doncaster miner fills the room.

The man is discussing the death of one of his co-workers, who was hit by a non-union truck during a local picket line in 1972. The anger in response to this killing was one of the prime reasons for the violent strike action that swept the country later that year, and the emotion in the man's voice as he recalls it all is something else. You get the sense this is the first time he has *really* talked about this stuff. His voice crackles and quivers as he describes watching his friend die in front of him. It feels so personal – so raw – that I almost feel uncomfortable listening to it. Like I'm overhearing something I shouldn't be.

It takes me a minute to realise what it reminds me of: a Green Shoots call.

Swetha reaches over to stop the recording and the man's voice cuts out abruptly. She smiles at me. 'So, that gives you a taste of the kind of thing we do here. A colleague of mine recorded that interview a while back; the gentleman being interviewed passed away a few years ago. But as far as we know he's the first person to have spoken about this incident in such detail. I'm in the process right now of trying to track down other people from the Doncaster area who were involved in those initial strikes. Trying to set up more interviews, gather more material for this big oral history of the trade union movement we're curating here at the Library later this year.'

'It sounds brilliant,' I say truthfully.

She shrugs. 'Well, it's not *all* brilliant. There's a lot of dull admin, too. But I'm very lucky – I love my job.' She shuts the laptop. 'Let's talk about you, though: Tanvi told me about that helpline caller you both went up to see. That sounded . . . intense.'

I laugh. 'It was.'

'But fascinating, too – hearing about his life afterwards?'

I nod. 'Tanvi and me had been speaking to him on Green Shoots for years. But in person, we actually got him to open up about all this new stuff he'd never told us.'

Swetha's lips twitch at the edges. 'Tanvi said it was mostly *you* who got him to open up . . .'

'No, not at all. We both did.'

'OK. She said he seemed very at ease talking to you, though.'

'Well, I wasn't faking my interest in what he was saying. Maybe that's why he was so eager to talk. It just seemed crazy to me that he'd been part of this really important movement – this group in the Eighties working to improve the lives of people with AIDS – doing incredible stuff, protesting, demonstrating, spreading awareness. And he hadn't really told anyone about it. Ever. All those memories were just cooped up in his own head. He had this fascinating story to tell that wasn't really being told.'

Swetha leans back in her chair and smiles at me. 'You've just described the ultimate goal for every oral historian: track down the fascinating stories that aren't being told. So, what do you think? Does this sound like a line of work you'd be interested in?'

'Definitely. Yes. One hundred per cent. But . . .' My heart sinks slightly as I remember that this is a big 'but'. 'I don't exactly have the qualifications.'

'Which qualifications?'

'Well . . . Any.' She laughs at that. 'I dropped out of uni before I could graduate. I was in a band, and I thought we were going to be massive, so I figured: what do I need a degree for? Great decision, I know. Hence working at a failing electronics store on Tottenham Court Road.'

Swetha wrinkles her forehead. 'Well, the way I see it, you've been training for this job for the past five years by volunteering at Green Shoots. From what Tanvi's told me about that line, it's not entirely dissimilar to what we do here: you perfect a technique of talking to people – or getting them to talk – without pressuring them or being judgemental or trying to stamp your own imprint on the conversation. It's a real skill, and it sounds like you have it: to just try to steer a discussion gently towards the areas you think will be most fertile.'

I nod as I consider this. 'I guess that is what we do on the helpline.'

'There you go,' she says. 'Now, I won't lie to you, Will, since this is a junior role, the salary is far from fantastic. And, as I say, a lot of your work would be administrative – archiving sound files, formatting them, transcribing them, booking interviews and so on. But at the same time, you'd be working alongside me and the other oral historians in the department, and ideally, within time, you could pitch your own projects. Perhaps even something about the ACT UP movement that Eric was involved in.'

The idea of this fills me with an excitement for the future that I didn't know I still possessed. 'Honestly, it sounds so up my street.'

'Great. Well, this was just an informal first chat. There'll be a second round of interviews next week with me and my supervisor. But I'll tell her I know you and put in a good word.'

'Amazing,' I say. 'Thank you so much, Swetha. Seriously.'

CHAPTER SIXTY-EIGHT

ANNIE

25th May
Walthamstow, London

'Jesus, I am *knackered*.'

Maya slumps onto the bare parquet floor and shakes her hair loose.

'Me too,' I say, joining her on the ground and staring at the mountains of cardboard boxes surrounding us. 'Thanks so much for your help, mate,' I tell her. 'Seriously. I couldn't have done it without you.'

'Or me?' Lexi's voice chirps up from the corner of the room. Maya and I both grin at her.

'Or you, Alexie,' I say. 'You've been a truly fantastic cheer-leader.'

She beams and makes an *oh, stop* face at us from the laptop screen. The whole having-a-six-week-old-bubba thing has understandably prevented Lex from helping out today. But she was extremely eager to play a supervising role over Zoom, while

Finn (aka The Baby Formerly Known As The Unit) alternated between snoozing and feeding.

'To be fair, the removal guys did most of the heavy lifting,' Maya says, rubbing the back of her neck. 'But I still think I carried about 300 of your bloody books up those stairs. One of the removal guys was actually quite hot,' she adds. 'Did you see him, Lex?'

'Yeah,' Lexi nods. 'Like a kind of beefier Richard Ayoade.'

'Exactly!'

I smile at them both fondly, zoning out for a moment as I gaze around my new home. Sixty-five square metres on the third floor of an ex-council block, with a rent that's *just* about affordable, even for someone who is technically unemployed (albeit with an eight-month's-salary redundancy package to protect me). The last few weeks have been some of the most hectic of my life, but I'm finally out of Dom's flat, out of Maya's spare room, and into my own place. Ready to move on. I have no idea what the future holds – and for the first time in a long time, that doesn't scare me. It excites me.

Maya clasps my hand. 'I'm so glad you're finally in, mate. But I'm going to miss you.'

I squeeze her hand back. 'I'll miss you, too.'

She hops up from the floor and grabs her rucksack off one of the towers of boxes. 'Right – let's christen the new place properly . . .' She unzips her bag and pulls a bottle of white wine out. 'Where are the glasses?'

'Er . . .' I stare around the room. 'No idea which box they're in, to be honest.'

'It's all right,' she says. 'We'll just swig and pass. It'll be like we're fifteen again, in the park.'

She unscrews the top, takes a large glug and passes it to me. Despite being room temperature, the wine is surprisingly tasty: light and fruity. I take another gulp and hand it back to Maya.

'Right, Lex – have you got a glass of something?' she asks. 'I want to propose a toast.'

Lexi raises her cup of tea at us through the computer screen.

'OK.' Maya turns to me. 'I just want to say, Annie, that you've been through the fucking mill in this past year or so. Everything with your dad, then all the stuff with your mum and Josie afterwards. And now this situation with that fucker Dom.'

'That fucker,' Lexi hisses.

I can't help laughing. While Maya and Lex still seethe whenever Dom's name is mentioned, I've worked through all the various post-break-up stages – humiliation, anger, sadness – and come out the other side. When I finally went back to the flat a fortnight ago to collect all my stuff, I didn't feel anything, really. I was just glad to be out and getting on with my life.

Maya holds the wine bottle aloft and continues: 'All of this horrible shit has happened, and you've got through it. And now I feel like a page has turned. You're in a lovely new flat, you've made up with your mum and Josie, you're shot of your cheating twat of a boyfriend – who, by the way, was never good enough for you, even before we knew he was a cheating *twat* – and you've got a nice little cash cushion from Marker that will give you the time to figure out what you *really* want to do in life.' She beams down at me, passing the bottle. 'So, here's to you, babe. To the future. You're amazing, and we fucking love you.'

'We fucking love you!' Lexi echoes, before adding: 'Is she crying? I can't see; the screen's too grainy!'

I wipe my eyes and laugh. 'I am crying, yes. I love you guys so much. Thank you.' I get to my feet, still blubbering, and wrap my arms tightly around Maya. 'Thank you,' I whisper again.

'I feel left out!' Lexi chimes. 'Bring me in for the hug, too!'

'You want us to hug a laptop?' Maya says.

'I don't see why we can't,' I say, taking another swig of wine.

'Yeah, all right.'

She grabs the laptop off the shelf and pulls it into our hug. We stay like that for a while, the three of us just laughing and laughing. I don't think I've ever felt so grateful to have such amazing best friends.

And then the moment is broken by my phone ringing on top of one of the boxes. I break out of the hug to answer it. An unknown number.

'Hello?'

'Oh, hey.' A male voice. 'Is that Annie Lucas?'

'Yes. Who's this?'

'This is Sim. Simon McGillan. I'm the – I *was* the drummer in The Defectors. You sent me an Instagram message a couple of months back?'

My stomach jolts. 'Oh. Yes. Hey!'

The past month has been so full-on – leaving Marker, frantically flat-hunting, picking up my stuff from Dom's – that I've barely had time to think about Will Axford. But now fate has arrived to drop him back at the forefront of my mind once again.

'Sorry I'm so late getting back to you,' Sim says. 'I barely ever check that account. I only saw your message today, and since you'd put your number at the end I figured I'd give you a call.'

'OK, right . . .' I signal to Maya that I'm going to take this in the next room. She shoots me an inquisitive glance before turning back to Lexi on the MacBook.

'Thanks so much for calling,' I tell Sim as I step into the kitchen, also full of unpacked boxes.

'No worries. I remember you from Paris,' he says. 'Anyway, I'm probably way too late – I'm guessing you've finished your article by now, have you?'

'I actually never wrote it in the end.'

'Oh?'

'Yeah, no. I got in touch with Mike and he wasn't up for being interviewed. And I couldn't get hold of Al or Will.'

'Oh shit,' he says. 'Well, if you still want an exclusive chat with the drummer, then I'm here for it.'

I laugh. 'Thanks but I think that ship has sailed now. I've actually left the site I was going to write it for.'

'Well, fair enough. It was nice talking to you, Annie.'

'Thanks. You too.' Before he can hang up, something strikes me.

'Sorry, Sim?'

'Yeah?'

'I was wondering – this is quite random – but on your Instagram page, one of your last posts was a black square with a phone number in it. I was just wondering what that was about?'

'Oh.' I hear him take a sip of something as he searches his memory. 'Ohhhh. Yeah, that was the number for this helpline. A crisis line that people call if they're struggling.'

'Right . . .' I open a box at random and start unpacking items onto the counter. I'm anxious for him to tell me more, but I know it's a sensitive subject. Did he used to call the line?

Or was he just advertising it because Will volunteered there? I let the silence drift, and luckily Sim fills in the gap.

'One of our mates – well, he was Will's mate, really. He used to call this line a lot. He had really bad depression, you see.'

'Joe . . .'

I don't say it as a question. Truthfully, I don't even mean to say it out loud at all. The name just escapes my lips. It's the first time I've thought about him in years. That boy in the hotel room, with the baggy hoodie and the dirty blond hair. The dark circles under his eyes. Will had talked about him a lot that day. His best friend.

'Joe used to call Green Shoots?'

'Will only found out a few weeks after . . .' Sim breaks off. I hear him swallow thickly. 'He died, you see. Joe died.'

My hand stops halfway to the box I'm unpacking. 'What?'

'Yeah. Fucking sad, man. I thought maybe Mike or someone might have told you? See, it actually happened in Paris, on that same day you interviewed us.'

I open my mouth to speak, but nothing comes out. Joe died . . . *that day*?

'We did the gig,' Sim says. 'And then Will went to look for Joe in the hotel afterwards, and that's when he found him. He'd taken these pills, and he'd been drinking . . . The doctors said it was impossible to tell whether he'd meant to . . . y'know? Or not.'

My eyes twinge and tears start to blur my vision. In that moment, I see myself on the bridge in Paris, at the end of that night. Hating Will Axford with every fibre of my being. Feeling sick with humiliation and regret and disappointment. I'd assumed he was just off shagging someone else. Or that he was so pissed he'd forgotten all about meeting me. But no. His best friend was dying. His best friend died.

'Annie?'

Sim's voice startles me back to reality. I scrub a hand across my damp eyes, and clear my throat. 'Sorry, yep, still here,' I say after catching my breath. 'God, that's so awful. I didn't know.'

'Yeah. It's shit. Will was never really the same afterwards. We tried to keep going with the band for a few months, but eventually he just stopped answering the phone to us. I haven't seen him in years. He cut everyone out of his life. But before that he did mention finding out about Joe calling this crisis line. I guess that's why I posted it on Instagram. A kind of tribute to him, I suppose. Even though I barely knew him.'

I grip the kitchen counter. My eyes are still streaming, but a sudden firmness has taken hold in my chest. Tomorrow is Sunday. I know what I need to do.

'Well, I'd better go, Annie,' Sim says. 'Like I say, it was nice talking to you.'

'And you. Bye, Sim.'

I place my phone face down on the counter, and take a moment to gather myself. When I'm done, I walk back upstairs, take a hefty gulp of wine, and tell Lexi and Maya everything.

CHAPTER SIXTY-NINE

WILL

26th May
Tottenham Court Road, London

I'd been hoping that Dev would be OK with me leaving.

That he wouldn't take the news about me being offered a new job too hard. That perhaps he'd nod stoically and sigh, tell me that he totally understood my decision, but MicroShop wouldn't be the same place without me.

As such, his actual reaction is mildly hurtful.

'What?! Yes! Seriously? This is fucking *brilliant*!'

He jumps up and down, punching the air and performing a celebratory robot dance.

'You're in shock,' I say. 'I get it. Take some time to process.'

He responds by increasing the speed of his robo-jig. 'To be honest, Will, I've been looking for a reason to boot you out for ages. This is the best news I've had in months.'

'Right. Thanks, mate.'

He stops dancing. 'I don't mean because I don't like you, William. I do like you. A lot.'

'Thanks for confirming, Dev. I like you too.'

'No,' he says, 'it's just that the shop's doing extremely bloody badly.'

We both glance around the entirely customer-free store we're currently stood inside. 'Yep. I sort of figured that,' I say.

'My uncle's been on at me for ages about us not needing two staff in here, but I didn't want to chuck you out on the street and leave you jobless.'

The fact hits me like a sledgehammer: Dev has been knowingly running his family business into the ground purely to keep me afloat. I feel a strong urge to hug him, which thankfully for both of us I manage to contain.

'Bloody hell, Dev. Thank you, man.'

He sighs. 'What can I say? I'm a terrible businessman.'

'Yeah, but you're a very good egg.'

'That's true. I'm a fucking *great* egg.' He sips his tea and stares wistfully around the shop. 'To be honest, I'm not sure how much longer I'll stick it out here either. That Caddystack gig is going pretty well, for starters.'

I smile. Towards the end of our mini-golf outing on my birthday, Dev had sauntered up to the Caddystack manager to complain about the quality of the tunes, and ended up sweet-talking himself into a semi-regular DJ gig there.

'I've already picked up a couple of extra slots, too, just from people coming up to me while I'm playing there,' he tells me.

'What for?' I ask. 'Club nights and stuff?'

'Mainly weddings, actually.'

'*Weddings*?' I laugh. 'You're a drum 'n' bass DJ, aren't you?'

He shrugs. 'Well, yeah. But the unfortunate truth, William, is that most drum 'n' bass fans are now in their thirties and forties.

We're *old*, man. But I don't mind. I quite like the idea of being London's only hardcore jungle wedding DJ. The pay's good, the crowds are fun and you get as much free cake as you can eat.'

'That's amazing, mate.' I clink my tea mug against his. 'You'll finally be living your dream. A professional DJ.'

He nods, beaming. 'What about you, then? What's this new gig you're leaving me in the lurch for?'

I tell him all about the British Library job – explaining the ins and outs of what I'll be doing as a Junior Oral Historian. I can tell I'm grinning like an idiot as I'm talking, but I can't help it. Getting that call from Swetha two days ago, telling me I'd actually got the job . . . it was the most excited I'd felt in forever.

'That sounds so awesome, mate,' Dev says, clapping me on the shoulder. 'I'm chuffed for you. Hey – lunchtime pint to celebrate?'

'I can't today, man, sorry. What about tomorrow?' It's Sunday, so I'm not even working today – I only stopped by to tell Dev in person about the new job before I headed to my Green Shoots afternoon shift.

'Tomorrow for sure, William,' Dev says, giving me another thump on the back.

*

An hour later, I arrive at the Green Shoots office, dump my bag and log in to the computer.

I check the log book to see that Eric phoned yesterday, apparently in 'very good spirits'. I hope he calls again this afternoon; I haven't spoken to him myself for a few days now. But Tanvi's right: it's a good thing that he's calling less and less. Green Shoots used to be his entire world, and now it isn't.

The same goes for me, I suppose.

It's been at the back of my mind to tell Eric about my British Library job, too. Follow up Tanvi's idea of proposing a proper interview with him about his activism, with a view to pitching an oral history project on ACT UP. But maybe I should give it a month or two: I've not even started the job yet. Should probably get my feet under the desk first.

My shift unravels quietly. There are only two calls over the course of the five hours; no Eric, no Sandra, just a couple of not-too-heavy first-timers. With quarter of an hour left before Tanvi arrives to take over, I start packing up the remains of my late lunch – what my mum would refer to as a 'picky tea', consisting of hummus, carrots, tomatoes and sausage rolls. As I'm washing the plate in the kitchen, I hear the phone ring. Drying my hands, I walk back to the office and lift the receiver.

'Hello, Green Shoots?'

There's a pause. And then I hear a voice. Her voice.

'Hey, Will,' she says. 'It's Annie.'

I stand rooted to the spot for a second, unable to speak. Since that evening at the Lamb & Flag, not a single day has gone by when I haven't thought about her. When I haven't wished she would call. And now, here she is, on the line, and I can't think of what the hell I should even say to her. All I can muster is: 'Hey.'

'I know you said not to call, Will, but I just—'

Those few words – and the urgency in her voice – are enough to shake me out of my stupor. 'I'm so sorry I said that,' I cut in. 'I acted like a total prick in that pub. I'm sorry.'

She laughs, sounding half-surprised, half-relieved. God, it's *so* good to hear her laugh.

'I would never have used this line to try and get at you for the article, Will,' she says. 'I honestly didn't know. I didn't know it was you.'

'I know, I figured that out.' I drop back down into the chair. My legs suddenly feel as rubbery as they did in that pub. 'It's just that whenever the band comes up I . . . freak out. Lose all sense of reality. And then, seeing you again – it made me think of that day in Paris, and that just scrambled my thoughts even more, and . . .'

'I get it, Will,' she says hurriedly. 'I spoke to Sim.'

I blink. 'You . . . what?'

'He called me yesterday. He was replying to the message I sent a couple of months ago, about setting up an interview. He told me, Will. About what happened that night in Paris. With Joe.'

I stare into the computer keyboard, feeling the tips of my ears burn. 'Oh. Right.'

'Will, I'm so sorry,' she whispers. 'I had no idea. I'm just so, *so* sorry.'

I clear my throat and try to keep my voice steady. 'Thank you. Yeah, it was . . . It changed everything.'

'Of course. I remember you talking about him. That day. I could tell how much he meant to you.'

A quiet, unhappy laugh escapes me. 'Yeah.'

'I just had to call,' she says. 'To tell you that. And to tell you I'm sorry. I hope that's OK.'

I swallow and take a breath. 'Of course it's OK. I'm so glad you called. I've . . . I've really missed talking to you.'

Her surprised, relieved laugh crackles in my ear again. 'I've missed talking to you, too. Which is why I've . . . Well, I've sort of done another "brave thing".'

'What do you mean?'

'I mean . . . I'm outside.'

CHAPTER SEVENTY

ANNIE

26th May
Limehouse, London

It was Maya's idea.

Last night, as we demolished the rest of that bottle of wine, it all came rushing out. I told her and Lexi everything. I told them about calling Green Shoots that very first time, about developing this strange bond with 'Jack' all while I was desperately trying to track down Will Axford. And then I told them about the night at the pub. The insane realisation that 'Jack' *was* Will Axford. Maya screamed so loudly at this reveal I was worried my new neighbours might call the police. But then I told them about the aftermath: about Will storming out with the wrong idea, how it led directly to me telling Dom I had feelings for someone else, and him telling me that he'd cheated.

And then, finally, I told them about the call I'd just taken from Sim. The truth about Will standing me up on the bridge that night. By this point, Maya was no longer screaming. She and Lexi were both staring at me with their eyes shining and their jaws set.

'Annie, that kind of connection doesn't happen every day,'

Maya told me. 'Being able to open up to someone, be totally at ease with them, talk to them about *anything*. You can't let this go. You just can't.'

That's when she suggested it: one last 'brave thing'. So, here I am, stood on an industrial estate in deepest east London, waiting for the door to open.

And then it opens.

Will walks towards me, smiling and shaking his head. My pulse flutters at the sight of him.

'How . . .?' he says.

I grin. 'You guys should really up your security. My friend just googled "Green Shoots charity registered address", and this place came up.'

He glances around the run-down estate and laughs. 'I can't believe you're here.'

He looks different from that night at the pub. The beard is gone, for a start, replaced by a light stubble that accentuates his cheekbones and reveals that single dimple, the shape of a teardrop, in the centre of his left cheek. I'd forgotten all about that. His messy brown hair is a little longer, too. He sweeps it out of his eyes, and smiles at me again, flashing that weirdly sexy gap between his front teeth.

I was *so* nervous on the Tube over here. I even considered turning back halfway. But the way Will is looking at me right now . . . I know it was the right decision.

'So,' he says.

'So,' I reply.

And for a moment, we just stand there, grinning at each other.

'It's been a while,' he says finally. 'What's been going on?'

'A *lot* has been going on.' I shift on the spot. 'I left my job.'

'No way!' His smile stretches. 'Me too, actually.'

'Seriously? Is this a good thing or a bad thing?'

'Good,' he nods. 'Really good. What about you: good or bad?'

'Good, too.'

'Good. So, what else?'

I clear my throat. 'Split up with my boyfriend.'

'Oh . . . OK.' He scratches his head. 'Good or—'

'Good,' I cut in quickly. 'Definitely good.'

He looks so relieved that I almost laugh out loud. 'Excellent. Also – snap,' he says. 'Kind of. Me and that girl Jess you met, we were . . .' He pauses long enough for my stomach to perform a triple backflip. 'I don't know what we were, really. But we're not anymore. I haven't spoken to her since that night at the pub. And before you ask: *definitely* good. I—'

He breaks off and glances behind me, raising a hand in greeting. I turn around to see a woman, maybe a little older than us, approaching.

'Hello,' she says brightly, dragging the word out, and raising her eyebrows at Will. She's wearing a bright-yellow raincoat, and there is an instantly likeable air about her.

'Hey, Tanvi,' Will grins. He turns to me: 'Annie, this is my friend, Tanvi. Tanvi, Annie.'

Tanvi sticks out her hand and beams at me as I shake it. 'So good to meet you, Annie.'

'You too.'

'Well, I'd better get in,' she says. 'That phone's not going to answer itself. I'll let you two carry on.'

She squeezes Will's shoulder affectionately as she goes, and he gives her a happy, bashful smile. The urge to kiss him is suddenly so strong that I have to take a step backwards.

We watch Tanvi unlock the office and step inside. As Will turns back to me, I suddenly realise I still haven't said the thing I actually came here to say. The thing I've been rehearsing in my head for the entire journey over here.

'So, look,' I tell him. 'What I really came here to say is that so much has happened to me in these last few weeks, Will. I really feel like things have changed – I've changed – for the better. But it all started here, on this phone line, with you. And I wanted to say thank you for that.'

His brown eyes widen and he rubs the back of his neck. 'I feel exactly the same, Annie. After what happened with Joe, I just closed myself off. From everyone. But talking to you . . .' He shakes his head and smiles. 'All these little chinks of light started opening up. I started letting people in. I started feeling . . . OK again. Happy, even. And honestly, it's all because of you.'

My heart thumps, my chest swells. 'Same here,' I tell him. 'I think speaking to you about Dom – my ex – made me begin to realise we weren't right for each other. And speaking to you about my dad made me see how much I was missing my mum and my sister, how much I needed them properly back in my life. Which they now are, by the way.'

'That's amazing, Annie. That's brilliant.'

Without realising I'm even doing it, I take a step towards him. 'So. Thank you,' I say. 'For changing everything.'

'Thank you,' he says. 'For the exact same thing.'

I gaze up at him and suddenly it's like I'm back on that bridge in Paris, five years ago, wishing that he would kiss me. Wishing I had the guts to kiss him. But then he moves closer and reaches for my hand, and as our lips touch, I don't need to wish anymore.

EPILOGUE

Eighteen months later
Kings Cross, London

The lobby of the British Library is packed to bursting point.

The hum of animated conversation fills the vast hall, as people continue to arrive, all of them dressed to the nines and hugely excited at the prospect of this opening night. Glasses of wine and nibbles are being studiously distributed by staff in black tie, and a small stage has been set up near the foot of the main staircase, beneath a smartly designed poster that reads, 'ACT UP: AN ORAL HISTORY OF RESISTANCE'.

Will is upstairs, on the second floor, watching the whole thing from the balcony.

This exhibition is his first as curator (technically, co-curator alongside his boss, Swetha), and he hasn't felt this nervous in years. The product of months of hard work from both of them, the show will document the activities of the direct action advocacy group ACT UP in Britain throughout the Eighties and Nineties. There are posters, photographs, flyers, newspaper clippings, as well as dozens of audio clips from brand-new interviews with the group's former members, all conducted by Will. In a few minutes, he and Swetha will head downstairs to formally open the exhibition. She'll say a few words, and then it will be up to him to address the crowd.

The knot in his stomach tightens, but it's not only due to the speech. After all, Will knows the show is good: he's prouder of this work than any he's ever done. No, the main cause of his steadily jangling nerves is something else entirely. He squints down and scans the crowd again. She's not here yet.

To distract himself from his butterfly-filled stomach, he picks out several other people he knows. His parents are here, beaming proudly around the beautifully decorated hall; Tanvi and her husband are talking excitedly to a few of the other Green Shoots volunteers; Dev is chatting to Maya by the gift shop; even Lexi and Gavin have made it – they must have found a sitter for little Finn.

Sim, Mike and Al are here, too, on the other side of the room, clinking their wine glasses and laughing. Will watches them, feeling a flush of fondness for his old bandmates. It was Sim he'd reached out to first, about a year ago. Gradually, over pints and dinners and film nights, Mike and Al had rejoined the fold, too, and the four have become firm friends again. They've even been making their way tentatively back to music. It began as a laugh – Mike's suggestion that they rent a rehearsal studio 'for old time's sake'. But the practices have been gaining momentum lately, each of them surprised at how much they're enjoying it, how much they've missed it. Their old Defectors songs have been ditched in favour of tried-and-tested classics by The Beatles, Buzzcocks and Elvis Costello. Dev has even suggested they might join him on the wedding circuit at some point. Will can't help grinning as he imagines what his younger self would have made of this idea. The lead singer of a wedding covers band – is there *anything* more tragic? At 34, though, the thought fills him with nothing but tingling excitement. God, it would be fun.

He takes a sip of water and continues scanning the crowd. He finds himself grinning broadly again as he spots another friendly face: Eric.

His interview had been the first one Will had secured for the exhibition: a five-hour, tea-fuelled conversation in Kirkmond-on-Crouch, where Eric had gleefully laid out his whole life in full colour, with particular attention to his ACT UP involvement. Since then, Will's research has uncovered many other former ACT UP members across the country, and he has gently suggested that Eric could perhaps drop them a line. After some persuasion, Eric has – and many have become close friends. They're all here tonight; a whole bunch of them have journeyed in together for the opening. As Will watches Eric banter easily with them, swapping stories and memories, he finds it hard to believe this is the same lonely pensioner who was once too frightened to leave the house.

But then, a lot's changed since those days. He glances fondly at Tanvi and the rest of the Green Shoots lot. Since he started attending the helpline's monthly Partage meetings, he's become close with a few of the other listeners, too. Tanvi was right: they're a lovely bunch. Life is getting busier as Will progresses in this new job, but he still manages to do at least one shift a week. He hopes he can keep that up. Keep helping people. Keep listening. At the back of his mind an idea is already forming for his next project here at the library: a sweeping oral history of crisis helplines in the UK. Perhaps he'll mention it to Swetha next week.

He heads back into the office, allowing himself a moment's proud reflection as he gives his speech notes a final glance: all these people, here to attend an event born from his ideas and passion and hard work.

He wonders what Joe would make of it. Whether he might be proud, too. He wishes, more than anything, that his best friend could be here to see it.

Will is shaken from these thoughts by a knock at the door. He opens it and is greeted by a pair of arms flung around his neck and a firm kiss on the mouth.

'Sorry I'm late,' Annie says. 'I thought I'd sneak up first and say good luck.'

He kisses her back, wondering if the pure joy her presence instils in him will ever dull with time. They've been together a year and a half now, and if anything it's getting stronger.

'You're not late, don't worry,' he says. 'How did it go with Rachel?'

Annie beams back at him, the tip of her nose still pink from the cold. 'Good. Really good.'

'Amazing!' Rachel is her agent. Annie signed with her a few weeks back, after months of writing and rewriting and sending cover letters to every corner of the country. She still can't quite believe it: she has a literary agent. Her! She's currently making good money as a freelance copywriter, but Will suspects it won't be long until Rachel weaves her magic and Annie has bigger fish to fry. He has read her latest stories: he knows how good they are.

She kisses him again, softly this time. They stay like that for a while, wrapped in each other's arms.

And then Swetha is at the door. 'Sorry, lovebirds, time to go.'

Annie laughs as she gives Swetha a hug. 'You'll both be brilliant. See you down there.' She presses her forehead against Will's and whispers: 'Good luck with your "brave thing".'

He smiles. He knows she means the speech, the exhibition, but he's thinking of what he's planning to do in the restaurant afterwards.

Will has given the matter serious thought over the past few weeks. He knows how he feels about her; he's never been surer of anything in his life. But still, is he jumping the gun here? After all, they've only been living together nine months. Recently, he has been thinking back to their Green Shoots conversations on the topic, and he remembers one thing she said very clearly: 'I like the idea of being married, but not *getting* married,' she'd told him. 'I hate the thought of a massive wedding.'

The idea appeals to him. A small, intimate day: best friends and family only.

His hand goes to the little velvet box in his jacket pocket. 'Thanks,' he says. 'I love you.'

She pulls him in for another kiss. 'Love you too.'

ACKNOWLEDGEMENTS

As ever, the first and largest portion of thanks goes to my brilliant editor Emily Kitchin, who gave me the chance to write this story in the first place, and was so encouraging of it right from the start. Emily – you're a stone-cold legend and an absolute joy to work with. I simply could not have written this book without your insight, guidance, enthusiasm and ability to conjure genius ideas from thin air. Thank you SO much!

Huge thanks are also due to Clare Gordon and Katie Seaman for their additional editorial wizardry, and to everyone at HQ for being so continually fantastic and supportive. Thanks to my awesome agent, Clare Wallace, and to all at Darley Anderson. And to Lucy Ivison, as always, for being a top-drawer idea-bouncer-offer. To Tanvi Rakesh: thanks for the loan of your name (and for just generally being a good egg). To Sarah Lowry: thank you for taking the time to give me some invaluable insight into the fascinating world of oral history.

Much love to the *real* Defectors – Chris Carroll, Harvey Horner and Neil Redford. Apologies for taking a dig at 'Wet

Like Water', which was – when all's said and done – a big tune. Band practices with you lads at Wacky Chris' were some of the best times of my life, and I miss them – and you all – very much.

Finally, a profound 'verbal nod' to all the great people I volunteered alongside at the crisis line Green Shoots is based on. And to all the regular callers, too, wherever and whoever you are. I still think of you all often, and hope you're doing OK.